Praise for USA TO[...]
Jennifer Snow[...]

"Heartwarming, romanti[...]
—*New York Times b*[...]
on *An Alaskan Christmas*

"This first title in the Wild River series is passionate, sensual, and very sexy. The freezing, winter-cold portrayal of the Alaskan ski slopes is not the only thing sending chills through one's body."
—*New York Journal of Books*

"Set in the wilds of Alaska, the beauty of winter and the cold shine through."
—*Fresh Fiction* on *An Alaskan Christmas*

"Jennifer Snow's Alaska setting and search-and-rescue element are interesting twists, and the romance is smart and sexy... An exciting contemporary series debut with a wildly unique Alaskan setting."
—*Kirkus Reviews*

"Readers will enjoy the mix of sexy love scenes, tense missions, and amiable banter. This entertaining introduction to Wild River will encourage fans of small-town contemporaries to follow the series."
—*Publishers Weekly*

"*An Alaskan Christmas* drew me in from the first page to the last. I tried to read slower so that I could savor the story and feel every emotion. I reveled in every nuance, felt the cold, the wind and snow, and loved the small town and the mountains... I can't wait to return to Wild River."
—*Romance Junkies*

Also by Jennifer Snow

Wild River

Wild River Novellas

For a complete list of books by Jennifer Snow,
please visit www.jennifersnowauthor.com.

JENNIFER SNOW

Alaska Dreams

If you purchased this book without a cover you should be aware that this book is stolen property. It was reported as "unsold and destroyed" to the publisher, and neither the author nor the publisher has received any payment for this "stripped book."

ISBN-13: 978-1-335-63982-0

Alaska Dreams
Copyright © 2022 by Jennifer Snow

An Alaskan Christmas Homecoming
Copyright © 2022 by Jennifer Snow

Recycling programs
for this product may
not exist in your area.

All rights reserved. No part of this book may be used or reproduced in any manner whatsoever without written permission except in the case of brief quotations embodied in critical articles and reviews.

This is a work of fiction. Names, characters, places and incidents are either the product of the author's imagination or are used fictitiously. Any resemblance to actual persons, living or dead, businesses, companies, events or locales is entirely coincidental.

This edition published by arrangement with Harlequin Books S.A.

For questions and comments about the quality of this book, please contact us at CustomerService@Harlequin.com.

HQN
22 Adelaide St. West, 41st Floor
Toronto, Ontario M5H 4E3, Canada
www.Harlequin.com

Printed in Lithuania

MIX
Paper from
responsible sources
FSC® C021394

CONTENTS

To all the creatives out there chasing a dream—
you've got this!

Alaska
Dreams

CHAPTER ONE

Santa Monica, California

THE RIGHT SCRIPT *will give you chills*. That was how Selena's movie star stepfather, Mel Hudson, knew when to accept a role. Well, if the goose bumps covering Selena Hudson's skin were any indication, *this* was the role she'd been looking for.

When her indie producer friend had first contacted her about the project, she'd been hesitant—Jay was fairly new to Hollywood, an Atlanta film industry transplant with impressive film festival achievements for writing. It would be his first time directing, and they'd be working with a minimal budget, the funds raised through a crowdsourcing site, and with a personal donation of her own salary, but now that she'd read the finished script, her fears had evaporated. The contained psychological thriller, *Alice Was Here*, was edgy, smart and full of creepy suspense. No happily-ever-after in sight.

Selena held her breath as she turned to look at her boyfriend, Matt Mayson, as he flipped the last page of the copy he was reading. His messy morning hair and sexy dark-rimmed glasses, which he only wore in front of her, had her struggling to stay focused on the movie script. "Well? What do you think?"

Matt's gorgeous grin, when he looked at her, had her

pulse racing even more than usual. "I *think* you have your breakout movie."

Deep sigh of relief. "*Our* breakout movie," Selena said, tossing both their scripts aside and straddling him on the bed. Work done. Now time for fun. Pressing her hands against his muscular, solid, freshly waxed chest, she leaned forward to kiss him, but his cell ringing on the night table had him turning his head just as her lips approached. Instead of his mouth, she got the stubble on his chin.

"Sorry, it's Arman," he said, picking up the phone.

His manager. Right. *He* still had one.

She, on the other hand, was a free agent after firing her entire management team a year ago. A decision she did not regret.

At all.

How could she work with a team that didn't believe in her? Just because she'd started her career as a child actor in family-friendly movies and sitcoms, and then evolved into one of Hollywood's most recognizable rom-com stars, did not mean she couldn't act in other types of films. Unfortunately, she'd been pigeonholed, and every audition she tried to get for an action or drama or thriller came back with the same reply from studio execs: silence.

It was worse than hearing no. The fact that they simply ignored her attempts to do something different, as if they thought she was kidding, grated on her nerves.

"I have to get this," Matt said when she made no move to get off him. He gently eased her body away and sat up straighter.

She took no offense. There was a time she had been a slave to her manager's ringtone as well. "Don't forget to tell him about the script," she whispered as she climbed off the bed and he answered the call.

Picking up her copy again, she left the room and stepped out onto the large deck off her bedroom, which overlooked the ocean in Santa Monica. Palm trees and blue skies as far as the eye could see. A soft, warm breeze blew her short dark hair across her face, and she tucked it behind her ear. The new chin-length bob was part of her reinvention. No more long, romantic-looking, wavy beach hair. This style was professional and sophisticated. Slightly harder to style, which annoyed her since it didn't quite stay in a ponytail when she worked out, but change took time to get used to.

A deep inhalation of the salty, warm September air calmed all her anxieties, and the familiar view gave her a sense of comfort. She'd lived in Santa Monica her entire life and there was nowhere else she wanted to be. The sun, sand, surf and vibrant, eclectic lifestyle California offered in the center of the bright lights was the only world Selena had known and the only one she needed to know—as long as she could hold on to it and still follow her own passions. The overseas film industry would welcome her with open arms, but she wasn't quite ready to walk away from this world.

She sat on the plush lounge chair, tightening her short, silky pink robe around her waist and extending her legs out in front of her. She adjusted the large umbrella for shade, then scanned the opening pages of the script again. The screenwriter had an incredible voice, an amazing way of capturing a character's essence with just a few short lines of descriptive writing, and by the end of the first page, she'd been drawn in.

This was going to work.

Never had she felt so confident in a project. It validated her decision to refuse the countless huge box office movie auditions for rom-coms that had come her way that year, and instead venture out into coproducing a project of her own. Before her near-death experience with her stalker the year before, she'd gone along with what everyone else wanted and expected from her. She'd played the game. She'd been that artist who politely and gratefully accepted the opportunities that presented themselves. She didn't make waves or demands. And she'd been happy to do it. Mostly.

After the scare, things changed. She'd changed. She'd taken more control over her life. She was determined to go after the career *she* wanted. Life was too short not to take chances and go after the "big dream." This indie project was going to help her do just that.

She glanced inside the bedroom, where Matt now paced nakedly, his cell phone to his ear. Damn, he was hot. Six feet, 170 pounds of muscle, blond hair, dark eyes, dimples for days and a solid, square jawline; he certainly turned heads and commanded attention wherever he went.

That phone call better be quick.

Having him agree to the indie film and coming on this new adventure with her made her feel that much better about it. Having him believe in her and support her meant a lot. These days, that support was tough to come by when she was refusing to be the cash cow everyone had come to depend on.

She watched him rake a hand through his silky blond hair, and her heart pounded in her chest. She was in love with him. Of course, she hadn't told him that yet. They'd met on the set of her last feature film. He was new to acting and, at twenty-one, six years younger than her. He'd been the best friend to the leading man in the film they'd worked on together, but he had real talent. He could have been the star. Their chemistry on set had had to be toned down so as not to overshadow the intended romance, and they'd held off on officially dating until filming was over. The wait had nearly killed her. She'd dated her costars often in the past. It was par for the course in this industry, but this time with Matt felt different.

It wasn't just his amazing looks, his sense of humor or natural charisma, but also his talent. A lot of the male leads she'd worked with were one-dimensional. They pretty much played the same character in all their films. Matt had depth. He was new to Hollywood, but he was going straight to the top.

She strained to hear what he was saying.

"Of course I want this opportunity…Yeah, no, I'll make it work." Pause. "Thanks, man…Yeah, talk soon."

Opportunity? New audition? That didn't surprise her. Matt's career was going to skyrocket, and she was lucky enough to have VIP access to watch it take off.

A moment later, he joined her on the deck and she studied him. He leaned back on the other lounge chair and closed his eyes. "Mmm, that sun feels amazing."

His rock-god statue-like body was amazing, but she forced her hormones to take a back seat. Business first. Pleasure later. It was their agreement. Careers came first. Relationship second. "Well? Did you tell him?"

"Yeah."

Her skin tingled with a sense of foreboding at the not-so-enthusiastic one-word response. "What did he say?" Normally, his business was his own and she could resist being inquisitive, since this industry required a lot of information to be kept confidential until press releases went out, but this particular project involved her, too.

Matt didn't open his eyes. "He's not convinced it's the best thing for me to do with my career on the rise."

Selena's jaw tightened. Managers. Thought they knew everything. If Matt wasn't careful, soon every career decision would be out of his hands. Getting advice and guidance as a new actor was essential, and with his limited résumé, he was lucky to be represented by one of the biggest talent firms in LA, but Selena knew the trappings of money and quick success in this industry. She didn't want Matt to get caught up in it all and lose sight of why he'd started acting in the first place. Still, she had to be careful not to be too pushy. They'd both agreed not to meddle in the other's career.

"He hasn't even read the script," she said carefully. "So, how would he know?"

"He just thinks we should keep reaching higher while riding the success of the last film. Backsliding might give the wrong impression or something." He shrugged like only a newbie deferring to the expertise of his manager could shrug.

"Backsliding?" Wow. Hollywood still couldn't appreciate the value of independent films. They truly believed actors took on these roles when they could no longer get top billing. Not because they might want to try expanding their skill set or be involved with something a little deeper, maybe more meaningful…

She certainly wasn't taking on this project as a way to pay off parking tickets or anything.

"You know *I* don't think that," Matt said, opening his eyes and rotating his head to look at her.

"Are you sure?" She hated the note of uncertain vulnerability that entered her voice. She didn't like that she cared so much about what he thought about her and her recent career decisions. She hadn't thought she had to prove to him that this new direction wasn't from lack of options, but out of a desire to move forward, reach higher, expand her talent further.

Matt sighed, sitting up and turning to face her. "Look, don't worry. I said I'm in and I'm in..." He paused, diminishing the strength of his commitment. "Arman just has another audition lined up for me as well," he said casually.

Too casually. He was obviously hiding excitement.

Be supportive. This is a good thing. "Can you talk about it?"

His smile was wide as he said, "Not officially...but between us?"

She nodded. She was a vault.

"It's the lead in the new Michael Miller action drama that was announced last week."

Her mouth dropped. Michael Miller was the hottest new director on the scene. At only twenty-five, he'd made blockbuster record sales with his last movie about aliens fighting robots for control over the human race. She'd reached out to him about this particular project months ago and had gotten the "no response means no" reply from his agent. And now Matt, the "one movie under his belt" Hollywood newbie, was being offered an audition to star as the lead?

Professional jealousy could destroy a Hollywood power couple. She took a deep breath and hoped her smile looked genuine as she said, "That is amazing. You deserve it." He did deserve it. He was supertalented. And it wasn't as though he was stealing a role from her. It just bummed her out that she wasn't getting an opportunity to audition to play the opposite lead. Working with him on a blockbuster film would be incredible. A boost both their careers needed. Walking a red carpet with him on a Michael Miller film would solidify their status in both their professional and personal lives.

He stood and joined her on her chair. He reached for her and pulled her close. As he buried his head into her neck, some of the tension evaporated. The man did things to her that turned her insides to mush. And how did he smell so incredible first thing in the morning?

"I'm a newbie, remember? I can't turn things down and still hope to get opportunities like you can." He kissed along her neck and shoulder, and shivers danced along her spine. The romance and attraction she'd portrayed on-screen couldn't begin to measure up to this real-life romance with him. Did he feel it, too? "You've proven yourself and have had an amazing career." His words were muffled against her ear. "You can afford to take risks. I can't yet."

Her body tingled with desire and his words reassured her. He was right. She was at the point in her career where she could take risks. He wasn't. And maybe if he got the role in the bigger film, it would actually help the indie project's success. A rising tide lifted all ships, right?

She turned to look at him, taking his face between her hands. "You are going to blow them away," she said sincerely.

He kissed her softly and grinned as he pulled back. "Rehearse lines with me?"

Her stomach twisted slightly. It was really no big deal, but rehearsing lines for a movie she'd been hoping to audition for might give her a mild anxiety attack.

Support. That was what they did for one another. "Of course. Do you have the script already?" If Arman had somehow managed to get his hands on the coveted script this early, the manager might actually be worth listening to.

Matt laughed as he placed another soft kiss to her lips. "I was talking about the indie film."

And she was supposed to *not* fall in love with this guy?

She wrapped her arms around him tight and pressed her body to his. "Have I told you how much I like you?"

"You have."

"Have you told me how much you like me?" she asked in her most seductive voice. She didn't want to sound like she was begging for him to tell her what she longed to hear, but she wished he'd just say the *L* word first. That was the way it always worked in her relationships. The men always said it first, even if in hindsight they didn't really mean it. The uncertainty from having strong feelings that she wasn't sure were reciprocated was new. And it was torture.

"I think it should be obvious," Matt murmured against her lips. "After all, I've agreed to freeze my nuts off in the middle of Nunavut to film this movie with you, haven't I?"

Not exactly the reassurance she was desperate for. But he was right. People showed love differently. While she was more vocal in her feelings, his love language might be acts of service.

"It's Alaska, actually," she said, kissing him. "Wild River, to be exact."

For the first time in a year, Selena was headed back to the place where her life had been in danger. But this time, she wasn't running away from something. This time, she was running toward her new future.

Seattle, Washington

THE STATION'S SECURITY GUARDS were a lot stronger than they looked.

At six foot two, two hundred pounds, Gus Orosco wasn't a small guy. Yet they had no problem carrying him out of the Sports Live studio, where his co-reporter was left scrambling to recover from Gus's on-air blackout.

There was really no other word for what had happened in there moments ago. Fully conscious, there was no way he would have sabotaged his career on live TV. "Guys, you can put me down," Gus said, struggling to free himself. With his feet three inches off the floor and their tight grip on his forearms, it seemed like he was actually dangerous or something. He smiled at an intern walking down the hall toward them, but the young college student avoided his gaze and stuck close to the wall as he passed.

Seriously? He'd helped the kid carry an impossible Starbucks order ten blocks the day before. He sighed. "Come on, guys…"

"Sorry, Gus. We're under strict orders to deliver you straight to Vern."

Vern Orosco. His boss…and grandfather. The head of Sports Live Studios. The one man on earth Gus hated to disappoint. "I can walk," he said, though he wasn't sure he'd be walking in the direction of his grandfather's fortieth-floor corner office if they released him.

Barry, the older guard who'd worked at the station as long as Gus had been there, eyed him, assessing whether he could be trusted.

"Seriously, I'm cool." Now. Five minutes ago, he'd been far from it. Not typically a hothead, his outburst on live television had shocked everyone, including himself.

Barry gave him a warning look. "Don't do anything stupid."

Gus held up a Scout's honor sign as best he could with his arms still restrained, and the two men released him. "Thank you," he mumbled as his feet hit the floor. "I can make it from here." This was embarrassing enough. Walking past all of the upper executive offices with security guard escorts would destroy him.

Darius, the younger, newer guard, hesitated. "If you bolt…"

Gus sighed. "Guys, I'm not going to bolt. I'm fine. And I need to face the music."

Barry nodded, allowing him to continue on his own, but the two men stood at the end of the hallway, watching, just in case.

Unfortunately, there was no escape unless he wanted to jump from the fortieth-floor window at the end of the hall, crashing onto the busy Seattle city street below, but his downward spiral hadn't quite reached that drastic point yet.

Though he might be close. The long walk along the studio hallway toward Vern's office was like walking the green mile. On the walls on either side of him were framed photos of the best sports athletes in the world. He'd spent hours in that hall when he'd first gotten the job as co-reporter of the three o'clock sports news, a dream job working for his grandfather. A sports fanatic, playing every sport and watching every professional game from a young age, this was the only career he'd ever wanted. Growing up in small-town Alaska, watching his grandfather on the Seattle studio news set, where he'd been a reporter himself, Gus had been in awe of the older man. He'd visited every summer, and as soon as he'd graduated, he left Wild River and headed south. A university degree and four years of interning at the station, and he had his dream career.

Up until five minutes ago.

Now the eyes of the athletes seemed to follow him down the hall. Disappointment and judgment he couldn't escape.

What the hell was he going to say to his grandfather?

None of the excuses coming to mind were good enough. Vern had always been firm but fair, and Gus knew not to expect any special privileges just because his boss was family.

Stopping in front of the door, he glanced down the hallway. Barry gave him a sympathetic nod, even as he flexed his tattoo-covered arms in warning. Gus opened the office door and stepped inside.

He gulped as he faced his fate.

Sitting in an oversize plush leather recliner, his grandfather had his back to him, the television remote in hand. The man didn't turn around as the door closed behind him.

Gus cleared his throat. "Vern…"

"Shh," the older man said. He rewound the studio footage from moments before, and Gus watched his outburst backward on full speed and winced. It would look even worse in slow motion when it became the next social media meme.

His grandfather hit Play and finally turned to face him. It was almost like looking into a mirror, one that showed you your appearance at an older age. The patriarch of the Orosco family barely looked a day over fifty, and his athletic build from being a former college football star was still impressive. With dark hair, only slightly peppered at the sides, and not a wrinkle to be found on his sixty-three-year-old face, he was still sought-after by the ladies. Everyone said Gus was the spitting image of his grandfather, a compliment he'd always appreciated, but their mirrored looks of anguish right now were almost too much.

"Sir, I'm…"

"Just watch," Vern said, staring at his grandson.

Gus shoved his hands into his pockets and forced his most neutral expression as the footage replayed. A train wreck he'd already witnessed crushing him all over again.

Only instead of the tiny studio screen where he'd had to

watch as his ex-fiancée, an infield reporter on location at the Climate Pledge Arena, get engaged to superstar hockey player Vince Fallon, his grandfather's eighty-inch high-definition flat-screen merely amplified Aileen's beautiful, breathtaking look of happiness as she'd accepted the lame-ass proposal from a man who didn't even have real front teeth.

The air in the office seemed to evaporate as he watched her tear up and hug Vince, still in his gear from preseason practice. How the hell could she actually love this dude? He was a thickheaded brawler with the IQ of an eight-year-old. And if her Instagram photos could be trusted, she'd only been seeing Vince for three months, which was three months and two days since she'd called off her engagement to *him*.

On the television, the camera footage switched back to the studio, and that was where shit went sideways. The camera zoomed in on his face—a very red, enraged face, one he didn't even recognize—and then the ensuing chaos played out on the screen. Finally, as the guards appeared on set and carried him off camera, his grandfather hit Pause.

"So, obviously, you're fired."

Gus nodded. Obviously. A few choice words he'd used on air alone would have the network coming down hard on his grandfather. The backlash the station would face for his behavior was definite grounds for dismissal. "For the record, if I could go back and redo the last twenty minutes, I would." Lately, he'd found himself wishing for a redo on the last six months, when things had started taking a turn for the worse with Aileen. When he'd started putting his career goals ahead of their relationship and she'd felt him drift away. When the arguments had escalated to a breaking point and he'd lost her. When she'd returned her engagement ring to him and he'd been too stubborn to beg her to reconsider. So many moments he'd like to do over again.

"Have a seat, Gus," Vern said, taking a deep breath.

He sat.

"What happened?" It wasn't his boss asking now—it was his grandfather. The firing would hold; there'd be no changing the man's mind. They both knew it. So, Vern immediately transformed into the caring role model he'd always been when Gus was in trouble or needed help.

He released a deep breath and ran a shaky hand through his hair. "I don't know. I mean, obviously I snapped, but… it's just, she makes me so crazy, you know?" His hands clenched into tight fists and he blew out a puff of air, expecting to see steam escape from his mouth.

Aileen always had that effect on him. Their relationship had been intense, emotionally driven, for better or worse. They fought, they made up. Then they'd fight again and it was a vicious cycle. But it was their thing. Passion in love and in anger. She got under his skin like no one else ever had, and he was addicted to the chaos she added to his life. Arguably, she was all wrong for him, but his heart refused to listen to his head. He'd proposed out of fear of losing her. He still loved her, and seeing her get engaged to someone else just months after she'd told him she wasn't ready to settle down with someone who loved their career more than they loved her was a kick in the teeth. And he was supposed to be okay reporting the goddamned story?

His grandfather nodded. "She is a firecracker, that one. Reminds me of your grandmother in a lot of ways."

Gus had never met his grandmother, who'd passed away from a rare brain tumor before he was born. He remembered stories his grandfather would tell about her, though, how she'd been an advocate for women's rights and how, as a black belt in multiple martial arts, she never took any shit from anyone, insisting on having her own career during a time when a lot of women stayed home to raise families and putting his grandfather in his place whenever he stepped out of line. Gus could see where maybe the attraction to wild horses could be hereditary. Unfortunately, his grandfather's heart had never recovered—he'd never remarried, had barely dated after that... Gus truly believed that maybe he, too, was destined to now be alone, pining after the love of his life forever.

The office door opened and his sister, Trish, walked in. Dressed in a pin-striped gray suit, pale coral blouse and six-inch heels, her straight auburn hair hanging down her back, she looked ten feet tall and on a mission. Gus's jaw tightened. Of course she'd be attending this untimely meeting. As head of publicity for the station, she'd be doing damage control for weeks. And she'd never let him forget all the extra work he'd made for her.

"You look like shit," Trish said, pulling up a chair on the other side of the desk, beside their grandfather. Apparently, the side where *still employed* family members sat. Despite not being directly involved in the running of the studio, he'd never felt like an outsider, never felt a divide until that moment. He realized they were essentially his employers, and the best interests of the studio outweighed family loyalty. He wouldn't expect it to be any other way, but it still stung.

"Thank you," he mumbled sarcastically.

"Here's a latte, which I absolutely did not spit in," she said, handing him the to-go cup with the station's logo on the side. A to-go cup. Nothing like saying, *Here's your coat, what's your hurry.* His sister was pissed, even if her even-keeled personality wouldn't allow her to show it in conventional ways like yelling or throwing things. Sometimes, especially today, he wished she would live up to her reputation as a redhead and lose her shit, just once.

He unbuttoned his sports coat and slumped in the chair across from her. "So, what do you need from me to help smooth things over?"

Trish glanced at their grandfather. "I assume you fired him already?"

Vern gave a simple nod.

She turned back to him, still in full professional mode. "Well, an apology statement would be the first step."

An apology to the network and his family wouldn't be hard. He already deeply regretted his actions. He could even muster enough strength to apologize to Aileen for ruining her engagement, though it had crushed his spirit. But the thought of an apology to Vince Fallon had his back teeth clenching hard. Proposing after three months? Doing it when he knew Gus would be forced to see it? The guy had been setting him up. Might have something to do with the uncomplimentary assessment Gus had made regarding the guy's preseason performance so far, but his job was to be honest. The fact that Vince was dating his ex hadn't at all influenced his commentating the week before.

"I'll put something together," he told his sister.

She shook her head, the auburn hair whipping back and forth across her back. "No, you won't. My new PR intern is already drafting it."

He nodded and sipped the latte. "Sorry to create so much work." He took a deep breath. "What else should I do to try to salvage my career?" If anyone had the advice he needed right now, it was Trish. The two of them hadn't been really close growing up, Trish being ten years older. She'd begrudgingly stepped into a maternal role after their mother left when Gus was three, but their shared love of sports had connected them. She had a great business mind and he trusted her.

She sighed and folded her hands on the desk. "Look, Gus. I love you like a brother..." She grinned, finally breaking her stern persona. "So, I want to help you." She paused. "But by now, every sports station from here to Alaska has blackballed you."

Ouch. Her bluntness was something he normally appreciated, but not when he was this vulnerable. "Already?"

"About seventy seconds after that shit show aired," she said.

"Well, what am I supposed to do?" He stood and tossed his empty cup toward the trash can and missed. His entire life he'd been taking the necessary steps to get where he was...or had been. What the hell did he do now if no other station would even look at his résumé? He hadn't taken any real time off since high school, always driven with an eye on the prize. Now he was suddenly unemployed and potentially unemployable in his field. From one mistake. Albeit, a monumental one.

"My advice is to lie low," Trish said. "Let this blow over. Cool off a bit."

"Do you think it will?" he asked, bending to pick up the coffee cup and placing it in the trash.

"Eventually."

He could work with *eventually*. It was better than *never*. "So, when should I start getting my agent to reach out to other stations?" He could definitely expect a step back. Maybe he'd have to settle for a lower position with a smaller, local sports network. Maybe even do some radio for a while, but he'd done the crime… "Two weeks? A month?"

Trish glanced at Vern, then sent him a sympathetic look. She rarely looked anything other than busy and slightly annoyed at the lack of competence around her, so he knew what was coming next had to be bad. Really bad. "Your agent called. He's out."

Wow. Six years working together and the man didn't have the courtesy to drop him himself? He swallowed hard. It had taken a lot of hard work to get that agent in the first place; after today's public fiasco and firing, it would be nearly impossible to get a new rep.

"Gus, take some time. Get away from the city and the negative attention this is going to draw. Take a breath. Clear your head," Vern said.

Gus looked back and forth between them. He knew them both well enough to read what was written all over their faces. "You two think my career is over."

Neither one answered, which was all the answer he needed.

"Great," he said as he headed toward the door. He needed air, and some time to think and process and figure out next steps. There had to be a way to fix this.

"Gus," Vern said. "You'll need to give up the apartment."

His apartment on the forty-first floor of the downtown building with the spectacular view of the city skyline. The one and only special *perk* of being the grandson of the studio head. They each had an apartment on that floor. But, apparently, now he was homeless. He understood. He couldn't exactly live above the studio, but… "Where am I supposed to go?"

"Home?" Trish suggested, and Gus's stomach dropped.

This was it. The end of the road. The end of his career

aspirations. He'd lost his job, his agent, his apartment and the respect of his grandfather in a matter of minutes.

And now it looked like he was dragging his busted heart back home to Wild River, Alaska.

CHAPTER TWO

Anchorage, Alaska
Three weeks later...

Airports always felt like the pulse of a city. The hustle and bustle of people leaving and arriving. Loved ones saying goodbye or welcoming home. Excitement about vacations to foreign destinations or anxiety about new life adventures swirling all around. Traveling was something that energized her, and being back in Alaska had Selena buzzing.

At the baggage carousel, with her Chihuahua, Unicorn, sleeping in the pet carrier strapped to her chest, Selena waited impatiently for her cell phone to connect to a service provider. "Come on, come on..." She petted the little dog's multicolored fur as she eyed the bags on the rotating belt. She couldn't wait to hit the road. They had a two-hour drive to Orosco Campgrounds. Getting to the filming site to check out the lay of the land and then heading into Wild River to see her friends were first up on her agenda. Alaska was the best place to film this movie. It also held the additional perk of her being able to see all the people she'd connected with during her time of need the year before.

Her indie producer friend and first-time director, Jay, and the rest of the crew were just as eager to get going as she was. Dressed in his fashionable faux fur winter coat and leather boots, Jay drained the contents of his coffee cup. "You good to wait for the bags while I go to the rental desk and pick up the van?"

She nodded. Normally, she had an assistant to gather the bags, but she could handle this. "Yeah. I booked the reservation in your name." She might not be gracing theater screens as frequently these days, but her name was still more recognizable than Jay's. And yet, after her stalker scare and with no security detail in tow this time, she was being cautious. No one besides her Alaska friends even knew she was coming. Her parents were overseas volunteering with one of their charities and were virtually unreachable, so they wouldn't even know she'd left California, and she'd told her agent that she was taking a vacation. He wasn't as supportive about her new career direction as she'd like, but the finished movie would show him she was right.

Assuming they pulled this off. They were running on a skeleton crew of five—two camera operators, a gaffer and two PAs, one of whom was also hair and makeup. Besides her character and Matt's, the other main character in the film—the villain—was being played by Jay's brother, an up-and-coming actor who'd won an award on the indie circuit for his performance in several risqué shorts. His role in the film was limited to three scenes and Jay was confident Justin could deliver a great performance. He was flying in the following week for two days of shooting.

The rest of the crew stood together on the other side of the carousel. They all knew one another, having worked with Jay on other movies, and Selena felt like the odd one out. It was definitely a first to be feeling like the outsider on a film set, and she was desperate not to think they were judging her or wondering why Jay had wanted a rom-com queen for the dark, edgy film. She was new to the genre, so she had to prove herself to them, along with everyone else.

That was the point, right? And once Matt arrived, she'd feel better. His audition for the Michael Miller blockbuster film was that same day, so he'd been forced to take a later flight.

The service bars lit up on her cell phone as Jay walked away, and she smiled as she immediately dialed Leslie's number. It was just after seven in the morning, but she knew her friend would be up, and she could use a familiar voice right now with everyone else ignoring her.

The first ring hadn't even completed its chime before her former bodyguard turned friend answered. "You're here?"

The sound of Leslie's voice coming through the phone had Unicorn's eyes snapping open and her ears perking up. The dog adored Leslie, and Selena always trusted her dog's opinion of someone. She hadn't warmed up to Matt yet, but that was probably because she didn't like sharing Selena's attention. It was natural for the pup to be jealous. Matt simply needed to try harder to win her over.

"Almost. Just landed. We should be at the campgrounds outside Wild River in a few hours," she said, her excitement rising again. On the plane, her anxiety had started to creep in, but she knew it was nerves about the new direction she was taking with her career. She'd have felt better if Matt had been on the flight with her.

By now, he should be in the air and would be there soon. He was planning on renting his own car and driving in, so that they'd have a vehicle separate from the crew to do things on their own. She loved the idea of exploring Alaska with him and introducing him to her friends in Wild River. Maybe this trip, she'd get the courage to tell him she was falling for him…

"Are you staying here in town?" Leslie asked.

Dare she hope that her friend sounded hopeful? Leslie wasn't huge on emotions and she kept her feelings close to her chest, but over the last year, since the two of them had relied on one another to escape Selena's dangerous stalker, they'd grown really close. They Skyped several times a week and texted almost every day. In secret, Selena always referred to Leslie as her *best* friend, but she'd never say that out loud to Leslie for fear of spooking her. "Yeah. At a B and B on Main Street—the Bluebird Inn?"

Leslie was silent.

She checked the cell reception to see if the call had been dropped. "You still there?"

"Yeah, I thought I heard you say you were staying at a two-star inn."

Selena rolled her eyes. "Yes, Leslie. I don't need luxury accommodations all the time." She would have loved to stay at the Wild River Resort, the posh, expensive hotel surrounded by beautiful, majestic scenery, where they'd spent a few nights the year before, but despite her own personal savings, this movie was being filmed on a modest budget and the rest of the crew were keeping costs low, so she would, too. She wouldn't alienate herself further by not staying at the same accommodations.

Again, Leslie was silent.

She sighed. "Fine. We're making this movie on the cheap," she whispered so the crew within earshot wouldn't hear. "At least we're not staying at the filming campgrounds." She shuddered. The location they'd scouted online for filming was forty minutes outside the small resort town. It was an abandoned campsite that, according to the old website, hadn't been open for years. From the photos, it looked creepy as shit when it *had* been maintained and operational. Jay had really found the perfect place for the thriller.

"Well, come to The Drunk Tank tonight around seven. We're throwing you a surprise party," Leslie said.

Selena laughed. "Way to ruin it." Leslie hated surprises and thought over-the-top gestures were unnecessary. The fact she was abandoning her own feelings on the subject and going outside her comfort zone to throw a party for Selena was endearing.

Seeing one of her four suitcases on the conveyor belt, she cradled the cell phone between her ear and shoulder as she yanked the bag out of the rotation. Her cell chimed with an incoming call as she set it down. "Hang on a sec. I have a call coming in." She moved the phone away from her ear. Matt's name lighting up the display made her heart race. Was he here already? Had he caught an even earlier flight? She looked around the crowded airport, but didn't see him. "Hey, Les, I have to go, but I'll see you soon," she said. "Big hugs coming your way."

"Fantastic." Her friend's sarcasm held the faintest hint of excitement, and Selena smiled as she switched to the other call.

"Matt? Are you here already?"

He cleared his throat. "Um…no."

Hearing Matt's voice now, Unicorn let out a low growl. Selena petted the dog's head affectionately. Another one of her bags appeared, but she let it pass by her as she asked, "Did you miss your flight?" She checked the time. Maybe his audition had gone late. Not ideal, but he could catch a later flight in and still be there by the next morning. It would mean he'd miss the party at The Drunk Tank that night and the opportunity to meet everyone, but there would be other chances to introduce him.

"No, I didn't miss it," he said.

Her heart fell to her stomach.

"Sorry, Selena. I'm not coming."

Her mouth dropped and she was at a rare loss for words.

What the hell did he mean he wasn't coming? He'd been planning on it right up to when he'd dropped her off at the airport. He had specifically said, "See you soon," and he'd kissed her goodbye as though he was missing her already… or maybe that was her.

"You still there?"

She blinked and cleared her throat. "Yes, I'm here. And you should be on your way, too. You said you were in, remember?" If she reminded him of his promise and commitment, he'd come through. It was probably Arman getting into his head again with the backsliding nonsense.

"I know and I'm sorry. The audition went better than we could have hoped," he said, his excitement making her feel both happy for him and selfish that she kind of didn't give a shit about the blockbuster film opportunity right now. She'd just flown thousands of miles to film a movie that was already a long shot, with a crew who weren't exactly welcoming, and now her costar, her boyfriend, the only other person besides Jay who liked her, was bailing?

"That's great," she managed to say through clenched teeth, "but I thought you were going to still do this movie, too. The other one doesn't start filming for months and I'm sure there are more casting steps. This was just a first audition. There's no guarantee that you'll get the part." She winced as the words flew out. She sounded like an asshole, but he was leaving her high and dry.

"Thanks for the vote of confidence," he said, his voice sounding hard.

She sighed. She wouldn't let this *setback* jeopardize their relationship, but he needed to know that this was a personal letdown as well as a professional one. He'd agreed to be in this movie. He'd signed a contract. Not one he couldn't easily get out of, though, with the additional clause his manager had added that stated if another project came up with a budget that superseded the indie film, he could bail. "I'm sorry. You know I think you've got this role in the bag," she said. "I just expected you here. I need you here," she added softly. He was a big part of why she was excited. She'd been looking forward to starring in a film with him. Working with him on set would make it more fun; the long days wouldn't feel like work. Besides that, all the plans she'd had for them when they weren't filming—discovering the beauty and excitement of Alaska and connecting in a more natural environment, away from LA—were all ruined now, too. She'd wanted to experience so much with him and now she wouldn't get that chance.

"You don't need me," he said. "It's a female-driven thriller. You're the star…"

Something in the way he said it made her wonder if that was the reason he was bailing. Had his manager warned him about playing second fiddle to her? Or was Matt not comfortable with it? He didn't strike her as someone who would feel intimidated by her success, despite it having been an issue with other actors she'd dated.

"You can cast anyone in the male lead."

In just the movie? Or in her life, too? Her pulse raced and her overthinking kicked into high gear, causing emotion to enter her reasoning. "I don't want to cast just anyone. I want to cast you. I did cast you." He'd committed to this. He'd committed to her. Or at least she thought he had. "Matt, please just get on a plane." She hated how desperate she sounded, but the truth was, her belief in herself and in the project only went so far. Having him on board had given her the security net she'd needed to take this leap. With him, the movie would be a success. With just her, she wasn't sure anymore.

Which sucked. Hard.

"Sorry, Selena," he said, and he did sound genuinely sorry. "My management team doesn't think it's the right step, and you know I need to listen to their advice right now."

She swallowed hard and nodded. He did. She couldn't argue with that. For years, she'd listened to everyone's advice and played the game according to their rules. And she'd had a fantastic career because of it. She'd achieved a lot by following the advice given, even if she was looking to branch out now and follow her own gut instincts. "I know," she said quietly.

"Look, the movie script is amazing. Jay is amazing. *You* are amazing. You're going to pull this off." He paused. "And honestly, wouldn't you rather pull it off without me?"

He was spinning it now. She recognized the manipulative move, but actually, she did want to pull this off without... maybe not him, but his name attached. Matt was right. If the movie succeeded with him in it, she'd always wonder. Now the success would all be attributed to her and Jay and the crew. Her determined, fiery spirit resurged. "You're right. I can do this on my own." Then her voice softened. "But I'll miss you." She held her breath. Now that the work stuff was settled, where did they stand relationship-wise? Was he bailing on the movie *and* her?

"I'll miss you, too," he said, to her relief. "But three weeks is nothing, right? Hollywood power couples last when they're apart longer than that."

Her heart warmed. Hollywood power couple. He saw them that way, too. "Three weeks is nothing," she said, missing him already. "And congratulations on the audition. That role is as good as yours." She meant it and she was proud of him, despite the pickle he'd just left her in.

"Thanks, babe. Now go make a movie that proves all the Hollywood execs wrong."

That was exactly what Selena planned to do. As soon as she found a new leading man.

Orosco Campgrounds, Wild River

THE POUNDING ON the cabin door had his eyes snapping open, then his head instantly throbbing from the violent action. It was still dark in the room, but this time of year in Alaska, that could mean six in the morning...or ten. The small television on the wall was on but muted, and the fire in the corner fireplace had long burned out. A crisp chill in the room had Gus drawing the blankets higher as his eyes closed again. Then muffled voices and the sound of a vehicle door slamming had him sitting up and peering outside the small window next to the bed. A thin veil of fog still lingered over the campgrounds and he couldn't see anyone from this side of the cabin, but he definitely had visitors. Ones he wasn't expecting.

Who the hell was it? Who the hell even knew he was there?

He hadn't told anyone he was coming back to Wild River. He'd gone completely off the grid three weeks ago, after leaving Seattle. Though several friends had reached out, he'd ignored them, unable to face anyone. Other than his sister and grandfather, no one knew where to find him, and the cabins weren't open to guests anymore. The campgrounds had been closed for years, since his father died and no one else had had any interest in running Gus's great-great-grandfather's old business.

The knocking resumed.

He'd ignore it. They'd go away. Must be in the wrong place.

He pulled the bedsheets back up around him as he lay back down on the old, thin mattress on the single wooden bed frame and tried to go back to sleep.

Only they didn't go away. More pounding on the door ensued. Consistent, unending pounding. More vehicle door slams and louder voices drifted through the cabin walls.

What the hell was going on out there? This was private property. Obviously, the Trespassers Will Be Shot on Sight sign on the busted gate hadn't been enough of a deterrent. And, unfortunately, there wasn't even an old prop gun he could use to reinforce the sentiment.

Tossing the thin sheets aside, he barged toward the door, tripping over empty beer cans on the floor and stepping in an old pizza box along the way. The place held a pungent stale scent. He sniffed his shoulder. Actually, maybe that was him. Showering had been an optional daily activity over the last few weeks. A glance in the mirror revealed food stuck in his beard and major bedhead.

Another loud knock as he reached the door had his temper flaring. "What?" he asked, nearly tearing the old weather-beaten door from the hinges as he flung it wide open.

A woman stood there, and her gaping expression as her gaze dropped to his junk had him shielding himself behind the door. Right. Clothes had been optional as well. And it wasn't that he worried about making her uncomfortable with his morning wood, since she was the one demanding his attention; rather, it was the lack of an impressive hard-on that had him acting modest. He'd run out of clean underwear days ago. The ancient coin-operated machine on the campgrounds didn't work, and a trip into town to do laundry didn't appeal to him at all. "What?" he repeated in her slightly stunned silence.

"I'm looking for the owner," she said, with a surprising sense of authority, her thin nose high in the air.

"I'm close enough." Hearing the other voices again, he peered outside beyond her to see a minivan parked on the overgrown gravel drive. Rental plates on the back. Two men, dressed in unseasonal bulky jackets and trendy, impractical hiking boots, were unloading what looked like camera equipment.

Oh, hell, no.

"We are here to film..."

He shut the door in the middle of her sentence and backed away from it. His thundering heart echoed the loud strides of his pacing as he tried not to panic. What the hell? Why were the media trying to harass him all the way here in Alaska? Why now after three weeks? Had Vince Fallon set this up? Revenge for the insults on the guy's skills he'd called out live on national television? His blood boiled. That prick. Not bad enough that he stole Gus's girl, instigating the meltdown that had led to his demise. Now he was trying to pour even more salt in the wound?

More pounding on the door.

"Go away!" What the hell kind of story were they after, anyway? *Sports journalism royalty throws it all away on failed relationship? Heir to the Orosco sports kingdom spirals into depression in the middle of nowhere?*

"Open up!" The woman sounded a lot stronger and bossier than her five-foot-six, hundred-pound frame would have led him to think. Her persistence was impressive, but still, she had to get lost. He had nothing to say to the media. He had expected they'd have moved on to a new scandal by now. So much for thinking the whole thing would blow over soon and he could get back to rebuilding his life and whatever career he could salvage.

"Hey—I need to talk to you!"

She was relentless. Probably made a great reporter. "No comment!" he yelled through the door and gave it a little kick for good measure, stubbing his toe in the process. *"Shit."* He hopped around on one foot, the pressure pulsing in the toe. Where the hell were his boots? He scanned the cabin. Discarded clothes littered the floor next to his open suitcase, but he didn't see the boots.

"We've already paid to use this location. Open the damn door!" the woman yelled.

Paid to use this location? What the hell was she talking about?

His cell phone rang and he groaned, seeing his sister's number. "Forget to tell me something?" he asked, answering the call.

"There's a film crew arriving today," Trish said, sounding preoccupied. The sound of the buzzing newsroom in the background made Gus's chest ache with longing. He desperately missed being in the studio, the thrill of breaking sports stories, the lively debates with his coanchors... the comforts of his bachelor pad. "Arrived already, actually," Trish continued. "I've got a movie star sending me text messages. All caps, about some jerk being uncooperative. I assume that's you."

Yeah, she was all-caps-ing him, too. Only in real life.

"Put some clothes on and get them settled. They plan to be there for three weeks," Trish said.

His older sister and her orders could kiss his ass. She couldn't boss him around anymore like she did when they were kids...or when she was higher on the chain of command at the studio. She wielded zero control over him at all anymore. "You said the place would be empty." No one had been there for years, and they chose now to need the campsite?

"It was. Now it isn't."

"I came here to get away from people...cameras."

"They aren't filming you. Relax," she said. "Just stay locked in your cabin and no one will even notice you." He could hear the sound of her desk phone ringing and papers rustling in the background. The news studio was always buzzing with activity and she was busy. He missed being busy. He missed the fast pace and the overall vibe of working in the world of sports. Three weeks away from it felt like forever. The longer he was away, the harder it would be to crawl his way back. The presence of the media had freaked him out; knowing they weren't here for him was even worse. A sinking feeling in his gut said no one gave a shit.

"Hello!?" The pounding on the door resumed. "We're not leaving!"

Jesus. "I'll take care of it," he told Trish. He ran a hand over his hair and disconnected the call. Pulling on a pair of jeans and a T-shirt, he rummaged through the mess until he found his boots. After shoving his feet into them, Gus threw open the door just as the woman's fist was about to make contact with it. The little holy terror fell forward, and he extended his hand to her forehead to prevent her from falling into him.

"Hey!" She swiped his hand away and straightened herself. With squared shoulders, she glared at him. "Nice of you to put clothes on this time." Her gaze swept over him and she wrinkled her nose as she sniffed the air.

His gaze landed on her chest. Or rather, the multicolored ratlike thing she carried in what appeared to be a baby carrier strapped to her chest. "Is that supposed to be a dog?" Who the hell dyed their pet's fur to look like some sort of unicorn?

"This is Unicorn," she said, obviously offended as she affectionately stroked the animal as though he might have hurt its feelings.

Apparently, someone who named their pet Unicorn.

"Follow me," he said, grabbing a rusted metal key from the hanger behind the door and stepping outside. He shut the door and pushed past her, his shoulder nudging hers not so gently in the process.

Her unimpressed humph behind him almost made him smile, but he wasn't sure his face knew how to make that motion anymore. Three weeks holed up in the cabin alone, he wasn't even certain he still knew how to form a complete sentence. He trudged through the overgrown, wet, dewy grass connecting the cabins, and she was close on his heels. He threw a glance over his shoulder to imply his need for some space, but she ignored it, and the smell of her soft, sweet perfume swirled around his head on the breeze. He held his breath against the feminine scent and the reminder of the cause of his current predicament.

Sure, she wasn't Aileen and the perfume wasn't even close to his ex's preferred eau de toilette—it was gentler, less harsh; it was actually kind of nice—but right now, he was painting all women with the same brush.

Reaching the storage shed, he unlocked the door and turned to face her. "How many cabins did you reserve?" He wouldn't put it past Trish to have rented out the entire place, including his cabin.

"We just need the one. For filming. We aren't sleeping out here." She shuddered as though she couldn't think of a worse fate.

She moved closer to peer inside the storage shed, and within the close proximity, her dog tried to lick him. He pulled back just in time to avoid the tiny pink tongue. "Gross."

Her eyes narrowed. "Right. Because my dog is the disgusting one. At least she's had a bath in the last decade."

He wasn't sure he could win a battle of cleanliness at the moment, so he ignored the insult. "There you go," he said, handing her the cabin key. He paused, then added, "Don't burn it down." He couldn't resist the comment. The new short haircut and lack of dramatic makeup had thrown him for a moment, but he recognized her now. Selena Hudson. Child movie star, now acting in sappy, tearjerker romance movies. Aileen had dragged him to every last one over the course of their three-year relationship. He'd endure the torture all again for another chance with her. He recalled that Selena was most recently famous for her near-death experience with an infuriated stalker. Aileen had been very worried when the news reports had claimed the star had been in a cabin fire in the Alaskan wilderness. One she'd reportedly caused.

Selena's piercing look erased all thoughts of his ex. "Think you know something about it?"

He shrugged. He actually didn't give a shit that she'd accidentally burned down her former bodyguard's family cabin, where they'd been hiding out. In fact, if she burned down these cabins, they'd probably make more off the insurance claim than if they sold the old business, something none of them had found the heart to do yet. "Only what was in the news," he said.

"Well, the news doesn't always get it right," she said defiantly.

If only that was the case. "Okay, then. If that's everything, I'm going to go back to bed now," he said as he re-locked the storage shed.

She looked like she was about to give him an earful about lack of professionalism or some bullshit, her tiny nose pointed sky-high, her "I'm better than you" attitude oozing from her. Hollywood actress all right. No question there. Before Aileen, he'd dated a couple of hopefuls. He'd quickly realized he preferred his women a little more down-to-earth. But then her eyes narrowed as she studied him.

Sweat gathered on his back, and he lowered his head as he tried to move past her.

"Wait!" she called from behind him. Again, way too close. "I know who you are."

Doubtful. Right now, even he didn't know who he was. He'd completely lost his sense of purpose, along with his career and his home.

"You're that sports broadcaster. That guy who lost his shit on TV."

When he kept walking, she quickened her pace behind him. She snapped her fingers several times as she tried to come up with his name. "Orosco Campgrounds... Orosco... Gus!"

He winced. So much for going unnoticed.

"My boyfriend watches your sports news segment. Or did. That was quite the meltdown," she said.

He stopped and turned, dodging her body as she almost collided into him. "Think you know something about it?"

She hesitated, then shrugged, a look of soft sympathy reflecting in dark blue eyes. It transformed her entire expression. Gone was the air of arrogance, replaced with an unsettling understanding that had him backing up, away from her. "Can't believe everything I see in the media, right?" she said softly.

Unfortunately, in this case, she could.

He turned quickly and continued walking. "If you need anything else while you're here, call Trish," he called over his shoulder. He wanted nothing to do with Selena Hudson, her movie or her sympathetic blue eyes.

CHAPTER THREE

"Stop squirming. I'm not letting go yet." Selena held tighter as Leslie tried to wiggle her way out of the hug a few hours later as they arrived in town for her not-so-surprising surprise party. Busy with their respective lives, they hadn't seen one another outside of Skype for a year and Selena was a hugger. Leslie would just have to suck it up.

Leslie gave up the struggle and went completely limp instead.

Selena laughed and reluctantly let go. She was there for a few weeks—she'd get in at least a dozen more. "Don't say you haven't missed me!" she yelled over the loud rock music playing inside The Drunk Tank, the local hot spot on Main Street. The place was packed for a Tuesday night and she loved seeing all the familiar faces around the bar, especially after the day she'd had so far. Ironically, Wild River always felt like a safe space for her.

Leslie tried to appear nonchalant as she tugged on her long blond ponytail. "You call me every day."

"I could stop…"

"I didn't say that," Leslie said with a grin.

Selena was happy to see Leslie, and even happier to see her so happy. That hadn't always been the case. The year before had taken an emotional toll on her former bodyguard as she'd struggled with letting go of the tragedy of losing her fiancé in a car accident on their wedding day and opening herself up to love again. During their wild adventure outrunning Selena's stalker, Leslie had reconnected with her former best friend, Levi Grayson, and had discovered that their feelings went well beyond friendship. She was learning to open up, not be so guarded all the time, and Selena liked to think she'd played a part in this new transition. Their intense near-death experience had changed them both for the better. Leslie was starting to enjoy life more, and Selena was starting to take a tighter rein on hers.

"Wow, what a turnout. I can't believe you threw me a party," she said, scanning the packed bar. The Drunk Tank's small-town charm combined with its hot, mountain-rugged bartenders made it a fun place to spend the evening. She'd gotten to know some of the locals and Leslie's family while she was there previously, and she knew this was a place she could relax and be herself.

However, next to her, Jay looked a little on edge as the rest of the crew headed toward the bar. She introduced him to her friend. "Leslie, this is Jay Kline. He is an amazing filmmaker and the director of the movie we're shooting here."

"I've heard a lot about you," Leslie said politely.

"Yeah, likewise. Selena hasn't stopped talking about this place," he said, still glancing around the bar. He pulled his fedora down lower across his forehead and looked at her like he wanted to wrap her in a cloak. "You sure about this?" he whispered. "I don't want any publicity about the movie yet."

Selena touched his shoulder. "Believe me, there are no paparazzi here."

A cell phone camera light going off in rapid succession nearly blinded her in the bar's dim lighting, and Jay shot her a look.

Selena laughed. "Okay, maybe just this one." She opened her arms wide as Kaia ran into them. Only now, the "little" girl and longtime fan of Selena's family-friendly flicks was almost as tall as Selena was. "You look even older than you did last week on Skype!" she said, standing back to look at the bar owner's daughter, then pulling her in for another hug. After helping Kaia with her lines for the school play the year before, the two had remained in contact. The young girl was smart and tech savvy, and living in Alaska had given her a strength of character rare in teens these days.

Seeing all the friends she'd been missing made Selena feel better after the not-so-great start to the day.

First, Matt bailing on her, and then that asshole, Gus Orosco, giving her a hard time. She'd always gotten a jerk vibe from the sports broadcaster. Gorgeous with a magnetic charisma, the guy was made for the camera, but he always seemed like he'd needed weights in his shoes to keep his overinflated ego from floating him away into oblivion. Unfortunately, it looked like his hotheaded temper had done the job. Exiled to his family's campsite outside Wild River.

How the mighty had fallen.

Still, she had felt a tinge of sympathy for the guy, seeing him look like such a hot mess. Obviously, he wasn't dealing with his massive mistake very well, but Selena could hardly blame him. If she had to see Matt with someone else—getting engaged to someone else—she might lose her shit, too.

And, unfortunately, the image of his naked body hadn't yet completely evaporated from her memory. Shock had imprinted the image—that was all it was. She definitely hadn't been attracted to the grumpy man who smelled like beer, firewood and cheese.

"I'm so happy you're here," Kaia said. "This place is so

boring, I could die." Kaia had practically gone from kid to
teen overnight, and Selena caught the look of irritation from
Kaia's father, Tank, as he poured a round of shots behind
the bar. No doubt the dad had to be wondering where his
outdoor-loving, baseball-cap-wearing daughter had disappeared to. Standing in front of her now, Kaia was almost
unrecognizable. Wearing slim-fitting jean capris with low
wedge heels and a tank top, her hair curled and with just a
hint of makeup that she obviously thought her dad wouldn't
notice, she looked so much more mature than she had just
the year before.

Not what any protective dad wanted to hear.

Unfortunately for Kaia, her dad's nickname was well-
earned. The guy made The Rock look small in comparison.
The boys around here were going to have to get creative if
they wanted to date her anytime soon.

"Please don't post those pictures to social media yet," Jay
asked Kaia, looking ready to confiscate the girl's cell phone.

She gave him a reassuring smile. "Don't worry. I know
the drill. And by the way, I saw that short noir you wrote
and produced set in that suspension club. It was fantastic."

"You saw *what*?" Tank asked, spilling whiskey as he
tried to eavesdrop from a distance.

"Nothing, Dad!" Kaia said, winking at Jay.

Jay immediately seemed to relax and relish the praise.
"Yeah? You saw that?"

Kaia nodded. "The cinematography was amazing. And
the way you captured the purity and essence of the extremists and told the story with such a compassionate eye, despite the edgy darkness."

"I like this kid," Jay told Selena, before heading toward
the bar, where the rest of the crew congregated.

Her gaze lingered on the group. It didn't escape her notice that they weren't all that eager to hang out with her and get to know her friends. Well, whatever. They could enjoy their time together and she'd enjoy her friends' company.

"Where's Unicorn?" Kaia asked.

"No dogs in the bar," Tank said.

Selena laughed. "Don't worry, Tank. She's at the B and B." She'd contemplated smuggling her into the place, but she suspected she was already on the bartender's shit list for offering Kaia the opportunity to help out on set. The young girl had really developed a passion for the industry, and Selena thought Tank should be happy that his daughter seemed to prefer behind the scenes to being in front of the camera. "You still okay with checking in on her and walking her while I'm filming?"

"Absolutely."

"Has school started yet?"

"Last week," Kaia said, wrinkling her nose.

"What's with the face? I thought you loved school." Kaia excelled at everything she did.

"Junior high is going to be torture. I don't know how I'm going to survive it," she said with a shrug. "When does the movie start filming?"

"Our table is free," Leslie said before Selena could explain their recent setback. She motioned for them to follow her toward the table in the back that her fiancé, Levi, was holding for them. Selena tried to sound unfazed as she answered.

"In a few days…" They'd been scheduled to start the next morning, but Matt's character was needed for almost every scene. They'd need to recast his role, and fast. Jay had had a full-on anxiety attack at the airport when she'd delivered the bad news. He'd wanted to sue Matt for breach of contract, but they both knew there was no money to do that and Selena wouldn't risk her relationship. Putting her career on the line for this movie was enough.

Unfortunately, despite spending the afternoon in her room at the B and B, calling every male actor she could think of in LA and beyond, so far she'd had zero luck securing an alternate. Most claimed to be busy filming other projects or in pre-pro or post on projects, but she knew the real issue was that none of them wanted to be part of the risk she was taking in case it blew up in her face. No one else attached to the project had an A-list "friends" list, so this was all on her. She hadn't told Jay yet that she was having no luck. She might have even lied and said there were a few more people she was waiting to hear back from. She hated to have to call her stepdad to try to use his name and success to find an actor willing to do this, but she was running out of options. Jay had trusted her with this project and her ability to pull it off. He was already stressed over losing Matt. She couldn't let him lose faith in her. She had to think of something, and fast.

Kaia's frown didn't make her feel any better. "The filming schedule you sent me last week said cameras needed to start rolling tomorrow if you're going to come in on budget."

Maybe sharing all the details with the preteen hadn't been a great idea. She took a deep breath and tried to sound unfazed as she said, "My leading man bailed."

"Matt ditched you?" Kaia asked, eyes wide.

Even Leslie looked pissed as she swung around. "For real?"

"It's not like that. He has another movie," she said, waving a hand. "And I'm not at all upset about it or mad at him. The blockbuster film offer wasn't exactly something he could turn down."

"Well…that's very unselfish of you," Leslie said carefully. "But he did leave you high and dry."

"I thought you being blissfully in love would take the cynical edge off," Selena said, hating to admit the truth of Leslie's words. Matt could have still filmed this movie with her. It would have taken three weeks, and preproduction for the other movie wouldn't start for months. She hadn't heard from him again since they'd spoken at the airport, despite calling him a few times. Obviously, he thought she might try to convince him to reconsider, so he was avoiding her until she solved the problem he'd created. *That* pissed her off a little…

"Just saying, no matter the reason, it was a shit thing to do." Leslie's cheeks flushed slightly at the mention of her fiancé, who stood now to greet them as they approached the booth.

"Hey, movie star. Nice to see you," Levi said, giving Selena a hug.

"Thanks. You, too." She released him and then slid into the booth next to Kaia. Levi already had their drinks on the table, so she reached for her apple martini and took a sip.

Levi glanced at them all, obviously sensing they'd been in the middle of a conversation. "Everything okay?"

"Matt ditched out on Selena," Kaia said.

Selena sighed. While she might be able to understand and forgive Matt, obviously her friends wouldn't get it. It should make her feel better that they had her back like this; instead, it made her feel defensive, as though she needed to reassure them that she wasn't dating a guy unworthy of her attention. "He has another film."

Levi seemed to sense her conflict as he nodded. "I guess that happens sometimes, right? Scheduling conflicts?"

She sent him a grateful smile. "See? Levi gets it," she said pointedly. "It's just business."

Leslie and Kaia exchanged a look that she chose to ignore.

"You're filming at the old Orosco Campgrounds, right?" Levi asked, sitting across from her and next to Leslie. He took her hand in his and kissed it almost absentmindedly. A slight sensation of jealousy hit Selena at the sweet, casual gesture. She wanted that. With Matt. Right now, their lives primarily revolved around work, talk of work, sex and more work. They had a real connection, but she wanted it to move beyond the fact that they were both movie stars and develop into something more real and affectionate...outside the bedroom. She wanted to go on road trips with him, introduce him to her family, meet his family. So far, they'd been too busy, or there was always an excuse...mostly on his end... to avoid these normal relationship milestones. But so what? They were moving at a slow pace, letting things evolve over time without pressure. There was nothing wrong with that, and she wouldn't start stressing over it just because their relationship didn't look like other people's.

She took a sip of her martini before answering Levi's question about the filming location. "Yeah, if a real murder doesn't happen there first," she mumbled.

He frowned. "What do you mean?"

"That former sports reporter, Gus Orosco, is licking his wounds there. It's an old family campsite apparently, and the guy is a class-A jerk face."

"Gus is back in town?" Levi looked far too excited at the news.

"There's no way you're friends with him." Levi was nice and caring and humble despite being a supersexy smoke jumper. Selena had made a play for him last year when he'd helped them hide out from her stalker at the smoke jumpers' cabin, but alas, his heart belonged to Leslie. The friendship between the two men seemed unlikely. Levi would have nothing in common with Gus. He didn't really seem all that into sports.

He nodded. "Well, we used to be. We went to the same school and were in Scouts together as kids. His dad was the group leader. We had drinks a few months ago when I was in LA battling those wildfires."

Selena's eyes narrowed. "You told me you were too busy to hang out!"

Levi laughed. "It was in the airport bar. He was flying back to Seattle after reporting on some sports story."

"Oh. That's okay, then," she said teasingly.

"So, how are you going to film the movie without a leading man?" Kaia asked, sipping her virgin martini. Obviously, the young girl was determined to keep her focused on the issue at hand.

Unfortunately, she had no idea. She'd exhausted the talent possibilities she could reach out to in LA. She hesitated, scanning the bar. There was no shortage of men in Wild River. Talent existed everywhere. Untapped potential could be all around her.

Selena pulled out her phone and opened her social media. It was a wild idea, but it was the only one coming to her at the moment. One that had to work—otherwise, they were screwed. Either way, it was worth a shot. "We're doing a casting call," she said, typing into her social media manager. She hit Post before she could rethink it, and there was no turning back. She showed the group the post that would go viral within the hour.

So much for keeping news about the movie quiet for now. *Sorry, Jay.*

Within seconds, his wide-eyed murderous gaze met hers across the bar. She shrugged and gave him a look that begged him to trust her.

"Here? You're doing a casting call here?" In contrast, Kaia looked like it was the best news she'd ever heard, as she opened her Twitter app and shared Selena's post with her followers.

Selena shrugged again, desperate not to reveal how desperate she actually felt. "I'm sure there's undiscovered talent here. We just need to find it."

THE FILMING CREW hadn't come back the night before after they'd finished scouting the campgrounds and marking where they planned to shoot various scenes, but late the next morning, Gus could see the crew setting up cameras and lighting equipment in the cabin across from his. So his unfriendly welcome hadn't frightened them away.

And the tiniest part of him was actually happy about that.

He hadn't realized just how far he'd spiraled, being out there completely alone for three weeks, and the sight of other humans—humans not from Wild River and who were involved in a similar industry—had him longing for some interaction. Just the sight of the film set had his bones twitching to get back to the career he loved, back in a television studio.

Unfortunately, it also reminded him that it wasn't up to him. He hadn't reached out to other sports networks or potential new agents yet. If he was being honest with himself, he wasn't prepared for the inevitable rejection. Nonetheless, either way, he had to know if he still had a future in sports broadcasting, and there was no better time than the present.

Pacing the cabin, he started with the person most likely

to accept his call—his former agent. His cell phone to his ear, he paced in front of the window as the call tried to connect. Three rings, then dead air. He looked at the phone to check the cell connection; he had full bars. He dialed again. Three rings, then nothing, not even a voice mail.

Unbelievable. The man wasn't even bothering to screen his calls. He'd simply set his number not to receive calls from Gus.

He sighed, rotated his shoulders and threw several jabs as he bounced on his toes. He wouldn't get discouraged. It was just one agent. There were hundreds more.

Hundreds more who apparently wanted nothing to do with him. Hours later, Gus had heard so many different versions of *fuck off*, his mood had gone from cautiously optimistic to devastatingly disappointed. No one wanted to give him a second chance. He wasn't employable in his field right now...and possibly not ever.

So much for the industry having a short memory.

With barely enough strength to dial the final number on his list, he shut his eyes tight as the call connected to the last agent. "This is Blair."

At least the man had answered. Gus cleared his throat. "Hey, Blair. It's Gus Orosco. Long time." They'd met at several sports conventions over the years and the man had actually tried to poach him once, so maybe this might be the one...

"Hey, Gus. Great to hear from you."

It was? "Yeah, hey, so I'm in the market for new representation and I was wondering if you wanted to chat sometime. Coffee or drinks?"

Blair seemed surprised. "Oh...um, I guess you haven't heard."

"Heard what?"

"I'm out of the game... Actually, I was forced out. Bullshit lawsuit from several clients about withholding funds. You know the crap we deal with in this industry..."

Gus rubbed his forehead and suppressed a sigh. "Yeah. Sorry, man."

"But, hey, we can still grab that drink if you want."

Gus cleared his throat. "Absolutely. I'm out of town right now, but I'll reach out when I'm back in the city."

"Sounds great. Anytime. I'm free," Blair said eagerly.

Gus disconnected the call, feeling worse than he had before reaching out. Guess he had his answer about where he stood career-wise. If agents weren't willing to take a chance on repping him, studios wouldn't be willing to hire him either.

An hour later, slumped in an armchair, one leg draped over the side, a bucket of day-old chicken wings on his lap, he flipped through the stations on the television. Depressed and bored out of his mind, he continued to glance outside the window whenever he heard the crew talking or laughing, and he fought the urge to go see if they needed any help.

He hadn't caught sight of Selena out there yet. He suspected the talent wasn't slumming it with the crew or about to get her hands dirty setting up. He'd sensed a disconnect between her and the others the day before as they'd toured the campgrounds. She didn't seem comfortable with anyone except the movie's director, Jay. She was obviously the only big name in the group.

Maybe she was doing the movie as a favor or something...

His cell phone chimed with the first new message in weeks, and reaching for it, he saw his friend Levi's number lighting up the screen. Opening the text, he read the only message from his buddy since three months before when they'd had a few drinks at an LAX bar. Coincidentally in the right place at the right time. It had been great to see his old Scouts friend again and they'd said they'd stay in touch, but life always got in the way of those promises.

Hey, heard you were in town. Let's get together, he read now.

Fantastic—that little Hollywood terror had spread the rumor about him being there. So much for lying low. She probably wasn't complimentary about him either. He could just imagine the way she must have described him, given the fact that he'd looked like hell when she'd woken him from his depressed slumber. Well, what the hell kind of greeting had she expected to get, especially after she'd recognized him?

Seeing Levi might not be such a horrible idea, though. He was starting to get cabin fever and he was out of beer.

A long cold shower later, he found the least smelly clothes he could find in the pile on the floor, threw on his boots and headed into town.

Wild River was an outdoor enthusiast's dream, with its amazing backwoods for hiking, camping and fishing in summer, and world-class ski hills in winter. It was one of the most amazing places in Alaska to grow up. Winter weather left something to be desired, but it was worth braving the cold to witness the show of the aurora borealis in those long months of darkness. The splash of color lighting up the night sky and the view of stars that seemed to multiply the longer you looked was something he knew he'd been lucky to have in his backyard. The small town was surrounded by mountain ranges that reached the sky, the white snowcapped peaks covered even in the summer months.

As a teen, when his father was alive, they'd spent most of their days hunting together. Trish had already moved to Seattle by the time Gus was eight, so it had only been him and his dad for a long time, until Gus moved south as well. His dad died a year later from a heart attack shoveling snow. The death had been sudden and unexpected, and he and Trish had only returned to Wild River long enough for a small funeral and burial. Gus hadn't been back since.

There wasn't anything left in Wild River for him now, with his career and remaining family in Seattle, but surprisingly, the familiar surroundings of Main Street, with the same stores and overhangs exactly the way they always were, and the faces he recognized as he passed on his way to The Drunk Tank, had him feeling better than he had in days. So many winters had been spent skiing the slopes in the distance and participating in the town's winter and holiday events. Summers were fun, with the town's population exploding with tourists coming to camp and explore the backwoods. The memories wrapping around him were like a comforting blanket after the rough, reality-hitting day he'd faced. Comfort he hadn't expected. Comfort he hadn't thought he'd needed. Of course, the high-altitude, fresh, cool, smog-free late-September mountain air probably helped as well. Coming to Wild River might have been the best thing for him after all.

He hated when Trish was right.

As he approached the bar, he slowed his pace a little. A long line of men stood outside, spanning several blocks and wrapping around the corner. They were all reading something either on their phones or on papers in their hands. A barricade had been set up on the sidewalk and Jay was standing at the door of The Drunk Tank with a clipboard and headset on.

What the hell were they doing? He thought they were only filming at the campgrounds. They were infiltrating the ski town as well?

Pulling out his cell phone, he texted Levi: We were meeting at The Drunk Tank, right?

Levi's response was immediate: I'm inside already. Got us a pool table in the back.

Gus frowned as he tucked the phone away and approached Jay at the door.

"Hey, man...no cutting," a guy yelled out from the line.

Others grumbled their annoyance at his perceived skipping of the queue.

Gus ignored it as Jay glanced up from his clipboard to give him a surprised look. "Hey, can I go on inside? I'm not here for whatever this is. I'm meeting someone in there." Though he'd rather meet Levi somewhere else. Anywhere else. This looked...ominous.

Jay eyed him, then pointed a black-painted fingernail at him as he recognized Gus's freshly shaved face. "You're the Orosco Campgrounds guy." He didn't look impressed.

Gus nodded and cleared his throat. He owed the guy an apology. "About yesterday... My sister hadn't informed me that I was to expect you. I had assumed I'd have the campgrounds to myself, so apologies for the inappropriate welcome." An image of Selena's shocked expression at his nakedness flashed in his mind and he immediately felt even more embarrassed. He might be down on his luck these days, but he needed to pull himself together.

The guy nodded and cocked his head to the side with a sympathetic look. "It's all good. We've all been there."

Gus didn't want to get into the meaning of that sentence, so he mumbled his thanks and pointed inside. "So, can I...?"

"Go on in." Jay held open the door and Gus entered the

bar, immediately wanting to cover his eyes from the blaring lights.

Unlike every other time he'd been inside the place, all the interior lights were on and the curtains were open. There was no music playing and he couldn't move farther into the bar without being stopped at a long table where Selena and two other women—or rather, one other woman and a teenage girl—sat.

What the hell was Selena up to? She'd been in town five minutes and she'd completely taken over the place?

Her smile faded slightly as she glanced up and saw him. She was cuter when she wasn't yelling at him or demanding to have her own way. She looked so different in real life than she did in movies. It wasn't just the new, shorter hairstyle; her features were softer without all the makeup. In jeans and a cashmere, V-necked sweater, she didn't look like Hollywood royalty at all. He might even be convinced she belonged here in Wild River. "Hey," he said awkwardly, giving an even more awkward wave.

Hands in pockets.

"You here to audition?" she asked, and he couldn't tell if she was intrigued by the idea or terrified, as her dark blue eyes scanned him and stopped at the hot sauce stain on the T-shirt he wore under his leather jacket. At least he'd showered and shaved. That had to be a step up from the last time she'd seen him.

Not a big one, if her expression told the story.

Well, unlike the rest of the men in town, he wasn't trying to impress her that day. He squared his shoulders and lifted his chin. "Hell, no," he said, glancing around. "I'm just meeting a friend."

The blonde woman next to her stood and extended a hand toward him. "You must be Gus. Levi's friend?"

He nodded, shaking her hand. When had things gotten so formal in Wild River? Selena's presence was already changing the vibe around town and he wasn't sure he liked it. "Yeah."

"I'm his fiancée, Leslie," the woman said.

Ah, the one Levi hadn't shut up about when they'd met for drinks at LAX months before. Back when Gus was still madly in love and happy as well. To anyone else in the bar that night, their conversation must have been nauseating as they'd basically gushed about their significant others. But his friend hadn't been lying about how attractive his fiancée was. Long blond hair pulled back into a tight ponytail and big brown eyes that seemed to miss nothing. It didn't surprise him that she was in law enforcement. She was Selena's ex-bodyguard and she looked like she could kick his ass, so he'd best be on his best behavior. "I've heard a lot about you," he said politely. "Can I come around?" He gestured to the barricades they'd created on either side of their audition check-in desk.

"Oh, sure," Leslie said, allowing him access.

He paused on the other side and, against his better judgment, asked, "What exactly are you doing, anyway?" He could hazard a guess...

"It's a casting call." The teenager spoke up, sounding like it was the most exciting day in her young life. She was practically vibrating on the seat, while obviously attempting to appear cool and unaffected. It wasn't working.

"For which role?" He hadn't seen many people at the campsite...mostly just the crew. Were they seriously hoping to cast a full movie with local talent? That was ambitious.

Selena hesitated. "The leading male character."

He frowned. "You left LA, where everyone and their dog

wants to be an actor, just to try to find someone to star in your movie in Wild River?"

She huffed, holding her pen in her hand like a dagger. "What's your point?"

He shrugged. It was none of his business, and that pen could do some damage. "No point. Good luck with it," he said as he turned to head toward the pool tables, where Levi stood waiting. He widened his eyes and sent the guy a look. Levi laughed.

"I still can't believe Levi is friends with that guy," he heard Selena mumble, and he stopped.

Just keep going. Who cares what she thinks of you?

He turned back. "I'm sorry—what?"

She shook her head and smiled pleasantly. "I said, have fun playing pool."

"Thought that's what you said." He continued on toward the back of the bar and glanced back over his shoulder. Unfortunately, she glanced over hers at the same time. The electricity vibrating between them was undeniable, and he wasn't sure why they continued to bicker. He could just steer clear of her and she could ignore him, but the verbal sparring had him feeling more alive than he had in weeks. Her stare burned with such an intensity it was almost impossible to look away.

Was she checking him out right now? Or plotting his death? Hard to tell. And damn if that didn't excite him.

Firecrackers was what his grandfather had called the women the men in the family were attracted to, and Selena Hudson definitely fell into that category.

"Watch your step," she said.

He frowned. "Huh?" He looked forward just as his foot met air, and he stumbled onto the sunken flooring where the pool tables were. He'd forgotten about that step. He refused to look her way. He knew she was probably laughing her ass off at his clumsy stumble.

"Hey, man. Good to see you," Levi said, handing him a beer and tapping him on the shoulder as he tore off his jacket.

"You, too," he said, taking a much-needed gulp. "Though you think you could have chosen a worse place?" Choices were limited in Wild River, but somewhere not holding movie auditions would have been preferable. Still, he couldn't honestly say he wasn't intrigued to watch how this would play out. He suspected the last-minute search for a lead hadn't been part of the plan, and he doubted Selena was going to find what she was looking for.

Levi nodded toward the check-in table. "I'm here for moral support." He lowered his voice. "This isn't exactly Leslie's thing."

"Well, why is she doing it? Is she back on the clock?" Had Selena rehired her former bodyguard? She didn't exactly need one in Wild River.

Levi laughed. "Not necessary. Everyone around here adores Selena."

"Can't imagine why," he mumbled against the rim of the beer bottle.

"And it's actually really fun to see the closet aspiring actors in our midst. Remember John Kiely from the auto repair shop?"

"No shit. He was here?" The guy barely spoke a word. Grunting was his preferred way to communicate, and now he wanted to star in a movie?

Levi nodded.

"What the hell is she doing here filming a thriller, anyway? I thought she only made rom-coms?"

"She's trying to get out of the box Hollywood has put her in. Prove she can do something different."

According to the *Gossip Now* reports Gus had read online when he'd googled her the night before, she'd dropped her entire management team after her stalker scandal the year before, which meant she was embarking on this new film project on her own. That took bravery.

His gaze fell on her, and a new feeling washed over him. Something like respect, maybe?

"Anyway, she's taking a gamble on her career, so try not to unnecessarily complicate things for her," Levi said, giving him a pointed look as he handed him a pool stick.

Gus averted his eyes as she glanced their way again. "Don't worry, man. I plan to stay as far away from those cameras—" and that pretty little firecracker "—as possible," he said, hitting the cue ball and sending the multicolored balls scattering.

CHAPTER FOUR

THIS WAS AN absolute nightmare.

"He wasn't this bad in auditions," Jay whispered to her as their first-choice substitute leading man, Marcos, a twenty-eight-year-old chef from the Wild River Resort and member of the local theater community, vomited his nerves into the trees.

"I don't get it," Selena said to Kaia, feeling her own anxiety rise. "I thought he did local productions?" He'd been fantastic the day before. So fantastic, in fact, that she'd started to feel validated in her belief that talent was everywhere.

The young girl typed on the phone. "He does, but it looks like he's more of a behind-the-scenes guy," Kaia said, turning her cell phone search of the local theater contributors toward Selena.

Obviously someone with a passion and talent for acting, but also crippling performance anxiety. During her career, she'd met dozens of people with big dreams—and fear holding those aspirations hostage.

"I'll just be a sec," Marcos said, holding up a finger before retching again.

Selena sent him a sympathetic look. "It's the cameras and the lighting freaking him out."

Jay checked his watch as the sun started to dip below the trees. "We are running out of daylight. Soon we will need to switch to the nighttime scenes." He undid his man bun, ran a hand through his long hair and redid the bun—a nervous habit of his. Then he placed his hands on his hips and shot her a pleading look. "You're sure there was absolutely no one else on your contact list you could have reached out to?"

"I tried everyone."

"Call your stepdad," Jay begged.

Tempting, but even if Mel was reachable in Somalia, her problem seemed irrelevant when her parents were off helping solve hunger. And besides, she really didn't want to rely on her stepfather's help. She'd always made her way on her own, as much as she'd appreciated his support and guidance in the early years of her career. And now, when so much was riding on this, including her self-esteem, she didn't want to feel as though she'd needed the boost from his household name. "They are overseas, working with one of their charities," she said simply, because she knew the humanitarian side of Jay wouldn't push for her to make the call.

"What about Matt? Any way you can persuade him to reconsider?" Jay's desperate look almost made her cave. Instead, she squared her shoulders and stood straighter. He thought they needed Matt, and she wanted desperately to prove to him that they didn't. They didn't need Matt or her stepfather. The movie had her and that would be enough.

Please, God, let that be enough.

"We don't need Matt," she said confidently. And besides, she'd already pleaded with his voice mail the night before. His quick phone call that morning had been just a reiteration of his spiel at the airport.

Better to succeed without him attached...prove to herself and Hollywood that this was the right direction for her future career…yada, yada, yada.

"Right now, we need someone who isn't throwing up." Jay paced, and the rest of the crew looked equally frustrated as they waited for instruction. Time and budget were being wasted the longer they stood around. And they were all pointing the finger at her over this predicament.

"Well, it's your call," she said to Jay. "Should we keep trying with him or bring in another one?" The auditions the day before had yielded three potentials, and in the interest of time and situations like this one, they'd tentatively "hired" all three. Of course, the actors were getting paid in experience and all the free coffee and doughnuts they could consume, but they all just seemed happy to be involved. Marcos had been the best at delivering the more dramatic lines in the script, and his physical appearance had been similar to Matt's—thin, tall, clean-cut—so she'd selected him as the favorite. Two other men sat on the sidelines, waiting. Hopefully with stronger stomachs.

"Marcos, honey! You think you can finish out the scene?" Jay asked as the man started walking toward them.

Marcos nodded, but one look at the cameras on the boom above his head sent him rushing back into the trees. "Nope," he said, before bending at the waist again.

Shit. She forced enthusiasm into her voice as she said, "Okay, well, he's out. Let's grab the next one and try to shoot from the top."

"God, I hope the dog isn't this much work," Jay mumbled, rubbing his forehead.

Kaia laid a reassuring hand on his arm. "Don't worry. Diva is a superstar. You're going to love her when you meet her tomorrow."

At least they could count on one role to be a success.

The search-and-rescue trained husky would be playing the part of the leading man's dog in the scenes the next day.

Jay reset the crew as Selena headed to the holding tent where the two alternates sat drinking coffee and eating doughnuts. She forced a big smile as she addressed them. "So, Marcos is a no-go."

The two men sat straighter and with eager expressions.

At least they were excited. Now, if just one of them could turn that into talent, they'd be okay. She eyed her choices. Truthfully, Marcos had been their first choice, and then the others were tied for second place. "Um…" Dan was shorter, stockier, and his longish hair suited the idea of a recluse who'd been out alone in the forest for too long. Joaquin was gorgeous with dark hair and crystal blue eyes, but he was a little younger than she'd envisioned the lead. It was a crapshoot either way. This whole idea was a long shot, and she was seeing that now, even if she was reluctant to admit it. If these men didn't work out, they were going to have to pack it in and head back to LA. Maybe film in a few months when they could recast. It meant missing that year's film festival deadline, but ultimately, it would be better to postpone filming than mess it up. She was still holding a thin thread of hope that one of the men sitting in front of her could pull off the unexpected miracle of an amazing, award-winning performance. "Dan, want to give it a shot?" The man performed regularly with the local choir, so at least he was comfortable in front of an audience.

"Sure," he said, standing and rotating his shoulders. He ran through a vocal scale, and they quickly read through the lines for the scene they were trying to film. It was one of the less dramatic, less intense scenes. They were trying to ease the actor in slowly, hoping to build momentum.

And Dan did great as he rehearsed with her. Really great,

actually. Even Kaia nodded her approval, joining them in the tent. His voice was strong and clear, and he didn't appear nervous at all. Wardrobe and lighting could help him look the part. She glanced at Kaia. "I'm going to freshen up. Do you want to bring Dan over to makeup, please?"

"Absolutely," Kaia said, leading the way out of the tent. "Follow me, please."

Selena turned to Joaquin. "Thank you for your patience."

"Let me know if you need me," the guy said, turning his attention back to a game of *Among Us* on his cell phone.

Selena hoped they wouldn't. So far, the movie wasn't working out the way she'd envisioned or hoped, and she really didn't want to be the reason Jay had to push the filming. This was his passion project, and it had all the right ingredients to be a huge success. When he'd approached her about starring in it, she'd been one of those ingredients, but her decisions in dealing with these setbacks had to be making him question his initial one of bringing her on board.

Twenty minutes later, she shook off the lingering unease and doubt as they restarted the scene. It was the part in the movie, about twenty minutes in, after the dramatic rescue scene in the woods. The morning after...

Dan swung the ax, chopping the wood outside the cabin. At least the action looked realistic. The ax came down hard, dividing the pieces with ease. Matt would have definitely struggled, never having held an ax in his life. Did everyone in Wild River know how to chop wood? Was it like a skill they were born with?

Selena approached him, falling into character, applying the slight limp from her injuries from escaping her abuser and having run through the forest all night. "Hey, I, uh... just wanted to say thank you. For yesterday," she said softly. She was aiming to sound slightly unsure, but added just a touch of strength to her voice, as this was the first turning point in her character's arc, where she started rebuilding her confidence and self-worth and will to live.

Dan turned to look at her, but as he delivered his line, he was looking past her. At the camera. "It was no problem."

Jay yelled, "Cut!"

Dan frowned as he glanced at Kaia, off-screen, holding a copy of the script, ready to give lines if needed. "That was the line, right?"

Selena nodded. "Yes, and you delivered it great!" Positive reinforcement went a long way. She paused. "It's just… you can't look straight into the camera." Breaking the fourth wall was something a lot of newbies did. Unfortunately, it was a hard habit for most to break.

Dan nodded. "Oh, okay. We did at the audition, so…"

"I know. You're right," she said calmly. "That was just for us to determine what you'd look like on camera, but now that we're actually filming, just talk to me."

"Okay. Got it," he said. He cleared his throat and they got into position again.

Selena delivered her line again.

And again, Dan's eyes met the camera. This time, *after* he delivered the line.

Selena fought for patience. These guys weren't professional actors. What did she expect? Dan was really great. If he could just figure out how to stop looking at the cameras, he had the potential to be good in the role.

"I did it again, didn't I?" Dan looked embarrassed as he ran a hand over his face, wiping half his makeup away.

"Don't stress. Just pretend the cameras are not even here. Just two people talking," she said.

He nodded. "Okay. I got it this time."

He did not, in fact, have it this time or the next ten attempts. Each time, his gaze seemed pulled to the camera lens like a magnetic force had taken over his line of vision.

Even Kaia looked exasperated as she rolled her head up toward the darkening sky.

Jay rose from his director chair and approached. "Selena, can we chat for a sec?"

"We will be right back," she told Dan with a forced smile.

Out of earshot, Jay looked ready to burst, and for a normally very calm and centered guy, Selena knew the seriousness of his impending meltdown. "We've lost the day," he said, gesturing to the disappearing sun. "This scene is supposed to be midday. Even for Alaska, this is getting too dark."

She sighed. "I know. I'm sorry! These men were the best options."

"*Matt* was the best option." Jay started to pace.

Great—they were back to that again. "I know, but we don't need him." She hated the idea that Jay was losing confidence that she could carry this movie herself. *She* had suggested Matt instead of holding auditions in LA, and now this was on her. But the movie really was about the strong female lead. For twenty scenes, she was completely alone, and she could blow those solitary performances out of the water. They just needed the other scenes to come close to being as good. If the movie did well on the film festival circuit and got picked up by a major studio, they'd recast and reshoot with a bigger budget anyway.

"These guys aren't actors and I'm putting my career on the line with this movie," Jay said, inhaling sharply through his nose, then releasing the breath in a rush through his mouth.

So was she, but she understood how important this was

to Jay as well and how close to the edge he was, so it wasn't the time to remind him that they were both in this together. "Okay, let's grab the last guy and try filming a different scene. Third time's a charm, right?"

"Hey, guys, hate to interrupt, but the third alternate just bailed," Kaia said, popping her head around the side of the cabin.

Selena's eyes widened. "What? Why?"

"Apparently, his girlfriend caught wind of the fact that there were…intimate scenes in the movie and she's not cool with it."

Someone, please just shoot me and put me out of my misery.

Jay looked more than willing as he stared at her for any other brilliant ideas she might have.

Selena's hand went to her forehead and she avoided Jay's gaze as she said, "Give me five minutes. I'll figure something out."

Otherwise, they were packing their shit and heading home.

HE HADN'T EXPECTED the entertainment when he'd arrived three weeks ago, but the filming mishaps in progress had to be the funniest thing Gus had seen in a long time. At least he knew he was capable of laughing. He wasn't completely heartless; he did feel bad that things were going so terribly wrong, but they had to have anticipated this wouldn't be an easy feat. None of these men had ever filmed a movie before. A lead actor was something they should have brought from LA.

He popped a piece of gum into his mouth as he watched the third potential male lead leave the set. Gus's eavesdropping had revealed that apparently the steamier scenes in the script had Joaquin's girlfriend kiboshing his acting debut.

He'd always wondered how Hollywood stars dealt with that element of their careers. If seeing Aileen get engaged after they'd broken up had set him off, he wasn't sure he was the type of person who could handle seeing their significant other be intimate with another person, even if it was acting. It was no mystery why the divorce rate was so high among the Hollywood elite.

"Thought you were hibernating." Selena's voice sneaking up behind him made him jump, and his gum lodged itself in his throat.

He coughed to clear it and turned to face her. "Even bears would wake up for this shit."

Her makeup-covered face contorted into a full on toddler tantrum, and he took a step back in case she punched him.

"This isn't funny," she said, sounding more than a little wound up.

"It kinda is," he said in an attempt to defuse her irritation, help her see the humor in the situation. He wished he hadn't when she *did* punch his arm. Hard. "Ow!" He rubbed his bicep. She was a lot stronger than she looked.

"These men are killing me. This is not that difficult." She rubbed her wrinkled forehead, her stress overtaking her annoyance with him. She was distraught and obviously in a slight panic, and Gus felt a tinge of regret for making light of the dilemma and enjoying the train wreck from the sidelines.

"Maybe not for you," he said. "You've been doing this your entire life. You excel at it. These men are amateurs at best."

She glanced up at him and her mouth gaped. "Did you just say something nice?"

He grinned. "Caught me at a weak moment. Don't get used to it." He paused. "Look, just try not to stress, and maybe cut some of the leading male scenes from the script. Shoot what you can with just you, and film the rest at a later date." Seemed like an easy fix. Hadn't he heard her tell Leslie the day before at the auditions that it was a female-driven movie anyway? Not that he'd been listening while he was supposed to be playing pool...

She groaned. "We're already planning to do that, but there won't be time or budget to film those scenes before this year's film festival submissions." She shook her head and her hands tightened in little fists. "This movie could be so amazing...damn, Matt!" she said through clenched teeth.

Matt Mayson. He'd discovered the two were an item through his googling. Images of the two stars at a rom-com premiere had been the interest of paparazzi for about seven minutes earlier that year. That was the way it went in Hollywood. The seven-year itch was reduced to seven minutes. He'd also learned through his non-eavesdropping that she had to go through this torture because the other man had bailed on her at the last minute, and he couldn't help but feel a sympathetic tug toward her. He knew what it felt like to be ditched.

"Hey, look, obviously he wasn't worth it if he let you down like this." Where had that come from? Giving relationship advice now?

Advice that wasn't appreciated, if the look on Selena's face could be trusted. "Matt and I didn't break up," she said curtly. "He's filming another movie. We're professionals. It happens. We get it."

"So you're not pissed at him?"

"No! Not at all," she said. Despite being an actress, she was the worst liar on the planet.

He raised an eyebrow. "Not even a little?"

"Not even a little." She waved a hand. "Our relationship doesn't revolve around our careers. We can totally separate the two. Our connection is based on mutual respect, admiration and trust."

Like she'd trusted him to follow through on this commitment to her? He bit his tongue, holding the comment back. She was already in a mood, and he could tell she was processing what she'd just said and was coming to the same realization anyway.

She sighed. "I don't know what I'm going to do. Jay is going to kill me and we're out of options."

Her wrecked expression made his insides twist in an unsettling way, and a need to put some distance between them overwhelmed him. "Well, good luck," he said awkwardly. This wasn't his problem, and the way he wanted to suddenly help her solve it had him retreating. Fast. He knew this protective instinct of his and it wasn't good. It was always the first step toward developing feelings. Some relationship guru that Aileen had dragged him to see when they were having problems communicating had enlightened him on the male process to falling in love. He deferred to the three Ps: Proclaim. Protect. Provide. The three things all men did when they truly loved someone. He'd felt all three for Aileen, but it had definitely started with the protection thing. They'd met on Santa Monica Pier when he chased down a guy who'd snatched her purse while she was on a date with another guy. Definitely a clichéd way to meet... Hell, Selena would probably love the story. Aileen had always said it was much better than telling people they'd met at a bar or online.

Either way, he had to ignore the same protective instinct that pulled at him right now. He was not getting involved in this one.

He started to walk away and ignored Selena when she called out to him.

"Wait!" she said.

He didn't.

"Hey, I have an idea!"

Uh-oh. He kept walking, picking up his pace, but she chased after him. He moved even faster, propelling his legs forward in an awkward speed-walking thing that had his hips swinging in an unmanly manner. He heard her gasp of shock as she followed. "Gus, wait!"

Nope. He was running now. Away from her and the idea that he knew was brewing in her mind. Three weeks of no real physical activity had him winded fast, but he kept going.

But so did she. And she was closing in. Fast. Superstrength and superspeed—what was she? A machine?

He glanced over his shoulder and his foot caught on a tree root partially covered under a thin layer of snow, and then he was stumbling forward, losing his balance. His hip crashed into the hard, cold ground as he rolled flat onto his back, and a second later, Selena was sitting on his chest.

Sitting. On. His. Chest.

His wide-eyed look of shock combined with his rapid pulse had his mouth going completely dry as her tiny little body pinned him to the ground and she stared down at him. "Did you just run away from me?" she asked, slightly out of breath. Her piercing eyes held disbelief, humor and, worst of all, a sparkle of challenge. Which he was a complete sucker for.

He nodded. "I did."

"So, obviously you know what I'm about to ask."

The impossible. "Save your breath. I'm not acting in your movie." He tried to thrust his body upward to shake her off. He did not want to touch her. Touching her would be a mistake. A big mistake. But she gripped his sweater like reins and held tight, refusing to be bucked off.

He felt himself harden in the front of his jeans and his voice caught in his throat. Now was not the time for his body to react. "Get off." It was more of a growl.

She ignored it. "Just hear me out."

"No."

"Stop being such a jerk!" She shook his upper body in frustration.

She was strong for such a small person.

"I need help, so just listen before you say no," she said more gently, changing tactics, yet still not letting him up. "You're bored out of your mind—otherwise, you wouldn't have been lurking around the set."

"I wasn't lurking. I was standing in plain sight." He should have just stayed in his cabin, out of the way. Why the hell hadn't he?

"You know how to act in front of cameras," she said. "You can project your voice, and you are familiar with lighting and spotlights and memorizing a script quickly."

"No." He wasn't giving excuses. He was simply refusing.

"Come on, Gus! Please."

"No. And get off me," he said. He grabbed her waist and instantly regretted the contact. The feel of her body between his hands had him fighting the wave of desire coursing through him. It had to be the fact that it had been months since he'd been with a woman, because there was no way he was this attracted to Selena Hudson. She was irritating and annoying and…and…irritating.

She clung to him as he lifted her off him, dragging him back down, this time on top of her. She quickly wrapped her legs around his waist and squeezed tight. He couldn't get away. He was being overpowered by a hundred-pound movie star. "What the hell? You some sort of ninja? Let me go." His face was inches from hers, and the freakishly strong woman shook her head.

"I'm a black belt in jujitsu. A woman should know how to protect herself."

"Apparently, I'm the one who needs protection."

"I'll make you a deal."

"No."

She glared up at him. "Just shut up for a second and listen."

His breathing was slightly labored, and he prayed she couldn't feel his hard-on. She did not need any more ammunition to use against him in whatever negotiating power she thought she had.

"You want another shot at broadcasting, right?"

He hadn't said that, but there was no point denying it. He didn't confirm or deny as he waited for her to get to her point.

"I know someone at Sports Beat in LA. A top reporter that I shadowed for a movie role early in my career."

Sports Beat? Okay, so maybe she had his attention. His dream had always been to work at his grandfather's studio, but the *secret* big dream was always Sports Beat. The LA-based studio was one of the top sports reporting news stations in the country. He'd even applied once or twice, but had never even gotten a look in. At the time, he'd eased the sting by telling himself it was a good thing; it saved him from having to make a choice between the dream station and his family's. But now that his family didn't want him working for them, there would be zero guilt. He cleared his throat, hating that she had him hooked. "Go on."

Her expression said she knew she'd won. "If you act in the movie, I'll get you an interview at the station."

After his meltdown, there wasn't a snowball's chance in hell that he'd get a shot like that...unless Little Miss Movie Star could actually deliver on her promise. He hesitated. Did she really have that kind of power? Getting someone at the station to overlook his recent faux pas seemed highly unlikely. "How do I know you'll follow through?"

"I never make a promise or a deal that I don't intend to keep."

He stared down at her, his emotions suddenly undecipherable, and unfortunately, the opportunity she was dangling in front of him like a carrot to a starving horse was only a small factor.

She stared back. Silent. Knowing this negotiation game well.

His heart pounded. Could he actually act in her movie? The trade-off would be worth it, but it would mean more time with her, and if his body's reaction right now was any indication, that wouldn't be a good thing.

Hadn't he heard her tell one of the actors that there were sex scenes?

The idea of kissing her...touching her... Damn, he had to get off her.

He took advantage of her weakened state and broke free of her hold, jumping to his feet and dusting himself off.

From the ground, she held up a hand for assistance, which he ignored. He was not touching her again.

She huffed as she stood. "So? Deal?" She extended a hand again expectantly.

He swallowed hard and pointed a finger at her. "You better follow through."

"I can get you the interview—the rest is up to you," she said, letting her hand fall back to her side.

If he could just get into those offices, he'd stop at nothing to secure the opportunity. His chest heaved in a deep, resolute sigh. "Fine. I'll act in your damn movie," he said. "But you better not be messing with me."

Needing the privacy of his cabin, he turned and walked away quickly, before her sexy, victorious grin made him erupt in his jeans in front of her, giving her even more to gloat about.

CHAPTER FIVE

SHE MUST HAVE been out of her mind. Or, more accurately, desperate.

Gus Orosco was the worst and he hadn't exactly wanted to do this. If she hadn't bribed him with an opportunity she now had to somehow make good on, he never would have agreed.

Jay's skeptical look as she overconfidently presented her fantastic solution to their problem the next morning was a wake-up call to the absurdity of what she'd done.

"You're messing with me, right?" he said, before launching into another lengthy lecture about what this film's success meant for all of them.

"…this is your one chance to prove you can do something different…the guy is a loose cannon…everyone knows we're making a movie together now, all eyes are watching…"

Her chest tightened and her palms sweat more the longer he spoke. It was a credit to her acting abilities that she kept her smile in place and maintained a calm, reassuring demeanor. Inside she was spiraling.

"Are you listening to me?" Jay asked, hands on his hips.

She nodded and placed her hands on his thin shoulders. "Just trust me, okay?"

He took far too long to answer, but finally sighed. "I

trust you," he said, before walking away to direct the crew for setup.

But could *she* actually trust Gus to follow through? She didn't really know the guy well enough to be putting the movie's fate in his hands. What if he bailed on the last day of filming? He hadn't said how long he was sticking around. What if he decided to head back to Seattle, leaving them high and dry?

As she returned to the set cabin, Jay's words continued to echo in her brain.

There was really no guarantee that he'd do this. And if he did go through with it, would he actually try his best to deliver a good performance, or just go through the motions, delivering the lines like a talking head? Her reasoning for thinking he was the best option was sound, but would he freeze up when he had to really act, not just give his opinion on something?

He'd certainly given his opinion on Matt the day before and it had unsettled her.

She entered the cabin and sat at the table, where her computer was already set up. Removing her jacket, she fixed her hair and took a deep breath.

Gus wasn't right in his assumptions. He knew nothing about Matt and their relationship. He knew nothing about *her*, just his preconceived notions. As far as she was concerned, he could keep his opinions to himself.

Still, she tapped her fingers impatiently as she waited for the Skype call to connect for her morning chat with Matt.

Where was he?

They'd agreed these early-morning sessions were the best time to connect, given the time difference and the fact that she was filming at all different hours of the day. She was desperate to see his face. She missed him. Even more than she thought she would. Which had to be a good sign. There was a thin line between the two sayings, "Absence makes the heart grow fonder" and "Out of sight, out of mind." Her stepdad always said he wrapped every movie ahead of schedule just to be home sooner to be with her mom. Their relationship, despite the pressures of a Hollywood spotlight, was inspiring, and Selena had seen firsthand that these marriages could work when two people put the effort in and put one another first. She wanted that, too.

Her cell phone chimed, and seeing Matt's name on the display, she shut the laptop harder than she'd intended. Obviously, he was texting to cancel the call. Otherwise, he'd just be dialing her on the computer. His casual dismissals of their agreements were starting to grate on her nerves. Didn't he want to see her just as much? Didn't he miss her? It had only been a few days; maybe her romantic nature had to chill a little. Seeming desperate and needy wouldn't help.

Something came up, babe. Chat later?

Something or someone?

What was wrong with her? She could trust him. He may not have followed through on this movie commitment, and so far he'd been mostly unavailable when she tried to connect, but that didn't mean he was untrustworthy on the relationship side of things. Right? He was busy with his own career commitments and was a rising star with dreams he was reaching toward. The fact that he was even in a serious, committed relationship at such a young age and the start of his career was a marvel. They were lucky to have one another. She wouldn't stress out or read too much into the text.

It wasn't like he knew she really could use his support or even just wanted to see his face or hear his voice right now. He didn't know that everything had gone sideways... partially his fault. Mostly his fault. He didn't know she'd just made a deal with the devil. Or that the movie she was counting on to save her career was now in jeopardy.

Her finger hovered over the call button as her chest tightened. He might be too busy for a Skype call, but a quick phone call would be okay. He was obviously near his phone. No one was ever too far from their phones.

Nope. He said he couldn't chat. She was never the needy type and she wouldn't start now. Sighing, she texted back:

Absolutely! Hectic day for me as well. xx

She checked the time. It was just after seven. Standing, she regarded her reflection in the small, dusty mirror in the old cabin they were using as a makeup and wardrobe trailer and then headed outside.

She shivered more from the eeriness that enveloped her than the morning chill. A heavy fog had yet to lift from the dewy, overgrown grass. She felt as though she were walking through clouds as she moved down the path. The trees in the distance looked like shadows against the mountain ranges all around them. Tall and ominous. It was still dark, and the crew were now setting up for the twilight shot. It was the perfect ambience for the scene they were planning to shoot first. Creepy and mysterious. The scene where the heroine was running through the woods after escaping the madman who had her held captive on his houseboat for two years. The first scene meeting the leading male.

Gus.

She looked around the campsite but didn't see him outside. She'd told him they were starting at seven. If he was still asleep...

"Question…" His voice behind her made her jump. The fog cover had completely hidden his approach, the soft, wet grass muting the sounds of footsteps.

This place was spooky.

He was dressed in wardrobe already. His hair was combed to the side and he wore the fake glasses his character was meant to wear. He didn't look so far off what she'd envisioned as she'd read the script for the first time. In fact, she hated to admit it, but his stockier build with muscular chest and shoulders was more the "mountain cabin in the woods hermit" look than Matt's younger, thinner, polished appearance. And the script in his hands prompted an indistinguishable feeling to wash over her.

He'd actually looked at the copy she'd given him the night before? Read it, even? She would not give him so much credit to assume he'd actually memorized his lines for that day's shooting schedule.

"What's the question?" she asked tightly. She was already regretting the decision to cast him. Almost as though his willingness to participate was a warning of sorts. A warning of what, she didn't know, but alarm bells were certainly ringing in her ears.

"In this scene we're about to shoot, you're running from your abductor, right?" He scanned the pages, a frown on his features.

She nodded. "An abusive abductor who has held me captive for two years, yes." It was the intensity of her character's fear in that scene as she was free for the first time but almost more afraid of her freedom that had struck Selena as the most powerful writing in the script. Stockholm syndrome was a fascinatingly terrifying reality for a lot of captives, and her character struggled with feelings of betrayal and abandonment toward her captor while desperately wanting to escape.

"And you stumble upon a recluse living in the woods?"

"All that is in the script." Was there a real question coming? She rubbed her hands together, suddenly eager to get on set. She wanted to channel all her fears and uncertainty and uneasiness about this entire situation—and her issues with Matt's unresponsiveness—into the scene. Fake tension to help ease her real tension.

"But she's not afraid of this stranger?"

Selena sighed. "She needs help and he can't be as bad as what she's running from."

"Right—" Gus nodded "—but the part I don't get is why this recluse would help her. If he truly wants to be left alone, which he obviously does, why risk his own way of life for this stranger?"

Selena sighed. "Because it's in his nature to be a protector." She would like to think most men would feel an urge to help someone in need. At least, the men in her life were that way. Her stepfather was a bear when it came to Selena and her mother. Maybe Gus was more of a live-and-let-die sort.

"But why?" he asked.

"Because he just does."

"That's not compelling enough. He needs more of his own backstory in order for me to connect with him." He flipped through the script. "There's no mention at all about why he's a recluse or why he's choosing to live this way."

Oh, God. The male ego surfaces. "The movie's not about him."

Gus shook his head. "But he plays a huge role, and I think audiences could connect with him better if he was more established as a key player."

Why did he care so much about a movie he had wanted no part of? Suddenly, he wanted creative control? "It's a female-driven thriller. No one cares about this guy's back-story."

He looked ready to argue, and then shrugged. "Okay. It's your movie." He turned to walk toward the crew, and she bit her lip as she watched.

It had struck her as a missing key element when she'd read the script as well, but when she'd talked to Matt, he'd claimed what she just had. That the movie was focused on the female lead, and adding too much to the male character would only detract from her story, put the emphasis on the male character once again. Now she wasn't so sure. She wanted the audience to connect with the movie on an emotional level, and having any undeveloped characters would leave the film lacking. And wouldn't viewers connect better with her if they could see why she felt she could trust this stranger in the woods? She hesitated... This was already a mess and they were behind on filming the content they already had.

"Wait!" she called after Gus.

He turned to face her as she approached him. "I'll talk to Jay and the writer about adding in a small flashback or something tied to his military days," she said casually, as though the addition was something to appease him rather than being a great idea.

He nodded. "That would work. Something about saving a life or being unable to would really solidify this protective instinct or a need for redemption, maybe?"

So he was an expert now. Unfortunately, she couldn't argue against the fact that it would only make the script stronger. "Glad you're happy."

He studied her. "You okay? You're not as perky this morning."

She was on edge, to be precise, and she needed to shake

it off. Matt was out. Three others hadn't worked. She was stuck with Gus for better or worse, and she needed to focus on making sure her performance was brilliant to cover up for his lack of experience. And if he had ideas that could strengthen the script, that was a good thing. They were now on the same side. She shouldn't fight him, but instead embrace his involvement as a positive. "I'm fine," she said. "This…you…are just our last shot at this. We're so far behind and over budget already. I'd hate to let Jay down even more by having to completely postpone the filming."

"If it helps, I'll talk to my sister about not charging you whatever it was you were supposed to pay to use the place," he said absently, staring at the script and making several notes along the margins.

Her mouth dropped. "You would?"

He glanced up at her. "Yeah. It's the least I could do for… um…the way I acted the day you arrived."

Huh. That was unexpected. Maybe he wasn't as bad as she'd originally thought. She nodded. "Well, thank you. Yes, that would help." The cost of the place wasn't as high as most shooting locations, but any funds they could save would help ease the strain on the budget.

"Consider it done," he said, and their gazes met and held for a long moment before the sound of a dog barking broke the silence around them.

She cleared her throat. "That must be Kaia with Diva, your character's dog."

"Okay, dog's here. You two ready?" Jay asked, looking apprehensive as he joined them. His thin face looked pinched, and the dark circles under his eyes revealed his stress. So much was riding on this for both of them, and if Gus couldn't pull this off, they'd have to reconsider the project for now. Neither of them wanted to do that. Hollywood had a short attention span, and Jay was riding some success from his previous short-film achievement on the festival circuit. Right now, Selena was still a household name. By next year they'd both be forgotten as new talent emerged, and a comeback would be that much harder.

"I'm good," Gus said, looking ready and, dare she say, eager to get started.

"Guess we'll see about that," she mumbled as they found their marks for the shot.

Standing in the forest about half a mile from the cabin with two members of the filming crew, Selena refocused her mind as she waited for Jay's signal. Getting into character was usually easy for her, but normally she was playing the role of a happy heroine falling in love. Not that big of a stretch for most actors. This raw, vulnerable, complex role was far more challenging.

She took several deep breaths and closed her eyes, envisioning the fabricated scenario of being held captive by a stranger. Feeling trapped and claustrophobic in tight quarters with a madman. It wasn't so difficult. Selena recalled the moment the year before, trapped in the car with Eoghan, her stalker, when he'd found them in Wild River. Leslie had been knocked out and she'd been bound and gagged in the back seat of the car as Eoghan had flown down the Alaskan highway, taking them farther and farther from safety. She'd never been so afraid in her life. That feeling of helplessness as she couldn't control her fate. There had been no one who could save her in those moments... Desperation and despair had set in.

Hearing "Action," she opened her eyes and started to run. She knew this scene by heart, as it was one of the most intense, pivotal moments in the movie. The heroine had finally escaped the houseboat where her abuser had passed out after she'd hit him in the head with a lamp.

She forced her panting to sound as though she'd been running for hours...all night through the forest. She knew the camera would be focused on her legs, then her hair flying behind her on the wind, then her face. Terrified. Wide-eyed. Wild.

Three, two, one...

She stopped. Turned. Frantic, panicked. Lost. In the middle of nowhere.

Then running again. Bare feet against the rough terrain. The script had suggested shoes or at least thick socks, but Selena had decided to brave the overgrowth. Make the scene more dramatic and authentic. A woman escaping, desperate to live, risking everything for freedom.

She kept running until the cabin came into view, and her heart started to pound for real. Could Gus pull this off? Could she?

She saw him chopping wood outside the cabin. The ax swinging overhead, then sending the wood scattering.

Diva, the beautiful gray-and-white husky, lying on the ground next to him, sat up on high alert as she approached. The dog's ears stood straight, and on cue she barked three times, alerting her owner.

Gus looked at the dog, bent to pet her affectionately, then stood and turned toward her.

Oh, please, God, just don't be complete shit.

She hurried toward him, and his gaze held caution and concern as he scanned the woods behind her. She fell against him, her breathing labored. "Help, please help." Exhausted and emotionally spent, her character was on the verge of collapsing. Her body sagged toward the ground at his feet.

Gus bent at the knees and scanned her for injury as the script dictated. She knew the camera would now be in his POV, taking in her bruises, her bare feet, the ripped clothing… His expression was one of genuine concern.

She was impressed and struggled to stay in character.

"Is anyone following you?" he asked, his voice gruff. He peered into the forest again, and Selena could almost believe he might be looking for someone in the fog.

The dog moved in closer, offering comfort and support. Kaia was right—Diva was a superstar.

Selena shook her head. "At least, I don't think… I don't know. Please just help." Her frantic-sounding pleading was good. Even *she* could feel the tension and powerful moment she was delivering. And it helped that she could feed off Gus's energy. She could feel it radiating from him. It was unexpected. It was good.

"Hey, hey…you're safe now." The genuine softness in Gus's voice had her mouth gaping slightly. She stared into his face, but all signs of the edgy and sarcastic jerk he'd been the last few days were gone. In their place was a concerned, caring, tortured hero.

"Cut!" Jay's voice had her blinking, then shaking her head.

Shit. She'd messed up the scene. "Sorry," she mumbled. She'd totally been caught up in Gus's transformation.

"Do you need your line?" Kaia asked from the sidelines.

She shook her head. Great—now *she* was looking like the amateur. "No. I'm good. Let's go again," she said, swallowing hard and rotating her shoulders.

The cameras started rolling again.

Gus gently touched her shoulder and gazed into her eyes as he'd done moments before, and Selena forced every ounce of professionalism to the surface. She wouldn't get thrown by his apparent closet acting abilities this time.

"Hey, hey... You're safe now." Gus repeated the line even better this time.

"I'll never be safe." She said her line and pretended to pass out as the scene came to an end. Unfortunately, as she lay there on the ground waiting for Jay to yell "Cut," that same unsettled feeling in the pit of her stomach really had her questioning her casting decisions.

"ADMIT IT, THAT was good."

"It was fine," Selena mumbled.

"Oh, come on... It was better than fine," Gus said, riding an unexpected high from his first performance. He'd killed it that morning, despite Selena's reluctance to admit it. The day before, he'd been totally against the idea, and the only reason he'd agreed was because of the Sports Beat opportunity she'd bribed him with, but when he'd reluctantly started reading the script the night before, he'd actually gotten caught up in the plot. The female lead was engrossing and complex, and he'd definitely connected with his character's desire to hole away in a cabin. Hell, it was as though he'd manifested the part. And he wouldn't admit how surprised he was that Selena was considering his characterization suggestion. Like it or not, he was part of this project now and he was going all in. Gus Orosco never half-assed anything.

The filming crew seemed happy, and even stressed-out Jay was pleasantly surprised. He'd expected Selena to be falling at his feet with gratitude. "What's next?" He bounced alongside her as they walked toward the cabin.

She shot him a look. "You are way too jacked up."

He shrugged. "This is more fun than I thought it would

be. So, which scene are we doing next?" He wanted to re-read the lines and get in the right mindset. He almost didn't recognize this burst of energy coursing through him. Having a sense of purpose obviously had a way of healing.

Selena blushed slightly. "We need to knock out all the present-day scenes first, the ones set here at the campsite. Then we will film flashbacks." She paused. "So the first night cabin scene is next."

He nodded. "First night cabin scene... Got it." He pulled his rolled script out of his back pocket and flicked through the pages to just beyond the half-hour mark of the film. His eyes scanned the page. "First night cabin scene," he mumbled to himself as he found the scene header. "Ah, here we go." He hadn't read this far the night before.

Selena stared at him as he skimmed.

Alone in the cabin...she showers...comes out of the bathroom in a towel...

Oh, hell, no. His gaze shot up to find hers. "They just met."

"It's called forced-proximity desire fueled by the element of danger and tension."

He scoffed. "And viewers will believe that?"

She frowned. "One-night stands happen in movies all the time."

He nodded, running a finger under the collar of his T-shirt, sweat suddenly pooling on his lower back. Maybe he should have read the entire script before committing. Now he understood why the other guy bailed the day before. This sex scene was pretty intense, and there was no fade to black as things heated up. "Right, but... I just don't think my character, Will, would do that."

She raised an eyebrow in amusement. "He wouldn't?"

"No. He's a strong, silent type. Good guy. Moral. Wants

to do the right thing. Sure, he might want to—" he cleared his throat "—but he won't. She's vulnerable and scared and just left her abductor."

"Right, and her newfound sense of safety combined with lingering Stockholm syndrome has her developing an attraction to Will in a twisted, disoriented way," she said. "The psychology supports it and its very intriguing characterization."

"Maybe for her…" He shook his head. "But it's just not true to his character."

"First, you want backstory. Now you're dissecting your character motivation?" She looked amused and mildly irritated, but if he was going to act in this movie and do it right, he needed to feel connected to his character, and having him jump on a vulnerable woman wasn't the kind of person he thought he could confidently and realistically portray. Jumping on Selena wasn't something he—Gus—could do either, even if it was make-believe. His body's reaction to her the day before had him terrified of the idea of this very intimate scene. Getting close to her, kissing her, being completely naked with her, was a little too much.

"You want this to feel genuine, right?" he asked.

She folded her arms across her chest. "Uh-huh. Of course."

"Well, I just think the sex takes it too far."

"Is this Will talking or Gus's insecurity about his—" she cleared her throat "—abilities?"

Seriously? She was questioning his manhood? Ego kicked common sense to the curb. He took a step toward her and his gaze burned into hers. "Believe me, sweetheart, I could blow this sex scene out of the water…" He moved even closer and touched her cheek. "In fact, why don't we film it and I'll show you, and then we can leave it on the cutting-room floor when you realize I'm right."

He saw her swallow hard and struggled to remind himself that he was trying to mess with her. Right now, his actions had his own pulse racing. The thought of acting out this scene with her had him turned on again. Which was bad. Very, very bad.

Conflict registered behind her dark eyes as she silently seemed to accept his challenge.

Shit, he'd expected her to retreat. He should, but he seemed frozen on the spot, unable to back down now.

A long, torturous moment passed between them. Then she stepped back abruptly and folded her arms across her chest. "Fine. We'll ask Jay what he thinks. He can decide."

He sucked in a breath of air. "Sounds fair," he said, shoving his hands into his pockets.

"Be prepared to put your money where your mouth is," she called over her shoulder as she headed toward Jay.

He stared after her, suddenly unsure which way he wanted the director to call it.

Diva sauntered toward him, and the dog gave him a look that suggested he was a coward for not wanting to act out the scene.

He shook his head as he bent to pet her soft gray-and-white fur. "What do you know about it?" he asked. "You have nothing to worry about. Audiences are already going to love you."

SHE COULD NOT believe Jay sided with Gus.

The dude was an actor all of five minutes and suddenly he had a say in the script? Unbelievable. If she'd pulled something like that with a director in her early days, she'd still be doing commercials.

It wasn't that she thought the movie needed a sex scene to fulfill audience expectations or to add nudity for a higher content rating. But after researching the psychology behind the writer's intentions for it, she thought it was fitting and realistic…though she'd been happier about it when she was starring opposite Matt. The idea of getting intimate on set with him had excited her and she'd known the sparks would fly, creating a moving and erotic scene.

She should be relieved that she didn't have to get naked with Gus. She should…

Sitting in the cabin hours later, she raised her eyes above her newly revised script from the on-call writer in LA to glance at Gus, pacing in front of the burning fireplace, inspecting his copy. He was really getting into this and trying his best. Despite her reluctance to give him an ego boost earlier that day, she had been impressed by him and she wanted to feel relief that the movie wouldn't have to stop filming. Unfortunately, the nagging unease in the pit of her stomach wouldn't subside. If she didn't know better, she'd think it was butterflies, but that would be silly. The guy gave her indigestion, that was all, and his idle threat to prove her wrong about his sexual abilities made her nauseous. Absolutely nauseous.

And not at all curious.

"Are you staring at my ass?" He'd stopped pacing and was staring at her.

And her eyes were indeed staring at his ass. How long had she been spaced out, checking him out like that? She quickly looked away. "Don't flatter yourself. I was visualizing."

"Glad my butt cheeks could help," he said with a grin, flexing them.

Oh, my God.

Jay entered the cabin, bundled in his warm faux coat, thick wool scarf and matching hat, despite the blazing heat of the fire. "It is so cold out there, I can't feel my face." He glanced between them and eyed them as though sensing an odd vibe in the air. "You two ready?"

Selena nodded as she stood, grateful to head back to work. Work kept her focused, and suddenly she was grateful for the script modifications. They were still filming the shower scene as planned, which would later be intercut with flashbacks of her abduction and abuse, but the scene would now end on a kiss instead of the full sex scene. She hoped Jay didn't regret this decision. Having to reshoot it later would be torture.

Gus rotated his shoulders and set his script aside as Selena disappeared into the bathroom. The film crew and Jay set the lighting as she undressed. There was no body double, there was no skin-toned body suit. She was going full nude for the first time ever on-screen. She was confident in her body, and she knew Jay was planning to shoot this from safe angles to protect her from anything she wasn't comfortable with. This was an art film. She was an artist.

Gus cleared his throat, appearing in the doorway as she reached behind to undo her bra. "Um…should maybe just the camera crew be in here?" He averted his eyes as she removed the bra.

"You're going to need to see her naked in this scene," Jay said.

"Right. Yeah…no…it's acting. I'm professional," he said awkwardly, but then turned to her. "You good? You're okay with this?"

"It's a movie set, Gus," she said, but she couldn't deny she appreciated his consideration. As Jay yelled "Action," she could see his gaze shift all over the room, everywhere but on her as she removed her underwear, climbed into the shower and pulled the curtain. The aerial cam overhead would capture her in her entirety, but it was an indie film and people expected raw. The waterproof makeup bruises covering her skin were so real looking, she was almost convinced they were as she lathered her hair and went through the motions of the intense, heartbreaking scene where her character recalled all her pain and fear until she spiraled in a pit of despair.

She sat in the tub and drew her knees to her chest, crying as the water cascaded down her body. In a moment, Jay would yell "Cut," and they'd move from the bathroom back to the living room, where Will and Alice would share a kiss.

Instead, the shower curtain pulled back, and Selena struggled to stay in character with the unscripted action as Jay motioned for her to roll with it.

Gus, holding a large towel, bent slowly, gathering her into his arms as he would a child, and carried her out of the bathroom. The cameras followed. He placed her onto the cot in the corner of the cabin, where the sheets were rolled back. He gently slid her legs beneath the covers and pulled the sheets up higher on her body.

She stared at him in real awe as he improvised the scene.

"Get some sleep," he ad-libbed, and Selena's heart raced. Everything she'd ever done had been scripted. Revised and edited and expected to be delivered word for word. She'd never improvised a scene in a real movie before, but her gut told her that this was working.

Jay was watching on. Intent. Almost as though holding his breath.

She had to go with it. Do what felt natural. Right in this new moment Gus had created, Selena reached for his arm as he went to walk away.

He turned and the same fiery expression from earlier that day blazed in his eyes.

That part was in the script, so why was she buying into it? Feeling like maybe it was less good acting and more real desire? She had to be losing it to think there was a real spark, real attraction and chemistry between her and Gus.

"Stay," she said softly, though not weakly. Her character might be breaking down, but she was surviving and growing. This breaking point was the first transition in her character from victim to survivor.

Gus looked pained, tortured, as he gave a Tom Hardy brooding hero performance, the semblance of a struggle between what he wanted to do and what he thought was the right thing. Then he was moving toward her, fast, gripping her face between his hands.

Her breath caught in her chest as his mouth crushed hers with an intensity that she'd never experienced on set before. His lips were softer than she'd expected. Maybe because of their tendency to always be in a frown or smirk. She pressed hers to his, and his grip on her face tightened, holding her in place.

His mouth searched hers with a hunger that caught her completely by surprise.

Maybe that threat hadn't been so idle.

She clung to him and deepened the kiss, even though it was unnecessary.

It's in the moment. It's raw passion.

Jay had said to roll with it.

Gus broke away first, his eyes snapping open, a look of unconcealed surprise reflecting in their depth. So, she wasn't the only one caught off guard.

"Get some sleep," he said hoarsely, with a look on his face that she knew wasn't just acting. No one was that good.

That kiss had just rocked his world as much as it had thrown hers completely off course.

Damn, it was definitely a good thing they'd decided to cut the sex scene.

CHAPTER SIX

SHE JUST NEEDED to see Matt. Once she saw him, things would be put back into perspective. Her world would be righted again. At least, it had better be, because right now, she was more than slightly shaken and needed to refocus.

It was a movie set. It was a scripted kiss. And Gus was turning out to be a much better actor than she'd assumed he could be. The way he'd looked at her right before his lips touched hers had almost stolen her breath for real. The intensity, the look of longing, the passion reflecting there... She'd almost swooned out loud. She shook her head. What the hell was wrong with her? She was an actress. She kissed people on set all the time and made the connection look real.

This was precisely the reason Hollywood made it difficult to have a long-lasting relationship. Getting into character, getting into the script and delivering a convincing performance required actors to really deep dive into the emotional side of acting, which sometimes made it hard to decipher real feelings and attraction from make-believe.

Kissing someone was personal, whether it was in front of a camera or not.

She'd expected to struggle to kiss Gus. She had not. Which was the major source of her irritation right now, and he didn't seem to have a problem with it either, which was even worse. After their bickering and lack of warmth toward one another since she'd arrived, she hadn't expected them to pull off a credible scene.

Heading back inside the cabin, after everyone had cleared out and the crew were loading the van to head back into town, Selena hurried to her laptop and took a chance that Matt was logged on to his computer. They'd only spoken briefly by text a few times that day... If he was online, maybe they could have just a quick chat. To clear the fog lingering in her mind.

The Skype connection rang, and a slight wave of guilt washed over her. She'd kissed another man that day, and while it was her job, it still felt a little wrong. Maybe that was a good thing. It meant her feelings for Matt were real. She'd never experienced this before with other men she dated. How they felt about what she did wasn't really a concern or consideration.

How would Matt feel about seeing her kiss other men in movies? How would she feel about seeing him kissing other women? Or doing more than kissing?

Her stomach twisted slightly. Especially if, after the cameras stopped rolling, he suffered this same odd sensation toward his costar that she was feeling right now.

"Come on, Matt..."

The call connected, and she leaned toward the screen and plastered a smile on her still made-up face. "Hi!"

"Selena?" He looked a little groggy and disoriented, as though she'd woken him, and a quick time check made her feel a little guilty, but she'd needed to talk to him. "Thought you were filming late today?" he asked, covering a yawn and then running a hand through his messy hair.

He looked so adorable. She wanted to be there with him. Crawl into bed next to him and cuddle into his bare chest.

Good. This was good. Gus who? Phew!

"Missed you," she said. She glanced toward the cabin door to make sure it was locked, then leaned in with a seductive smile. "You still in bed?" Skype sex would be exciting. Her body was already reacting to the thought, and it had zero to do with the lingering tingling in her body from Gus's kiss. Zero.

"Should be getting up... Late night." He checked his watch.

Late night? He'd texted around ten o'clock and said he was calling it a night. She'd tried to reach him to say goodnight, but the call had gone to voice mail, so she'd assumed he was already asleep. "Oh, did you go out?" Was that casual enough?

"Yeah," he said over another yawn.

"Where did ya go?" Did she sound curious or controlling?

"Just Disco on 10th. Arman called around eleven and wanted to meet up..."

Arman. She wasn't sure why Matt's manager bugged her so much. Maybe it was his influence over Matt...or the way he obviously didn't think Matt should be tied down right now with his career on the rise. He was that single, on-the-prowl male friend that women hated their significant others to have. The one who made it no secret that they'd do anything to cause a breakup to have their wingman back. But Matt wasn't in Hollywood to hook up with every available actress. He was there because he was serious about his career. Meeting Selena had been just icing on the cake for him, he'd said... She was an opportunity he couldn't pass up.

She bit her lip. Had he really said "opportunity"? Had she thought that was romantic at the time? Maybe he'd used a different word.

"Meet anyone interesting?" Disco on 10th was a hot spot for A-listers. She'd spent a lot of time there when she'd turned legal age. She'd always been desperate to go, but like everything else in the vibrant city, the glitter had faded over time. She'd worked with a lot of impressive people and had been surrounded by movie stars her entire life. Celebrity encounters didn't impress her anymore.

Matt, however, was new to the industry, and he'd find all of that exciting.

He nodded. "A few people," he said, his tone noncommittal. "Hey, Selena, I should get moving. I'm meeting my trainer in an hour."

"Trainer?" They usually worked out with her trainer in her home gym. He was still staying at her place while she was gone, so she'd assumed he'd continue training there.

Why did this bother her so much?

"Arman set me up with Alex Mitchell. He wants me to be ready for the role in case I get it."

Alex Mitchell was the most sought-after trainer in The Valley. He hadn't taken on a new client in years. Selena had tried reaching out to him when she'd been wanting to audition for this action film herself and her agent had gotten his voice mail. And no callback.

"Wow. That's great," she said, but she knew her voice lacked enthusiasm. This Skype call had been meant to uplift her, reenergize her, make her feel more comfortable and settled. It hadn't helped at all.

"Hey, you okay?" The concern on Matt's face did make her feel a tiny bit better. He did care about her, and he had every right to party and get a new trainer. That didn't mean he liked being with her any less. She was on location, after all. What did she expect? That he'd sit around bored stupid, pining for her and missing her? It was just a few weeks, and things would return to normal once she got back.

"I'm great," she said. "Like I said, just missing you."

She heard her home front gate chime throughout the house behind him and then it abruptly shut off. He'd let someone in. She frowned. "You expecting someone?" Okay, that sounded controlling, but it was her house. And he was still in bed and had just said he was planning on heading out.

"Food delivery," he said quickly. "I signed up for one of those premade meal delivery services. You know I can't cook." He grinned.

"Oh." She hated how suspicious she was feeling. He couldn't cook. She did all the cooking for the two of them, along with weekly meal prep according to their diets and all their juices for detox weeks. Matt would starve without her. A meal service made sense.

"Just make sure you reset the lock on the gate when you head out, okay?" After the previous year, she had become more cautious about her home security. Without the large detail she used to have, the state-of-the-art home-monitoring system Leslie had helped her decide on was her main protection.

"Don't worry—I will. I should go," he said.

"Yeah. Me, too." She hesitated. Should she say she missed him again? She wanted to say the L word, but she didn't want to say it for the first time on Skype, and in that moment, she felt as though wanting to say it was coming from a place of feeling desperate to connect with him, gain some sort of reassurance, not from the actual desire to say it. "I'll talk to you later?"

He smiled. "Of course. We can chat all night."

She breathed a sigh of relief. "Okay." She was worrying for nothing. He'd just been busy the last few days. He wasn't intentionally distancing himself. Everything was fine. "'Bye."

"'Bye," he said, and she saw him stand quickly and head out of the room. In his haste, he didn't log off the Skype chat or close his computer.

She almost did, but something in her gut made her pause.

A minute later, that same gut feeling had her pulse racing and heart pounding as Matt reentered the room...with a tall, thin blonde.

Food delivery, her ass. This woman was *not* a meal service driver. In fact, Selena recognized those high cheekbones and amazingly lush hair extensions from the billboard advertising along the highway for a lingerie store. She'd bought the two-piece bra set the woman had advertised.

Apparently, Matt had decided to go with the woman and all.

Her mouth was dry and she swallowed hard as she sat watching the train wreck unfold, like a bad B movie.

There was no way they were just friends. Her body wrapping itself around Matt's as he removed her shirt was definitely not friendly. She watched in horror as her boyfriend's hands massaged the lingerie model's bare breasts and he lowered his head to her neck.

She wanted to say something, but her voice got stuck in her throat. She was almost embarrassed to be witnessing this, and her instincts were to shut the laptop and pretend it had never happened. Return to happy oblivion.

"Selena's not home?" the woman asked, and it seemed to awaken an intense feeling of betrayal. Suddenly, she was seeing red. Anger verging on rage replaced all other emotion.

No, Selena was *not* home. But that was her home. Her bedroom.

What the hell? Was Matt seriously planning to have sex with this woman in *her* bed? No f-ing way. She couldn't watch any more. The sight of him with this woman had her chest tightening so much she could barely breathe.

Anger diluted the hurt long enough for her to clear her throat loudly on the screen.

Matt jumped away from the blonde and swung to face the computer, surprise and fear on his face. No remorse, though. Not the slightest hint of guilt. "Shit, Selena? You're still there?"

She swallowed hard and raised her chin. She refused to let him see how he'd just destroyed her. "Get out of my house right now."

He sat at the screen. "Selena, come on. This is nothing."

The blonde in the background didn't look impressed by Matt's assessment of their situation. Her thin arms folded across her abs, she pouted.

"We're done. Get your things and get out." It was amazing how strong her voice sounded. Inside, she was crumbling.

"Selena, this is Hollywood. This is what we do."

This was not what she did. She was loyal and committed in her relationships. She treated people with respect and trust. She'd thought she had found someone who felt the same way. Who had the same outlook. Turned out she was wrong. That realization hurt. "I want you out in five minutes, or I'm calling security."

He sighed, running a hand through his hair. "I'll tell her to leave," he said, as if he was doing her a favor by not cheating on her in her own bed.

The blonde scoffed and grabbed her shirt off the floor. "Don't bother. I'm out." She slammed the door as she left the room, and Matt looked pleadingly at Selena.

"There. She's gone."

Until the next one. She wasn't naive enough to believe there wouldn't be more. Oh, God, had there been others? Previously? Her bedsheets were headed for the trash as soon as she got home. Matt obviously wasn't as serious about Selena as she was about him. He didn't have the same feelings at all. Thank God she hadn't told him she loved him. "You need to be gone, too."

He looked panicked as he moved closer to the screen. "I gave up my rental. I thought you and I…"

"What?" She had to know what he thought they were, whether living with her but not being exclusive was his ultimate plan. In what universe did that work? How was that at all fair to her?

"I don't know…" He shrugged. "Having fun, I guess. Keeping things casual."

Wrong answer. "Out in…" She checked a watch-less wrist, hoping he couldn't see her hand shake. "Three minutes."

"Selena…"

"Time's ticking."

He sighed as he stood, and she watched him hurry to collect his personal items from her room and en suite. His clothing from the drawer she'd given him in her dresser, his toothbrush and shaving cream from the bathroom, his jackets hanging in her closet… All the things she'd liked seeing, things that meant they'd merged their lives together in at least a small way. The tightening in her chest begged her to reconsider, forgive him and let him stay if he promised not to cheat again, but her pride, common sense and self-respect prevented her from doing it. Her parents hadn't raised her to put up with shit from people, especially not men who claimed to care about her. People made mistakes, but that didn't mean she had to allow toxic people the chance to hurt her over and over again. As much as she cared about Matt, she wouldn't be a fool.

With everything he owned in his arms, he stared into the screen. "Once I'm gone, I'm gone."

Moving on to threats. Right. That was love. He'd only further confirmed her decision and made it that much easier. "That UCLA hoodie is mine."

He stared at her in disbelief before dropping her favorite sweatshirt onto her bed. Then his image disappeared as he slammed his laptop shut and the call disconnected.

Selena slumped back in the chair, feeling as though she'd just run an emotional triathlon. She took several deep breaths, the air getting trapped in her throat. "Shit." How could she not have thought he'd be this way? He was a young Hollywood heartthrob, up for a blockbuster role, with women falling at his feet. He was gorgeous and charming and could have any woman he wanted. She'd thought he was different. She'd actually believed him when he said he was happy with her. Breaking up with him was the right thing to do, but that didn't make it easy. He'd really meant a lot to her.

So much for thinking she was anything special to him.

MAN, HE WAS a moron for suggesting they cut the sex scene.

Selena's body, when he'd seen her in the shower, had been such an incredible turn-on. Gorgeous with her clothes *on*, he should have expected the delicate, porcelain skin, soft-looking muscle tone, the curves of her breasts and hips to be completely mesmerizing, but damn, he hadn't been prepared for the sight of her at all.

Covered in what he knew were fake bruises, she'd worn the look of vulnerability, distress on her features, and he'd almost believed for a second that she was the tortured, battered woman she was portraying. She'd been eerily believable, and it had once again invoked this sense of protection in him. He hadn't really thought it through when he'd decided to improvise the changes in the scene. Truth was, he had forgotten all about it. Watching Selena's shower scene unfold through the camera angles and monitors, he'd reacted with his gut.

Jay had been on board and had claimed the new direction of that scene was even more powerful than the original. The new director was buzzing by the time he yelled "Cut," and even the crew had offered up a round of applause. More likely out of relief for a successful filming day rather than anything to do with his performance, but there was still pride in having helped them out of the jam they'd been in.

Contrary to the others, Selena had been quiet, and that seemed completely off brand for the star. He wasn't sure why, but her silence was making him nervous.

He knew they'd sizzled on set that day, but it was all just acting. Selena was good at it. Real good. He'd almost believed she'd been into that kiss. Her soft lips drinking him in had him forgetting all about the film crew hovering around them. He'd instantly wanted to abandon his character's moral motivation and go back to the original plan in the script.

He swallowed hard now as he watched her leave the set cabin as that day's filming was done. They'd pick up in the morning with several of the less intense scenes. Apparently, they'd filmed the tougher, emotional ones that day. Most likely to see if he could pull them off. She and the crew would be heading back to the B and B for the night, leaving him out there at the campsite.

Suddenly, he didn't want to be alone, and it had nothing to do with the chilling thriller script.

A minute later, Gus paced outside the filming cabin. He licked his lips and could still taste Selena's cherry-flavored lip gloss. His worst fear in that moment was having the taste disappear.

Which was both irrational and idiotic. He wanted nothing to do with the star except for holding her to her promise of securing his interview with Sports Beat. So, why he couldn't stop wishing they'd needed a second or third…or fourth take on that kiss scene, he couldn't figure out.

Pent-up sexual tension, along with the friction simmering in the air whenever they were around one another—that was all it was.

Still, did she want to talk about it? He stopped and stared at the cabin door.

Man, he was a moron. Of course she didn't want to talk about an on-set fake kiss. He needed to get his head on straight. He started walking away, but the sound of unmistakable sobs and a loud crashing noise had him barreling back toward the door and reaching for the handle.

It was locked.

Shit. If she was hurt in there, they'd be screwed. He was fairly certain there was no real insurance on the place to cover any injuries. And protecting his family from a lawsuit was the only reason he was concerned and banging on the door. The only reason. "Selena!"

Silence.

"Selena! You okay? Open up."

"Go away!"

Well, she was conscious and obviously in a mood again. His heart raced. Had he done something wrong? Something to piss her off? Had he crossed a line in meddling with the movie script? Or with the intensity of the kiss? His improvising the scene might have gone a little too far… "Just want to know you're okay in there," he said cautiously.

The door swung open and her raccoon, bloodshot eyes had him all sorts of conflicted. Crap, she was still crying. What had he done? Tears weren't really his forte. Growing up with his hard-ass sister, he hadn't really had to deal with female tear ducts erupting very often. "Did you hurt yourself?" he asked, scanning her body and then immediately regretting it. She'd removed the sweater from wardrobe and was standing there in a pair of leggings and a black bra top. And that was all. His mouth went dry as he tried to look anywhere other than her amazing rack and tiny, toned waist. Luckily, he didn't see any bruises or blood. Even the fake ones were washed off.

She shook her head. "I'm fine."

"You don't look fine," he said carefully. Hell, in fact, she looked fine as hell, but that wasn't what he meant. "What's going on?"

"It's nothing, Gus."

He hesitated. Take her at her word and go away, leave her to deal with whatever was going on, or probe for answers? What was the right move here? What did women really want a man to do when they said they were fine, with tears streaming down their faces? He was in a no-win situation here. He knew what he wanted to do and it went against all logic. He cleared his throat. "If this is about today…"

She frowned, the tears halting instantly. "What about today?"

"Well, you know…" He shifted from one foot to the other. This was awkward. "The thing on set…" The intense, fiery chemistry between their mouths and bodies. The way they'd stared hungrily at each other like they wanted to rip one another's clothes off, even after the scene was over.

She looked confused.

Man, he was an idiot. Of course she'd been able to separate the on-set connection from real life. "Never mind. I'll go." It was an on-set scripted kiss. Nothing more.

"Wait. What are you talking about?" she asked. "The kiss?"

He sighed. This was embarrassing. Obviously, that wasn't the reason she was upset. His ego had invented a problem that didn't exist. For her, anyway. "Well, I just... I, uh, hope I didn't overstep or do anything wrong."

Her expression softened and changed to something completely different. "The kiss was fine."

Fine wasn't the word he'd use, but okay. Shot to the ego delivered and received. "Okay... So you're good?"

"Yes." She started to close the door, but it was clear she wasn't *good.* Normally, he would mind his own business, but the kiss had changed the dynamic between them. For him, anyway. She might make out with a shit ton of movie stars and have it not mean anything, but he wasn't used to mind-blowing kisses with strangers. He'd only ever dated three women seriously in his life and he didn't do casual, so this was odd for him. And the way he wanted to make sure she was okay was absolutely terrifying. He should not be applying a stubborn protective instinct to a famous, wealthy, black-belt-in-jujitsu movie star who could take care of herself better than he ever could.

"Hey, do you want to go into town and grab something to eat?" he asked before he could stop himself. The rest of the crew were packed up and gone. He'd noticed she'd had her own rental car the day before, to do things on her own. He sensed she still wasn't really fitting in with the others, and he hated to think that she might be upset all by herself that evening.

She frowned as though he'd asked her to go squirrel hunting. "Eat?"

"Yeah. You know, that thing people do when they're hungry?"

She hesitated, and a hint of a smile tugged at one corner of her mouth before she quickly sucked her bottom lip in. "I'm not really hungry or feeling up to going out anywhere, but thanks."

Why was he disappointed? Why did he even want to spend time with a woman who already had a boyfriend and, further, had essentially blackmailed him into acting? "Okay."

He turned to go. Looked like another night of ramen in his cabin.

Her voice stopped him. "I might have my appetite back in an hour or so. Maybe we could order something to my B and B and just hang out there?"

Her B and B. He felt as though his tongue had swollen in his mouth. She was inviting him back to her room at the inn. What did that mean? Should he say yes? What would her boyfriend think of that? Maybe they were one of those supercool couples who weren't at all jealous. Or maybe he posed zero threat to her and her relationship because she wasn't dealing with this sudden attraction the way he was.

"Gus?"

He was still standing there, staring at her as though this was the biggest decision he'd ever had to make. He nodded. "Sure…okay. Sure, yeah." God, he sounded like a moron.

"Okay, just give me a second to get my things," she said, closing the door.

Gus blew out a deep breath. What the hell was he thinking? Hanging out with her in public wasn't the best idea, given his attraction to her, but at least it was safe. The privacy of her B-and-B room wasn't a good idea. He should bail, tell her that something came up.

He was reaching for the door when it swung open. She gave him a grateful smile and closed it behind her. "Thanks for wanting to hang out tonight. I don't know if you've noticed, but the rest of the crew kinda abandoned me," she said with a laugh, but he heard the mild hurt in her voice.

And damn, he couldn't abandon her, too.

CHAPTER SEVEN

SHE WASN'T A fantastic driver.

In LA, she didn't need a car. She only had a driver's license for ID purposes. She'd had a driver her entire life up until the year before, and now she used Uber or public transit to get everywhere she wanted to go in the city. Snowy, icy roads were definitely not something she'd had to deal with when she'd picked up her own rental. But she was a competent, capable woman. She could handle the thirty-minute drive from the campsite to the B and B.

Even with Gus sitting in the passenger seat, his long legs looking cramped in the small space.

He'd changed from wardrobe clothing into jeans and a sweater under a well-worn leather jacket, and he'd put on cologne. It was all she could smell in the close quarters—the rich, smooth scent of the brand Matthew McConaughey was the spokesperson for. Gus looked slightly uncomfortable, as though he didn't know what to do with his hands as he sat next to her.

But it was his perceptive gaze and offer to hang out that had her battling a fresh batch of tears. For the first time in her life, she'd felt alone after her breakup with Matt. Sitting in the cabin after the Skype call, a hollow loneliness had enveloped her. The crew were all heading out to the local steak house that night. She'd overheard them talking about it. But she hadn't let their lack of invite bother her because she'd hoped to be busy talking to Matt anyway.

After catching him cheating, she'd wished there was something she could do, someone she could hang out with to try to feel better. Leslie was working the night shift, patrolling the highway, and Kaia had school the next day... And she really hadn't wanted to tell either of them about the breakup anyway. Not yet. They already thought Matt was a bit of an asshole for bailing on the movie. This would only confirm their feelings about him. While they were right, she didn't need them reminding her of her poor judgment with regard to him. Neither of them had really been pro-Matt to begin with.

She couldn't handle an I-told-you-so right now.

"Are you sure you don't want me to drive?" Gus asked, startling her.

Sitting there, staring off at the light snowfall, she'd almost forgotten he was there. She was still surprised he was. His offer to hang out had shocked her, but she appreciated it, even if it was out of pity. "No. I got this," she said, putting the car in Drive and heading down the trail toward the campsite gates.

He cleared his throat and glanced at her.

She waited. He obviously expected an explanation for her tears, but he remained silent, turning his gaze out the window instead.

She clutched the steering wheel as she turned onto the highway, hitting the gas to pick up speed on the glistening road. The back end of the car skidded slightly before righting itself into the lane and she relaxed a little.

Gus cleared his throat again and she sighed. "Could we maybe not talk about it?" Just the day before, he'd expressed his opinion on Matt and she'd delivered a speech about how committed they were to one another, how they trusted one another. She'd feel like a fool admitting she was wrong.

He looked relieved. "Fine with me." He hesitated. "But I'm here if you want to."

Strangely enough, that was all the comfort she needed. She shot a glance at him quickly before turning her attention back to the road. "You did really good today," she said.

"Thanks. It was a lot more fun than I thought it would be."

Yet he'd been worried about the on-set kiss, thinking he might have crossed a line or something. He was actually a really decent guy. One who had set her pulse racing earlier that day on set and now was helping to make her feel less alone.

"And, uh, you were absolutely incredible," he said, admiration in his tone.

And the rush of heat flowing through her at the genuineness of his compliment had her feeling another level of connection to the most unexpected costar. She definitely needed to be careful.

THE ROOM AT the B and B was admittedly a lot nicer and more comfortable than the cabins, but the intimacy of the quiet, close quarters had Gus squirming. Why on earth had she invited him here to eat? And why had he agreed? The drive in her rental car from the cabins to Main Street, where they'd picked up takeout from the diner, had been strained. He'd had no idea what to say to her, and for the first time since meeting her, she hadn't been talking nonstop.

Oddly enough, he'd missed the sound of her high-energy, incessant chatter. Something had obviously upset her that day. Enough that she hadn't wanted to eat out or hang out with her Wild River friends, but somehow wanted to spend time with him.

He glanced around the room as Selena removed her jacket and tossed it onto the chair in the corner. "Where should I set up the food?" There was just a four-poster bed and several armchairs in the room. No table or desk. The high dresser was the only real piece they could convert into a table, and that wasn't ideal.

"On the bed, I guess," she said with a shrug, as though she ate takeout on beds with strangers all the time. Maybe this *was* standard costar stuff.

"Okay."

"Where's my baby?" she said, and a second later, the multicolored Chihuahua he'd seen the first day she'd arrived at the campsite came running out from under the bed. The thing practically dived into Selena's open arms as she bent to gather the pup and cover her in kisses.

Lucky dog.

"How's my girl? Mommy missed you so much," she said. She glanced at him. "Gus, meet Unicorn."

"She's...cute." The little mutt wasn't exactly the type of dog he'd choose for himself, but she definitely suited Selena. Small, perky and adorable. Even the rainbow hairdo seemed on brand.

The dog squirmed in her owner's arms and Selena set her down. She immediately ran toward him and jumped up onto his leg. Tiny little paws and the sweetest face stared up at him, tongue hanging out of the corner of her mouth.

Selena smiled. "She approves."

Why on earth did it make him feel better that her dog liked him? He bent to pet the animal and Unicorn danced excitedly around his legs. "Does she need to go outside?"

"She shouldn't. I have doggy pee pads in here, and Kaia's

been stopping by to walk her and spend time with her so she's not alone."

"You don't want to bring her to the set?"

Selena laughed. "She'd be too much of a distraction, demanding a lot of attention."

"Makes sense," he said.

"Just give me a minute to freshen up," she said, heading into the bathroom. She only closed the door partway, and he watched as she turned on the water in the sink and removed the rest of the heavy makeup from her face.

There was something intimate about watching a woman remove her makeup, almost as if watching them slowly reveal themselves. He'd only ever lived with one woman—Aileen—but it was that small ritual at the end of the day that he looked forward to the most. The moment when she left the rest of the world behind and revealed herself to him.

But this wasn't Aileen; this was Selena, and he felt like an intruder observing her.

He quickly looked away and opened the bag. He took out the hamburgers and fries they'd ordered. Then he removed his jacket and shoes before climbing onto the bed. He sat with his back against the headboard and waited.

She'd completely transformed when she reappeared. Makeup-free face and her short dark hair in a messy ponytail, the too-short tendrils escaping to frame her face. And she was back to wearing the leggings and bra top. Completely comfortable in her own skin and completely oblivious to the fact that she was hot as hell in this casualness, she was without a doubt the sexiest woman Gus had ever had to resist.

How the hell was he supposed to concentrate on eating? Food was the last thing on his mind.

Luckily, she opened a dresser drawer and pulled out an

oversize gray sweatshirt. As much as watching the incredible body disappear beneath it sucked, it was definitely for the best. He had to somehow get this attraction in check. She was off-limits for a lot of reasons, and he'd do well to keep those at the forefront of his mind.

"Hungry now?" he asked as she sat cross-legged on the bed next to him.

"Not really."

That feeling was mutual. But if they didn't eat, what *did* they do?

He wouldn't mind taking another shot at occupying her mouth...

Despite her words, she reached for her fries and started eating. She closed her eyes and moaned, and he was ready to run out of the room. How could she not know the impact her sexy body and eating enjoyment might have on a guy? On him?

Maybe because this was completely Hollywood normal. Or maybe it was because he'd given her the impression that he found her irritating and annoying and not the least bit attractive, so she'd placed him in the nonthreatening, barely friends category.

Which was good. That was where he should be. Where he would remain.

He reached for his hamburger and unwrapped it. He took a bite, and the familiar taste of the best hamburgers in Alaska had him momentarily forgetting the awkwardness of the situation. "I missed these," he said, his mouth full of food.

Selena nodded. "If I lived here, there would be no way I could keep up my strict diet."

He was happy to see she was indulging, though he suspected this was comfort food. He cleared his throat. "So, want to talk about what upset you today?" He'd try one last time, and if she said no, he'd drop it.

She sighed as she shot him a look. "I'm sure it's the last thing you want to hear."

He shrugged. It should be, but for some reason, he did want to hear about it. Even worse, his protective instincts had kicked in again and he wanted to help.

Women don't want you to solve their problems; they want you to listen.

Wow, that guru book had really stuck with him.

"I know I probably can't help, but I can listen if you just want to vent."

Her mouth fell open, and she stared at him as though she'd never seen him before.

He laughed. "What? I'm not a complete asshole. Not all the time, anyway."

She looked like maybe she almost wished he was, and then set the fries aside and took a deep breath. "Okay, well, I'm not going to get into the gory details, but Matt and I are done."

His heart raced, and he wanted to punch the flicker of hope that rose in his chest in the face. Nope. Single or not, Selena was not his type. She was not someone he'd get tangled up with. He was in Wild River to process, re-group, heal—not take another shit-kicking from another wild horse. "Sorry to hear that," he said.

She shrugged. "I'm over it."

Really? That fast? He searched her face for signs of whether or not she actually was, because he still felt the hurt and heartache over Aileen even months later…though less so the last few days. He hadn't really thought about his ex at all in days, which was a rarity.

"I mean, obviously I'm not over it," she said, shoving

three fries into her mouth at once. "Him bailing on the movie was tough, and what bothered me most was that I'd been looking forward to spending time with him here in Wild River. I had so much planned, things I wanted to check out with him, experience with him. I wanted to spend an entire day doing the fun winter stuff that we never get a chance to do in California." She sighed. "But what can I do?"

He didn't think he was supposed to answer the question, so he just nodded.

Unfortunately, she was staring at him expectantly. His eyes widened. "Oh, were you actually asking me?"

She nodded, unwrapping the hamburger. "You recently went through a breakup and heartache. What did you do to get over it?"

He wasn't sure he really had. Up until he'd met her, he thought his heart was never going to pound for a woman again. "Um, well, um... You could still do all of those things you wanted to do. Might make you feel empowered?"

"I think it will only make me feel depressed, doing them alone."

"Okay..." Did she want advice on getting the guy back? Or simply moving on? He hoped it was the latter, but he asked. "Well, is it something you two can work out?"

"He was about to have sex with another woman in my bed."

The dude what...? Why the hell would she even want him back after that? And what guy would cheat on a woman as hot as Selena?

Show me a hot girl, and I'll show you a guy sick of her shit.

Bro logic was obviously still ingrained in his mind, too. And he couldn't say that Selena was an angel, easy to deal with. She'd practically tackled him to the ground and demanded he do what she wanted the day before. His lower body twitched at the memory of her sexy, tight body straddling him in the forest, and he shifted on the bed.

"Look, any guy who would do that to you isn't worth your time," he said. It was a standard answer, and yet it was the simple truth. If a person could cheat once, they could do it again. Everyone deserved someone they could trust, depend on. No one should be mistreated or taken for granted that way.

She studied him over a bite of her burger. "Have you ever cheated?"

"No."

Her eyes narrowed as though not believing it as she chewed.

"It's true." He paused. "I've only had three serious long-term relationships." Aileen had been the shortest. His high school sweetheart had been with him through college, though at a distance as she was studying to be a dancer at Juilliard. After that ended, he'd dated a *Sports Illustrated* model for five years. She'd turned out to prefer women, and then he'd met Aileen.

"Well, your girlfriends were lucky. I'm not sure I've ever dated a guy who didn't cheat. In hindsight, of course."

"Tell that to my girlfriends." Aileen hadn't appreciated his loyalty to her. She'd demanded even more, and then when she'd gotten it, she'd dropped him as if he didn't matter, as if his commitment to her was easily replaceable. He wasn't perfect, but he was starting to think maybe he'd deserved more, too.

Selena looked like she wanted to say something and was holding back.

"What?"

She sighed. "Nothing. I'm just trying to figure out what your ex could possibly see in that hockey player that she couldn't see in you."

His pulse raced, and the way she was looking at him had his fight-or-flight instincts kicking into high gear. Unfortunately, despite common sense, he didn't want to do either.

Instead, he pushed the food out of the way and moved toward her. Her eyes widened, and a second later, she'd tossed the burger aside and her hands were reaching for him.

He wrapped an arm around her waist and fell on top of her on the bed. Her hands gripped his face and her mouth crushed his. The same unsettling wave of desire hit him again. It had to be physical attraction and chemistry that had him reacting this way. He wasn't actually into her. She was irritating and annoying and demanding, although that one wasn't really a negative attribute right now.

He cupped her face between his hands as he deepened the kiss, savoring the taste of her lip gloss and the salt from the fries. He must taste like pickles and ketchup, but she didn't seem to care as she licked his bottom lip and then separated his lips with her tongue.

Her hands slid beneath his shirt and her fingers tickled along his abs, upward over his chest. She lifted the base of his sweater, and he broke contact with her mouth long enough to allow her to remove it over his head.

She clearly wanted this. Wanted him. But the passion in her kiss could be the result of anything—their on-set chemistry earlier that day, her recent breakup, her conflicted opinion of him…

Unfortunately, he wasn't sure he could keep going any further if that was the case.

Otherwise, she'd regret it the next day, and they still had to work together on the movie. That was what was important to her, and he didn't want to mess up this major career move for her. His mind reeling with reasons to put on the brakes completely destroyed his impulsivity. He reluctantly pulled back and she frowned. "What's wrong?"

"This doesn't feel right," he said. It felt more than right—it felt amazing—but he knew he couldn't actually have sex with her. He barely knew her, but he knew her well enough to suspect she might have an impulsive side as well, and, in her vulnerable state, he wasn't sure he wanted to contribute to her abandonment of common sense.

"I thought it was feeling pretty damn good," she said, slightly breathless. She trailed her fingers over his chest, and he placed a hand over hers to stop her. If she kept doing that, his moral compass might not keep him on the straight and narrow.

"It was... It is. I just don't think you're in the right emotional space right now. You just broke up with someone." She was single. That was definitely going to make things harder.

She looked amused. "Emotional space?"

He nodded.

She propped herself up on her elbows, and all trace of humor left her expression as she asked, "What do emotions have to do with sex?"

Oh, snap. He'd never had casual, no-strings-attached sex before. And while he wasn't opposed to the idea right now, he didn't completely believe that was what it would be. For him, at least. The kiss earlier that day, the way her vulnerability had hit him and the way he wanted to rip her clothes off right now—and then stay to cuddle afterward—were definitely telling him that he needed to put on the brakes before he was left recovering from a double heartache. This whirlwind of a woman blowing through his life could leave him a complete wreck if he didn't safeguard himself. "Well, I just...um... Well, I at least like to like a woman before I sleep with her."

One perfectly shaped eyebrow rose. "You don't like me?"

Oh, my God. How was he supposed to explain this without sounding lame? "I don't not like you. That's the problem with a one-night-stand situation."

"So you do like me?"

She was enjoying his squirming and that made him want her even more. She was tempting and fiery and spirited and playful. And combined with her determination, talent and commitment to her career and those beautiful dark eyes and smoking body, she was definitely a threat to his heart. And how she'd already weaseled herself in there through a crack when he hadn't thought it was open to new intruders was a mystery.

"I do like you, yes," he said, climbing off her and off the bed. Safer to put some distance between them. He tried to hide his erection as he stood near the door. "I like you enough not to want to mess this up—the movie," he said quickly.

She looked surprised and even more attracted to him as she nodded. She sat up and straightened her sweatshirt. "You're right. This could have jeopardized the movie. I don't know what I was thinking."

"I don't think either of us were really thinking just now," he said. He'd started it. There was no way she should be feeling at all guilty or responsible.

He also didn't want her to think she was undesirable to him. She'd just been hurt by one jerk. He approached her on the bed and brushed a strand of dark hair away from her face. "Believe me, this is taking every ounce of my gentlemanly strength to resist you," he said. "Which is why I should go."

She nodded slowly. "Agreed." She stood and walked him to the door, and he hesitated there.

Should he at least kiss her cheek? Give her a hug?

"Good night," she said, opening the door. Then, handing him her car keys, she added, "Take the rental. I'll get a ride to set with the others tomorrow morning."

"Thanks," he said, accepting them. "Good night. I'll see you tomorrow on set," he said as he stepped out into the hall.

As the door closed behind him, he took the stairs two at a time and bolted through the front door. The fresh mountain coolness was a huge relief to his overheated body. He released a deep breath, the white cloud floating on the night air around him as he headed down the street toward the rental car.

He might have been successful resisting Selena's body that evening, but he wasn't so sure his heart had escaped the firecracker's sparks.

THAT WAS A FIRST.

Selena could not think of one other time in her life when she'd come on to a man, offered no-strings-attached sex and gotten turned down. And she wasn't insulted. She was actually more intrigued by Gus Orosco than before. He'd clearly wanted her just as much as she'd wanted him. It was good to know she hadn't imagined their intense chemistry on set. His kiss that evening had been even more passionate and desire filled than the one in front of the camera, and she'd been more than willing to take things to the next level. He'd surprised her that day in a lot of ways. His commitment to the role, his caring and compassion toward her… his asking her to hang out.

As she stood in the window of the B and B and watched him walk along Main Street, she had a hard time remembering that she'd just broken up with a man she thought she'd been falling in love with. Compared to Gus, Matt paled on so many levels. Had she simply been blind to his true nature or had he delivered a great performance?

Either way, it was going to be tough to trust her instincts when it came to her heart anymore. Physical connections like the one she'd just had with Gus were easy. Attraction was almost animalistic. Passion was harder to fake, but it, too, came from a more impulsive, instinctual place. She needed to be more careful with her emotions moving forward, guard her heart a little better, not be so open and willing to trust. And maybe no more dating actors for a while.

Unicorn placed her paws on her leg and Selena bent to pick up the dog. She snuggled into her soft fur as she saw Gus climb into her rental. The dog yipped at the window and Selena sighed.

"I know exactly what you mean," she told the dog.

CHAPTER EIGHT

GUS HAD BARELY made it back to the campsite the night before when the writer in LA had emailed the new version of the script with Gus's suggested backstory elements. It was just one flashback scene and a heart-to-heart conversation with Selena's character, Alice, but it made a big difference. At least, he thought so. Will was more believable and relatable, and Gus thought viewers would connect with him better now, knowing where he'd come from and why he was living as a recluse.

His character was no longer one-dimensional, which meant Gus couldn't be either. He knew he'd done a good job the day before, but now the pressure was really on to deliver. He couldn't ask for changes to the script and then not pull them off.

Filming that day started at noon because Jay needed daytime scenes, so he had the morning to himself and he was on a mission.

A bell chimed above his head as he entered Flippin' Pages Bookstore on Main Street just as they opened. The two-story bookstore had been on Main Street as long as Gus could remember. They'd always picked up his school textbooks from the store, and he and his sister bought their grandfather one of their gift cards for every occasion. Vern made a habit of reading every sports biography ever written. One of the things that made him so great at his job.

He not only knew the sports, he knew the players and the people running the teams. He was a lifetime student of the psychology behind the sport, always craving more knowledge and encouraging his grandchildren to do the same.

The bookstore was also the site of Gus's first kiss with his junior high school girlfriend, Candace Jones. Hidden behind the comic book section, he'd taken that first leap. She'd tasted like bubble gum and had kissed before. He was awkward and terrified. She'd told him afterward she just wanted to be friends, so for years he'd lacked confidence in his kissing abilities and had striven to be a better kisser in future relationships. She'd probably done him a favor by crushing him that day. He smiled at the memory. How different things looked in hindsight. Being in the bookstore now definitely brought a new wave of nostalgia for his hometown.

"Hello! Welcome to Flippin' Pages," a pretty brunette said from behind the counter. She glanced his way quickly with a friendly smile, and then her attention was pulled back to the laptop screen on the desk. "Anything I can help you find?" she asked, not seeming eager to help as she typed furiously on the keyboard.

"If you can just point me to the history section, that would be great," he said. She looked busy and he could find what he was looking for.

"I've got you," said a tall, dark-haired guy wearing a name tag that read Callum. He was coming from the back room with two cups of steaming black coffee. He was a doppelgänger for Clark Kent with his dark-rimmed glasses, square jaw and light blue eyes. Gus didn't recognize him, but he was probably ten years younger. He placed one of the mugs on the counter for the woman and kissed her cheek affectionately. "You keep studying."

She sent him a grateful look as he approached Gus, and Gus felt a slight tug at his heart at the casual yet meaningful gesture. He missed being in a relationship like that. Not that he'd ever had a calm, rational, peaceful relationship that included bringing one another coffee and quick cheek kisses. His were more demanding of attention and dedication and a need to constantly reaffirm the connection. His were exhausting, actually. But, someday, he'd like to have what these two obviously did.

"History section is right over here," Callum said to him. "Anything in particular?"

Gus browsed the long shelves of books about historical figures, events and moments throughout the last century. So many options. The small indie bookstore in Wild River had a vast selection. It had been voted one of the top bookstores in America for a reason. The store was as much a draw for tourists as the mountains and ski slopes. "I'm looking for war books in particular. Biographies of military leaders, that kind of thing." He really wasn't a history buff, and he knew nothing about serving in the military. He had no idea what his character might have endured to make him the man he was, retreating from society and struggling to connect with other people.

His own retreat had had nothing to do with valor.

But he needed to get in the right mindset. He wanted to understand his character in order to portray him properly— do the character justice.

He also wanted to impress Selena.

After leaving her room at the B and B the night before, his attraction to her was obvious, but these unexpected growing feelings were also undeniable. He liked her a lot more than he'd expected to and hadn't been able to get her out of his mind all night. The way she'd looked, the way she'd tasted, the way she'd touched him… He never wanted to do anything halfway, and he wanted her to see how committed he was to helping her with this movie.

She deserved this break. She was so talented. As he'd watched her on set the day before, her work ethic and drive had shone through. It had made him want to work harder, push beyond his own comfort zones.

She also deserved to have someone else believe in the movie the way she did. Matt was obviously an idiot for letting her down in so many ways. He hoped she knew that. He hoped she was feeling better about everything. She'd put on a brave face the night before, but he knew her desire to be with him had come from a place of hurting and maybe not wanting to be alone, not wanting to feel rejected, at least partially.

"Here we are. *The Life and Reflections of Sergeant Ramsey*," Callum said, reaching for a book and handing it to him. "I think this is really the only one we have…"

Gus turned the thick hardcover book over in his hands. "This is great." It might take him a week to read it, but even a few chapters might help. He paused. "Do you have any how-to books? Reference books?"

"Three aisles over," Callum said, as an older woman entered the store carrying two heavy-looking boxes. He recognized her as Levi's grandmother, the woman who owned the store.

Both men hurried to help her, each taking a box.

"Aw…sweet boys," she said, stomping snow off her boots. She eyed him and smiled, deep creases appearing around her eyes beneath cat-eye glasses. "Gus! I didn't know you were in town," she said, but he suspected it was a white lie, based on the glint in her eyes.

Everyone knew he was there by now—and why.

"Hello, Mrs. Grayson. So nice to see you again," he said, carrying the box toward the counter.

"How's your grandfather?" she asked.

"He's good. Still running the studio and running circles around men half his age," he said.

"Still single?" she asked in a teasing tone that he suspected also held genuine interest. Women all over the world had a thing for Vern Orosco.

"He is," Gus said with a laugh. "I'll get him to call you?"

She grinned. "You do that." The phone rang and she waved at him as she hurried off to answer it.

He set the box onto the counter next to the one Callum carried and dusted his hands. "So, three aisles that way?"

"Yep. I'll let you browse. Let me know if you need anything else," Callum said.

"Thanks," Gus said, heading toward the section. He perused the shelves and found what he was looking for on the top one. *Acting 101* and *Drama for Dummies*. He grabbed both, then headed back to the counter. He'd binge-read as much of these books as possible to deliver the performance of a lifetime.

This movie wouldn't fail on account of him.

SELENA DRUMMED HER fingers on the table in Carla's Diner on Main Street and checked the time on the neon-rimmed clock on the wall. Leslie had suggested the fifties-style diner, complete with its teal-and-pink leather booths and jukebox in the corner, for breakfast that morning. Coffee was about all Selena could consume. And based on how jittery she was already, maybe she should stop. She pushed the coffee cup away and looked out the window facing Main Street.

It was just after nine, and the store owners were putting out sidewalk displays and flipping their Closed signs to Open. The reflection of the sun rising over the mountains created a beautiful glisten over the frosty streets and sidewalks. Normally, she'd be happy to sit back and take in the charming small-town sights, but that morning, she was too anxious to really appreciate it.

Come on, Leslie!

She needed a voice of reason. Someone to tell her that this thing with Gus was just a lightning-speed rebound. Unfortunately, she'd had these butterfly type feelings around Gus before her breakup with Matt, and her attraction had only gotten stronger after filming the day before.

What would it be like that day on set? Would they be able to be comfortable around each other after the night before? Would things be awkward? For the first time in her career, she was nervous about going to work, a place that usually felt like a second home. Thank God, she had a few hours to get her mind straight, as they weren't filming until noon that day.

Leslie entered the diner, still in her state trooper uniform, her blond hair pulled back in a tight bun. Her makeup-free face gave an air of authority, as though she was forever on duty. Selena relaxed a little. She always felt better around Leslie. Safer. Even though she wasn't her security detail anymore. Her friend was a safety net for more than just her physical well-being. Her no-nonsense, blunt, straightforward demeanor helped to balance Selena's more fantastical, romantic side. Leslie made decisions with her brain, not her heart.

"Hi. Sorry I'm late," she said, sliding into the booth across from her. She placed her gun and badge on the table, and it was a reminder that Selena's problems probably paled in comparison to the shit Leslie dealt with on a daily basis, so she tried to downplay her eagerness for her friend's advice.

"No problem. How are the night shifts going?" she asked. She also needed to ease into this conversation with Leslie, as her friend was sure to have opinions on Selena's recent life developments that Selena might not be thrilled to hear.

"They aren't ideal with Levi at the station during the day, but I need to work my way back to the good shifts. No free rides around here, despite my family connections." Everyone in the Sanders family was in law enforcement, from Leslie's mother to her siblings. The altruistic gene had run in the family's blood for generations.

Leslie reached for the menu and scanned. "I'm starving. What are you eating?"

"I made out with Gus!" Blurting it out seemed easier than easing into it. She winced and waited for the earful from her friend.

Leslie continued to scan the menu. "Eggs Benedict sounds good, but so does the Denver omelet." She bit her lip, absently reached for Selena's coffee cup and took a sip, and then grimaced as she swallowed the liquid.

Selena reached across the booth and lowered the menu. "Didn't you hear what I just said?"

Leslie nodded. "It was bound to happen."

"Excuse me? Do explain." Her hooking up with Gus certainly hadn't been a given in her mind. She'd found Gus irritating and annoying when she first arrived. Not at all attractive. Though the image of his naked body opening the door the day they arrived had replayed in her mind more often than she'd admit, especially after the day before. Last night, she'd been hoping for another glimpse.

"The chemistry between you two was off the charts the other day at the bar," Leslie said, as if it was obvious.

"We were bickering," Selena mumbled.

"Still chemistry," Leslie said, returning her attention to the menu. "What are you having?"

Selena released an exasperated sigh. "I'm *trying* to have a conversation. Can you forget your stomach for two seconds?"

Leslie shook her head. "I don't think so." As if to confirm her point, her stomach growled loudly. She set the menu aside and waved the waitress over. "Let's order first. Then we can talk."

"Fine." Selena tapped her foot impatiently under the booth and sucked in her bottom lip to avoid speaking.

As soon as they'd placed their breakfast order, she leaned forward, cradling her coffee cup in her hands. "I'm not even sure what happened. We had this tension-filled connection on set..."

Leslie held up a hand. "Wait. Hold up. He's in the movie?"

Oh, *that* part her friend found odd. She hadn't had time to fill Leslie in on this latest film development. Her friend was supportive, especially since she had a closet talent for photography and film, but the whole Hollywood scene didn't draw her interest. "Yes. The other three didn't work out and I was desperate." She shrugged. She wouldn't tell her how she'd convinced him to do it. She was still stressed about how she was going to deliver on that promise. "Turns out he's not a bad actor."

"Okay, so maybe it's just a costar thing." Leslie shrugged as the waitress filled her coffee cup. She took a sip, and once again her face screwed up as though her usual favorite coffee was bitter. "You said it happens all the time. If you're worried about telling Matt..."

She shook her head and took a deep breath. "Yeah, that's over." She couldn't believe it had been just the day before that she'd ended things. Felt like a lifetime.

Leslie's eyes widened. "I saw you less than forty-eight hours ago. How does your life change so quickly?"

For her friend, Selena's quickly changing life was no doubt hard to digest. Selena was used to a fast-paced, exciting existence, but even *she* was dizzy after the last few days. In Wild River, the pace was slow and predictable. Leslie and Levi lived a normal, simple life, despite both having dangerous, lifesaving careers. Selena knew what her life must look like to them. Thankfully, she also knew they were the kind of people who would support her and not judge. Unlike a lot of her friends in the city, where appearances and gossip were sometimes more important than being there for one another.

"I caught him cheating on Skype," she said, waiting for her friend's "I told you so" speech.

"That asshole," Leslie mumbled. "Can I say you're better off without him?"

No speech, just support. Selena nodded. "Agreed. The weird thing is, I'm not as hurt as I know I should be. I think it's because I know he obviously wasn't the man I thought he was anyway." Healthy, mutual breakups because things just didn't work out were harder to get over because there was nothing wrong—it just wasn't right. This one was easier because she couldn't miss something she'd never really had. Her feelings for Matt had been real, but a relationship couldn't thrive if it was one-sided. And anyone who could casually dismiss her that way wasn't worth crying over.

Leslie nodded, scanning the restaurant for the waitress as her stomach let out another big rumble. "So, maybe this thing with Gus is just a knee-jerk reaction to the breakup?"

Gus thought so, too, but Selena knew that wasn't it. "I don't think so. I was really into him last night. He's not at all the way I pegged him when I first arrived." She played with her nearly empty coffee mug. What exactly did she want to happen? She'd been open to taking things further the night before, and she was certainly open to spending more time with him and getting to know him. There was no reason not to. Unless he was still pining for his ex, and *that* was the real reason he hadn't gone for her the night before.

He was there in Wild River to get over his breakup and failed career. She'd offered to help with the career issue. Maybe she could help heal the broken heart, too? He'd certainly come back to life a little over the last couple of days.

"But you two didn't have sex?" Leslie asked.

"Nope." As their food arrived and Leslie immediately dug in, she filled her friend in on Gus's reasoning for putting on the brakes the night before.

"So, he didn't want to have sex because he likes you too much?" Leslie looked confused.

"Apparently."

"I thought you two were constantly butting heads?" Leslie sipped her coffee and sent her a questioning look.

"Turns out you're right   that was sexual chemistry."

Leslie nodded. "Wow." She filled her mouth with eggs Benedict and chewed slowly. Then her face paled, and she quickly climbed out of the booth.

Selena frowned as Leslie made a beeline for the restrooms, nearly colliding with an elderly couple entering the diner.

The waitress approached with a concerned look, coffeepot in hand. She scanned their dishes on the table. "Everything okay with the food?"

Selena hadn't touched her French toast and Leslie was

running for the bathroom. "Everything's great," she said with a reassuring smile. The food at the diner was amazing; they were both just having an off day. "I'll go check on her."

Entering the washroom a moment later, she heard the unmistakable sound of Leslie being sick in the last stall. She made her way to the door and knocked gently. "Hey, you okay?"

"No," Leslie said, before retching more.

Selena winced, and after reaching for a paper towel, she poured cool water over it as Leslie opened the stall door. She handed it to her with a grin. "How far along are you?"

Leslie's face took on a slight look of panic that Selena had guessed her secret, but then it was replaced with a look of happiness so bright that tears gathered in Selena's eyes. She was right. Leslie was pregnant. She'd suspected it when her friend was sticking to virgin martinis the other night, thinking no one was noticing the lack of alcohol. They said pregnant women had a glow, and, despite vomiting, Leslie was beaming as she washed her face and rinsed her mouth in the sink. She wiped her face and forced several deep breaths.

"Three months," she said. "So I guess the morning sickness is right on time."

Selena hugged her tight. "This is the best news. I'm so happy for you!" Her friend had changed so much that year since being in a relationship. She was still the badass she always was, but there was a slight softening to her edges these days. She pulled back reluctantly. "I bet Levi is excited."

Leslie looked away. A guilty look spread across her slightly pale face.

"You haven't told him yet?"

She sighed. "I'm terrified to tell him."

"Why? He will be over the moon about this." Selena had

never met a man more in love than Levi. He'd pined over Leslie for years. He'd been in love with her since the second grade and had had to watch while she fell for his best friend instead. Getting another chance with her had been a dream come true for the smoke jumper, and this news would make his life.

"I'm not worried about his reaction." Leslie paused. "I'm worried that things might go wrong with the pregnancy, that something might happen."

Selena felt a tug at her chest for her friend. A lot of women had that worry, and of course Leslie was still worried about the rug being pulled out from under her now that she'd found happiness. Losing her fiancé years before on their wedding day made her cautious about the good things in her life. She was afraid to let go and enjoy in case something bad happened. It was completely natural.

She touched Leslie's shoulder. "I understand why you're worried, but I think you've had your share of life tragedy. I think you can relax and be happy."

Leslie still looked uneasy, but her shoulders relaxed a little. "I've just never wanted something so much in my entire life," she said, touching her barely visible stomach.

The rare showing of vulnerability had Selena's chest filling with emotion once again. She was happy that she could be there for Leslie. "Everything is going to be just fine," she said reassuringly, wrapping her arms around her friend's waist. "And I can't wait to be fun Auntie Selena and spoil this kid rotten."

Leslie wiggled free and a hand covered her mouth. "Hold that thought," she said, diving back inside the stall.

Selena sent a sympathetic look as she turned away to give Leslie some privacy. She stared at her reflection in the mirror and puffed out her own flat stomach. She'd never really thought about kids in her future. Too busy building a life and career to even entertain the thought. But maybe someday she'd want to have kids, which would require a partnership with someone she could truly build a life with.

An image of Gus flashed in her mind, and she quickly pulled her stomach back in and shook away the thought.

For now, she was perfectly happy being Auntie Selena.

CHAPTER NINE

THE TEXT MESSAGE from Levi as he left the bookstore and strolled along Main Street brought back even more waves of nostalgia.

Snow Football Game. Homer's Park in an hour. We could use another player. Join in if you're free.

Snow football used to be his favorite winter sport. He liked to ski and snowboard and play hockey, but growing up in Alaska meant the snow and cold weather lasted a lot longer than in other places, so the summer sports season was always too short. Snow football solved that problem. It was the one game his father would play with them as well, and it was always more fun to have an adult play. They'd invite all the Boy Scouts and their fathers and form two teams to play in the wide, open area on the Orosco Campgrounds. They'd dress in so many layers it wouldn't hurt when they were tackled, and attaching snow cleats to the bottoms of their shoes helped give them traction on the slippery ground. They'd play for hours, until everyone was soaking wet, exhausted and hurting. Then his dad would serve hot chocolate near the firepit. He hadn't really thought about those games with his dad until now, but they were some of the best times of his life.

Levi would probably remember those days as well.

Maybe that was why he'd invited him to play. Reconnecting with his old friend since being back had been great. He wished he'd reached out to him sooner when he'd arrived in town.

He checked his watch. He still had two hours before filming. Spotting SnowTrek Tours a block away, he texted back that he was in, and then he hurried to the store. If he was going to play, he needed the right gear.

The locally owned adventure tour company was one of Main Street's gems. Despite the larger chain store opening a block away, SnowTrek was still thriving due to their ability to adapt and add additional services for tourists and locals, including a BASE jumping program for extremists. It scheduled tours for all ages and skill levels, and they had a small but smart selection of snow gear from Alaska-owned companies.

"Welcome to SnowTrek Tours," the owner, Cassie Reynolds, said from behind her messy desk as he entered.

"Hi." He'd gone to the same school as Cassie and her brother, Reed, for about a year in elementary school. He was older than they were, so they'd never been close friends. But he'd recognize her anywhere, as she hadn't changed a bit. Short blond hair, bright eyes that always looked excited and a warm smile. He knew through the rumor mill that she was engaged to The Drunk Tank's owner and was Kaia's stepmom-to-be. That little movie assistant didn't know how lucky she had it with the amazing role models and support she had in her life.

"Is there something I can help you with?" she asked as he scanned the display racks.

"Hey, Cassie, right?"

She nodded. "And you are Gus Orosco, the sports broadcaster. Heard you were visiting. How are you?"

He winced. Former sports broadcaster, but he ignored it. No need to get into it if she was the only person on earth not to have seen his on-air meltdown or the subsequent trending social media memes. "I'm good. I'm actually looking for boot cleats...the snap-on kind for snow sports."

She nodded with a knowing smile. "Snow football game over at Homer's Park?"

His stomach lurched and his jaw dropped. "Tell me your boyfriend's not playing."

Her laugh filled the space. "He never misses a game."

"Great, so I'll be needing extra padding as well," he said with a sigh as he selected some warmer clothing from the sale rack.

"The cleats are in the back room. I'll just be a sec," she said, leaving him alone in the showroom, only to return a second later. "Here they are. Anything else you need?"

"Actually, yes," he said, grabbing a piece of paper off a SnowTrek notepad on her desk. He scribbled something and handed it to her.

She laughed as she signed the note and handed it back to him. "Good luck."

Half an hour later, he arrived at Homer's Park, dressed in thermal underwear under thin ski pants for mobility, a thermal, long-sleeved shirt under a padded winter jacket, and short boots with cleats attached to the bottom. He clapped his hands together, feeling his excitement rise as he approached the group waiting to get started on the field.

He missed sports. Missed playing them. Missed watching them. Missed talking about them.

This was good. Between Selena setting his heart racing and this pickup football game, he might actually start feeling better.

Or...he might die.

As he reached the group, he swallowed hard. Everyone looked a lot bigger now than they had when they were kids. Gus had always been one of the stockier, heavier kids for their age group, besides Levi. Now it seemed many of the men on the field dwarfed him. He recognized most faces as members of the ski patrol or search-and-rescue volunteer teams. So, they were obviously in good shape, and he'd last worked out... He couldn't remember.

And, yep, Tank was playing. Seeing the guy stretching, he quickly approached Levi. "Hey, man. Are teams decided yet?"

Levi grinned, obviously reading his mind. "Don't worry. Tank's big, but he's not fast."

Either way, Gus wasn't taking any chances. Reaching into his pocket, he produced the note Cassie had graciously signed for him, requesting a place on Tank's team. Levi laughed as he read it. He tapped him on the back as he handed him back the note. "Saved by the girlfriend, huh?"

Gus would take it.

An hour later, Levi picked a book off the table in Gus's cabin, where they were enjoying a celebratory drink after their team won the snow football game. "What's this?"

He had about ten minutes before the film crew was scheduled to arrive and he'd yet to binge-read the biography or try to acquire years' worth of acting skills from the *Drama for Dummies* book in record time. Maybe he should have skipped the football game.

"Books to help me not look like a complete idiot in this movie," he said, pouring two cups of coffee, adding a splash of a liqueur and carrying them to the table.

Levi laughed. "So, the rumors are true. You're going to be a movie star now?"

Had Selena told Leslie about him being in the movie?

What else had she said about him? Had she told her friend about their evening together the night before? If so, he would have loved to be a fly on the wall for that conversation. Might help him figure out how he was supposed to act around her, what to say that day when he saw her. His palms were damp just thinking about it. At least there were no scheduled kissing scenes that day.

"Not a chance. This was a onetime thing…and I only agreed because she promised to get me an interview with Sports Beat," Gus said, sitting at the table and sipping the hot liquid. That had been the only reason, and it was still a pretty damn important one, but now there were others as well.

He sipped the coffee, allowing the hot liquid to warm him after the football game in the snow. He was on his second pot that day and soon he'd been shaking, but he hadn't slept well the night before, and he needed to bring his A-game on set, no matter what kind of reception he received from Selena, especially now that she'd had time to process his apparent rejection.

Truth was, it wasn't so much a rejection of her advances as it was a terrified fleeing. He wasn't sure what to do with the emotions and attraction that were catching him off guard. And he needed to be careful. She'd just gotten out of a relationship, and he'd come to Wild River to regroup and figure out what he was going to do next.

Complicating things with a fling might not be the best move.

But he did like her, and he wanted to make sure they could still work together on the movie. That they were still…cool.

Levi let out a low whistle. "Sports Beat—man, that would be amazing."

With or without Selena's input in securing him the interview, the opportunity would be a long shot, but he had to start somewhere trying to rebuild his career. Without an agent, reaching out to the key players at the studios would be a challenge, and unfortunately, his highlight reel would now always include his blunder on set. The internet lasted forever.

"It really would." He ran a hand over his hair and sighed. "It's been the elusive dream position for as long as I can remember."

"How would your family feel about it?" Levi asked, studying him over the rim of his own coffee cup.

"They'd be cool." He wasn't worried that his grandfather would feel betrayed. Vern was the most supportive person in Gus's life. His grandfather had built such an amazing career and legacy, and he'd want Gus to do the same. Firing him couldn't have been easy on his grandfather, and he'd love it if Gus landed on his feet with a great opportunity. "And just so you know, your grandma was asking me to hook her up with a date with Vern."

Levi shuddered. "I don't think your grandfather could handle her," he said with a laugh.

This Levi certainly seemed much happier than the military brat who'd been shy and reserved when he'd first moved to Wild River. He seemed calmer, more settled now. Evidently, being in love suited the man.

"Speaking of amazing women, Leslie's pregnant," he said, and the wide beam of his smile lit up the whole cabin.

Gus let out a whistle. "Wow! Shit, man, that's awesome. Congrats."

Levi shook his head, an amused grin on his face. "She doesn't know I know."

"She hasn't told you?"

"No. But I can tell. She's different," he said pensively.

"Are you going to tell her you know?"

"Not yet."

"Do you know why she hasn't told you yet?" Levi didn't seem upset by it, but Gus wasn't sure he'd be so cool if the woman he loved wasn't telling him something so important. So life changing.

Levi sat back in his chair and sipped his coffee. "Leslie hasn't had the most fairy-tale life."

Gus nodded slowly. He'd heard about Dawson's death on their wedding day and Leslie's struggle to move back to Wild River and make a new start, a new life with Levi. The story was tragic, but things seemed great for the couple now, despite both of them mourning the loss of a good friend. "But she's happy with you now. You two seem really solid." And Gus wasn't at all jealous of that.

Levi nodded. "We are and she's terrified of losing that. It's hard for her to trust that things won't go sideways. That our relationship will last. So, I know she's worried that something might happen, and not telling me right now is what she's comfortable with. If we could keep this between us, I'd appreciate it."

Levi was a good dude. One who obviously knew his fiancée well.

"You got it, man, and congrats. I hope everything goes well," he said. "Keep me posted. Let's actually keep in touch this time."

"You'll be begging me to stop sending baby pics." Levi smiled as he stood to leave. "I should get going. I think the crew is here."

Gus's heart raced as he heard the vehicle pull into the driveway.

"Break a leg, man," Levi said, leaving the cabin.

It wasn't a broken leg Gus was worried about.

SEEING LEVI EXIT Gus's cabin, Selena fought the urge to hide.

She was complete shit at keeping secrets, especially one this big. But she'd promised Leslie she wouldn't say a word to anyone. Not even the father of the baby.

Lying by omission is still lying.

Her loyalty to Leslie ran deep and it wasn't her place to say anything. News this big and fantastic had to come from the source. Now, if only she could act normal and hold a conversation with the man without letting something slip or her guilty expression setting off his spidey sense that something was up. He knew she was having breakfast with Leslie that morning.

Maybe she should hide until he left…

Too late. He saw her.

She waved as he approached. "Hey, you came by to see Gus?" she asked, thinking that keeping the topic off her breakfast with Leslie might help, but just the feel of Gus's name on her lips had her blushing. Had Gus told Levi about the two of them? About her jumping him the night before?

"Yeah, we played football this morning. Was hoping to catch you as well."

She narrowed her eyes. "You were? Why?" She knew nothing. She would reveal nothing. She was a vault. He could try to shake her down, but he'd get no information out of her.

He laughed. "To say 'bye before you headed back to California in case I don't get a chance to see you," he said carefully.

Oh, right. Okay. "Oh, sure… That makes sense."

He studied her. "You're acting really odd."

"I'm always odd."

"True story," Jay said with a grin, coming up behind her. He motioned to his watch. "We're starting in ten minutes."

Saved by the director. She turned back to Levi. "Well, I have to get to makeup, but it was great seeing you both." She moved in for a hug and he squeezed her quickly. She immediately realized her mistake in mentioning both of them. She should have just said, *Great seeing* you. Now she'd opened a door.

And he walked right in. "Hey, by the way, how was Leslie this morning at breakfast? How did she seem to you?"

Her heart raced and her mouth was a desert as she swallowed hard. "She was good. Great. Totally fine. Why?" She was sweating. The interrogation was torture. How was she supposed to keep this amazing secret under his intense, burning, quizzical gaze?

"How was breakfast?" he asked, his gaze piercing a hole through her.

So many questions! "It was good. Great. Totally fine."

"What did Leslie eat?"

"Eggs Benedict."

"Did she have coffee?"

She nodded, pressing her lips together so that the truth couldn't escape them.

He grinned and nodded slowly. "Okay. Well, that's good. Great. Totally fine, even."

Uh-oh. Had she just inadvertently revealed something? Why was he looking at her like he knew she knew he knew something? *Did* he know something?

"Well, I'll let you get to work. Keep in touch, okay? I have a feeling Leslie might need your support more than usual in the next little while," he said with a wave as he headed to his truck.

"Shit. Did I just reveal the secret?" she asked herself, watching Levi walk away.

"What secret?" Gus whispered into her ear.

She jumped so high her shoulder hit him in the nose. "Ow!"

"Sorry," she said, her heart racing. "You really shouldn't sneak up on someone like that." He was lucky she hadn't turned around and slugged him. Hard.

"Sorry," he said, rubbing his nose.

"You okay?" She meant more than just his nose. Was he freaked out about what had happened between them the night before? He shouldn't be; technically, nothing had happened.

He nodded. "I'm good. Great. Totally fine," he said with a sarcastic grin. It was clear he'd heard her floundering, talking to Levi.

And just like that, she knew they'd be fine on set that day. Things didn't need to be awkward between them. They were costars and that was it. Nothing had happened the night before.

Only it didn't feel that way. It might almost be less awkward if they *had* had sex. Sex was simple. Or at least simpler than the alternative—that they might actually like one another. She'd just ended things with Matt the day before. She wasn't going to jump headfirst into this…whatever this attraction was to Gus. He was surprising her, that was all. In a good way.

His grin faded a little as he asked, "So, we're okay?"

She nodded. "Absolutely." She checked her watch. "I should get to makeup. I'll see you in a bit."

She turned toward the cabin, but his voice stopped her. "Selena…"

She forced a casual smile as she turned and walked backward. "Yeah?"

"If I could go back and redo last night, I would."

She nearly stumbled over her feet as she cleared her throat. "Well, who knows? Maybe if you're lucky, you'll get that chance," she said, turning away before he could see the look of pleasure on her face.

CHAPTER TEN

HE WASN'T QUITE sure where the words had come from, but from the moment he'd laid eyes on her that day, the overwhelming urge to be near her, hear her laugh, touch her—hell, even bicker with her—made it clear that given another chance, he wouldn't turn down the opportunity to get closer to her again. With or without clothes on.

His gaze drifted to her now as they gathered around the firepit outside the shooting cabin to discuss the day's schedule. A light snow fell and the air was still around them, and the way her cheeks flushed in the glow of the fire had his pulse racing. She caught his stare and he looked away quickly.

"Good news—today should be an easier filming day, as we captured most of the intense shots yesterday," Jay told the group. He checked his clipboard and continued, "We're going to start with the montage shots of Will and Alice getting to know one another, show the passage of time. Quick and dirty. These shouldn't take more than a few hours. Then once night falls, we will move into the second night cabin scene, where we learn more about Will." Jay turned to smile at him. "Courtesy of the new script that, in my opinion, is fantastic. Thank you to Gus."

A round of applause from the crew had him blushing. He avoided Selena's gaze as he mumbled a thanks. Oddly, the crew had welcomed him with open arms while they were still cool and standoffish around Selena. He didn't get it. It had to be bothering her, but she seemed to accept being the odd man out.

"Okay, everyone in positions. Let's get the cameras rolling," Jay said.

An hour later, Gus was literally sweating, despite the cold Alaska air.

These might be easier scenes emotionally, but this montage filming was a lot harder than it looked. The rest of the crew moved effortlessly from one staging to the other, but the quick transitions and refocusing were making Gus dizzy. Everyone was moving at a lightning pace, and he could barely catch his breath, as though he really were living these days in the span of mere seconds of film time.

By the fourth transition, he raised a hand, and Jay motioned for the cameras to stop. "What's up?" the director asked.

"I, uh…just need a quick break," he said.

Jay checked his watch, then looked to the sky. It was almost three, and they needed a few more daytime shots before moving into the nighttime cabin scene. "Five minutes?"

Gus nodded. "That's great." He headed into his own cabin and shut the door.

There was a knock almost immediately. "Hey, you okay in there?" Selena called out.

He turned and opened the door to her. She was dressed in wardrobe, which consisted of leggings and an old red-and-black-checkered jacket that she'd supposedly borrowed from Will. Her fake bruises were now just a yellowish hue along her cheekbone. The sight of her character still unnerved him, despite knowing it wasn't real. "Just needed a breather," he said, allowing her to enter.

She sat on the arm of the couch as he turned on the tap

at the kitchen sink and poured a glass of warm water. He guzzled it, refilled it and gulped it down before facing her. "I had no idea how hard this was."

She laughed. "You get used to it."

"Definitely not planning on that," he said, collapsing on the couch beside her. "These whirlwind shots are tough. We're supposed to have been together for two weeks, and trying to switch gears for each scene is killer."

"Jay's trying to reduce the amount of editing in post by filming the shots in the order he wants them to appear in the film. It's easier working with a bigger budget when the director can film out of order more and focus on shots in one location at a time. We're doing that for the bigger scenes. I'll talk to Jay and see if we can film the last three with a bit more flow."

He shook his head. "No, it's okay. I'll survive." He stared at her in awe. She did this all the time, and had since she'd been a kid. As a movie viewer, it was easy to critique a film, never understanding the amount of work, effort and talent that went into making a seamless film from start to finish. All the person-hours and dedication it took from everyone involved. And these lower-budget indie films had to be even harder.

"What?" she asked.

"Nothing…" His cheeks flushed with heat. "You are just impressive, that's all. You started acting at what age?"

"Well, as a baby, I did a few commercials, but I don't remember those," she said with a grin. "I officially started acting at four years old."

"Four years old on a movie set." He studied her. "Did your family push you into it or was it something you wanted?" He'd heard of that happening with a lot of child actors and Hollywood heirs. The decision was essentially made for them.

She shook her head. "Are you kidding? I had to beg my parents to let me audition for my first role in a family film. While most kids played with Barbies to dress them up, I acted out scenes with mine. I built my own sets for them. In a way, I was studying acting even before I really knew what I was doing."

"That's incredible. To know from such an early age what you wanted to do with your life. What you were meant to do." Drive and ambition from an early age were a recipe for success. It made him feel better knowing this was a life she'd always wanted, not something her family's legacy had forced upon her.

"It's the same with you," she said. "You always loved sports and knew you wanted to be a broadcaster, right?"

He did, and not being able to do it the last month had nearly killed him. If it hadn't been for Selena and this movie, he might still be falling deeper into a hole of despair. He nodded. "I guess it is, yeah." Who would have thought the two of them would have this in common?

"So, your grandfather and sister are in the business. What about your parents?"

He shook his head.

"Did the love of sports skip a generation?" she asked.

He cleared his throat. "No. Actually, my dad played hockey. Minor leagues, but he had amazing talent. He met my mom through the sport. She was a cheerleader." He paused. He hadn't talked about his mom in a long time. He'd been a toddler when she left, but Trish had been a teenager and had taken it hard. A young girl needed her mom during those tougher years, and he knew his sister still wasn't over the fact that their mother had left. She refused to acknowledge her; therefore, no one really brought her up.

"They got married and had my sister, and then me, ten

years later," he continued. "Dad never quite made it to the big leagues, playing for the minors here in Alaska. Got close a few times, according to my grandfather, but always came up short. It wasn't enough for my mom. She had envisioned a life a little more grandiose, I guess, traveling the world as an athlete's wife, and Dad didn't measure up." He cleared his throat and Selena's hand touched his shoulder. "She left when I was three. Dad gave up hockey a few months later. It was as though his drive to succeed left with her. He took over running this campsite, until he died a few years ago from a heart attack and we shut it down." His father's broken heart had ultimately killed him, never having gotten over their mother leaving.

Apparently the Orosco men fell hard, and recovering from heartache wasn't something they really knew how to do.

"I'm sorry, Gus," Selena said gently.

He took her hand in his and shook his head. "I haven't told anyone any of that before." He'd never even told Aileen about his father's hockey career or his mom leaving. She'd never asked much about his family beyond Vern and Trish.

"Well, thank you for telling me," she said, and their gazes met and held.

Damn, she was beautiful.

A tap on the door meant time was up, breaking the moment between them.

"I guess we better get back out there," he said.

"Daylight's fading," she noted, standing up.

On impulse, he reached for her hand again as she started to walk away. She stopped and turned with a surprised look.

He pulled her toward him and gently touched her cheek. He stared into her eyes, and an overwhelming urge to kiss her flowed through him. "Thanks," he said.

"For what?"

"More than you know," he said, satisfying himself with a quick, soft kiss to her forehead before releasing her and opening the cabin door.

IT WAS A simple kiss to the forehead.

Siblings kissed one another that way. She kissed her grandfather that way when he visited during the holidays. And yet that simple kiss from Gus had rocked her. She'd had passionate, desire-filled kisses with him and had felt their effects, but this one was somehow even more powerful. The way he'd opened up to her about his family, the way he'd reached for her hand, the way he'd stared at her with a complexity of emotions in his expression after they'd shared a moment of connection, getting to know each other deeper, and then the gentle press of his lips to her forehead...

She'd practically turned to mush.

The cabin was set for the scene as they entered, and contrary to the first nighttime cabin scene, this time there was a warmer, cozier vibe to the space. The crew had added more ambient light, there were handmade quilts on the cot, and the kitchen was clean and tidy. The space definitely now held the effects of a woman.

A log was burning in the fireplace, and, as if by Hollywood magic, soft thick, fluffy flakes fell outside the windows as darkness settled.

Kaia came hurrying in with Diva, slightly out of breath. "Sorry I'm late. Hockey practice ran longer than scheduled," she grumbled. She put on her headset and shook off her coat.

"That's okay. We did montage scenes this morning, so we didn't have many lines," Selena said, giving her a quick hug. Then she bent to pet Diva. "Hi, gorgeous girl." The thick gray-and-white fur ball was an amazing search-and-rescue dog, but she was a pampered pet first and foremost. She lay on her back and soaked up the attention.

Kaia shook her head with a sigh. "Better not let Dad see you act like that," she teased the dog.

Diva slowly sat back at attention, and Kaia directed her to lie on the rug near the fireplace where she'd be "sleeping" in this final scene they needed her for. The preteen turned her attention back to Selena. "So, rumor has it, Gus was at your B and B last night." She gave her a what-are-you-doing? look.

"We just had dinner…as costars. Get to work," she said gently. She wasn't sure what was happening with her and Gus yet, but she refused to worry about the opinion of a young girl who was far too mature for her age.

She sighed as she watched Gus read his lines on the sofa. Small towns spread gossip faster than Hollywood gossip rags. Luckily, she wasn't a local, so most people wouldn't have given it another thought. But Selena cared about Kaia, and she knew the impressionable young girl looked up to her. She didn't want her thinking that Selena was hooking up with Gus. As far as Kaia knew, Selena was still dating Matt.

"Places!" Jay yelled, and Selena refocused her attention as she sat next to Gus on the sofa. This was the new scene the screenwriter had added the night before. She wasn't as confident in it as the others she'd read and rehearsed over and over, but the success of this scene was mostly on Gus.

He looked nervous, and he didn't glance up from the script until Kaia gently tugged it out of his hands. He breathed heavily and rotated his shoulders.

"Don't worry. If we have to retake this one a few times, it's not a big deal," she said reassuringly.

He nodded.

But after Jay called "Scene," and Gus started his personal monologue about his past, Selena felt herself being drawn into his story. His tone, his believability as a tortured veteran who'd lost everything, his phrasing… It was all on point. Some of the lines she couldn't remember reading, which meant he was improvising again, but it was working.

She was so caught up in the emotionally heartbreaking story that she almost missed her cue. This was where she comforted him. She touched his shoulder gently as directed and he sprang up from the sofa. He approached the fireplace, where he stood with his arm against the stone wall, staring into the flames for a long beat, before bending to add more logs to the fire.

Selena watched, her expression one of sympathy as required by the script, but inside, she was full of awe. Where the hell had this secret talent come from? He was not only delivering the script as it was written, but his additions were making it that much better. Had his opening up to her in real life earlier that day sparked a vulnerability in him that he was tapping into for the scene?

She was honored that he'd opened up to her, trusted her with the story about his past, his mother leaving. He'd never told anyone before.

"Ow," he mumbled, and she saw him yank his hand away from the heat of the fire.

She frowned. Getting burned wasn't in the script. Her eyes shifted to Jay, and he nodded at her to go with it.

She'd never improvised before this movie, but some of their greatest performances were coming from those unscripted moments. She stood and hurried toward him. "Let me see," she said, bending next to him.

He reluctantly gave her his hand, and Selena's reaction to the sight of the burn was completely genuine. Gus stayed in character as she led him to the bathroom and carefully tended to the wound. She applied burn ointment and a thin layer of gauze...

His stare burned into hers, hotter than the flames sizzling in the fireplace, as he swallowed hard. "Thank you," he said in a low, growly voice.

Selena extended a hand and touched his cheek, and their gazes held.

Jay called, "Cut!"

Gus still didn't look away, and it was only when Kaia appeared with water for them that the moment was broken and Selena remembered to breathe. "Thanks," she said to Kaia.

"Okay, that's a wrap, guys. Let's pack it up," Jay said. A quick round of applause was given for a productive filming day, and then everyone packed up to leave.

Selena was riding the high of an amazing scene and the new connections she'd formed with Gus that day as she gathered her things and followed everyone outside. Feeling hopeful for the first time in a week, she stepped outside into the cold night air.

Then she stopped short. "Matt?"

She blinked, but he was still there. At the campsite. In Wild River. What the hell?

Next to her, Jay looked like a kid on Christmas morning. "Matt! Hey!"

"Hi, Jay..." Matt said, his gaze locked on Selena, who seemed frozen in place as she stared back in disbelief. "Hey..." Matt glanced almost sheepishly at Gus standing next to her. Gus didn't make any motion to leave her side; in fact, he only moved closer.

Did he realize he'd done that?

She snapped out of her haze. "What are you doing here, Matt?" she asked, her tone chilly, but a heat rose inside of her. The day before, she'd been so angry and hurt, her decision to break up had been firm. Today, however, her anger was diluted, especially after seeing Matt there in the flesh amid the thick snowflakes, looking incredible in ripped jeans and a black sweater under a thick thermal vest, his blond hair gelled above his sleek, dark-rimmed glasses. Those damn glasses—what the hell was it with her and those spectacles, anyway? Maybe it was that they made him seem more humble, less arrogant.

She'd never seen him behave arrogantly—until the day before on Skype. *That* guy had been almost a stranger, but they said a person's true colors emerged when they were cornered, and Matt's weren't something she wanted in her life.

She would not weaken or give in to his apologetic expression. The guy was a cheater and that was something she couldn't forgive.

"Can we talk?" he asked, looking nervous.

"There's not much to talk about." Still, he had flown all this way...

Nope. She wouldn't cave. He was untrustworthy. His presence there now was too little, too late. He'd bailed on the movie. He'd bailed on them...on her.

Jay glanced at her questioningly. She shook her head, motioning for him and the crew to go on ahead without her. She still hadn't told Jay about the breakup. It had seemed irrelevant, given their bigger issues regarding the movie, but now the director looked confused as he headed toward the van.

"Come on, Selena. I'm here," Matt said. "I should have been here before. I realize that now." He glanced at Gus again, with unconcealed jealousy that would have made her over-the-moon delirious before. She'd have taken it as a sign that he was really into her, but not so much anymore. Now the jealousy made her annoyed that he'd assumed she'd immediately moved on with Gus, though he wouldn't be completely wrong.

"Can we get a moment alone?" he asked Gus.

Gus looked at her and she nodded.

He hesitated, then shot Matt a look as he shouldered past him. "I'll be over here if you need me," he said, still glaring at Matt.

She couldn't help the way it warmed her. She didn't need his protection. She could handle this herself, but it was nice to know he cared. They'd gotten so close over the last two days. It was almost inconceivable. Yet it felt like she had known Gus a lot longer than a week. Oddly enough, it felt like she knew him better than she knew the man standing in front of her, asking for a second chance. She knew Gus's passion for a career he wanted to get back, she knew the flaws that made him that much more relatable, she knew his struggles getting over his heartache, and she knew his family dynamics, which made up part of who he was. All she really knew about Matt was that he was an incredible actor, who'd fooled her with his performance.

When Gus was still within earshot, but pretending not to be listening, Matt sighed and moved closer to her, lowering his voice. "Look, I'm sorry about what happened. It wasn't what it looked like. She meant absolutely nothing to me."

"That's supposed to be better?"

"Well, isn't it? It was just physical. We both know that happens all the time. Wouldn't it be worse if I had a true connection with someone else?"

It would, but only by a fraction. Cheating physically or emotionally had the same devastating effects on a relationship. They both weakened trust bonds between two people and raised the level of suspicion and doubt. A relationship would never be the same. "A true connection with *someone else* would imply that you had one with me."

He reached for her hands and they fell limp in his. She refused to give in to his charms, his apologies, his twisted reasoning for another chance. "We do have one," he said. "A very strong one. At least, I thought so, anyway."

Her heart wavered. She'd longed for him to say that. Waited for it. Now it sounded like bullshit to try to win her back. And she didn't trust his motives. Whatever accommodation he'd found in LA probably wasn't of the same standard he'd grown accustomed to at her house. He couldn't afford the lifestyle he'd had with her. And he certainly wouldn't have found the loyal, genuine support she'd always given him. No doubt, he wanted another shot at all of that. Who wouldn't?

"I thought so, too," she said, "but I'm not a fool, Matt." He'd be using her until his own fame and fortune made her unnecessary. It hurt, but the truth sometimes did.

"Of course not." He squeezed her hands and stared pleadingly into her eyes. "Just give me a chance to prove myself."

"You had one. You blew it." Why did he think he deserved another one? Because she cared about him? Had thought the two of them were great together?

"I flew all the way here. Big gesture. Doesn't that count for something?"

In the past, it probably would. Selena the rom-com queen, with stars in her eyes and wearing rose-colored glasses, might have been so impressed and touched by the fact that he'd gotten on a plane and flown to her that she'd take his sorry ass back. But new, post-stalker Selena thought it was something he was supposed to have done days ago. Before groping another woman in her bedroom. "You know, I always thought it would. But I'm starting to realize, it's the little things—" *like not sleeping with other people* "—that actually matter." Her gaze landed on Gus, and she knew he deserved part credit for her new resolve. Comparing Matt to Gus, there was no contest. The realization was baffling, that she could have been blinded by her own emotions and not see what was in front of her. It took meeting someone genuine and honest and vulnerable to open her eyes.

"Please, Selena. I'm here. You don't have to forgive me and take me back. But at least let me be in the movie with you and I'll show you how much this matters. How much you matter." His voice softened.

Having him as her costar was what she'd wanted, what she'd thought was best for the movie. They didn't have to get back together, but maybe he was still what the movie needed to succeed.

Nope. She shook her head and pulled her hands back, folding them across her chest. "We've cast someone else."

"That guy?" He jerked his head toward Gus. His soft, caring attitude switched abruptly. "You can't be serious."

"Actually, I am." Thank God she hadn't just fallen for the fake remorse. He wasn't getting his way, so he was back to bullying tactics. Unbelievable.

"But what about my contract?"

"The one you broke when you didn't show up to the first

day of filming?" she asked smugly, grateful for their own clause additions.

His scowl deepened as he scoffed. "Gus Orosco is a sports broadcaster, not an actor," he said.

Ah, so he did recognize Gus.

Selena couldn't resist. She fought a grin as she leaned in closer, her confidence in her decision strengthening her resolve. "Maybe not," she said, "but he's actually turning out to be better than you."

HE DIDN'T MEAN to eavesdrop. Okay, maybe he did. He wanted to hear the guy's lame apology. Thank God Selena hadn't fallen for it. Matt had an agenda, and it had nothing to do with being in love. If Gus were a betting man, he'd put his money on the fact that Matt saw Selena as someone who could help him get ahead, or at least open some doors and pave the way for him with some influential people.

His gut twisted. Not so unlike what he was doing.

But his situation was different. He wasn't supposed to be in love with her. They weren't together. They were costars and friends. Friends who were attracted to one another and developing feelings.

But their business dealings had been agreed upon before he knew her, before he started to like her more than was safe. And she'd offered her help because she needed something from him in return. Which he was delivering.

Though, it did surprise him that she'd turned down Matt's offer to take his place in the movie. Sure, she was personally pissed at the guy, but Gus would have assumed she'd eagerly accept him back to the cast to ensure the movie was a success.

He didn't for a second believe what she'd said about him being the better actor.

She'd just wanted to get back at Matt. Still, her choosing him made him feel good. Which was a little weird, considering he had no interest in acting or being in this movie. Or at least he hadn't previously. Things were different now. He still didn't want to be a movie star. But he desperately wanted to nail this role so that the movie could have the best shot at being a success. He didn't want to be the weak link that caused it not to do well.

Selena was absolutely killing it, and he couldn't wait for all the naysayers to see the film and see what level of acting she was capable of.

He caught sight of her from the corner of his eye as she spoke to Jay. The director had immediately hurried over to her when he'd seen Matt drive off, obviously not used to slippery, icy trails, skidding all over the road.

He strained to hear what they were saying.

"Are you out of your mind?" Jay's voice was about an octave too high.

"No. He didn't want to be a part of this, and now it's too late," Selena said calmly.

"We can reshoot the scenes. Going over budget is worth it to have him attached."

"I disagree. I think we are doing just fine with Gus," Selena argued. But he could sense she might be rethinking the decision to send Matt packing even as she was defending it to the director.

"Gus is fantastic," Jay said evenly. "I'll give you that, but Matt's name will help get the finished product into the festivals."

Ouch. Selena's name should be more than capable of that. Why didn't Jay have more faith in her? It annoyed Gus that everyone kept dismissing her when she was proving she had more talent than any of them. He resisted the temptation to join in the conversation. This was her battle, and she was more than capable of handling it.

"I don't think we need him," she said.

"Selena, whatever personal issues you two have going on, you need to put them aside. Think about the movie. Think about your future career and what this means."

Obviously, the man also wanted her to think about what it meant for his career. Jay was desperate to make a name for himself, too, and Gus knew the industry was all about connections and who knew who. Hell, his own opportunity was coming through the same channels.

He swallowed hard. He should back away. Be the one to bail so that the decision was easier. Tell Selena to recast Matt so the movie had the best chance of success. He started their way, and then stopped when she said, "No. Jay, you've trusted me all along. Trust me now. I know we can do this without Matt, and I really think we should."

Jay looked unconvinced as he stared at her, but finally, he nodded. Hands on his hips, he looked away. "Fine. Seeing as how you are coproducing the project and essentially not getting paid, I'll defer to your judgment. But if this doesn't work out—"

"I'll take full responsibility," Selena said.

Man, she was a beast. Standing up for what she knew was the right thing for her when Matt was trying to gaslight his way back into her life. Standing up for Gus and the movie against Jay—there was so much to admire about her. So much he could fall for...

He shook his head and walked away. He needed to get his head on straight. The last few days had completely messed with his emotions and his mind. What was going on? He still wasn't over Aileen, and yet this new attraction to Selena bubbling up couldn't be denied.

"Hey, wait up!" Selena's voice behind him made him slow his pace. From the corner of his eye, he saw Matt's rental car still struggling to make it through the snow.

And no one was chasing after it.

"He seems pissed," he said, nodding toward the vehicle.

"Good," she said, linking her arm through his as they walked.

The gesture was casual, yet his heart pounded, feeling her body so close to his. He welcomed the smell of her soft perfume drifting on the breeze and the feel of her hair blowing against his shoulder.

He cleared his throat. "So, you sure about this?"

"About sticking with you?"

In more ways than one perhaps, but he'd focus on the movie. The easier part. "Yeah."

She nodded. "Without a doubt." They'd reached the rental van, where Jay and the crew were packing up for the day. In a minute, she'd be gone again until the morning.

He cleared his throat. Should he invite her to dinner? To stay and hang out?

Sure, 'cause the cabin was cozier than her B and B. What was he thinking? *Just let her go.* He should spend the night alone, clear his mind, sort out these feelings before they got even more complicated.

"We'll meet you at The Drunk Tank in an hour?" she asked as she climbed into the van, surprising him. "I'll leave you my rental so you can drive in."

Wasn't exactly a date invite…more like an assumed group thing. A movie crew-and-cast thing. But it beat staying out here alone. Bored. Thinking about her.

He nodded. "Sure. Why not?" He did not give off the casual vibe he was going for.

"Okay, see you soon," she said as he shut the van door.

A second later, they drove off, and Gus headed back inside his cabin to shower and change for the definite not-date with the costar he was definitely not falling for.

CHAPTER ELEVEN

"I HOPE YOU'RE not mad at me," Selena said, as she and Jay stood at the bar two hours later, waiting on their second round of drinks. Since their differing of opinions on the Matt issue, he hadn't said much. Quiet in the van on the way to the B and B and seemingly lost in his own thoughts so far that evening. Not fully engaged in the conversations, checking his cell phone more than usual.

It was hard not to internalize his mood as her fault.

"Why would I be mad? Just because you turned away a guy on the verge of mega superstardom to keep grumpy but lovable Gus in the movie?" Jay asked with a sarcastic tone that said he was annoyed but not mad.

Selena could live with that. "I'm sorry! I just couldn't give Matt the satisfaction of feeling like he'd somehow saved the day. Like we were lost without him." The way he'd shown up expecting her to take him back so readily, both in her life and in the movie, just further infuriated her the more she thought about it. Never again was she going to give in to the wants of these fickle men. Not when she knew there were good, solid, caring, respectful guys out there. Her gaze shifted past Jay to the door.

Gus hadn't shown up yet. Had he changed his mind?

"And of course, you're totally into Gus," Jay said with a smirk.

Selena hoped the neon bar lights hid the rush of color to

her cheeks. "No, I'm not. That's the most ridiculous thing I've ever heard." She wasn't ready to talk to Jay about the pull she felt toward her costar just yet. It would appear that she was transferring her feelings from Matt to Gus without any kind of cooling-off period, and she wasn't the type to jump from one guy to the next.

"I know he was in your B-and-B room last night." Jay's cell chimed and he immediately reached for it, his eyes skimming across the screen.

She waved a hand. "Nothing happened. I was upset about Matt, and it turns out Gus is a good listener." Unlike Jay, who was now completely engrossed in his text message.

"So, you don't like him at all?" he asked, his fingers flying over the cell phone.

She forced a strangled fake laugh. "Have you not seen the two of us at each other's throats from the moment we arrived?"

Jay nodded. "I have. I've also seen a shit ton of chemistry and physical attraction…and not just on set."

"I'm an actress. I'm pretending."

Jay put his cell back in his pocket with a shrug. "Okay, I'll buy that, but in case you were into Gus, I think he's into you, too."

Yeah. She knew exactly where she stood with him. Somewhere in the middle of *like* land. Not too much, not enough. He'd been as clear as mud.

"Anyway, there he is," Jay said, nodding behind her.

She swung around so fast she nearly grew dizzy.

He wasn't there.

Jay grinned. "Thought you weren't into him." He picked up several drinks and nodded as he headed toward the pool tables in the back, where a group of local search-and-rescue members were playing a game. The following day, they were going to be extras in the scenes being filmed, and their shoe-string budget was paying them with drinks that night.

Selena sighed as she checked the time on her phone. Maybe Gus had realized spending time together might not be the best idea. There was definitely an attraction there, but they were both still getting over breakups, and a rebound wasn't something either of them wanted.

Best to give things some space. From now on, no more hanging out away from filming.

The bar door opened and he entered and she released a deep breath.

Oh, thank God.

He scanned the bar, and she started to raise her hand to flag him down, then lowered it and looked away. Let him find her. Let him come to her. Her days of chasing after men were over. She'd already put herself out there with him. Now the ball was in his court. Whatever happened, happened. She wouldn't move too fast or force anything.

She heard his boots approach on the wooden bar floor and faked a look of surprise when he stopped next to her. "Oh, hey, almost forgot you were coming." Okay, that was a little much.

He grinned. "My sister called and, well, she's a talker."

"Trish, right?" The woman who'd rented them the cabins.

"That's the one," he said as Tank approached.

"What are you drinking?" the bartender asked.

"Scotch, rocks, please," Gus said, scanning the bar. "Is that Jay and the crew over there?"

She nodded, tapping the bar stool next to her. "Yeah, but we don't have to join them right away." So much for playing it cool. Truth was, she wanted to talk to him for a bit. She was curious about him, and most of what she knew she'd learned from Google, which wasn't always a trust-worthy source.

Gus sat on the stool and removed his jacket, draping it over his legs. Her eyes fell to his biceps in the tight gray T-shirt that still had the sales tag on it. Aw, that was why he was late. He was buying new clothes. The shirt still held the folding wrinkles. Had he wanted to impress her by looking good? He needn't have bothered with the shirt. The biceps were good enough.

She averted her eyes from the temptation to touch one. *His family. Ask more about his family.* "So, Trish is head of publicity for the sports station?" she asked.

He nodded. "Among other things. She is kinda Grandpa's go-to for almost everything, but primarily, she takes care of marketing and publicity."

"And your grandfather is Vern Orosco?"

"Yes."

"And he actually fired you?" She'd read about it, but it had been hard to imagine family firing family. It was one of the reasons she'd never hired family to be a part of her business. Her stepdad taught her that. He said the fastest way to destroy a family was by working together in this business. There were more than enough examples of it to trust the logic.

Maybe the Oroscos had it figured out...or *had* it figured out.

"He did." Yet Gus didn't seem to hold any ill will. He didn't sound bitter at all. He'd taken responsibility for his own actions, and that said a lot about who he was. Putting the family's name and business above his own personal disappointment.

"That must have been hard," she said gently.

He nodded. "It wasn't easy, but the hardest part was

knowing I'd let him down. He's always been this huge role model for me."

Tank arrived with their drinks and they each took a sip. She searched her mind for a new topic. Something more upbeat. Something less gloomy...

"So, what about you?" he asked before she could come up with something. "I read that *you* were the one doing the firing last year."

She nodded slowly. "Yep. My entire management team. I kept only my agent." Her agent handled deals and contracts. He was the logical, practical, sign-here, don't-sign-here guy. He helped secure auditions without trying to persuade her one way or the other. His advice was blunt, direct, sentiment-free. The management team had been responsible for guiding her career. They were the ones pushing her in the rom-com direction and ultimately pigeonholing her in Hollywood. They'd helped her make some great choices along the way, and also bad ones, ones she didn't want to repeat, ones that had benefited them. A year ago, she'd decided she needed that decision-making power in her own hands.

"That was brave," he said.

"It might have been stupid," she said, her honesty surprising even herself. But she was starting to wonder. Maybe she'd been hasty.

"I don't think so. I think you went with your gut, and your gut can always be trusted." He took another sip of his drink.

She thought so, too. "I just hope this movie is a success so that I can at least feel somewhat validated," she said, playing with the stem of her martini glass.

"It will be," he said.

She laughed. "You said that before, and then admitted you actually had no idea."

He took another sip of his drink and his gaze locked with hers above the rim of the glass. "That was before I saw you act."

Her heart raced at the compliment. Having him believe in her shouldn't have such an effect, but after the disappointment with Matt and the challenges so far with filming, it did. She could easily fall for him, and she was desperate to pull back a little. She looked away and cleared her throat. "How did your family end up with the serial killer campgrounds, anyway?" From what she knew of the Oroscos, they were all career sports industry people, even his dad at one time, apparently. His opening up to her about that earlier that day still warmed her, the fact that he trusted her.

He shook his head. "The grounds weren't always that bad. They've been in my family for five generations. I think some of the original decor remains," he said with a laugh.

"You said it, not me," she said with a smile, a deep warmness flowing through her at the fun, flirty banter.

"It was kinda just passed down from one generation to the next. Whoever stepped up and wanted to take over running the money pit was welcomed to it. My dad was the last one to run the site, but after he died, no one in the most recent generation has stepped up. Now they just sit there. Looking creepy."

"And serving as an amazing location for this movie." She turned in her stool to face him. "Jay showed me some footage from today and it's incredible." A good deal of editing would be done in post, but so far, they'd kept the filming clean and precise, and from what she'd seen, everything was coming together the way they'd envisioned.

Gus stared at her and she grew embarrassed. "What?"

He looked away quickly and shook his head. "Nothing.

So, tomorrow, I noticed the schedule said we're filming on the coast?"

The next day they were scheduled to film in Port Serenity. They were a little off on the scene order, but they'd receive assistance from the local coast guard, and several of the local search-and-rescue crew had signed up to be extras, so they needed to shoot those scenes as per the original schedule, then return to the campsite for the rest. "Yes. We'll film the last three scenes there, then come back to wrap up." The idea of wrapping this movie made her stomach twist. She was having fun. She felt herself growing as an artist, felt her creative muscle expanding, knew she was delivering the best performance of her career. The thought of it being over made her a little sad. She wasn't sure what was next. That uncertainty between films had never really bothered her before. She knew something else would come up. Now her career was hinging on this indie success.

"Do you need me for those?" he asked, sounding somewhat hopeful.

He wasn't actually in them, but… "Maybe you should come with us, just in case," she said with a casual shrug. Okay, so she wanted him there. It would be nice to have him along and he'd be able to see the full movie being shot. "Only if you want to. If you're not busy. You've almost fulfilled your end of the bargain."

His handsome face moved closer to hers as he said, "I want to, I'm not busy, and I'm no longer seeing this as just fulfilling a bargain."

"Sure you don't want to drive?" Gus asked, tucking his neck lower in his leather jacket as they left The Drunk Tank two hours later. Wind cut through the thin coat. The rest of the crew was still inside, but Selena was calling it a night.

Reluctantly. They'd been having such a great time chatting together at the bar, they hadn't even made it over to the pool tables with the others, which was fine with him. She, too, hadn't wanted to leave, but an early-morning shooting schedule required it. She had to be on camera. The rest of the crew could look like hell behind the scenes if they enjoyed an all-nighter.

Once again, her commitment to her career impressed him.

"I'd rather walk," she said, inhaling a deep breath of cool, fresh mountain air. "I love Main Street at this time of night. So quiet and still. There's never a time like this in LA. The city is always awake and glowing in neon. Here, you can actually see stars and hear your own thoughts." She really did seem at peace. Her expression relaxed as she tucked her bare hands into the pockets of a formfitting puffy bomber-style coat.

"It is nice out here. I'd just forgotten how cold it can get in the fall." Living in Seattle, where the weather was generally mild with lots of rain, he'd somehow blocked the Alaska chill from his memory. "If it's this cold now, I can't imagine winter here anymore."

She nodded. "I'll admit, it was a bit of a shock to the system."

He glanced at her. "You were here in March last year, right?"

"Yes. So, I guess it was technically almost spring, but it certainly didn't feel like it," she said with a laugh.

He walked in silence for a moment, unsure whether to ask her about it or not. She was back in Wild River, so maybe she'd gotten over the traumatic experience. The place didn't seem to hold bad memories for her. He cleared his throat. "It must have been kinda terrifying…being here, not knowing what was happening back in LA—whether they'd catch the guy or how long you'd need to stay hidden for your safety." As a man, he couldn't imagine the dangers women faced on a daily basis. His sister had once laid it out for him in a play-by-play of her day, from checking the back seat of her vehicle before climbing in, to holding pepper spray in one hand and her keys interlaced between her fingers of her other hand as she walked anywhere at night. And Selena had had it so much worse than just the average, random attack. This man had been stalking her for years, moving in closer, threatening her safety, even in her own home. The violation of privacy and feelings of vulnerability had to be torture.

Selena's short dark hair blew across her face as she nodded. "It was…unnerving. To be honest, I hadn't really taken it seriously—the threats and the extra precautions my security team had put in place. It just seemed par for the course. I'd had stalkers before. Over-the-top fans who overstepped boundaries. I thought this was no different."

Wow, he couldn't even imagine a career where a stalker might be just another accessory or rite of passage of sorts. He was on television, but he'd never thought himself a celebrity and he'd never dealt with overzealous fans or anything. His career in the spotlight was the perfect balance of exposure and platform without the stardom that made it impossible to live a normal life. Grocery shopping, vacations or a session at the gym were all paparazzi-free for him.

He doubted Selena had ever had that luxury.

"But this one was personal?" He'd read the news articles about the case. Selena's stalker had been obsessed with her since he was a troubled teen and she'd starred in an after-school teen special. He'd connected with her fictional character and hadn't been able to distinguish real from fantasy.

"Yeah. I actually feel bad for him more than anything." She laughed when he shot her a look. "I mean, *now* I do. In hindsight. At the time, I was scared. But he has mental health issues and he had a rough life. He deserves to be getting treatment, not a prison sentence, but such is the reality of our flawed legal system."

Gus let out a slow breath. "That's very generous of you."

She shrugged. "My therapist says my forgiveness is what helped me move on, process the trauma and get over it quickly. Can't live in fear, right?"

He studied her. "Is that what this leap of faith is about— this indie film? Not wanting to let fear dictate your life? Your career?"

"That's a big part of it, yeah. It's also a sense of feeling like *what's next?* I love making movies and I've enjoyed every part of my career so far, but I don't want to settle or grow complacent..." She shook her head. "I don't know. Maybe this movie won't do as well as I think, and all the naysayers and critics will be right. Maybe sticking in my own lane would have been the better choice..."

This rare display of doubt had him stopping her. She looked at him in surprise as he reached for her hands, removing them from her pockets. "No. Do not even for a second think that this was the wrong decision. You are killing it in this movie, and I'll do whatever I can not to hinder its success."

Her gaze locked with his, and her expression was one he'd seen a few times already, one he was desperately trying to avoid because acknowledging it would have him grabbing her and kissing her. And he still wasn't sure what to do about those desires. He quickly released her hands and gave a shaky laugh. "Sorry, that was intense."

"Don't be," she said, then cleared her throat as they kept

walking. "It means a lot to have someone support…this movie."

They'd reached the B and B, and he turned to face her. He hesitated. "Hey, if you change your mind about wanting Matt…" He'd understand if, now that she'd had time to think about it, she realized reshooting the scenes with the actual actor made sense. He wouldn't be offended if she wanted him out.

She shook her head. "I don't want Matt," she said softly but firmly enough that he knew she meant it. But did she just mean in the movie?

He cleared his throat. "Okay, well, I guess this is good night."

"Yeah, good night." She reluctantly headed up the walkway, then turned back. "You sure you want to tag along tomorrow?"

More than was safe. He actually hated the idea of not seeing her at the campsite the next day. What would it be like once they were done filming and weren't forced to be around one another? He already knew he'd miss her, and he was even more grateful for the job opportunity she was securing for him in LA. He'd always been open to the idea of moving anywhere for the right career opportunity, and now LA held even more appeal. But he was getting far too ahead of himself. They'd both taken a step back in their attraction to one another—just some flirting and a casual touch here and there that evening, so maybe the initial sparks were starting to fade on her end. He nodded. "Absolutely. Can't wait."

She glanced at her watch. "Well, you won't have to wait long. See you around four a.m.?" She cringed at the early hour.

"See you then," he said, waving and waiting until she

was safely inside the B and B before heading back down Main Street toward the rental car. Four o'clock might only be five hours from now, but for Gus, the early-morning wake up couldn't come fast enough.

CHAPTER TWELVE

IT TOOK LESS than thirty seconds for Selena to fall in love with Port Serenity, Alaska. The fascinating coastal town had a rich folklore that drew tourists from all over the world. Tales of Sealena, a mysterious half-woman, half-serpent creature, rumored to protect boats at sea, had become the focal point, and the local businesses were definitely capitalizing on the mythical creature's lure. From the large serpent statue in the center of town, to the bookstore-museum nestled among several pubs and restaurants along the coastline, the residents here knew how to bring in tourists.

"Hey, did you know they'd named their mysterious sea creature after you?" Gus said, his tone teasing.

She laughed. "It's pronounced *See-ah-lena*." She'd done her research.

"Well, you're definitely prettier," he said with a wink.

"Really? What tipped the scales in my favor?"

"The lack of a tail," he said. "How on earth did Jay get approval from the coast guard to film here for free?" he asked as they got out of the van at the small air rescue station. It was one of the things she loved about acting—she got a chance to live many different lifestyles, and her research for roles had resulted in a lot of unusual skills and interests over the years.

Selena grabbed her makeup kit from the back of the van

and whispered, "Apparently, he and one of the captains of the cutters had a…thing."

Gus nodded. "Ah…" They glanced over at a nervous-looking Jay, fixing his hair in the side mirror. "Looks like maybe the thing isn't quite over?"

"That's what I'm thinking," she said. "It didn't take much convincing for him to agree to film in Alaska, and it was his idea to have the last few scenes of Alice escaping on the water with the help of search and rescue." She saw the Wild River Search and Rescue van pull into the parking lot, and she waved. It was still hard to believe that these men and women were happy to volunteer their time and expertise to make these pivotal scenes look authentic. Life was definitely different here in Alaska, where people banded together to help and support one another with no agenda, without looking for anything in return.

So different from most of her friends in LA.

So different from Matt. Six text messages from him the night before had all gone ignored. He was staying at the Wild River Resort Hotel and he'd assumed she was staying there, too. He'd tried to lure her back with talks of couples massages at the spa and champagne breakfast in bed. He'd tried appealing to all her sensitivities, reminding her of the fun activities she'd wanted to do with him on this trip. But she saw the temptations for what they were and finally shut off her cell phone for the night. Turning it back on now, she sighed. Four new texts.

"Matt's still trying, huh?" Gus asked, and then looked embarrassed. "Sorry, didn't mean to look."

She tucked the phone away as they headed toward the building. "He's persistent." Until he got what he wanted and sufficiently used her. Then he'd be moving on. Her newfound clarity was actually refreshing.

"Any doubts or second-guessing this morning?" he asked, sounding nervous.

She smiled at him. "Nope."

He smiled back.

Jay caught up to them as they reached the door. "I'm freaking out."

"Don't worry. It's going to be fine." These scenes would be the most exciting ones in the movie, and with the help of the coast guard, they were going to look so much more real than if they'd used a green screen and special effects.

"I mean about seeing Doug again," Jay said, taking a deep breath.

She studied him. "What is the situation between you two?"

"He's the one who got away," Jay said. "We were high school sweethearts back in Atlanta. Of course, no one knew we were actually together. Neither of us had come out to our parents. Douglas's family was all military and he knew his old-school, narrow-minded father would lose his shit if he knew, so I was always just Doug's buddy." Jay rolled his eyes.

"But he's out now, right?" she asked.

He sighed. "Not exactly."

Her eyes widened. "Really?"

"He's just as nervous about coming out now as he was before. He's wanting to get through the ranks and prove himself, and he's afraid…"

"That his career might be jeopardized?" She shook her head. The world had come a long way with acceptance and *love is love is love*, but there were still those who refused to acknowledge people who may not share the same beliefs, the same values. "Sorry, Jay."

He sighed. "I just can't be with someone who refuses

to be honest with themselves. I was tired of hiding all of this," he said with a laugh as he gestured to his faux fur jacket and silver leggings.

Selena had a hard time believing anyone could ever think Jay was straight. He was brilliantly out with his sexuality, and the idea that he may have had to hide who he was, hide his fantastic self to have others accept him, made her chest hurt. She had multiple gay friends and their coming-out stories ranged from heartwarming acceptance from their families, to rejection.

"You shouldn't have to," she said, linking an arm through his. "Let's go show Doug what he's missing."

HIS DECISION TO tag along that day was definitely the right one.

He'd wanted to spend the day with Selena, but now that he was there, it was so much more than that. He'd never been to Port Serenity, and while the town's touristy vibe wasn't really his thing, getting a tour of the coast guard facilities and learning the different protocols was fascinating.

Jay's friend Doug had welcomed them all, and now they were headed down to the water to the cutter they were using for the getaway scene. The weather was made for perfect filming that day. Dark, ominous-looking sky, a thick mist covering the ground and snow clouds looming heavy above the mountain ranges. Rough, violent-looking waves were capping on the ocean, and a strong wind blew through his jacket as they reached the dock. The atmosphere would enhance the mysterious, dangerous scenes without many effects needed in post.

Selena was in wardrobe and makeup, and they were eager to get the cameras rolling as they boarded the vessel and the crew set up for filming.

Gus found a spot off camera to watch the action.

Selena had told him the boat would only go out a little ways from shore and that Jay would add minimal CGI in post to make it seem as though they were in the middle of the Arctic. Either way, being on a coast guard cutter was a once-in-a-lifetime experience. If he wasn't careful, he might catch this acting bug for the sole purpose of getting an up-close look at some cool-as-shit professions.

Once the cutter had left the shore, the cameras started rolling and Jay started to direct. Gus couldn't take his eyes off Selena as she performed, delivering her rehearsed lines perfectly. Confident, talented and focused, she commanded the set. He'd read the script, so he knew what was coming, could almost recite her next line himself, but it was in the delivery that the true magic happened. Her movements, her mannerisms, so different from the way she was in real life, captured this fictional character and brought her to life. Watching her, he almost forgot where they were and that it was all make-believe. Even with the cameras and lighting all around him, he felt himself pulled into this woman's desperate journey for freedom. Her portrayal of Alice was nothing short of award-worthy. By the time Jay yelled "Cut!" Gus was mesmerized.

"You were amazing," he said, when she joined him after a quick watch of the replay.

"Thank you. We just have one more scene to shoot, and then we are done for the day," she said.

"I'm having a great time."

"I'm glad you're here," she said softly.

His attraction to her only grew stronger and stronger the more time he spent with her, the more he got to know her. She was nothing at all like he'd expected privileged, rich Hollywood royalty to be. He'd wrongfully assumed she was a spoiled brat, and she was the complete opposite. She had everything she could ever want, but she was sacrificing it all to follow her gut and take a chance on herself.

A loud beeping sounded over the speakers in the boat as Doug started to head back toward the shore.

Gus frowned. "What's that?"

Selena shook her head. "No idea. Not part of the movie."

They approached Jay and Doug at the wheel. "What's going on?" he asked. The young cutter captain's demeanor had completely changed from the easygoing, relaxed guy they'd met. Now he was focused and moving at lightning speed as he reached for the radio and communicated with the station.

Codes they didn't understand were exchanged, and next the boat was headed away from shore and out to sea.

"The watch stander just received a call on the VHF radio from a rescue coordination center. There's an overturned twenty-one-foot vessel and we are the closest unit, being out of port already. We need to respond," Doug told them.

Selena's eyes widened. "We're going on a real rescue?"

Doug nodded.

"Holy shit, this is exciting," Jay said, clutching Doug's arm. The two men shared a strained gaze that was full of complex emotions and so intense that Gus and Selena slowly retreated to give them privacy. He felt for Jay. He knew what it was like to want someone and not be able to be with them. Maybe this reunion might help Doug realize what he was missing out on with Jay and help the two reconnect.

"I really hope they can work things out," Selena whispered, echoing his thoughts.

Gus reached for the railing on the side of the boat as the vessel picked up speed. Bobbing close to shore was one thing, but the breakneck pace over the ocean waves was making his stomach lurch.

Next to him, Selena tipped off balance as the boat crested a wave, and he caught her around the waist. "Got you," he said into her ear, pulling her body closer to his. It was the first time he'd held her since the night in her B and B, and the feel of her in his arms was something he didn't want to let go of. "I should probably keep holding on to you... for safety purposes."

She turned her face toward his. Her mouth was mere inches from his. "You think I need protection?" she teased softly.

"No. It's for my protection. I'm not so good with water." He'd never been a fan of swimming, and the ocean's mysteries could remain that way, in his opinion. He had no interest in meeting Sealena.

Selena looked surprised, but the boat crashed down over another wave, preventing her next words.

He held her body tight to his with one arm and held on to the railing with his other as the boat continued to the site of the overturned vessel. The feel of her against him, the smell of her soft perfume and peppermint-scented shampoo, combined with the exhilarating ride, was intoxicating. A rush of excitement flowed through him as they neared the accident, and Selena's flushed expression and the way she held tight to his arm around her had him experiencing more than just a little lust.

The cutter started to slow and Gus peered out the window. An overturned fishing vessel was several yards away. It was being tossed around on the waves and it was a marvel the thing was still in one piece. He spotted two men bobbing next to it, fighting the frigid, icy current and trying desperately to hold on and not be swept farther out to sea.

Doug and his crew sprang into action, tossing out life-saving buoys and reaching to bring the men toward the cutter. The boat rocked and swayed, and they battled the elements to haul them aboard the boat in the fastest show of bravery and skill that Gus had ever witnessed.

"These men are real live action heroes," Selena said in awe.

Suddenly Gus wished he was part of the team.

The crew assisted with helping the two men out of their soaking, freezing clothing and wrapping them in heated blankets, checking them for injuries while Doug and the other officers continued their search for the third man, who'd drifted away from the boat.

"What color is his jacket?" Doug asked the more lucid and calm of the two men.

"Dark blue," he said, his teeth chattering and his hands shaking as he held a steaming cup of hot coffee.

Not the best color to be wearing out there in the frigid ocean. The call had come in over ten minutes ago. It would be almost impossible to survive in these water conditions for long. Everyone knew it.

"Was he wearing a life vest?" Doug asked, as his crew continued to scan the surface.

The other two men weren't. Neither of them answered.

"To the left!" one of the crew said. "Object in the water."

Doug turned the wheel sharply and Selena clutched Gus even more to keep from falling. They blazed ahead through the waves and the other man came into view. He was face down, floating on the surface, and Gus held Selena's face to his shoulder as the crew members dived in to recover him and bring him on board. He could feel her tremble in his arms, and his own heart rate was dangerously high as the crew performed CPR on the lifeless body. The pale blue coloring of the man's skin wasn't promising.

His friends huddled together, looking more and more devastated as each second ticked by with no change. No sign of life.

"Oh, my God," Selena whispered. Her bottom lip quivered slightly as they all silently watched while Doug and his crew tried to save a life.

"Come on!" Doug said, applying more compressions to the man's chest.

Jay stared on in disbelief, and there wasn't a sound throughout the boat as Doug physically exhausted himself in his attempts to revive the man.

As Doug bent to give mouth-to-mouth a final time, the man sputtered, coughing up what seemed like an ocean full of water. His eyes snapped open with a look of panic and the entire group released a simultaneous breath of relief. The man was alive. Not out of the woods yet, but alive.

"That was the most terrifying thing I've ever lived through," Selena said.

For someone who'd been abducted, that was obviously saying a lot. He held her tight as the crew cared for the man and the boat returned safely to the port.

EMS was waiting near the dock to take the three men to the hospital for treatment for hypothermia and ensure no serious injuries had been sustained in the accident.

As the film crew disembarked, they thanked Doug and the crew. "It was definitely an adventure," Selena said. "You and your team are heroes, and we will make sure the movie honors you all."

Doug nodded. "Thank you. Sorry for the detour," he said with a tired-looking smile, his attention focused on Jay.

"We'll meet you at the van," Gus told Jay, leading Selena

away to give the two former lovers some privacy. They watched as the two men talked in hushed tones and Doug quickly touched Jay's cheek.

Selena gave a swoon-sounding sigh next to him. "I really hope they can work things out."

Gus did, too, but in that moment, he was more concerned about working out his own feelings for Selena. And fast.

"THAT WAS ABSOLUTELY EXHILARATING," Selena said. Adrenaline still had her buzzing even hours later as they pulled up in front of the B and B. The filming had gone great and they'd gotten to experience a real coast guard rescue. Unbelievable day. Doug had updated Jay on the men's condition an hour ago. They were all doing well at the hospital in Port Serenity, where they were being held overnight for monitoring and expected to be released the next day. Thank goodness the cutter had already been away from port and was able to reach them quickly; otherwise, that day might have ended in tragedy.

Gus laughed. "It was exciting, I'll give you that."

"I can't believe you're afraid of water." That confession in the midst of the rough waters during the rescue had surprised her. Gus didn't strike her as someone fearful of much. His strong, muscular build obviously housed a softer, vulnerable side.

"I'm not afraid of water. I'm afraid of drowning," he said as he carried her bag for her up the front walk toward the door.

"Fair enough." She was secretly afraid of escalators, as irrational as it sounded, so she wasn't judging his legitimate fear. She stopped outside and hesitated. "Did you want to come in?"

Please say yes.

She liked spending time with him. More than any other man in a while. She used to think she and Matt had a fun, playful way of bouncing off each other, but her conversations with Gus were both fun *and* meaningful. They could tease one another one moment, then have a deep conversation about career, family…fears, the next. His words from the night before in the bar had stayed with her all day. He believed in the movie. He believed in her. And that support had her more than a little falling for him.

"Um…" He glanced at the inn and then back at her. "I'm not sure."

"What's the issue? You like me too much? Or still not enough?" she asked, stepping nearer and placing a hand on his chest—his muscular chest, where his heart pounded beneath her hand. At least she wasn't the only one with an accelerated heart rate.

He swallowed hard. His Adam's apple bobbing as his gaze burned into hers. "I honestly don't know."

She moved even closer. "Well, maybe if you came inside, it might become clearer?" She'd never had to work so hard to get a guy naked before. Gus was a challenge she hadn't expected. She was enjoying the rare chase, but she was starting to want to catch him. She longed to take things between them to the next level. She liked him. She was attracted to him.

And if his hungry expression could be trusted, she wasn't alone in those feelings.

"Selena, are you sure? I mean, you and Matt just ended things…"

"This has nothing to do with Matt."

He hesitated and she let her hand fall away. He wasn't resisting her because of Matt. He was resisting her because he was still hung up on his own ex. On Aileen. "Sorry, I thought maybe things between us were…" Their spark had been growing, not fizzling out the last few days, but maybe she felt its heat more than he did. Feeling stupid, she turned quickly and reached for the front door.

Gus's hand on her arm made her stop, and he pulled her into him. His mouth found hers with zero hesitation, and he kissed her long and hard. The passion and excitement of the day paled in comparison to the thrill of kissing him. He tasted like mint gum, and the scent of the fresh, salty ocean air still lingered on his hair and clothing. She sank toward him, wrapping her arms around his neck, and he held her firm to his body.

She stood on tiptoe, driving her torso even closer. She couldn't get near enough and, in her opinion, there were far too many layers of clothing between them. She knew what she wanted and she wanted Gus. Now.

He broke away and his stare made her shiver. "You sure about this?"

She nodded quickly, and within seconds, they were inside the B and B and racing up the staircase to her room.

Jay, already inside, called to them from the lounge, where he and the crew were having a celebratory drink in honor of the three fishermen. She ignored him. After opening the bedroom door at the top of the stairs, she practically dragged Gus inside, grateful that Unicorn was still with Kaia.

He laughed at her urgency, yet wasted no time tearing off his jacket. He reached for hers, but she unzipped it herself. Undressing one another could wait for the next time. "Undress yourself. It's faster."

It was, and thirty seconds later, they were falling onto the bed together. Naked. So very naked. She wished she had more hands as they roamed over his shoulders and back and ass and hips. He was built like an athlete, and it was obvious that sports and health and fitness were a big part of his life. She'd always been attracted to a stockier, muscular build in a man, and Gus's body was a thing of fantasies.

His own hands were taking in every inch of her as well. They slid over her shoulders, down her chest…lower…then pausing. "You sure?"

"Stop asking."

"Consent is sexy," he said with a grin, rolling on top of her.

"Only so much," she said, dragging his head back down to hers and kissing him again. These lips. What the hell was it about these lips that she found so incredibly irresistible? She'd kissed dozens of men—on- and off-screen—and no other set of lips had her wanting to devour them the way Gus's did.

He wedged himself between her legs, and she lifted hers to wrap around his waist. Resting his elbows on either side of her head, he pressed his erect penis against her mound. A groan escaped her and she bit his bottom lip.

He pulled back, a look of surprise registering first in his eyes before being replaced with intrigue.

She grinned up at him seductively. She liked sex and she liked to have fun. Too many women she knew felt that they couldn't express their desires, their wants, their secret passions to their lovers. Selena was not one of them. She liked to be satisfied and, in turn, she was a giving partner.

Gus seemed even more turned on by her lack of inhibitions as she reached between their bodies and touched herself.

"Shit, Selena, you're so hot," he growled, stroking the length of himself as he watched her turn herself on even more. It didn't take much to get herself wet. The last few days had been torturous foreplay.

He kissed her as they both continued to play with themselves, and soon she couldn't take it.

"Condom?" she asked, knowing she wouldn't last long. They could savor each other next time. Right now, she craved him inside of her. Craved him more than any other man she'd ever been with.

He moved away and retrieved one from his wallet. He frowned. "Shit, it's expired."

She blinked. "They expire?" she asked. Since when?

"Apparently."

She grinned. "Been a while?"

"Too long, obviously," he mumbled. He tossed it into the trash can and took a deep breath. Clearly, he thought they were giving up.

No chance in hell. She wasn't letting this opportunity slide from her fingers. Rising from the bed, she walked toward him and wrapped her arms around his neck. "There are other ways…" she whispered against his lips. She slid a hand between their bodies and her hand gripped his cock.

He moaned and his grip on her waist tightened. He moved them back toward the bed and they collapsed onto the soft, down-filled comforter. Selena straddled him and continued to stroke him up and down. Precum escaped and she used it as lube as she increased her pace.

He was instantly hard, and his size had her wishing he could be inside her body, filling her. She pumped up and down and massaged his balls with her other hand.

Gus's eyes closed as his head rolled back against the pillows. "Damn, that feels good."

She quickened her pace, but he placed a hand over hers to stop her. "I want some of this action, too," he said, flipping them so they were facing one another, lying on their sides. He massaged her breast gently, his thumb flicking over her hardened nipple, and then ran his hand down her body until he found the opening between her legs. The feel of the pressure of his fingers against her folds had her craving much more. "You're so wet."

"Well, you kept me waiting long enough," she said with a teasing grin as she wrapped her hand around the base of his cock again, sliding gently upward, then torturously back down.

He stared into her eyes with such an intense look of longing that her breath seemed to be trapped in her chest. This was beyond physical for both of them. The instant connection they'd formed, even when they were bickering, was unique, rare. This kind of chemistry didn't come around every day.

"I've never fallen for someone this fast before," Gus said, echoing her thoughts.

Her chest filled with emotion. Knowing they were on the same page and that he was no longer fighting it had her turned on even more. His finger slid inside her body, and she swallowed hard as she clenched tight around it, needing more, desperate for more.

"I'm glad I'm not the only one feeling this way," she said as her pace quickened.

Gus's breath was labored as they continued to pleasure one another. She felt the first ripples of orgasm build and opened her legs wider for him. He slipped another finger inside and pressed his palm to her mound, applying stimulation to her clit as he drove his fingers in and out in a steady pulsating rhythm.

"I'm coming," she said as she stroked him up and down, faster, harder.

"Me, too," he said gruffly.

Seconds later, she felt him explode in her hand just as her own pleasure toppled over, and she cried out in release. Her breath came out in a short succession of pants as she rolled on top of him and kissed him, riding out the aftershocks of her orgasm.

He held her face between his hands and stared into her eyes. "You are the most unexpected person I've ever met."

She laughed. "I think that's a compliment?"

He kissed her again, softly. "Definitely a compliment."

Unexpected. She'd gotten a lot of compliments from men before, but none so unexpected as this one from Gus.

WHAT THE HELL was happening to him?

A month ago, he'd been brokenhearted enough over Aileen that he'd jeopardized his career and had to escape the city. He'd thought she was the love of his life. And yet he wasn't sure the feelings he had for her had ever run this deep. These new emotions bubbling up for Selena were terrifying.

She was a firecracker for sure, but unlike Aileen, she was the kind that brought joy with her vibrant, uncontrollable energy and spark, illuminating everything around her. Not the kind that lit everything in her wake on fire. Aileen loved the drama and conflict that her spirited nature created. Selena was so self-assured that she didn't need the chaos to feel relevant or seen.

Lying in her bed at the B and B, he stroked her hair as she slept on his chest. She was beautiful and smart and talented and successful. Suddenly he had the desire to fight harder for his career, the way she was. She was inspiring him to try harder, not give up.

He stared at the ceiling in the dark room and held her

tight. He wanted to make this work with her, and for the first time since Aileen, he felt himself opening up to the possibility of a new relationship. One that was stronger than any he'd had before.

Hours before, he'd almost told her he was in love with her.

Thank God she seemed to be falling equally hard and fast.

She stirred in her sleep, and he smiled at her when her sleepy gaze met his. "Hi," she said. "Can't sleep?"

"Don't want to," he said softly. He almost didn't recognize the soft sap he seemed to be with her. She brought out a gentler, more relaxed side of him.

She propped herself up on his chest. "What are you thinking about?"

"Just having a hard time realizing this is real, that I'm actually here in bed with you," he said.

"Because I'm such a megastar?" she teased.

He squeezed her tight and grinned. "That. And the fact that I hadn't planned on leaving the cabin when I arrived." He hadn't planned on a lot of things that he was suddenly grateful for. Selena's unexpected arrival into his hiatus from living was breathing new life into him.

She studied him. "Why did you leave the city?"

"Because I was homeless," he said with a laugh.

She frowned. Confused.

"My apartment was above the studio. Kind of a perk of the job." Who was living in it now? Would his grandfather even rent it out, or would he take it over as an additional space to his own?

"Oh, what a double blow," she said sympathetically.

A triple blow in one day, actually, but he just nodded. He didn't want to bring up Aileen right now.

"So, was it the fact that you wanted to escape the press and had nowhere to go that spurred this retreat, or was it about your ex? Aileen?"

Fair enough that she was asking. Everyone knew he'd been destroyed by his ex becoming engaged on television, and Selena had a right to know where his heart stood on that issue now. He wasn't completely sure, but he knew the aching longing for her had disappeared. He cleared his throat. "I always thought breaking up in a city would be much easier than a breakup in a small town. Seattle is definitely big enough, but apparently working in the same industry makes it just as difficult to escape seeing one another."

Selena nodded. "I get it. I've had a few of those. Having to work with an ex after a breakup isn't easy."

The fact that she got it made it easier to open up to her. She didn't seem threatened by his past relationship or any lingering feelings he might have; she was just curious and a source of support.

"What happened between you two, anyway?"

Ah, such a complicated question. "Short answer—she fell out of love with me."

"And long answer?" Selena asked gently, a genuine interest reflecting in her eyes.

"We weren't right for one another from the start. I always believed our fiery conflict and ability to come back together was a sign that we could survive anything life threw at us. But now I realize that we created the tension and the problems between us because we just weren't right together and it was exhausting."

"Passion in love and war?"

"Something like that, I guess."

"What was she like? What drew you to her in the first place?"

"Do you really want to talk about this?" he asked, trailing his fingers along her back. He didn't. For the first time in a long time, he felt himself healing, moving on.

"Not really. What would you like to do instead?" she asked suggestively, suddenly wide-awake.

"I can think of a few things," he said, flipping them so he was on top. "You sure you don't want to sleep?"

She reached up and cupped his face. "Absolutely," she said, drawing his head down to hers.

As her soft, delicious lips met his, all thoughts of Aileen and his past evaporated. He knew fighting these feelings for Selena was futile. He was already a goner.

CHAPTER THIRTEEN

IF THERE WAS an award for happiest actress in Hollywood, she'd win it hands down.

The night before with Gus had been everything she'd wanted it to be. It had blown way past her expectations. They hadn't slept a wink and had gotten very creative in their sexual intimacy due to lack of protection. It had been one of the best nights of Selena's life. Matt had been good in bed, but selfish, the way most hotshot up-and-coming male movie stars could be...but Gus was giving and attentive, and he'd said he was falling for her.

She wasn't sure how her feet were staying on the ground as they filmed several of the remaining scenes for the movie. Jay's brother, Justin, had arrived, and even having to film the darker, abusive scenes with him didn't bring her down.

"Hey, Selena, do you have a sec?" Kaia asked, approaching with an apprehensive look on her face.

"Of course. Everything okay?" Selena held out an arm to wrap around her.

"I'm guessing you haven't seen this yet," Kaia said, sounding apologetic as she handed Selena her cell phone.

Selena squinted to read the news headline on the Hollywood gossip site.

Despite rumors of filming a thriller, rom-com queen Selena Hudson can't distance herself from romance.

What the…?

Under the headline were individual photos of her and Gus, obviously pulled from the internet, that had been connected by a photoshopped heart.

Sources say the actress recently split from up-and-coming megastar Matt Mayson.

Sources. Matt. No doubt he referred to himself as a megastar. What an ass. It had to be him. No one else knew about the movie or her and Gus. At least, not anyone vindictive enough to leak it to the Hollywood media hounds.

The star, who has been struggling to break out in other genres after her near-death experience last year with a stalker, is rumored to be shacked up—quite literally—with defamed sports broadcaster Gus Orosco, somewhere in Nunavut.

Her teeth clenched. *Alaska, Matt! At least get the facts right.*

The isolated thriller is being coproduced by the star and directed by Jay Kline and is set to release later this year. Let's hope Selena knows what she's doing; otherwise, this may be the last we see of her on the big screen.

That final commentary was unnecessarily harsh. She handed the cell phone back to Kaia and forced a shrug. "It's nothing."

"Really? I thought you wanted to keep the movie quiet for now?"

The good news was that the article hadn't really focused on the movie. It was mostly about her and Gus. Matt had obviously been aiming at her with the shot. Not Jay. At least he hadn't revealed the film's plot or leaked the script or anything. Her stomach turned.

That wasn't a good thing either.

Damn. What if the media chose to do the same when she

and Jay were trying to promote the film? What if reporters were only interested in the more personal story of her love life? This new relationship with Gus might be more appealing fodder for the gossip rags in California than an indie movie…

She swallowed hard. "They had nothing to report. It's all good," she told Kaia, her gut still uneasy. "Just don't show Jay, okay?" Hopefully, he hadn't seen it yet. "Or Gus!" she added quickly, and suppressed a groan. What would Gus think seeing the article? He'd come here to get away from all of that.

"Sure," Kaia said. Glancing over Selena's shoulder, she grinned as she quickly moved away.

Out of nowhere, Gus's arms wrapped around her waist from behind and he pulled her into his body. Some of the tension seeped away, but not all. "Do you have plans for tonight? 'Cause I had a few ideas." His head buried into her neck, and the kisses he placed along her skin made her shiver.

Unfortunately, their alone time would have to wait, as she had agreed to dinner at Leslie's family home that evening. She was looking forward to seeing everyone again, but she knew she'd be itching to call it a night to spend time with Gus.

Leslie would understand if she canceled, right?

She reluctantly pulled back a little. "Leslie's family invited me for dinner tonight. We're only in town a few more days."

He nodded. "Oh, yeah… Of course. Well, can I meet you later?"

The fact that he wanted to see her whenever she was free had her heart racing. It was a great feeling to know they were on the same page. Unfortunately, they'd also been on page one of a tabloid.

"Or you could come with me?" she said.

He hesitated and she immediately wanted to retract the invite. Of course he didn't want to come. She was being totally presumptuous, imagining that he wanted everyone in Wild River to know they were…what? Dating? A thing? Shit, how was he going to react when he found out everyone in Hollywood knew? "I'm totally kidding," she said quickly. "I'll meet you at the inn later tonight."

He kissed her and grinned. "I want to come with you," he said.

"You do?" Her heart soared.

"Yes. As long as you're cool with everyone knowing about us," he said.

"You're cool with that?"

"You're not?" He frowned and retreated slightly.

"No, I am. It's just, well, I'm not sure what we're doing. Is there an 'us'?" For the first time in her life, it seemed the tabloids had a better grip on her love life than she did.

He stared into her eyes for a long, deep moment. "I know that I want there to be," he said huskily.

She held her breath, waiting for him to continue. She refused to be the one put herself out there first this time. Emotionally, at least. She'd initiated the physical stuff. He could label the relationship. She waited, and her pulse quickened in her veins the longer the silence lingered. His gaze burned into hers, and she swallowed hard.

"Gus?" A female voice behind her caught his attention, and he immediately released her and took a step back.

Selena frowned as she turned to see a beautiful blonde woman in a designer, belted, knee-length plaid winter coat and thick-heeled leather boots that came above her knees.

The surprised look on her face at finding Gus holding another woman was all the introduction Selena needed.

Aileen.

"What are...? Why...? What's going on?" Gus stammered.

Evidently, Aileen's arrival was as much of a surprise to him as Matt's had been to her.

"What the hell is up with all the exes showing up in Alaska?" Jay whispered, appearing out of nowhere next to her and making her jump.

"They can sniff out happiness and feel the need to create drama, is my guess," she mumbled under her breath as Aileen approached them. From what Gus had revealed, Aileen seemed to thrive on drama and chaos.

"Hey, Gus," Aileen said carefully.

He stared at her.

They all stared at him.

He shook his head as though trying to wake himself from a dream. Except this was real. His ex, the woman he was so busted up over that it cost him his job and made him retreat to serial killer cabins in the middle of Alaska, was standing there, looking breathtakingly gorgeous. And people didn't fly all the way to Alaska just to say hello. It was obvious Aileen had a similar agenda to Matt's.

Selena's gut tightened. She must have seen the tabloid article.

"What are you doing here, Aileen? How did you even know I was here?" Gus asked her.

Uh-oh... Selena's heart raced.

Aileen glanced at their captivated audience before saying, "It's kinda all over the media."

Jay's eyes widened and Selena leaned closer. "Don't freak out. It was just one article."

"What are you talking about?" Jay hissed.

"I'll fill you in later," she said, her attention completely focused on Gus and Aileen, who were both standing there, still staring at one another, obviously expecting the other person to make the first move.

Selena cleared her throat when Gus remained silent. "Hi, I'm Selena." She extended a hand, and Aileen looked grateful for the brief show of welcome.

"Yes, I know exactly who you are. I'm a huge fan. Gus must have told you that I dragged him to every one of your movies," the other woman gushed.

Dragged him. Great. The idea of the two of them watching her rom-coms made her stomach tighten even more. Selena smiled politely. "Thank you."

Aileen looked around and her gaze landed on the film crew. "You're filming here?"

Selena nodded. "A different type of movie."

"Hope there's still a romance in it somewhere," Aileen said, looking slightly awkward as her gaze shifted to Gus, who had yet to say anything more.

"Not exactly," Selena said. "Um…anyway, we were just wrapping up for today, so we will leave you two alone." The idea went against her gut instincts. She wanted to stay and tell Aileen she was too late, that Gus had moved on, was over her, but she couldn't speak for him. All she could do was hope their connection was real and that he'd tell Aileen things were over between them.

Meanwhile, he looked at a loss for words, conflicted and confused.

She shot him a quick look. "Text me later." She needed to get away from the awkward, tense situation. This had nothing to do with her. He needed to sort this out.

He frowned, shaking out of his haze. "No, wait. I was going to dinner with you."

Aileen's look of annoyance was evident.

"It's okay. You have a…guest," she said tightly. She wanted to grab him and kiss him and show Aileen that the two of them were together, that the tabloid had been right and she'd missed her opportunity with him. But Gus's hands were dug deep into his pockets, and it didn't escape her notice that he'd taken several steps away from her since seeing Aileen.

She wouldn't show them she was frazzled. Wouldn't let him know that she was spiraling inside. They'd only just gotten together, and it would be devastating if he decided Aileen was who he still wanted, but that decision was his and there was nothing she could do about it. Without closure, any chance they had at a relationship would be in jeopardy anyway.

"Stay and chat," she said. "Catch up."

Gus studied her. "You sure?"

Her chest tightened. Of course part of her was hoping he'd tell Aileen to take a hike, but she'd had her time with Matt. He deserved this time with Aileen.

She only hoped he was seeking the same closure and not another shot with his ex.

GUS TOOK AN extralong time putting a new log in the fireplace inside his cabin moments later. He needed a second to process the fact that his ex was there in the middle of nowhere Alaska. She'd never shown any interest in visiting his hometown before.

What did she want? He could kind of figure it out based on her reaction to seeing him with Selena. But why now? She'd mentioned a tabloid, which wasn't ideal. Jay had wanted to keep the movie quiet for now. But having everyone know he was with Selena didn't faze him.

He replaced the metal fire screen and turned to face Aileen. She'd removed her coat, and he noted that the thin, lacy-looking bodysuit she was wearing, which disappeared beneath her dark skinny jeans, wasn't exactly weather appropriate for Alaska in the fall. She was on a mission. One she planned to see succeed. Aileen always got what she wanted.

He wished he could say the sight of her had no effect on him, but Aileen had always turned heads. Especially his. She was gorgeous. But right now, all he could think about was the look of uncertainty in Selena's gaze as she'd left the campsite with the rest of the crew. She'd been cool about the whole thing, even polite and welcoming to Aileen, while he'd just stood there, dumbfounded, like a moron. She was incredible. He was an idiot for not sending Aileen away immediately and going to dinner with her.

Aileen scanned the cabin, taking in the rugged interior as though he were exiled to a dungeon. "I'm sorry you thought you needed to get away from the city," she said softly. "I reached out but I couldn't reach you."

That was because he'd been ignoring her calls and texts. He hadn't wanted to hear her apology for breaking his heart and moving on faster than lightning with a new fiancé. At the time, he'd believed her ability to jump into a new relationship meant she'd never really cared about him. Now he wasn't so sure.

"I needed some space after everything that happened," he said, shoving his hands in his pockets. The heat from the fire was almost too much as sweat gathered on the base of his spine, beneath his shirt.

"I understand that, I guess. But I was there for you… even if you didn't want the support."

Of course he hadn't wanted her support; it would have

been more like sympathy. She'd dumped him. She'd gotten engaged mere months later.

His eyes shifted to her hand, where there was no engagement ring. His stomach twisted. So much for hoping she was there only to get closure. "What are you really doing here, Aileen?"

She looked surprised by his bluntness, but nodded slowly. "I guess I should cut to the chase." She took a deep breath, which he knew was her way of drawing his attention to the heaving breasts above the lace of the bodysuit. She'd always had a way of distracting him with that gorgeous body whenever they had an argument or he wasn't prepared to give in to something she wanted. How much of their relationship had been manipulation, not love? "I was wrong. When I called things off with you, called off the engagement, I was scared. I wasn't sure what I wanted and I made the wrong decision."

"What happened to Vince?" he asked. He wasn't buying the scared story. Aileen was fearless. She went after what she wanted and rarely let anything stop her from getting it. If she'd wanted him—wanted them—she would have made it all work, the way he'd been trying to for so long.

She sighed. "That was a mistake, too."

"Sounds like a lot of mistakes are being made." Including coming here to see him. A month ago, maybe he would have fallen for her apology and fake remorse, but not now. Now he was seeing everything clearer. It was amazing how being with a genuine, caring, honest woman had enlightened him and woken him up to the kind of relationship he wanted, needed and deserved.

She rushed toward him. "Yes, and I want to fix them," she said gently. When she reached for him, he took a step back. "Come on, Gus. Give me another chance to show you that I'm all in for us. You wanted to be with me forever, remember?"

"That was before you decided to spend forever with Vince," he said. Did she really think that after all this time, all these months of pain and missing her and feeling as though a part of him had died, she could waltz back in and demand that he forget all of the hurt and welcome her back into his heart to destroy him all over again?

"I told you, that's over." She shuddered. "It should never have happened." She tucked her blond hair behind one ear, and he saw, dangling from her ears, the earrings he'd given her for Christmas—or rather, the earrings she'd bought for herself when she returned the ones he'd bought. If she thought wearing them now would evoke memories of a better time together, she obviously remembered that holiday season differently than he did. They'd spent most of the season arguing because she'd wanted to go to Hawaii and he'd wanted to stay in Seattle for a traditional Christmas with his family.

"I'm sorry, Aileen. I've moved on," he said.

Her mouth dropped. "With Selena Hudson?" she said, as though the thought was absolutely ridiculous.

He agreed he barely deserved the actress, but he knew Aileen's incredulousness was for other reasons.

"She's an actress, Gus. She's playing you," Aileen said gently, as though he were a child to whom she was breaking the bad news about Santa.

His jaw tightened. "You don't know her. You have no idea what you're talking about, and I think you should go."

She huffed. "Oh, for God's sake, Gus, wake up. Stop being so stubborn. If you wanted to punish me, you did. Seeing you with another woman hurt, okay. You won. Now, let's talk about us and how we can make things work. I know you want that. I want that, too."

She really thought she could bulldoze him. Maybe in the past, but not now... Not ever again. "No." He checked his watch. "And I have to go. You can stay if you want— I'm late for a dinner." He grabbed his jacket from the chair and stalked past her, ignoring her openmouthed expression.

"Are you serious?"

"Yep." He opened the door.

"Gus, I'm not offering this again. It's now or never," she said.

He picked up her coat and tossed it to her. "Never."

CHAPTER FOURTEEN

SHE WOULD NOT stress about the fact that the man she was falling in love with was with the one who got away. She wouldn't even think about Aileen's perfect complexion and beautiful hair and amazing fashion sense. And she definitely wouldn't envision them tearing each other's clothes off.

Nope. She would enjoy her time with her friends and not think about Gus at all.

"How are things with Gus?" Leslie whispered as they helped set the dining room table for dinner.

Selena sighed. So much for not thinking about him. "Complicated," she said, hating that she was wrapped up in drama. Just once she'd like a normal, conflict-free relationship. Nothing in the spotlight, nothing that her friends questioned as genuine, nothing she had to worry about. Just hours before, she'd thought maybe she'd found that.

"I thought things were going okay?" Leslie asked, moving her shirt away from her body. The oversize garment was meant to hide the tiny baby bump developing, but it wasn't quite doing the job. If anyone else noticed, they weren't saying anything. They knew Leslie well. When she wanted to reveal her secret, she would.

Selena shook her head with a smile. "Everything's fine. I'd rather not spoil the day talking about it." She only had a few days left in Wild River, and she might not see Leslie and the others again for who knew how long. She couldn't let the unknown of what was or wasn't happening out at Orosco Campgrounds ruin her day.

Moments later, everyone took their seats around the table, and surrounded by the warm, welcoming Sanders family, she did feel better. The delicious smell of the home-cooked meal and the good-natured family banter around the table were things she hadn't experienced often growing up. Her family was close, but their lives were hectic, pulling them in a lot of different directions. Her time with the Sanderses meant a lot and she needed it that day.

Seeing Leslie laugh with her mom, she almost didn't recognize her. After years of being estranged, the mother and daughter were slowly rebuilding their relationship and making up for time lost. Selena liked to think she'd had a part in that. After all, if she hadn't burned down their family cabin, the Sanderses may not have even known Leslie and Selena were hiding out in Alaska the year before. They would never have had an opportunity to reconnect and see that what truly mattered was forgiveness and family.

"How's the movie filming going?" Leslie's older sister, Katherine, asked from across the table as she passed the lasagna. The homicide detective was the quieter, more serious sibling and a bit of a mystery to figure out. She kept to herself and was fairly reserved, though not unfriendly.

"It's amazing," Kaia answered for her. "Definitely the best movie of Selena's career."

The praise from the preteen made her blush slightly. "Here's hoping," she said with a laugh. "We're actually almost done. Just a few final scenes to shoot." While she'd be sad to see the project come to an end, she was proud of what they'd accomplished, despite the setbacks in the beginning. She owed a lot of that to Gus.

Nope, not thinking about him.

"Can't wait to see it," Katherine said.

Hopefully, they'd all get a chance to. If they made it into the film festivals and the movie got picked up by a major studio, she'd have a premiere party and invite the whole town of Wild River.

The conversation flowed easily around the table as they ate, and she was successful in only checking her cell phone for text messages twice. Not that she was looking for messages from Gus... Unfortunately, the only ones she was receiving were from Jay, freaking out over the tabloid article. She'd told him not to stress over it, that any press was good press for the movie, and he'd calmed down a little. She wasn't happy about it either, but there wasn't much she could do.

After dessert, she tried to help clear the dinner table, and she was shooed away to relax in the living room. "You're our guest," Grandma Sanders said, taking the plates from her.

She felt more like family than guest, but she didn't dare argue with the older woman.

"Let me see the ring again," she said to Montana, Leslie's soon-to-be sister-in-law, as they moved into the living room. Leslie's brother, Eddie, beamed brighter than the rock on her hand when he looked at his new fiancée. The two were the perfect example of how opposites attract and how two very different people could complement one another so well. The single mom, who was an adrenaline junkie and former BASE jumper, and the straitlaced cop were so much in love the entire room could see it.

Montana extended her hand toward her, and Kaia said proudly, "I helped him pick it out."

Eddie winked at his soon-to-be stepdaughter and it reminded Selena of her relationship with her own stepdad. They were really close, and not having that with her real father, she'd really appreciated that male role model in her life. Kaia was lucky to have an amazing dad and future stepdad.

Selena took in the solitary stone set in a rose-gold band and smiled. "It's perfect." Selena loved this family. Leslie didn't know how lucky she was. Selena had always wanted siblings and big family events like the ones her characters always had. A fictional set was as close as she'd come. Until now.

The Sanderses had basically adopted her, even if they didn't know it.

"Have you set a date yet?" she asked, drawing her legs up under her on the comfortable, well-worn fabric of the plush sofa. She placed her cell phone on the arm of the sofa and glanced at it. No new messages. Her phone had been eerily silent since she'd left the campsite, and she couldn't help the feeling of dread washing over her, despite her resolve not to worry about it. She'd seen the look on his face when Aileen arrived. His shocked speechlessness had spoken volumes.

But there was nothing she could do about it. What would be would be. Sure, she'd been excited about him joining her for dinner that night, and sure, she'd been disappointed when he'd chosen to stay behind to talk to his ex, but just because they'd finally had sex didn't mean they needed to be joined at the hip—or any other body parts—every second. And it certainly didn't mean that they were officially together, even though he'd said he was falling for her.

No matter what happened, even if he didn't end up in Aileen's arms, she wouldn't go all in this time. She wouldn't assume her feelings were real and fall headfirst into the trap of falling in love first. She'd tried to keep her head with Matt, and she'd only been fooling herself. She fell hard and fast. And a lot.

She wouldn't do that this time. Especially not when Gus might still be conflicted.

"I'm thinking summer," Eddie said, in response to her question about a wedding date.

Lost in her own thoughts, she'd forgotten she'd asked the question.

Next to her, Montana's eyes widened as she stared at her fiancé. "*This* summer? Like nine months from now."

Eddie laughed. "You're right. That's far too long of a wait. Spring would be better." Sitting in his wheelchair next to the sofa, he reached out and squeezed Montana's knee. "Don't freak out. I'm kidding."

Montana shook her head. "No. I'm cool with spring," she said.

Looks of happiness around the room couldn't compare to the one on Eddie's face as he took her hand and kissed it.

Selena had to glance away. Surrounded by all the love was wonderful, and also a little hard on her own heart that day. Leslie and Levi were expecting a baby, even though no one knew it yet. Eddie and Montana were getting married. She was still technically single, trying to rebuild her career, and she hadn't realized time was ticking so fast, but seeing what her friends had, she knew she wanted that, too.

"Well, then we better get started on the planning," Grandma Sanders said, entering the room with a tray of baked goods. The matriarch of the family was an older version of Leslie, and there was no question as to who ruled the roost.

Levi glanced at Eddie, then kissed Leslie's forehead and stood up. "I think that's our cue."

Eddie nodded as he rolled his wheelchair closer to Montana. He kissed her and gave Kaia a quick hug. "Have fun planning."

Montana clasped his hand as he tried to move away. "You're leaving?"

Eddie laughed as he faced the room of his female relatives. "Do any of you care about my input into the wedding plans?"

Leslie shook her head. His mother waved him out of the room.

"Not in the slightest," his grandmother told him, reaching for a day planner, a wedding cake brochure and several wedding dress sample fabrics from her oversize purse. She'd come prepared.

"See?" he said to his fiancée.

Montana laughed. "Fine. Go."

Levi paused to kiss Leslie again on his way out of the room, and the way he affectionately laid a hand on her stomach made Selena wonder if Leslie had told him yet, but Leslie looked at him with suspicion and he pulled his hand back quickly.

"We'll be at The Drunk Tank if you need us," he said as he and Eddie left the living room.

Across the room, Leslie's gaze met hers and she mouthed, *Did you tell him?*

Selena shook her head. She might not be great at keeping things to herself, but she did value her life. Should she tell Leslie that Levi already knew? Nope, not her place. And it was kind of humorous watching the two of them keep their respective secrets, though she did wonder when Leslie planned on telling her family. Knowing her, she'd probably try to keep it to herself until the baby was a year old.

As the men opened the front door to leave, she heard Levi say, "Hey, man, what are you doing here?"

"Selena invited me…"

Her heart soared at hearing Gus's voice, and immediately her palms sweat as she heard him enter the house, his boots sounding on the hardwood floor of the entry. He was there. He'd left Aileen—before or after they'd had passionate makeup sex?

She sat straighter and tucked her cell phone into her pocket, then ran a hand over her hair.

He entered the living room, and she swallowed hard when his gaze met hers. His expression gave nothing away. No hint of whether or not he'd gotten back together with his ex. Damn, he looked gorgeous in a pair of jeans and a black crewneck sweater under a leather jacket. If he was there to break her heart, he could at least have had the decency to look worse.

"The ladies are about to plan Eddie and Montana's wedding," Levi said, filling him in. "We were escaping to The Drunk Tank. You in?"

Gus hesitated, his eyes still on her. "I suspect the ladies don't want me around…"

She did! But he'd have to leave with the men. He'd be bored out of his mind discussing cake toppers and satin versus lace.

"I'll join you guys. Just give me a sec," he said, striding across the living room toward her.

She held her breath as he leaned down, captured her face with one hand and kissed her softly but with a deliberateness, the quick, gentle peck holding so much unspoken reassurance. When he pulled away, her heart echoed in her ears. "What was that about?" she whispered.

"Just to make sure you know you have nothing to worry about," he said with a wink as he stood and followed the men out of the living room.

The collective swoon of the women watching had her blushing, and her happiness overflowed. Montana was getting married. Leslie was having a baby. And Selena was starting something special, too. With Gus.

THE DRUNK TANK was quiet, and Gus appreciated the nearly empty bar and the company of two dudes who might under stand what he was going through in matters of the heart. Eddie and Levi were both blissfully betrothed now, but he knew their journeys to this point in their relationships hadn't been smooth sailing.

"That was quite an entrance back there," Levi said, lining up the cue ball to break the colorful racked pool balls at the back of the bar.

It wasn't exactly in his nature to do something like that. He wasn't big on public displays of affection or elaborate gestures, and walking into the home of people who were almost strangers and then kissing a woman was a little out of character for him.

Or maybe he was more of a hopeless romantic than he thought.

All he knew for sure, all he'd known in that moment, was that he needed to reassure Selena that things between them hadn't been derailed by Aileen's surprise visit. Despite her cool, calm and extraordinarily mature reaction to the sight of his ex, he could tell she'd been worried as she left them alone at the campsite, and he hadn't wanted her worrying a second longer than necessary that he might have relit an old flame.

It had been the contrary, in fact.

Seeing Aileen again had momentarily made his heart lurch, but it quickly became obvious that her effect on him wasn't a positive one. It was his heart's way of telling him to run away. And fast.

His heart beat in a different way for Selena. She set it thumping without the instilled, unvoiced threat that at any second she could break it. And not because he cared any less for her, but because she gave him a sense of reassurance that he'd never gotten from Aileen.

"Yeah, sorry about that, Eddie," he said. "Didn't mean to steal any of your wedding-prep thunder." He watched two of the solid-colored balls sail into opposite pockets and Levi set up another shot.

Eddie laughed as he drank a mouthful of beer. "I think you just enhanced the moment in the room. I almost fell in love with you back there. With skills like that, next you'll be acting in a rom-com."

Gus shook his head. "One and done for me." This was an experience for sure, and now he needed to get back on track with his own career. As soon as he got back to Seattle, he planned on reaching out to the studios on his own, without an agent. He might have had a career blunder, but he was desperate to get back in the game. There had to be a small sports network somewhere that would be willing to take a chance on him.

"How's the movie going, anyway?" Eddie asked. "It's all Kaia talks about."

"That kid has been amazing on set. The crew love her," Gus said honestly. Kaia might only be twelve years old, but her work ethic was incredible. A testament to her parents and stepparents for sure.

Eddie beamed like a proud father. "She's a good kid. Adores Selena."

Kaia wasn't the only one.

"You two going to try to make things work after the movie is done?" Levi asked as he sank another ball.

"I hope so," Gus said, taking a gulp of his beer.

If they didn't, he wasn't sure what he'd do. The campsite now held far too many memories of her to be safe if he had to hibernate to heal another broken heart.

CHAPTER FIFTEEN

SELENA WOULD RATHER poke her own eyeballs out than make this phone call.

Brock Smithfield was a top sports reporter for Sports Beat in Los Angeles and a top class-A asshole. He'd only tried to sleep with her a half a dozen times in the three days she'd shadowed him for a role in a movie where she played the intern to an arrogant sportscaster. In the movie, she'd naturally fallen in love after discovering she was wrong about the man. In real life, she'd punched Brock when he grabbed her ass and Selena had barely escaped an assault charge.

She bit her lip as she stared at the number on her cell phone. She had to suck it up, put aside her personal feelings and her pride, and make the call. A promise was a promise, and now that she knew Gus—was falling in love with Gus—she not only needed to pull this string for him, she wanted to.

If only she thought Brock would be happy enough to hear from her to at least give Gus an interview. She paced the woods near the set. It was the final day of shooting, so she couldn't put this off much longer.

True, Gus hadn't seemed to be hating this whole thing over the last two weeks, but she knew he was really only doing it for the opportunity to save his own career. And he deserved it.

Squaring her shoulders, she took a deep breath and dialed the Sports Beat station.

"Hello! Thank you for calling Sports Beat, where sports are life. How may I direct your call?" a receptionist whose voice Selena didn't recognize said. The network cycled through receptionists who looked like they came from a modeling agency as fast as they cycled through plastic watercooler bottles.

Would the girl know who she meant if she said *Direct me to the biggest jerk in the building*? Probably. But just to be safe. "Brock Smithfield, please."

"Can I tell him who's calling?"

Preferably not, if she wanted him to take the call. But she knew this process well. Without a name that mattered, she'd be going to an unmanned voice mail somewhere in the mail room, and telling Gus that she'd left a message just wasn't good enough. He deserved her giving this her best shot. "You can tell him it's Selena Hudson."

Dead silence on the other end.

"Hello?"

"Hi… Yes, I'm here. Selena Hudson? As in the movie star?"

Selena scanned her surroundings, taking in the ultra-low-budget film set. More like the "hopeful she was resurrecting her career" star. But for all intents and purposes… "Yes, that's me. Is Brock in?" She didn't want voice mail. He'd never call her back, and she needed to secure this for Gus.

She peered through the trees to where he talked with Jay. A script in his hands, he was obviously preparing for that day's scenes. He'd really come through for her, and she wanted to return the favor.

And not just because she'd made the promise, but because he was a really great guy, and while she knew nothing about sports, she knew he was a really good reporter. He hadn't used his family name to just coast—he'd gone to university, he'd interned, he'd worked his way up like everyone else, and one mistake shouldn't define the rest of his career.

"He's in his office, just finishing up a meeting," the receptionist said. "I'll try to connect you."

"Thank you."

She waited for the hold music, but a long pause later, the woman was still there. "Um, Selena?"

"Yeah?"

"I want to apologize."

Huh? Did she know this woman? She hadn't said her name upon answering. The voice didn't sound familiar, but she'd known a lot of people in her lifetime. Not many people she was expecting an apology from, though. "I'm sorry—do I know you?"

"Not exactly... The thing with Matt... I had no idea he was seeing you," she said. "At least, not until I saw it was your house he invited me to. And then I naively assumed you two were just friends."

Selena's mouth gaped. Holy shit. It was the Skype woman. The billboard model whom she'd caught with Matt. She cleared her throat. "It's fine," she said, surprising herself with just how fine it actually was. "That's over."

"Well, I am sorry."

"Apology accepted. You helped me dodge a bullet, obviously." If she'd fallen any deeper for Matt, the heartache at the end would have been harder to heal from. If she'd said *I love you*, if he'd officially moved in...and then she'd learned of his true nature, things would have been that much more difficult. As it was, it hadn't been all that hard, thanks in large part to a certain sexy man waiting on her to shoot the final scenes of this movie.

"Yeah, he's a bit of a creep," the woman said.

"Speaking of creeps…"

"Right. You needed to speak to Brock."

So, the sports reporter was still living up to his reputation. "Yeah. The thing is, I'm not sure he'll take my call." She bit her thumbnail. "Think you can help me with that?"

"Don't worry. I got you," she said confidently, then lowered her voice. "I'll tell him it's his mom."

Ah, Brock Smithfield was a mommy's boy. "Thank you."

Less than ten seconds later, his voice came on the phone. "Hey, Mom, did you get through my laundry?"

Wow. The level of assholery had no bounds. "Your mom does your laundry?"

"Selena?"

He recognized her voice. She braced herself for the dial tone, but he was still there, so she spoke quickly. "Yes. Hi, Brock. Long time…"

"The scar on my cheek suggests otherwise, but okay." His voice was cold, and she knew defrosting him wouldn't be easy.

"Hey, about that…" What? She wouldn't apologize. He deserved it. He was in the wrong. Sexual harassment in the workplace was a big deal, and the guy shouldn't even be able to keep his job. She wouldn't grovel for this guy. Not even for the opportunity for Gus. But she needed to address it before they could move on to the reason for her call. "I should have handled things differently," she said. Like filing a sexual harassment lawsuit to hopefully prevent future victims.

"It's okay," he said, surprising her. "My sex therapist

said it was a reaction to my dismissing your advances and that I need to realize my own power over women."

His power over women was called sexual abuse, and he was completely delusional if he thought she'd ever wanted him. Her teeth clenched so hard she could barely form the next words. "Okay, yeah…so I need a favor."

"You need to shadow me again?"

Oh, hell, no. She'd get her information from inaccurate, misinformed Google searches before spending time with him ever again. "No… I have a friend. A sports broadcaster… really amazing at what he does. He was hoping to get an interview at Sports Beat." She paused, cringing at her next words. "And I thought since you are such a high-powered influence there, maybe you could help." Only for Gus would she suck up to this guy's ego like this.

"Oh, about that… No. I'm actually not allowed to hire anymore. A few lawsuits…" His voice trailed off.

Oh, God, the guy was slime. She wouldn't be deterred. "Well, do you think you could help get me in touch with someone who can?"

"Maybe. Who's the broadcaster?"

She hesitated. "Gus Orosco."

Silence. She waited. He hadn't immediately hung up, so she held her breath and continued to hope.

"I'll make sure he gets an interview with Malin."

Her mouth dropped and the phone nearly slipped from her hand. "Malin Kirk?" Head of the network?

"Yeah. She's my cousin."

That explained why he still had a job.

"And the dude's a legend. He deserves another shot. And besides, I hate that hockey-playing son of a bitch who stole his girl on live TV."

She smiled. Whatever twisted reasoning Brock had

didn't matter as long as she could tell Gus he had the interview. "Okay... Well, thanks."

"No problem and, Selena, I'm sorry..."

Again, she almost dropped her phone. He was apologizing? She'd never in a million...

"You just weren't my type, sweetheart."

Ah, there it was. "'Bye, Brock." She disconnected the call before she could blow Gus's opportunity with the earful she'd like to deliver, and she sighed in relief. At least she'd fulfilled her promise. The rest was up to Gus.

SNUGGLED IN BED at the B and B a few days later, Gus stroked Selena's bare arm. The last few weeks had been the craziest of his life. Fired. Heartbroken. Revived. And now optimistic. With filming wrapped, she was heading back to LA soon, and he'd be returning to Seattle. He couldn't keep hiding in Wild River, putting his life on hold any longer.

He hadn't asked her about the Sports Beat interview opportunity or whether he should be booking a flight to LA with her instead, and she hadn't mentioned it. He still wanted the shot, but he wasn't holding her to the promise if it had been just a ploy to get him in her movie. He liked her and he never would have gotten a chance to realize that, to get to know her, if it hadn't been for working together. The chemistry on set had lit a fire between them off camera, and he was wondering what came next for them.

Would she want to see him once they both left Alaska?

"So, I was thinking you should come to LA with me," she said.

His heart pounded so loudly it was probably causing her forehead to vibrate on his chest. "You were?" Going back to LA with her meant taking their relationship to another level. He wanted that, but he still wasn't sure where her head and heart were. It had taken him months to get over Aileen; her breakup was just weeks old. Maybe when they got back to regular life, she'd see that he didn't quite fit into hers. The bright California sun would only high-light his shortcomings.

"Yeah. You could stay with me if you want."

Stay with her? She was inviting him to move in? Shit. Was he ready for that? It seemed hella fast, yet he wasn't completely opposed to the idea. At all. He wasn't clammy or trying to think of a way to let her down easy. The idea actually didn't terrify him at all. "Okay."

"And I can hook you up with my tailor to get a new suit."

New suit? He frowned. She must mean for the movie premieres at the film festivals. Right. She was expecting him to come to LA to do movie promotion with her. She wasn't talking about their relationship's next steps. Thank God he hadn't said anything to that effect. He cleared his throat. "Sure, yeah, you'll have to guide me through all this red-carpet stuff."

She leaned on an elbow and glanced up at him, an ador-ably confused look on her gorgeous face. "The movie stuff won't be for a few months… We still need to finish it in post."

"Oh." So was she thinking about them as a couple?

"I was talking about your Sports Beat interview. It's scheduled for next week with Malin Kirk."

His eyes widened. Malin Kirk? How the hell had she pulled that off?

She grinned. "You really thought I was bluffing, huh?"

He grinned. "Yes." And he wouldn't have held the white lie against her. She'd been desperate and needed him, and he was happy he'd stepped in to help. But this was defi-nitely icing on an already delicious cake.

"I promised you I would." She kissed his bare chest and he held her tighter.

"You did." He paused. "But just so you know, I wouldn't have been upset if you hadn't gone through with your end of the bargain."

She lifted her head to look at him, and his breath caught in his chest. "I know. Even more reason for doing it."

He reached for her and lifted her body on top of his. The blankets fell away, exposing her naked, sexy curves. The soft roundness of her breasts and the thin waist and muscular stomach. She was breathtakingly stunning and she was offering him the opportunity of a lifetime to get his career on track—the opportunity to once again be good enough for her. He didn't want to blow this. He wouldn't blow this.

Her hands roamed over his chest and shoulders as she lowered her upper body and pressed it against him. Her hands tangled in his hair as she kissed him. Soft at first, small, teasing pecks...then more demanding.

His grip on her waist tightened as he deepened the kiss, his tongue separating her lips and then exploring her mouth. She always tasted so good. Her hips pressed forward and rocked slightly, her pelvis grinding against his lower half. He felt himself harden immediately and his entire body came to life in anticipation.

He'd thought this might be their last night together for a while until they figured out what was happening between them, but now he was heading back to LA with her, and the idea excited him more than the job interview.

She moaned against his mouth as she quickened her grinding against his penis. The feel of her wet folds against his skin had him breathing hard. "Condom," he said, reaching for one on the bedside table. After their first time together, he'd made sure to stock up.

She took it from him, tore it open and slid it on over the length of him, and the sensation had him closing his eyes and his fingers digging into the flesh of her thighs. She lifted her body up and over him and he slid effortlessly into her tightness. "That feels incredible," he mumbled.

She pressed her hands against his chest as she rode him up and down slowly, bringing him all the way out and then all the way back in. Her breasts bobbed with the motions and he was almost mesmerized by them. He reached out and massaged them, rolling his thumbs over the nipples and pinching gently until she was moaning and tossing her head back in pleasure.

She quickened her pace, gripping the headboard as she moved faster and harder. He grew even thicker, and the feeling of her tight, wet body wrapped around him had him dangerously close to the edge. He stopped her motions. "I don't want to come yet," he said, flipping them over so he was on top. In control.

Taking her hands, he lifted them above her head on the pillow and started slowly pulling out of her body, then plunging back in. Over and over, a steady, slow, rhythmic pace that he knew was driving her wild.

"Gus, please…" She arched her back to get closer, but with one hand, he pressed against her lower stomach, enabling her movements, her desperate search for release. He continued the torturous, slow, deliberate movement, bringing his cock to the very edge of her, then sliding back in, filling her.

She swallowed hard, and her beautiful, sensual gaze locked with his. "I'm falling in love with you, Gus," she said.

His entire body stilled, and a wave of emotions mixed with intense desire ran through him. A long beat fell between them as he processed her words and reconciled them with his own feelings. "I'm already in love with you," he said softly.

The look of relief and happiness on her face was almost too much. As though she hadn't thought his emotions ran as deep as hers.

"So wildly in love with you," he said again as he resumed his movements, quicker now. He gripped her hands in his, their interlaced fingers clenched together as he brought her to orgasm.

Her back arched and she released a cry of pleasure as she came and her body trembled around him, the ripples of her orgasm bringing him over the edge. He plunged in as deep as possible and held, allowing the desire to take over completely. He closed his eyes as relief flowed through him, and then his body collapsed onto hers.

He rolled them to their sides and held her tight. He brushed a strand of dark hair out of her eyes and kissed her forehead. "I love you," he said again. Now that he'd said it once, it was as though he couldn't stop.

She smiled up at him, her expression full of love. "I may have lied when I said I was falling. I'm so far beyond falling I can't even remember the fall," she said with a laugh.

Gus held her tighter. Never in his life had he felt more alive. This right here, with her, was everything he'd never known he needed. And he wouldn't let anything or anyone ruin this new shot at happiness.

CHAPTER SIXTEEN

"I'M GOING TO miss you so much!" Kaia's arms around her waist almost brought Selena to tears as she hugged her tight the next day at The Drunk Tank. The little girl nearly squished Unicorn, whom Selena had smuggled into the bar in her winter coat.

The bar was closed, but Tank had opened it for them to have one last round of drinks before she left for the airport. The burly bartender watched from behind the bar now as his daughter refused to let her go. Selena sent him a pleading look. She'd asked Tank if she could invite Kaia to visit her in LA next summer, but he'd said he had to give it some thought. Keeping the idea to herself was torture.

He sighed and tossed a dish towel onto the bar. "Fine. You can visit her during your summer break," he told his daughter.

Kaia's look of surprised happiness rivaled her own. The young girl swung around to look at her dad. "For real? I can go to LA?"

Tank shook his head. "*We* can go to LA. Cassie and I talked about it and we'll take you to Disney and Universal Studios, and you can visit Selena while we're there."

Kaia nodded eagerly. "Thank you so much!"

Selena sent a grateful smile to Tank as well. "Thank you."

The bartender nodded. "And by the way, I can see that

dog poking out from underneath your jacket," he said, but he returned to stacking beer mugs behind the counter as Leslie and Levi entered the bar.

Now, if she could only convince those two to come visit, leaving that day would be a lot less difficult.

"Hey, can we get in on this hug?" Levi asked as they approached.

Kaia reluctantly pulled away. "I guess so."

Selena accepted a hug from the man, and then Levi joined Gus, who was seated at the bar. He glanced at Leslie. "Your usual?" he asked with just a hint of challenge in his voice.

Ah, so they were still playing this game. Selena hid a grin. They had to be two of the most stubborn people she'd ever met.

Leslie sighed. "No, I don't want my usual and, fine, I'll break first! I don't want alcohol because I'm pregnant," she said in exasperation.

Selena's and Levi's matching fake looks of shock were comedy gold.

"Oh, fuck off, you two. You both knew," Leslie said with a slight annoyance that quickly faded to a look of happiness. "I guess my secret is officially out."

Levi walked toward her and wrapped his arms around her waist. He kissed her before saying, "You have made me the happiest man on earth."

Selena swallowed a huge lump in her throat as she watched them. Her gaze met Gus's at the bar and her heart pounded. They'd said they loved one another. He'd said it first and more than once, and that day they were headed back to LA together.

Her heart was so full of happiness right now she didn't think this moment could possibly get any better.

"And we have a favor to ask of you," Leslie said to her, her arm still wrapped around Levi's waist.

"Okay…"

"Will you be the baby's godmother?" Leslie asked.

Tears were impossible to hold back as she nodded and said, "Really? You want me to be the godmother?"

Leslie nodded. "I mean, if you're not religious…"

Selena shook her head quickly. "I was baptized! I can totally do it. There's a church in my neighborhood where I can go for training or whatever…"

Leslie reached out a hand and touched her arm to silence her. "Relax. There's not a test at the ceremony or anything. All that's required is a willingness to love this baby as much as we do." She touched her stomach and glanced up at Levi, who looked dangerously close to waterworks.

She hugged both her friends, squishing Unicorn again in the process. "I already do."

From across the bar, Gus winked at her, and in that moment, successful movie or not, she knew this trip to Wild River had changed her life for the better.

As HE SECURED and locked the cabins at the campsite later that day, Gus had an odd feeling of nostalgia for the family property. Coming to Orosco Campgrounds had been out of necessity, a lack of direction for what to do next with his life and an escape from the mess he'd created. He'd gone through the most depressive time in his life as uncertainty had swallowed him up in a pit of despair. But being there had completely changed his life. For the better.

His cell phone rang as he locked the gates, and seeing Trish's number on call display, he paced the trail as he answered. "Hey, sis."

"You're going to LA?"

Trish didn't waste time with idle pleasantries. "I am."

"So, the rumor is true? You are acting in a movie?" She sounded like him going to the moon would be easier to believe.

He understood her skepticism. If someone had told him a month ago that he'd be starring in an indie film opposite Hollywood's sweetheart, he would have pissed himself laughing. But here he was. Life really was unpredictable. "I am."

"Gus, what the hell is going on?" A rare display of concern in her voice made him laugh. He heard her close her office door, and for the first time ever, she wasn't distracted by a million things going on behind her. Somehow, he'd secured her full attention. .

"Nothing. I'm fine. Better than fine, actually."

"Did Aileen find you? She called asking if you were in Nunavut?" she asked, sounding even more concerned. "I refused to tell her where you actually were."

He scoffed. Obviously, she still had a tracking app on her phone to locate him. "She did find me, but that's officially over."

"Thank God. So, why do you sound...happy?"

Because he was happy. Happier than he'd been in a long time. And he had the beautiful woman watching him from behind the wheel of her rental car right now to thank. He'd told her he loved her and he'd never meant those words more in his life. This feeling with her was fast, but it was real. He knew the difference now.

"Hey, sis, I have to run. I'll explain everything once I get back to Seattle, okay?" He didn't want to tell her about the Sports Beat interview just yet. It would make it that much harder if he didn't get the job. He'd tell his family if it worked out.

"Okay," she said reluctantly. "But, Gus, don't do anything stupid, okay?"

"I'll try," he said, disconnecting the call. He checked the gate a final time and took a second to look at the family campgrounds, where so much had happened in such a short period of time. Eventually he knew they'd have to let go of the land, but at least it would be forever immortalized in the movie, and that gave him a sense of relief.

A second later, he climbed into the passenger seat of the car.

"Everything okay?" Selena asked as he pulled on his seat belt.

He reached for her hand and held it tight in his own. He brought it to his lips and kissed her palm as he nodded. "Everything's perfect."

CHAPTER SEVENTEEN

IT WAS HARD to believe that just three weeks ago, she'd been on the flight to Wild River feeling nervous, unsure and excited, and now she was headed home with only the excitement lingering. Had a lot to do with the man sitting next to her. Who now looked like he was the one who was nervous and unsure.

"Stop stressing. You're going to do great." She was choosing to believe Gus's anxiety was regarding his interview and not about them flying back to LA together. She'd invited him to stay with her in Santa Monica, and she really hoped it hadn't freaked him out. It wasn't an actual invite to live with her or anything; it was just a place to stay while he was in town. It made sense. No point in him getting a hotel when they both knew they'd be spending their nights together anyway. Though, she didn't mind how long he decided to stay.

"I don't know. I'm not sure I can erase public image," he said, his knee bouncing as he stared out the plane's window at the clouds below.

She leaned her shoulder into him. "You changed my opinion of you."

He cracked a grin. "That wasn't hard. You couldn't resist my acting abilities."

Her chest tightened. Had he been acting off-screen as well? Would the connection between them fade now that the movie was done and they were returning to everyday life? Nope, she wouldn't let overthinking destroy what they had going on. They weren't official or anything. He'd told her he loved her, but he hadn't exactly asked her to be his girlfriend. They were having a good time.

Speaking of...

Reaching under her seat, she retrieved the thin blanket and unfolded it, draping it over their laps. Gus tried to remove his portion. "I'm sweating already."

She reached above their heads and turned on the air, directing the breeze toward him. Then she replaced the blanket over his lap. Whispering in his ear, her breasts reaching his chin, she said, "Drop your chair back and relax."

His eyes widened as he caught her intentions, and he glanced around the first-class cabin. "Someone could see," he whispered, but he did as she instructed.

"Let me worry about that and you just try to relax."

"Not sure this is going to work," he said, scanning the cabin again.

"Challenge accepted." Selena slid a hand beneath the blanket, and starting at his knee, she ran it along the inside of his thigh, higher, until she cupped him through his jeans.

His sharp inhalation as she gently squeezed the bulge made her whisper, "Shh... You don't want us to get caught."

She saw his jaw tighten and his breathing became slow and controlled as she undid the button on his jeans and slowly unzipped them. "Selena..."

A flight attendant pushed past the curtain, and she sat forward and reached for her magazine with her free hand. Gus seemed to hold his breath in the seat beside her as the attendant walked past. When she disappeared behind the crew cabin curtain, Selena resumed her mission.

Sliding her hand inside the fabric of Gus's underwear, she gently wrapped her hand around him. He blew out a slow breath and closed his eyes, resting his head against the seat.

She grinned as she felt him get stiffer beneath her touch. "See? That wasn't so hard," she whispered.

"Oh, I don't know about that. You have no idea the effect you have on me," he said, clutching the seat rests.

She actually did have an idea and he had the same effect on her. A simple touch from him had her body reacting in ways it never had before. She slowly stroked up and down his thick, hard penis, feeling her own arousal mount as precum escaped him. She used it as lube and increased her pace.

Gus's Adam's apple bobbed up and down, and his hands gripped the seat rests on either side of him. He grew thicker in her hand and she swallowed hard, feeling herself get wet.

His breathing grew slightly labored, and he reached beneath the blanket and shoved his hand between her thighs. The pressure he applied through the fabric of her clothing had her clit responding to his touch. She might come before he did.

She quickened the pace of her stroking and felt him throbbing in her hand a second later. He turned his head and pressed his mouth to her bare shoulder, stifling a groan against her skin. Her own orgasm erupted, and she pressed her lips together to suppress her own moan of pleasure.

Pulling his hand outside the blanket, Gus gripped her face between his hands and kissed her hard. "That was a first."

"What can I say? I'm full of surprises," she whispered against his lips.

"I'm excited to see what else is in store," he said, staring into her eyes.

And she absolutely did not fall in love with him even more in that moment.

IT HAD TO be half a mile from the front security gates to the three-story Santa Monica home, tucked in a posh, expensive neighborhood near the ocean. Streets lined with palm trees and perfectly manicured grounds with amazing views all around had him feeling like he'd stepped into a different world. Nothing in Seattle could compare to California's scenery, and the weather that day was warm and breezy.

The Uber driver pulled up in front of the door and they climbed out. He caught a view of a large pool and cabana in the backyard as they removed their luggage from the trunk and headed up the front walk. He gazed at the house as Selena disarmed the alarm system and unlocked the front door.

"Come on in," she said, holding the door open as he entered with her suitcases. "You can just set them down there."

Gus left the suitcases near what appeared to be one of several guest rooms on the main floor and scanned the interior of the home. "You live here alone?"

She nodded. "Alexa, lights on," she said. "Well, with this adorable little fluff ball," she said, setting the pup down. Unicorn's tail wagged, obviously excited to be home. She danced in a circle, then ran off to find a doggy toy.

"Ever get lost?" he asked, taking in the expansive foyer. A spiral staircase led to the second floor. To his right was a long hallway where he could see several more rooms and what looked like a home gym at the end. To his left was a huge open-concept kitchen, dining room and living room.

Selena laughed. "It's not that big."

"It's not small." He hadn't really recognized how different their worlds must be until he was standing in her California mansion. In Wild River, at the B and B and at the cabin, it had been easier to close the gap between their lifestyles. His bachelor pad in downtown Seattle above the studio had been impressive, the most luxury he'd ever experienced, but it paled in comparison to Selena's home, one he knew she'd bought for herself at eighteen.

Impressive, but also very intimidating.

"Hungry?" she asked, leading the way into the kitchen.

He half expected to see a chef standing at the kitchen counter; instead, she went to the fridge and took out a package of frozen meat. "You cook for yourself?"

She laughed. "If I want to eat."

Man, he was being a dick. "I'm sorry. That was insulting and I didn't mean for it to be." He scanned the kitchen. "I'm just a little out of my element."

She reached for a pan over the island and placed it on the stove. "It's okay. I actually did have a cook and a nutrition coach up until last year. After I downsized my team, I decided to take over other aspects of my life, too."

"Want some help?" he asked. He was more of a take-out kind of guy, but he could chop veggies or something.

"You could open some wine," she said, nodding toward the wine chiller.

Wine. Wine was good. "I'm on it." He went to the chiller and removed an expensive bottle of white. "Corkscrew?"

"That machine on the wall does the work," she said.

He placed the wine on the impressive contraption and watched as it removed the cork. "Wow. That's cool."

"It was a Christmas gift from my mom," she said, adding seasoning to the meat.

He poured two glasses and handed her one, watching as she cooked. "You really are full of surprises." The more he got to know her, the more she kept amazing him. Watching her in movies and in the limelight definitely didn't capture who she really was. But then, a lot of actors portrayed a different persona to the public. He was honored to get to know the real her.

She laughed. "Turning down roles this year, I had a lot of free time to acquire new skills. I took a cooking class and learned Russian."

He'd managed to sabotage his career and gain ten pounds. He sipped his wine. "So, you've lived here for a while?"

"Yes. I fell in love with it when I came to a party here with my parents when I was five years old. It was owned by a famous screenwriter back then. He decided to retire in Italy the year I turned eighteen, and I convinced my parents to let me buy it."

"Mortgage-free and all, I bet." He meant it as a compliment, a testament to her early success, but a shadow seemed to cross her eyes when they met his.

"Should I apologize for my success or something?" she asked carefully. Not upset or angry, but evidently annoyed.

He set his wine down and reached for her, taking the spatula from her hand and setting it on the counter. "Not at all. I'm sorry. I just…uh… Well, you're intimidating."

She smiled slowly. "Well, get used to it," she said before kissing him.

He kissed her back, savoring the taste of the sweet wine of her delicious lips. His hands on her waist crept beneath her thin cashmere sweater and inched higher over her sexy rib cage and up over her breasts. He loved the feel of her. She was the hottest woman he'd ever been with, though it wasn't her physical attractiveness that had him a complete mess. She was smart and talented and funny and determined and driven.

Way out of his league.

He lifted her up onto the counter and wedged his hips between her thighs. He pulled her sweater off over her head and buried his head into the crook of her long, slender neck, placing a trail of kisses along her soft, deliciously scented skin. Massaging her breasts through her lacy bra had him hardening in his jeans.

The sizzling of the frying pan caught her attention. "Dinner."

He reached behind him, moved the pan off the burner and turned off the stove. "I'll finish making dinner later," he said. Right now, he was hungry for something else. Lifting her off the counter, he wrapped her arms around his waist and headed out of the kitchen. "Where's your bedroom?"

"Up the stairs. Seventh bedroom on the right."

His eyes widened and she laughed.

"Kidding. There's only a total of seven bedrooms in the house. It's the room at the end of the hallway," she said as he hurried up the stairs with her in his arms.

He made his way down the hall and into her bedroom. The sheer curtains on the glass doors leading out onto the large deck did nothing to shield the view of the ocean with the sun setting in the distance. It was impossible to resist. Instead of laying her on the bed, he carried her outside onto the deck.

The warm, salty breeze blew her hair across her face as he set her down on one of the sun loungers. He removed the bra and tossed it aside, then reached for her jeans. She raised her hips to shimmy out of them, and he gently removed her underwear, dragging the lace slowly down over her thighs and calves, and off over her pretty manicured toes. He captured her big toe in his mouth and sucked on it, before biting it gently.

"Ow," she said with a laugh, pretending to kick him.

He grabbed the leg and kissed along her calf, behind her knee, all the way up the inside of her thigh. She lay back against the sun lounger and closed her eyes as his lips found her opening between her legs. Their escapade on the plane had been nothing short of amazing, and now he wanted to give her the same pleasure she'd given him.

He softly licked the folds and his cock throbbed. "You taste so good."

Her legs shook slightly as he buried his head between them. Her moan drove him wild as he licked and sucked, but then she pressed a hand to his forehead, stopping him. "This is okay?"

She nodded. "It feels amazing...but, um, I can't usually come this way."

He blinked. Challenge accepted. He slowly rotated her body on the chair so that she was lying on her stomach. He straddled her on the lounger and gently started trailing his fingers over her back and shoulders.

"What are you doing?" she asked, though she settled in, not fighting it.

"Relaxing you." In his limited experience, a little relaxation with a partner went a long way. He increased the pressure as he massaged her tense shoulders and neck, then lower back.

"I haven't had a massage in a million years. That feels amazing."

He shimmied lower and massaged her buttocks and hamstrings. The feel of her curves and muscles beneath his hands was making his mouth water. He massaged her inner thighs and ran a finger along her wet folds.

Good—she was at least turned on.

He continued massaging her entire body until her arms were hanging limp at her sides and her eyes drooped closed. He gently placed a hand between her legs and played with her clit until her breathing grew labored. Then he wedged his body between her legs and softly lifted her hips into the air. He positioned his face below her and buried his head against her again.

He heard the sharp inhalation of air as he held her ass cheeks and pressed her pelvis into his face as he licked and lapped at her folds. He slid his tongue in and out, and her moaning increased.

"Oh, my God, Gus… I'm getting close."

He didn't stop. He savored her juices, feeling his own body desperate for release the louder she moaned.

He dipped a finger inside her body and felt her clench around it as he flicked at her clit with his tongue. He was driving himself wild.

"Gus… Oh, Gus…"

Her hips pressed down against him and his fingers dug into the flesh of her ass as he held her in place to finish her off. Her body trembled and she cried out as her orgasm tipped her over. She raised her body, and he inched up to lie under her as she collapsed against him. Spent. Satisfied. "That was a first," she said.

"Glad I could be of service," he said, smoothing her hair away from her face and holding her tight as the sun met the sea in front of them. Breathtaking view. Breathtaking woman.

She glanced up at him and then grinned, seeing his full-on erection in the front of his jeans. "We should probably do something about that," she said, starting to slide her body lower.

He stopped her and shifted their weight until he could climb up from the lounger.

He was rock-hard, but that had been all about her.

"Where are you going?" she asked, the satiated look on her face tempting him to go back and make love to her.

"To finish dinner," he said with a wink, and quickly left before his good-guy nature lost the battle with the throbbing in his pants.

THERE WAS A brief, blissful moment upon opening her eyes, cuddled into Gus's sexy, naked body under her soft duvet, before Selena's day went to shit. Rolling to her side, she opened her eyes and screamed as the flash of a camera nearly blinded her.

Snap, snap, snap. One after another before she could fully register what was happening.

Next to her, Gus's eyes popped open and he sat up straight. "What? What's happening?"

Selena sighed as the man on her bedroom balcony disappeared over the side. She hoped he broke a leg on the way down to the ground.

Jumping out of the bed, she grabbed her robe and slid into it quickly. "Paparazzi," she said with a sigh. So much for hoping that the one news article about her and Gus would be the one and *only*. Now it wouldn't just be speculation. There was no denying they were intimate when the shots showed them in bed together. She reached for her phone and dialed her publicist. Her *former* publicist. She'd let the woman go the year before when she'd suggested Selena play the victim in the press conferences regarding her stalker, to garner more public sympathy.

Please answer.

"Selena?"

"Angel, hi… I need your help." If anyone could reach out to the media outlets and get them to not run these photos, it would be Angel. Additionally, of course, there would be a hefty payout to that sleazy photographer with no guarantee that the photos wouldn't magically surface anyway.

"I thought my advice didn't mesh with the new image you're trying to create," the woman said smugly.

Selena's jaw clenched. Okay, maybe she deserved that. "I'm sorry we ended things on a bad note, Angel, but you are the best in the business and I need you." Five minutes of groveling later, she collapsed onto the bed.

Gus still sat there, looking helpless, apologetic. "I'm sorry. Maybe me staying here wasn't such a great idea."

Keeping the deck's blackout exterior blinds open was the bad idea. She shook her head. "This shit happens and I'm not surprised." Maybe it was time to increase her on-site security again, since she was suddenly back in the spotlight.

Regarding her love life…not the amazing indie film.

"Do you think your publicist can stop the photos from being printed?" he asked.

"I'm not sure. I hope so," she said, running a hand through her messy hair. "I don't even know how they knew we'd be here." The man had probably camped outside her home for weeks. She'd had it happen many times in the past, but in those days she'd acknowledged her lack of privacy as a price for stardom. Now it irritated her that her reinvention would be overshadowed by her relationship status.

Gus looked guilty as he reached for her. "I might be responsible for that."

She frowned. "What?"

"Well, not me. Aileen."

"What?" He'd been in touch with his ex? When? They'd been together 24/7 for days.

"She tracks my cell phone," he said with an annoyed head shake.

Not annoyed enough. "And you're okay with that?" Maybe he wasn't as done with Aileen as he claimed.

"No. Of course not. She's just strange like that. It's not a big deal. I'd forgotten she installed the app."

Not a big deal? The woman had tipped off the paparazzi that Gus was in Selena's home. The photographer had captured private shots of the two of them together. She was trying to rebuild her career and her reputation, and Gus thought it was no big deal that things might now be compromised? "It kinda is," she said.

Climbing out of bed, he approached and reached for her. When she pulled away, he sighed. "I'm sorry about Aileen. I'll put a stop to that right away."

She nodded. That made her feel a little better, but they still had the bigger issue of saving the movie promo from being all about the two of them falling in love on set. Two people looking for a comeback finding each other. Envisioning the kinds of headlines the media would come up with was making her nauseous. She rubbed her forehead. "This is a disaster."

Gus looked confused. "So, the media will say we're together. We are—right?"

She nodded and sucked her bottom lip in. Of course, Gus wouldn't get it. He was a man. In Hollywood, men could switch girlfriends every other day and they were called a baller. Women were expected to act differently. Not only would the public claim she was bed-hopping from Matt to Gus, but this new relationship would definitely take priority over the movie promotion. Any press would be diluted with stories of their on-set romance. "It's just I wasn't ready for that to be public knowledge yet."

He frowned. "I'm a secret now?"

"No. Trying to be private about my personal life has nothing to do with you."

"It kinda does," he said, his tone slightly chilly.

Seriously? He was getting annoyed at her for wanting to stay out of the spotlight for once? "I just didn't want my personal life to overshadow the movie," she said calmly.

He nodded slowly. "I understand that…" He touched her shoulder gently. "But the media would find out eventually and maybe this is a good thing? Being back on the press's radar before the movie press starts. We'll step out onto the red carpet as a power couple."

At one time, hearing a man say that would have made her heart sing. She'd wanted that kind of status in her relationship with Matt, but now she wanted to stand on her own, independent of a man on her arm. Once again, she'd be promoting a film with a man on her arm, and once again, her performance would be diminished as a result.

She folded her arms across her chest and swallowed hard. "Maybe we should cool things a bit."

"You're breaking up with me?"

"No!" She was in love with him. Ending things wasn't her intent. "No, just a step back so that we're not drawing as much attention."

He frowned as his hand dropped away. "What? Why?"

"Because I'm trying to rebuild my career, and I…got distracted from what's important." It hurt to say the words, but she hated that once again she'd fallen into a trap of putting her career on the line for the sake of a relationship.

Gus's pained expression made her chest ache. "I'm a distraction?"

She sighed. "I just mean I wanted to make this comeback on my own. Not as part of a couple, not relying on a male lead to help the movie succeed."

"You'd been prepared to do that with Matt."

She heard the disappointment in his voice and it weakened her resolve. "I…" Her cell phone chimed, and she glanced at Angel's text message, her heart falling into her stomach.

Sorry, Selena. This vulture was quick.

She clicked the link, and the photo taken just an hour ago of her and Gus in bed together appeared on *Gossip Now*'s online site, with the caption:

Selena Hudson hits rock bottom in her career and love life with disgraced sports broadcaster Gus Orosco.

"Shit."

"What's wrong?"

She shook her head. "Angel couldn't help." She tucked the phone away without showing him the headline. He had his interview that day and he didn't need a blow to his confidence. "Anyway, you should probably get ready. Traffic into downtown will be a mess."

He nodded slowly, taking a step toward her. "I'm really sorry, Selena. I guess I just don't see why me being involved in the movie, and your life, is such a bad thing. You're helping me with my career. Why can't I help you with yours?"

Because of society's unfair double standards. "I think it's best if you stay in a hotel while you're in town. Just until this blows over," she said.

"Until this blows over," he repeated slowly, looking defeated. "Okay. If that's what you want."

It wasn't what she wanted, but when were women not forced to choose between their careers and personal happiness? "Good luck with your interview," she said, heading into the bathroom before she could make the wrong choice.

CHAPTER EIGHTEEN

ONE GOOD THING about almost breaking up with someone before the biggest interview of his life was that he was too preoccupied to be as nervous as he should be.

Small, shitty silver lining.

Selena had been pissed, and rightly so. Gus was annoyed, too, but he'd be lying if he said he completely understood what the big deal was. And it was difficult not to internalize it somewhat. Her previous relationships were always a topic for the gossip rags, and she'd never mentioned it bothering her before. Why now? Why him?

He released a deep breath as he opened the door to the Sports Beat studios.

This was the big one—the dream he'd never imagined turning into reality. As tough as it was, he needed to put Selena and the paparazzi and their issues out of mind for the next hour. Once the interview was over, he'd figure out a way to make things right with her.

He checked in at the front desk and then scanned the studio's large, posh reception area and waiting room, taking in the sports history and memorabilia on the walls and the studio's awards lining the shelves behind a new receptionist, who was being trained.

He'd never thought he'd be there, waiting to see Malin Kirk. Even his grandfather looked up to the sports broadcasting mogul. His family would be so proud if he could pull this off.

And he owed this shot to Selena. He really didn't want to let her down. Maybe if it went well, they'd have a reason to celebrate and get things back on track. Maybe, after she'd had some time to cool off, think about things, she'd feel better.

The day before at her place had been amazing. After his initial struggle with feeling out of place, he'd started to feel more comfortable, relaxed…at home. Million-dollar mansions weren't supposed to feel homey, but Selena's stardom didn't seem to define her. Nowhere in the house were her awards or accolades. When he'd asked about a glory room, she'd just laughed and said she let her parents keep all that stuff at their place. She wanted her home to feel like a home, not any type of museum. He liked being there with her… Staying in a hotel would suck, but if she needed the space, then he could respect that. They hadn't ended things…just taken a little step back.

His gut twisted.

"Gus Orosco?" the receptionist said.

He raised a hand, then embarrassingly lowered it. He wasn't a five-year-old in kindergarten. "That's me."

"Ms. Kirk is ready for you now," she said, leading the way down a long hallway toward the corner office. Just the sight of the woman's nameplate outside the double doors leading to her office was surreal.

Malin was a legend. She'd built the network from the bottom up. Excelled, thrived and then conquered in a male-dominated industry. She had a reputation of being firm but fair—like his grandfather—and Gus felt honored just to have her attention.

The receptionist opened the door. "Good luck," she said

with a smile. He entered and the doors closed behind him. The executive stood reviewing footage on a large flat-screen on the wall above a long boardroom table. Wearing a red tailored pantsuit and four-inch heels, she seemed to fill the thousand-square-foot space. He swallowed hard as she paused the footage on a close-up of his red, angry face. He didn't need the sound on to know what insult he was throwing at Vince in this particular moment. He could read the word on his still lips.

He cleared his throat. "Not my finest moment," he said.

Malin turned and walked toward him. "Have a seat," she said, sitting in the chair next to him instead of behind her desk. She crossed one leg over the other and stared at him. "You really fucked things up for yourself."

Cutting straight to the chase. Okay. He could own his mistakes. Better to clear this elephant from the room right away. He sat straighter and nodded. "Yes, I did. Big-time." He paused. "Apparently, losing your shit on live television is a detrimental career move… But the good news is, I've done that and learned the tough lesson the hard way."

She laughed and he relaxed.

"Look, Gus, about the meltdown…"

He braced for impact.

"I thought it was hilarious," she said. "One of the most entertaining things I've seen on sports TV since those end-of-the-year blooper shows. It was shared over five hundred thousand times on social media."

She thought it was funny? She might be the only one in the industry. He didn't relax yet. It didn't mean she'd hire him, just that he'd provided her with a source of amusement. "Well, I'm happy you can see the humor in it," he said, shifting in the chair.

"Obviously, we can't have those kinds of outbursts on *our* network," she said, sobering.

"Obviously, and I can assure you, it won't happen again. I'm a professional and I'm confident that—moving forward—I can keep my personal feelings in check at all times." Even with regard to Vince.

Malin nodded. "That's good…"

He pushed on, sensing it might be his only shot. "Ms. Kirk, I've wanted to work here forever. It's always been the dream, and I applied more than once…"

She nodded, her long, whip-straight red hair falling over her shoulder. "I know."

"You do?"

"I saw your résumé come across my desk a few times over the years. Usually someone from the office would bring it by and suggest we interview you."

"But you never did."

She shook her head and folded her hands together on her lap. "Look, Gus, you're an amazing reporter and your credits speak for themselves, but you're an Orosco."

He frowned. His family legacy wasn't usually something holding him back. His grandfather's reputation in the industry had gained him respect and credibility when he was a newbie, opened doors for him over the years, not shut them in his face. "Do you know my grandfather?"

She smiled and it completely softened her features. "I adore him. And I respect him. And I would never steal his grandson."

Ah. That made more sense. But his grandfather had to suspect he had aspirations that went beyond the family network. He never would have held Gus back. "Well, he fired me," he said. "And he'd never want to keep me from this opportunity…"

She hesitated, staring át him for a long, excruciating moment. "Okay, well, I'll be honest with you. I wasn't expecting to even really be considering you for this position, given your family and such, so I'll need some time to review your résumé again and watch some of your demo reel—but I will, and if I like what I see, I'll be in touch." She stood and extended a hand toward him.

She was going to seriously consider him for the position. She wasn't turning him down immediately based on his past mistake. It wasn't a yes, but it wasn't a no. He'd take it. He could barely contain his excitement as he stood and accepted the handshake. "Thank you so much, Ms. Kirk. I'll look forward to your call."

"Um, one more thing," she said, picking up her cell phone and turning it toward him.

Seeing the photo of him and Selena in bed together on *Gossip Now*'s website, he tensed, and his face flushed with a mix of anger and embarrassment. If he got his hands around that photographer's neck...

"Is it true that you and Selena Hudson are a thing now?"

He sighed. He hoped they still were. "We were dating... while filming an indie movie together." He sighed. "She's not exactly thrilled about those photos or the media attention."

Malin nodded, putting the phone away. "Of course she isn't. She's a professional, trying to rebuild her career, and all the press cares about is who she's in bed with." She shook her head, looking disgusted.

"Yes, exactly. That's what she said." He hesitated. "I thought all press was good?"

"For men." She gestured around her. "For me, this came at a cost. No permanent relationships, just discreet flings, no kids, no pets. My personal life isn't private. It's nonexistent. Women in this industry can't afford to let their guards down for a second. We can't show emotion or weakness or make a mistake. Men are given second chances," she said. "Women aren't."

He swallowed hard. Men who messed up—like him. She was right. If he was a female reporter, he wouldn't be getting this opportunity, no matter who called in the favor. It was easy to think that society was changing when he wasn't on the suffering side. "I get it," he said with a sigh.

Now he just had to try to make it right somehow.

As he left the office, Malin's words haunted him. The media wanted the inside scoop and they'd publish any story they could get their hands on, but what if he went to them and claimed it was all just a publicity stunt? Claim that he and Selena knew they'd be a source of conversation if they were spotted together? Claim to just be friends, maybe hint at a secret collaboration without providing any details.

Feeling better than he had all day, having a plan to fix things, Gus stepped out into the bright California sun and headed south three blocks toward the *Gossip Now* offices.

SELENA PACED THE lobby of the upscale hotel that Gus had checked into before his interview. She checked her cell phone, but there was still no reply from him to the message she'd sent an hour before asking how the interview had gone.

She'd overreacted that morning, and guilt had plagued her since he'd left her house. He'd had the biggest interview of his career, and she hoped their argument hadn't thrown him off his game. It was still best for him not to stay with her, more paparazzi were sure to be lingering around her home now, but she hadn't meant the hurtful things she'd said, like referring to him as a distraction. That wasn't true. He was so much more to her than that, and her casual dismissal of what they had been was unfair and far from the truth.

The media would always look for dirt. No matter what she did, who she was with. The industry wouldn't change. She needed to change the narrative in her favor. Own her choices in her personal life as well as her career and block out the unimportant opinions of the public.

Her cell phone rang, and seeing Jay's number lighting up her display, she cringed. Obviously, he'd finally seen the *Gossip Now* article.

"Hey, Jay," she said, answering on the second ring. "Listen, I know these articles are frustrating—"

"Frustrating? You think that's the right word?" he asked, sounding even more upset than she'd been. Strange, the photos hadn't been of Jay in bed with a man. She understood his annoyance, but the press was messing with her life, not his.

"A few hours ago, I was really upset, too," she said evenly, "but we both know these things happen. It's impossible to stop these vultures from publishing this garbage." If she sounded unfazed, maybe he'd realize it wasn't such a big deal.

"Not giving them the information in the first place would be a start," Jay said, his voice rising.

She frowned. Why was he blaming her for this? Her friend was not someone she expected to be victim shaming. "Some guy scaled the side of my house for those shots, Jay. I didn't invite him in!"

Several hotel guests turned her way, and she moved closer to the revolving door and lowered her voice. "Look, my personal life shouldn't negatively impact the movie. There's still months before we need to start press, and Gus and I have agreed to try to lie low until then." They could still see one another, and try harder to keep things private.

"Selena, I don't give a rat's ass about you and Gus on the cover of every gossip rag in town," Jay said. "I'm talking about the leaked plot summary Gus gave *Gossip Now.*"

Her cell phone nearly slipped from her hand. "The what?" Her voice was more like a croak as her heart raced.

"You didn't see it?" Jay's voice was slightly calmer as he realized she'd had no idea what he was referring to.

"No."

Jay sighed. "So, you didn't authorize it?"

"Of course not." She rubbed her forehead as she fought for a calming breath. What the hell? They had one argument and he went running to the press? What the hell was he thinking? "How much did he say?"

"Let's just say, if someone wanted to film their own version, they'd even have some of the dialogue."

Damn it! *Stay calm.* "Okay, well, maybe it's not so bad. We'll just start our promo sooner than we originally planned. Keep the momentum Gus started." She said his name through clenched teeth. How dare he get the momentum started? This wasn't his movie. He was just in it, and only because she'd been desperate.

"I don't think we want to keep this particular momentum going," Jay said wryly.

She was afraid to ask. "Why not?"

"You need to read the article for yourself, but here's one sentence that pretty much sums it up—'Any thriller that stars Selena Hudson is sure to be an over budget, glorified women-in-peril TV movie, forced upon us as must-see filmography, by paid-off reviewers.'"

Her stomach dropped and she thought she might throw

up. What the hell had Gus told *Gossip Now*? Was he so upset that he'd shit-talked the movie?

She paced the lobby, her heels clicking against the marble flooring, the swirling pattern of black and white making her slightly dizzy. She shut her eyes tight as she said, "Is that the worst of it?"

"Nope. We're fucked, Selena, unless we can turn this around."

She groaned and, seeing Gus walking down the street toward the hotel entrance, her heart pounded in her chest. Her attraction to him was off the charts and he looked amazing in a fitted charcoal suit and light blue collared shirt, but right now, she wanted to kill him. "I have to go. I'm sorry about this, Jay. We'll figure out damage control, I promise. Trust me, okay?"

"I did trust you, Selena."

The dead air on the line was deafening as she tucked her cell phone into her purse and headed toward the revolving doors as Gus entered. "Hey…" he said with a nervous-looking smile.

"Can we talk outside?" She refused to give the tabloids more fodder with a public argument in the middle of the hotel lobby. Right now, she was so fuming mad, smoke must be coming out of her ears. Her hands clenched into fists at her sides as they stepped into the hot sun.

"You're pissed." It wasn't a question.

"Yes, I'm pissed. You went to *Gossip Now*?" she hissed.

He nodded. "Yes. I just thought I'd try to spin things. Make it sound like we were working together on a project."

"I can't believe you did that," she said, unable to conceal her frustration.

"I was trying to help…" He ran a hand through his hair.

"Help? Gus, you just leaked info about the movie before we were ready to release anything."

"I didn't mean to, I swear. I was just trying to give the tabloids something other than us—our relationship—to focus on," he said. "Those gossip reporters are tricky, and before I knew it, I was answering far too many questions."

"You're a reporter! You should know how this works!"

"I know. You're right. I'm sorry." He sighed. "But let's look at the positive—you said you wanted the attention on the movie."

"I do! When the time's right." She ran a hand through her hair and took several deep breaths. He'd gone to *Gossip Now* because of her meltdown earlier that day in an attempt to save their relationship. While she knew the gesture was coming from a sincere place, it upset her that he still assumed the relationship should be her priority, the only thing that mattered. How could he not understand that she was taking a massive risk and she needed it to pay off? "Jay's lost all trust in me now."

"This was my mistake," he said. "I'll call him and apologize."

"No. Let him cool down." Besides, this was her mess to clean up. Bringing Gus on to star in the movie had been her decision as well. She'd convinced Jay that trusting the loose-cannon sports broadcaster was the right thing to do.

He took a step toward her but kept his hands in his pockets as he said, "I thought I was doing the right thing. I was trying to fix things…so you wouldn't feel the pressure."

Fix things. She held up a hand, her blood boiling anew. "No one asked you to fix anything, Gus." Why couldn't he just lie low the way she'd asked? They could have continued seeing one another privately until the press moved on to more interesting drama. Now she was on damage control, and the first real promotion for the movie was a biased, negatively opinionated piece by a sleazy source that, unfortunately, everyone read.

Gus nodded slowly. "You're right. I just thought you and I had something great and you were considering throwing it away for the sake of the movie and your career and..."

That was what he thought? "I wasn't considering throwing it away, Gus. I was trying to figure things out."

"It didn't sound like it this morning," he said, his voice turning slightly hard.

Her spine stiffened. "So instead of working *with* me, being understanding and giving me time to process, you decided to take matters in your own hands?" That was not how a relationship worked. Sure, she'd been upset that morning and maybe she'd overreacted, but Gus had way overstepped. He'd jeopardized the movie's chances for success, and, worse, he'd done it without talking to her, without giving her a say on how to solve the issue of how they moved forward. She was so done with the male chromosome and its ego, especially when it impacted her career, her life.

"I made a mistake," he said, staring at the ground.

"Yeah," she said with a defeated sigh. "Maybe I did, too." Trusting him, believing in him, hoping he was different.

"So, that's it? That's what we are? A mistake?" he asked, and the hurt in his voice echoed the hurt in her heart.

She had no idea what to say. This wasn't a rom-com, and there was no one to write her lines. No guarantee of a happily-ever-after. Unscripted and raw, this breakup was the real thing. She couldn't be with someone she couldn't trust.

"'Bye, Gus," she said, and turned and walked away.

CHAPTER NINETEEN

HE WAS STILL kicking himself hours later and wishing he could travel back in time for another shot at fixing things. Selena had every right to be pissed at him and so did Jay. He'd really messed up. Going to the tabloid had been impulsive and he hadn't thought it through.

Seemed to be his fatal flaw these days.

That evening should have gone so differently. The interview had been short but it had gone well, and he was in one of the most exciting cities in the world. If he hadn't been so stupid, he could be celebrating the possibility of another shot at the career he loved with the woman he loved.

When did he ever get things right lately?

He sighed, running a hand through his hair as he collapsed on the bed. He missed her so much already. He understood her "one strike, you're out" policy. She'd been messed around with enough that year. First Matt had hurt her, now him. Inadvertently, but that didn't matter. Why on earth had he tried to be the hero? Save the day?

Selena Hudson wasn't some damsel in distress. She did not need saving. He'd been the one feeling as though he was losing her after their argument. Going to the press had been a selfish attempt to keep her in his life.

He groaned as he sat up and reached for his cell phone. He scrolled through his contact list and stared at her number. He desperately wanted to apologize, let her know how deeply sorry he was and, more than anything, make sure she knew how much he really did believe in the movie and in her. He'd read the article and they'd twisted everything he'd said for their own purpose. Why the hell had he thought he could trust a sleazy magazine to do the right thing?

He stared at the photo of her beautiful smiling face, and his chest hurt. She'd been a light in the darkness for him. She'd brought him back to life and made him want to be better. Nothing shone as bright without her. He'd thought getting over Aileen had been hard. Getting over Selena might kill him.

He opened his app for the airline and scanned the available flights back to Seattle for the next day. He didn't expect Malin to get back to him about the position quickly, so he was better off going back to Seattle while he waited. He knew he could stay with Trish, and he did have to let his family know about the interview.

He booked an early-morning flight and set the phone on the nightstand. Lying on the bed, he stared up at the ceiling and shook his head.

Just once, it would be great if he could get something right.

SELENA'S FEET POUNDED the treadmill and loud music blasted through her earbuds. Physical exertion and Alanis Morissette blaring in her head were the only way through this. She cranked the machine as she neared the five-mile mark, sweaty and exhausted.

Ignoring Gus's text and phone call that day had been hard. Part of her thought maybe she was overreacting. But each time she reread the *Gossip Now* article, her resolve returned. How on earth could Gus have done that? Trust and communication were the foundation of all good relationships, and his actions had her questioning him…questioning them together.

Definitely best to cool things for a while.

But he had been trying to help, and she had said she wanted the press focused on the movie.

She turned the volume even louder. No. She wouldn't do what she always did. Internalize it or gaslight herself into believing she was somehow at fault. He'd gone to the press. He'd gone behind her back and Jay's.

Sighing, she hit the emergency stop on the treadmill and yanked the earbuds from her ears. She climbed off the treadmill and fought to catch her breath as she toweled off.

Unicorn sat on her doggy bed in the corner, and the pup whined and pouted at her.

"Look, it wasn't my fault. He just wasn't the right one for us."

Unicorn shot her a disappointed look and turned away, curling her tiny paws under her head.

Her phone chimed with a new text and the puppy's ears perked up. Selena glanced at the display and saw her agent's name. "It's not him," she told the dog.

Unicorn went back to ignoring her and Selena read the text.

Sending you a new script. Really think you'll like this one.

Leaving the gym, she headed into her office and logged on to her laptop. Opening her email, she saw the message from her agent.

She clicked on the link attached and read the title of the screenplay—*Love on the Coast*.

Another rom-com. And his not-so-subtle comment: Think you should really consider this one. Xx.

Translation: If she kept turning down these opportunities, there may not be many more offered. She knew her agent was at the end of his rope with her. If she didn't return to being a lucrative client soon, she'd find herself without an agent. But what good was one who couldn't get her the movie roles she wanted, anyway? Unfortunately, she couldn't blame him for the fact that Hollywood saw her one way...

Maybe they were right. She was really great in these movies. She'd won awards and received amazing reviews. Why wasn't that enough? Why couldn't she just accept her place in the industry and continue doing what she was good at? Why couldn't she just be what everyone needed her to be? Expected her to be?

She took a deep breath as she downloaded the script and hit Print. She may as well read it.

Her cell phone rang over the sound of her printer, and seeing Jay's number lighting up the screen, she almost felt a sense of betrayal even considering the new rom-com script and a surge of relief that he was finally willing to talk to her again. She cleared her throat as she answered, "Hey, Jay. About yesterday—"

"We're in!"

She frowned. "What?"

"Three festivals so far," he said, his excitement making his voice almost shrill. Clearly, he wasn't upset anymore.

"How is that possible? We haven't finished the movie yet." They were starting post the next morning. Her stomach tightened thinking about it. Gus had been excited to come into Jay's studio with her to see how the behind-the-scenes magic worked. Would he still show up? Should she text him and tell him not to?

A part of her really just wanted to see him. Which was stupid.

"After that disastrous article, I sent some rough-cut footage along to the festival organizers. I thought, what the hell? And the response has been amazing."

Her breath caught in her chest, and she eyed the pages of the rom-com script that were sliding out of her printer onto the floor.

"Selena? What's going on? Why aren't you shrieking with joy?" Jay asked.

She laughed, and a sense of renewed determination flowed through her. "I'm shricking on the inside."

"Well, let that shit out, darlin', 'cause we're taking this movie straight to the top," Jay said.

And, with any luck, her career with it. Because right now, with her own love life in shambles and her heart a big mess, she wasn't sure she could read one page of the script scattered all over her office floor without wanting to vomit.

CHAPTER TWENTY

Seattle, Washington
A week later...

THE RAIN IN Seattle hitting the penthouse windows of his sister's flat above the studio was right on par with his mood. A week had passed, and there was still no word from Malin Kirk. And worse, no word from Selena. Gus was losing his mind. The silence was killing him.

He'd thought that maybe she'd reach out when he didn't show up at Jay's home studio the day after their argument, but only Jay had texted to say he was forgiven and missed. He doubted the director was speaking for Selena.

He stood at the counter in the kitchen, arms folded across his chest as he waited impatiently for the Keurig to brew. He scanned his sister's home. It was an exact replica of the apartment he'd once occupied down the hall, now inhabited by one of the other reporters who'd moved in during Gus's Alaska hiatus.

He needed to find his own place and start thinking about alternate careers. His savings were quickly depleting and he was losing hope about the job with Sports Beat. It had been such a long shot.

The Keurig finished brewing and he carried the studio-branded mug to the window. Gazing out at the city used to make him feel inspired. A year ago, he'd thought he'd finally made it—the perfect career, the perfect woman. Things had gone to shit so fast.

Then things had started to look up. Even better than he'd ever imagined. But maybe he was destined to self-sabotage everything good that came his way.

A crack of thunder in the distance nearly drowned out the sound of his cell phone ringing, but his heart pounded in his chest seeing the LA Sports Beat office number lighting up his call display.

It was Malin.

He took a mouthful of coffee and then spit the scalding liquid back into the cup.

"Damn," he muttered, taking a deep breath before answering, "This is Gus."

"Gus, Malin Kirk here from Sports Beat," her authoritative voice said.

As if he needed the clarification. He'd only been desperate for this call every second of every day for a week. There was only one other he'd have been more relieved to get. His heart echoed in his ears as he tried to sound casual. "Yes, hi, Malin. How are you?"

"Good. You in town?" she asked.

"I could be…" He was already removing his sweatpants in anticipation of a mad dash to the airport for a last-minute flight.

"Oh. No need. I just thought if you were around, we could meet to discuss this in person."

He swallowed hard. Why had he left LA?

Because staying in the city and not being able to see Selena would have been far too difficult.

"I had some things to wrap up in Seattle," he said. In truth, there was nothing left for him here in Seattle. His heart had already started to anticipate a new life in California. A future with Selena. But he needed to start moving on. As much as he'd cared about her, loved her, he'd messed up, and clearly she hadn't been in the same place. At least, not enough to give him another chance.

Malin's words about men getting second chances echoed in his ears and he checked himself. She was right; he was lucky to be getting this shot at his career. Expecting Selena to give him another one was too much to expect.

"Well, when can you get to LA?" she asked now.

He hesitated. "That depends…"

"What if I said we'd like you in studio next week?" Malin said.

Oh, thank God. He cleared his throat and tried not to sound too desperate. "Then I'll be there next week."

"Great."

"Thank you, Malin, for this opportunity. I can't tell you how much it means." So much for sounding cool and reserved. He was beyond grateful for this second chance, and not just at any small studio, but at his dream studio.

"Save your gratitude. Just don't make me regret this decision."

"I promise you won't," he said, before he heard the dead air on the other end of the line.

He stood staring at the phone for a long moment. Then, dropping it onto the sofa, he did a touchdown, end zone victory dance. Finally, some good news. Something was coming together. Unfortunately, it felt like a consolation to the second chance he really wanted.

Twenty minutes later, he knocked on Trish's office door. And ten minutes after that, his sister was staring at him wide-eyed, mouth agape.

"Unbelievable. You mess up and you get an opportunity of a lifetime." Trish glared at him from across her desk.

"Obviously, still a man's world," she mumbled, echoing the sentiments of all the other women around him.

He couldn't disagree. He felt like he'd been given an undeserved second chance, thanks to Selena. Who had refused to answer his calls and texts since his major mistake the week before. He just wished she'd let him apologize.

"When do you start?" Trish asked.

"Next Monday. I'm flying back to LA tomorrow." He already had several apartments lined up to view near the studio, and he was desperate to try reaching out to Selena again. She couldn't avoid him forever, could she? He at least had to tell her about the job and thank her again.

"So, this actress who hooked you up, did she become… someone special?" Trish eyed him. For a week she'd been scrutinizing him, drilling him about his time in Wild River and the movie.

Amazingly special. How had he not realized how much until she was ignoring him? He'd known he liked her a lot. Their physical chemistry was undeniable, and he enjoyed being around her so much, there now felt like a Selena-sized hole in his chest. He hadn't realized how hard he'd fallen for her until she'd walked away from him.

He sighed. "Yeah, she did."

"So, this LA thing is about her?"

He wished. If he could choose only one reason to move to LA, it would be to be with her. The job seemed more like a consolation prize now. But maybe if he was in the same city, he could find a way to connect with her again. They did still have a movie to promote, and maybe after enough time had passed, she'd forgive him? He wouldn't hold his breath for a second chance, but his heart desperately wanted one. "Unfortunately, the only thing waiting for me in LA is the job," he said.

His sister studied him. "So, let me make sure I get this straight. You run away to Alaska to heal a broken heart and you come back with a new source of heartache?"

He nodded. Only he could pull off such a feat. "You got it perfectly straight."

Los Angeles, California

"So, you're just going to keep ignoring him?" Jay asked as Selena ignored the ringing cell phone on the desk in her home studio. The display lighting up read "Gus Who?" and it was the only way she could remind herself to be strong and continue to ignore his attempts at contact.

So far, it was working, though she wasn't sure for how long. Blocking his number was the best thing to do, but what if she had movie business to discuss with him? She couldn't avoid him forever and yet wasn't ready to talk to him. Even though she was dying to find out if he'd gotten the broadcasting job with Sports Beat. That company and its staff might not be her favorite, but it would be a huge boost to Gus's career. And despite herself, she still cared enough about him to want that for him.

"Yes," she told Jay. Then, staring at the computer monitors, she pointed to a scene. "Can we see the second take of this one? I think the delivery of the last line was better." Working on post for the film and staying busy was the only way to keep sane. She was more determined than ever to make this movie a huge success. She'd turned down the audition for the rom-com as more film festivals selected their movie, and she refused to second-guess the decision.

She'd given the performance of a lifetime on this one. *That* she was confident about, and right now, she needed all the confidence she could get.

Jay sighed and searched for the footage, but he wasn't done talking about Gus. "You know, people make mistakes."

Someone was quick to forgive. She resisted the urge to remind him that he'd been just as furious with Gus initially. "I'm aware. I've been the unfortunate recipient of many." Two breakups in a month. That was a record for her. No more. She was off men and focused 100 percent on her career. This movie in particular. She bit her lip as she watched the scene play back. "Do you think we could green screen him out?"

Jay shot her a look.

"I mean, like CGI another actor in."

"Do you have that kind of budget lying around?" He shook his head. "And besides, he did amazing. And I don't mean just for a nonactor. I hate to break it to you, but he really brought it."

She sighed. She could be pissed at Gus without denying his performance was good. But looking at them together on-screen was torture.

Her phone chimed with a new voice mail message. By now, her inbox must be full, but she couldn't listen to the messages yet. She was afraid the sound of Gus's voice— not in character—which she was missing so much, would make her question her resolve. Make her weak enough to forgive him and give him a second chance.

"Let's wrap this up for the day," Jay said a moment later. "I've got a meeting with a studio to discuss some freelance postproduction work on a film."

Selena nodded. Until this movie made them all millionaires, Jay still had to find work where he could. "Good luck," she said.

"Thanks." He packed up his things and headed for the

door. "And consider talking to Gus. If you think he was only doing it all for the Sports Beat opportunity, you're wrong. I saw how he looked at you and that was real."

Selena sighed as Jay left the studio. If only she could trust in her own feelings.

Her cell rang again, and she was about to throw it across the room before seeing Leslie's number on the call display. She hadn't spoken to her since she'd left Alaska, and emotions welled up inside. She wished they could have a girls' night and sit around and drink wine—nonalcoholic for Leslie—and she could spill out her turmoil to her friend. Things just weren't the same by phone or through a computer screen. "Hey," she said, answering the call and sounding as upbeat as possible.

"Can you please call Gus?"

Selena rolled her eyes. Obviously, Leslie had heard the news through the grapevine. It annoyed her that Gus had gotten to them first. They were her friends. Technically, Levi was a better friend to Gus, but she liked to think she ranked higher since they'd all shared a near-death experience together. "No. That's over."

"Only he doesn't think so."

"Well, it's not up to him," she said, shutting down the film footage.

"He's driving Levi crazy, who in turn is driving me crazy…"

"Tell Levi to ignore his calls." Not that it was working for her. He was persistent, she'd give him that. Most men would have taken the hint after being ghosted for a week. Nonetheless, persistence didn't mean love. It could mean guilt or desperation or a need for closure. She'd dated one guy who sought her out for a second chance only to dump her himself halfway through the meal, so that he was no longer the dumpee.

Bizarre.

"What happened?" Leslie asked, her tone gentler.

Selena pressed her fingers over the bridge of her nose. Pouring her heart out might make her feel better momentarily, but then she'd be confirming that she was a bad judge of character and that she fell too hard, too fast, and right now, she wanted to be more like her levelheaded friend. In her situation, Leslie would just suck it up and move on. Keep her feelings private, and no one would know the depths of her sorrow. Selena would steal a chapter from that book this time. "Nothing. It was just a filming thing," she said casually, and the lie literally made her chest hurt. "Happens all the time. On-set chemistry and all that fools the brain into thinking it's real attraction. Totally faded once we were done with the filming."

"Why are you torturing yourself?" Leslie asked, not fooled. "You like him."

She loved him, actually. "I've liked a lot of guys."

"Not like this," Leslie said. "This one was different, and even I, your emotionally stunted friend, could see that."

"I think I just need a break from relationships for a while." She was done with men. She wouldn't be that woman who needed one. A full year. She'd enjoy singlesville and concentrate solely on her career. No matter how gorgeous, how charming, how seductive the man, she would refuse to date anyone for a full 365 days. A cleanse of sorts. "How are you doing?" she asked.

Leslie wasn't thrilled at the change of subject, but she said, "I'm sick from the time I wake up to the time I go to bed."

"I thought morning sickness only happened in the morning, as the term implies."

"Try telling that to this baby," she said with a laugh that conveyed she'd happily spend the day draped over the toilet for this child.

Selena felt a tug at her chest. Leslie had suffered through heartache and the loss of someone she loved, and now she was engaged and expecting a baby. She'd found her happily-ever-after. It gave Selena hope that maybe someday she would, too.

But not within the next 365 days.

"Levi's already started on the nursery. We're thinking a jungle animal theme that will work whether it's a boy or a girl, and he wants to build the crib himself," she said.

"That's amazing." Levi was such a great guy. Clearly, they were out there—she'd thought she'd found one. "Hey, Leslie, I'm just here with Jay." She felt bad about the lie, but the longer she stayed on the call, the more fearful she was that she'd break down and confess all about her broken heart, and she didn't want to ruin the call.

"Oh, right. I can't wait to see the movie once it's done."

"You'll be the first to see it," she said. Their first film festival was that December in Anchorage. "Take care of yourself and my godchild, okay. I'll call you later?"

"Don't call me, call Gus!"

As Selena disconnected the call, she sighed. Opening up her voice mail, she cleared the new messages from him without listening to them and then put her cell away.

Three hundred and sixty-five days. She could last that long without falling in love again. After all, it would take that long for her heart to heal.

CHAPTER TWENTY-ONE

HE WOULDN'T MESS this up this time. Getting the opportunity to prove himself on Sports Beat, even as a junior reporter on the late-morning broadcast, was the opportunity of a lifetime. Malin was putting her trust in him. This wasn't just a comeback; this was a dream come true.

But as he stood in the busy, fast-paced studio, he felt slightly hollow, when it should have been the most exciting highlight of his life so far. He'd been in LA for almost a week. He'd found a small apartment in the downtown area, close enough to walk to the studio, and he'd been busy setting up his new life, though it was impossible to forget about a certain brunette avoiding him a short drive away along the coast. He checked his cell phone again... hoping. Nothing.

"We're going live in ten minutes," a production assistant, wearing a headset and carrying a clipboard, told him.

He nodded. "Great. Thanks." This was it. He needed to focus. Get his head in the game. So far, he'd noticed the lack of warm welcome from the other broadcasters. He'd seen the snickers and the looks of disbelief over the fact that Malin was giving the meltdown guy a chance. He hadn't expected anything different—he just needed to prove himself. He knew the games they were covering in that morning's broadcast as well as if he'd played in them himself. He knew the highlight moments they'd be discussing in their Final

Five Round Table at the end of the broadcast, and he'd rehearsed his opinion down to something intelligent, critical, but maybe a little less passionately honest than he would have in the past. This was his first time on air in months, with a new network; it was best to ease in. Test viewers' acceptance of him. He wouldn't go all in and be too much, too soon.

His cell phone vibrated in his sports coat pocket and he frowned seeing the unfamiliar Alaska number lighting up the display. "Hello?"

"Gus? It's Leslie, Levi's fiancée."

Selena's secret best friend. His heart raced hearing from the no-nonsense state trooper. He'd felt as though she was on the fence about him dating Selena, a protective instinct that had been endearing. Obviously, she hadn't wanted to see her friend get hurt. By him. And he'd never thought he would be giving this woman a reason to tear him a new one right now. "Everything okay?"

"No. You need to fix things."

He sighed and ran a hand through his hair. "I'm trying. She won't answer my calls or texts. I'm in LA now, but I don't think she'd appreciate me stopping by her place." He had thought about it, but the last thing she deserved was him invading her space or being too pushy. She'd set a boundary and he wouldn't hurt her further by crossing it. "She's made it clear she doesn't want anything to do with me."

"She's upset and she's pushing you away because she doesn't want to get hurt."

"Three minutes," the production assistant said, motioning for him to put the phone away.

"I didn't mean to hurt her," he told Leslie. "It was a

dumb, impulsive move and I can't take it back. I let her down."

"We all make mistakes," Leslie said. "Selena is one of the most forgiving people I know. You just need to find a way to prove to her that you really do care."

"What do I do?" He'd take any advice Leslie had on the subject. He was caught in limbo between wanting to give her space and being terrified that she was seeing that as him not caring.

"I don't know, but she's a hopeless romantic, so think big gesture."

"Big gesture?"

"You've seen a rom-com, right?"

Too many. All week, he'd been watching Selena's movies. Seeing her fall in love on-screen had been torture, but it was the only way to see her, hear her voice. It was pathetic, but he missed her. He'd started to convince himself that things with him hadn't meant more to her than the on-screen performances. Anything to dull the ache in his chest.

"Two minutes. We need you in chair," the production assistant told him, an annoyed expression on his face as he tapped his watch.

Shit. He had to focus on saving his career. Not easy now that Leslie had put the more pressing, more important issue front of mind again. "Leslie, I'm on set, first day at the new studio. Live in less than a minute, so I have to go, but I'll think of something," he said quickly.

"You better, 'cause if you hurt my best friend again, I'm coming to LA to kick your ass."

He fully believed she would. And if only Selena had heard Leslie refer to her as her best friend, she might be happy enough to let her guard down and let him back in.

He put the phone on silent as he headed toward the set,

where the two senior sports reporters sat drinking coffee and discussing the football game they were going to be covering.

Big gesture? What the hell could he do? Selena had everything. He couldn't exactly propose or anything. They weren't quite there just yet.

Though the idea of being with her, living with her, sharing a life with her, hit him with such an overwhelming sense of longing that maybe they weren't too far from it. Was she in the same place?

Leslie's call had given him hope, but he was at a loss as to how to get her attention.

A makeup woman applied pressed powder to his forehead as the lighting crew checked the spotlights focused on him. Big gesture…

"Hey, man… Just out of curiosity, you don't have any other ex-girlfriends we should be concerned about, do you?" Myca, the lead broadcaster, asked with a grin. His tanned skin made his superwhite teeth almost glow. Aileen used to say that the guy reminded her of an Oompa-Loompa from *Charlie and the Chocolate Factory*. But right now, he was too new for a snarky comeback. He needed to earn their respect.

"Nope. All clear," Gus said, suppressing a sigh. Eventually, they'd accept him; at this moment, he was the new guy with the history.

"Thirty seconds to live," the production assistant informed them.

Gus sat straighter, checking his tie and clearing his throat. He scanned his notes but couldn't get his mind completely in the game. Would Selena be watching? The words on the teleprompter blurred as he stared at the crew, waiting for the signal that they were live.

Despite her ending things, he knew she cared about him. She might never admit to watching, but she wouldn't miss this.

"And we're live," the production assistant said.

Cameras rolling, Myca launched the broadcast with a recap of the previous night's hockey game. Gus had watched it. He'd rewatched the goals and the fights. He was holding his own in the discussion. Myca was even agreeing with his take on things. So far, so good. He started to relax, settle in…

Big gesture. Leslie and her call were still in the back of his mind.

They moved on to the football game and Gus's heart pounded in his ears. He could do this. He could get Selena's attention and maybe earn himself another shot with her. It was worth the massive risk he'd be taking.

"That play by Shepard was killer…" He paused. *Here goes nothing.* "And speaking of killer…" He cleared his throat. "Coming to film festivals late this year is an amazing new thriller featuring Selena Hudson and, well, me. You all need to see her in this performance. It's unlike anything she's ever done and she'll blow you away." He swallowed hard. "She blew me away with her talent and her heart. Her commitment to this moving story and her portrayal of a complex, wounded character. I'm just so proud to be a part of this incredible project. Check out *Alice Was Here* at a film festival near you," he said, staring straight into the camera as he delivered the movie plug.

The cameraman sighed as he cut to commercial, and next to him, his fellow broadcasters were looking at him with matching expressions that suggested they really couldn't believe he'd be so stupid. Throwing away this second chance, this dream job. He swallowed hard, not regretting his actions for a second. It was the only way to get Selena's attention and prove to her that he was truly sorry for hurting her. Putting everything he ever wanted on the line for her was his big gesture.

He could only hope she was watching.

"Did he just flush his career down the toilet again?"

Jay's disbelief echoed in Selena's ears as she stared, dumbfounded, at the eighty-inch flat-screen in her living room as Sports Beat cut abruptly to commercial. She'd known he'd gotten the job from Jay. And she'd known that morning was his first day on set from Jay. And it was Jay who'd practically forced her to tune in. She'd expected the tug at her chest in seeing him, but she hadn't expected the massive anxiety attack threatening to kill her after what she'd just witnessed.

"I think he did," she croaked.

For her. He'd just plugged their indie film on live TV, during a live broadcast, on one of the most popular sports networks on the planet. Her gut twisted and her palms sweat. What was he thinking? He'd gone on and on about Sports Beat being his all-time dream station. He'd been offered a second chance at the career he loved. He'd been given the opportunity of a lifetime and he'd just blown it. To get her attention? To apologize publicly? To show her he really did care about the movie…about her?

"I can't believe he plugged the movie on TV," Jay said, looking ecstatic as he paced in front of the television. "I mean, the tabloid thing was a huge mistake, but this is incredible exposure." Immediately his cell phone started chiming with new messages.

"Yep," she said, sitting there staring at the television.

She bit her lip as she waited for the broadcast to resume. Would he still be sitting in that third chair?

Jay sat next to her and reached for her hand as they waited. "Guess he was desperate to get your attention, huh?"

She swallowed hard. "Guess so." Maybe she should have taken at least one of his calls or responded to one of his texts. But she'd never thought he'd do something so drastic.

"Feel bad for ignoring him now, don't you?" he said, shooting her a knowing look.

"Little bit." She sighed. "But what the hell was he thinking? He wanted this so bad! He deserved this second shot!"

Jay eyed her with a lovesick look. "Obviously, he wants you even more. He wants to deserve a second shot with you."

Her pulse raced. Holy shit. Gus had basically chosen her over his career with no guarantee that she'd forgive him or give him another chance. He cared about her that much? "Oh, God..." She pressed a hand to her chest.

The sports broadcast came back on and Gus was no longer on set. Her heart sank into her stomach as she fell back against the sofa cushions. "Oh, no, I think he just threw it all away."

Jay stared at her in disbelief. "Then why are you still sitting here? Go make it worth it!"

Could she? She wanted to, but she also wanted to kill him for jeopardizing so much. "I'm going to strangle him," she said, unable to suppress the pleasure of knowing he must love her.

"Make sure you kiss him first," Jay said with a wink as she stood and hurried out of the room. "And give him one for me!"

CHAPTER TWENTY-TWO

WAITING IN MALIN'S office twenty minutes later, Gus searched within himself for feelings of remorse for what he'd just done. He couldn't find any. There was no doubt he'd be fired. He wasn't even sure why Malin had requested to see him. He'd expected security to just escort him straight out of the building from the studio set.

Unlike his last career suicide move, he wasn't feeling nauseous or anxious this time. He'd known the consequences of his actions and had been fully cognizant of what he was doing this time. And he'd gone for it. One last-ditch attempt to get another chance with the woman he was in love with.

He checked his phone. The only thing bothering him was that he still hadn't heard from Selena. Maybe his actions hadn't been enough. Maybe she really had moved on, or maybe he'd hurt her too bad for her to forgive him—or maybe she hadn't seen it. Maybe she hadn't watched.

If so, she was the only person in his life to miss it.

Three text messages from his sister, all caps asking whether he'd lost his mind; two from Levi, one praising him for going after the girl, the other telling him he was a moron; one from his grandfather that was just one word: firecrackers; and one from a potential new agent he'd reached out to earlier: Lose my number.

Everyone had been waiting, watching with bated breath.

And he'd essentially let everyone down…but not himself. Leslie was right. Selena had needed a big gesture from him after his mess-up in order to believe in him—in them—and he didn't regret it.

He just wished she'd seen the damn thing.

What if she had, and she still didn't care?

His palms sweat at the thought that maybe she really just wasn't into him as much as he thought. As much as he was into her. He checked his cell phone again—still nothing.

Malin entered, followed by her assistant, Tam, and he cleared his throat, preparing his apology and "thank you for the opportunity" speech. She closed the door and sat behind the desk this time.

Tam's expression was unreadable as she sat next to her boss, her fingers flying over the keys of her cell phone. No doubt she was preparing a media statement to the effect that Sports Beat did not endorse the thriller or Selena Hudson's career in any way and they had released Gus Orosco from the position on the reporting desk.

Malin stared at him, her dark eyes almost expressionless. *Here it comes.*

Nope, still just staring. Was she waiting for him to say something first? "Malin, I…"

She held up a hand.

"Give her a minute," Tam said, not looking up from her phone. "She's working through something."

His hopes rose a little. No immediate firing? Could he really be getting away with this most recent on-air stunt? No freaking way.

Malin turned to Tam with a nod of her head. "Okay, let's go with it," she said.

Go with what? Gus turned his attention to Tam, and she

set her phone aside. "Hashtag Romantic Reporter," she said in a serious, strategic tone.

He frowned. "What?"

"It's your new social media hashtag." She picked up the cell phone and glanced at it. "Yep. Already trending."

Malin's smile was wide. "Tam's a social media genius."

He was still confused. "I'm not sure I know what's going on," he said. In fact, he knew he had no idea what was going on. He'd expected to have been kicked to the curb by now. The final nail in his backup coffin secure.

"We've put a spin on what just happened on air. You are now known as the hopeless romantic sports broadcaster who can't keep his personal life off air," Tam said.

Was she serious? He was happy not to be losing his job, but he wasn't so thrilled that they'd spun it that way. They hadn't even discussed it with him. Though he hadn't ex-actly enlightened them to his plan either, and it wasn't like he could deny the truth of the new social media handle. He was a hopeless romantic who couldn't keep his personal life off air.

"From now on, we want more of your relationships on air. Find a way to weave it into every broadcast," Tam said, looking at her phone. "The broadcast clip has now been turned into a meme."

At least it was better than the last one, but he still wasn't completely clear on what they wanted from him. "Every broadcast? Talk about my relationships?" That could be a problem, seeing as how he didn't currently have one. A quick glance at his phone revealed that, nope, Selena still hadn't called or texted.

Tam nodded. "Yes. Viewers love snippets into famous people's lives, so this will work as long as we support it here at the network and make it fun."

"Sports fans would be into this?" He wasn't convinced.

Malin leaned forward. "Most of our viewers? No. Absolutely not. But new viewers will start to watch because of you. People who really don't care about sports will tune in to see the latest love update from Gus Orosco."

He sighed. That was one way to increase viewership. He wasn't thrilled that this was the new direction for his career, but he wasn't being fired. That was what mattered. Unfortunately, now he would need to invent relationship updates.

"Are you in?"

Did he really have a choice? He was already trending. "Right... Yeah, absolutely."

"Great. So, we're good. Tomorrow you can move to a prime-time spot," Malin said.

He blinked. Not only was he not getting fired, he was getting a promotion? "Are you serious?"

Malin nodded. "Yes. But make it interesting."

Interesting. Right. Maybe he could start by pouring out his heartache on set. He checked his phone again as he stood. Radio silence from Selena echoed in his chest.

This day really hadn't gone as he'd hoped.

PULLING UP ONTO the studio lot, Selena quickly turned into Brock's private parking stall and cut the engine. Would Gus even still be there? Unfortunately, she wasn't sure where else to find him. Her ghosting him had resulted in not having a clue where he was staying in LA. Was he even still here? Or had he headed straight to the airport after jeopardizing his career again?

The entire thirty-minute drive over, her mind had reeled and her desperation to see and talk to him had grown. She hadn't been wrong about him or what they had together.

He did love her, and she was so in love with him that she could barely breathe. Would he be regretting his actions?

"Call from Leslie... Call from Leslie..." Her Bluetooth announced the incoming call, and she hit Ignore, cutting the engine and climbing out of her car.

Her heart raced as she hurried toward the front doors of the studio and nearly collided with Gus as he exited. "Whoa," he said, bracing her before she crashed into him. Then his eyes widened, recognizing her. "Selena?"

Relief in his voice made her wish she'd called him, but she hadn't wanted to say this by phone. She wanted to tell him to his face how she was feeling about him—about them—and what he'd done.

"Hi," she said sympathetically. She felt great that he'd done what he had for her, and simultaneously terrible for the fact that he'd lost his dream job to get her attention. No guy had ever done anything so selfless and wonderful for her. She swallowed hard. "I saw the broadcast."

He nodded, studying her. "I was desperate to get your attention."

She slapped his shoulder softly. "Well, you could have sent a million roses or something..."

He shook his head. "That wouldn't have worked. Anyone could have done that. You deserved much more than that." He took a deep breath. "I wanted you to truly know..." He paused and her heart raced.

"Know what?"

"How sorry I am and how much I love you," he said, reaching out to touch her cheek.

She'd missed his touch, missed seeing him, missed hearing those words. She stepped closer, into his arms. "I love you, too. Ignoring you was torture."

"I deserved the silent treatment," he said, pulling her into him and holding her tight.

"Maybe… But now I feel terrible that you ruined your career again." She sighed. Maybe there was a way he could talk to Malin…or another station.

He grinned, reaching for his phone. "I assume you haven't been on social media."

She frowned. "What am I missing?"

"Hashtag Romantic Reporter."

"Who's that?"

"Me. They decided to put a spin on things instead of firing me," he said with a laugh.

"Are you okay with that?" she asked gently. It was definitely better than losing his dream job, but not if he was going to be a joke. He deserved to be taken seriously in the industry. He was an amazing reporter.

"I got bumped to a prime-time spot," he said with a shrug. "And the idea is actually growing on me. I am a hopeless romantic, so I might as well go with it."

She kissed him and savored the feel of his mouth pressed to hers, his arms holding her close. She was where she belonged, where she wanted to be. She was so in love with him and she couldn't wait to share a life with him.

"There's just one thing," he said.

"What's that?"

"They want me to share relationship info on air… So are you going to be okay with me publicizing us that way?"

She grinned. "I'm sure we can provide some newsworthy content," she said, kissing him again.

He stared deep into her eyes, and she felt all the love in his heart. Love that equaled her own. "I love you."

"I love you, Hashtag Romantic Reporter. Now, let's get out of here and start creating content."

So much for singlesville. Instead of 365 days alone, she planned on spending every minute of every day falling more and more in love.

EPILOGUE

Six months later...

"I DON'T THINK I've ever been so nervous in my life."

Selena laughed as she glanced at Gus, sweating in the theater seat next to her. He was dressed in a dark suit and white dress shirt, his red tie matching her bodycon dress, and she knew they looked amazing together at the first viewing of the film at the Alaska International Film Festival. They'd decided it was the obvious choice for the first showing, and she was excited to be premiering it where it had been made and to be able to share it with her friends and those who'd worked on the film. "You're nervous? It's just the make-or-break of *my* career about to happen."

He reached for her hand and held it tight in both of his. "This is going to be great. The movie's great. You're great."

He looked close to an anxiety attack, and it was so endearing she had to resist the urge to kiss him. "Gus, relax. We've seen the postproduction version. This movie is amazing." Funny that having to calm him down was making her less nervous. Reassuring him with the truth helped it to reflect in her own confidence.

He looked around the theater. "This place is packed."

That was the only unnerving part. She was one of the bigger names on the indie film fest circuit that year, and everyone was waiting to see what she'd put her entire career on the line for. Success or failure, there would be nay-sayers and there would be supporters.

Either way, she was going to be fine. Sitting next to her was the only opinion that mattered, the only support she needed. The last six months with Gus had completely put everything in perspective. Her career was still so important to her, a huge part of who she was, but now it was relationship first, career second. Their love for one another was what mattered most and they each put the other first, above all else.

She looked past him to where Jay sat next to Doug. The two of them hadn't exactly figured out how to move forward with another shot together yet, but they were working on it, and Selena smiled seeing Doug reach for Jay's hand. This movie had already changed lives, hers definitely for the better.

Behind her, Leslie squeezed her shoulder, and she turned to smile at her friend, the nine-month baby bump filling her with even more joy. *Good luck*, Leslie mouthed. And next to her, Levi gave a thumbs-up.

Selena glanced at Kaia, sitting with her double set of parents in the next row, and the little girl looked like she was vibrating. She winked at her and then settled back in her seat as the theater lights dimmed. She took a deep breath as Gus clutched her hand even tighter in his. They'd done their best. They'd left everything out there on-screen.

Now it was up to this roomful of movie enthusiasts, critics and reviewers to decide its fate.

As the movie credits rolled an hour and forty-two minutes later, silence echoed throughout the theater. Selena stared at the white letters scrolling on the black screen, and a sense of pride and accomplishment had the words blurring.

Then the eruption of applause all around her was the validation she actually no longer needed, but it was a huge source of relief and happiness, nonetheless.

"They loved it," Gus said, standing and pulling her to her feet. They turned and waved to the crowd. Next to her, Jay and the rest of the crew stood and accepted the well-deserved show of appreciation.

She beamed at Gus. "We did it."

He took her face between his hands and kissed her gently. "You did it."

And in that moment, it felt like there was nothing she couldn't do. She cleared her throat. "I have something else to tell you," she said.

He held her tight and stared into her eyes. "What's that?"

"Hudson Productions would like to place an offer on Orosco Campgrounds," she said with a wide smile.

He frowned. "Hudson Productions?"

"My new production company." She'd made the decision the week before. Whether this indie film was successful or not, she now had the courage to pursue her own passions, her own path. "I'm thinking that other companies will want to film there as well, so it would be a great investment."

He nodded. "I can't imagine a better future for Orosco Campgrounds," he said, kissing her gently. "I can't imagine any future for me without you in it."

Her heart filled as she kissed him again. "So, you'll consider my offer?"

"Only if you'll consider mine," he said, releasing her and dropping to one knee.

Her eyes widened as he reached into his jacket pocket and pulled out a Tiffany blue box. He looked nervous as he slowly opened the lid, revealing the most beautiful diamond solitaire engagement ring she'd ever seen. Its sparkle reflected off the walls of the theater.

Her hand covered her mouth as emotions welled in her chest. He wanted to marry her? He loved her that much?

"Marry me?" he asked.

She nodded quickly. "Yes! Definitely yes!" She pulled him to his feet and hugged him tight as another round of applause erupted around them in the theater. She could feel all the love and support around her, and it was the most uplifting feeling she'd ever experienced.

"I love you," Gus said, staring into her eyes as he slid the ring onto her finger.

"I love you more," she said, taking in this moment where everything was absolutely perfect. Taking a chance on herself had paid off and taking a chance on them was the first step to Selena's very own happily-ever-after. She shivered as goose bumps covered her skin.

Turned out, the right life choices also gave you chills.

* * * * *

ACKNOWLEDGMENTS

THIS SERIES WAS so much fun to write, and it wouldn't have been possible without my wonderful agent, Jill Marsal, and my HQN editors, Dana Grimaldi and Susan Swinwood. I am forever grateful for all the support, feedback and insightfulness that made each book so much stronger. Special thank-you to Kate Studer for her editing on this series and wonderful notes! The HQN art department did such a fantastic job on the covers and I couldn't possibly decide which one is my favorite. A huge thank you to the beautiful and talented Maeve Quinlan for all the film industry insight. All mistakes are my own. Thank you so much to my readers who have followed the series and reviewed the books and sent emails to let me know that you love Wild River and its community as much as I do (or almost ;)). And thank you to my family for always believing, always encouraging and always being the support I couldn't do this without. XO Jen.

An Alaskan
Christmas
Homecoming

CHAPTER ONE

IT WASN'T THE sight of her sister blissfully in love that bothered Jade Frazier. Or the fact that Maddie was in love with a guy Jade had dated first. She'd gladly given her blessing on that union. Heck, she'd been responsible for setting them up on the Valentine's Day Blind Date Ice Fishing event hosted by SnowTrek Tours the year before. No. It wasn't her sister's happiness driving Jade to the brink. It was *her* single status after the last several failed relationships. Staring at another upcoming holiday alone was depressing.

Ho ho, holiday loneliness.

It was this damn small town. She'd lived in the ski resort town in Alaska her entire life. Which meant she knew every man in town and had dated at least half of them. The ones her age, the ones a few years older... If she kept climbing the age scale, she'd either be dating divorcés or look like she had daddy issues.

She scanned The Drunk Tank, the local watering hole on Main Street, hoping for new blood... She'd even settle for a holiday fling with a tourist. But the faces illuminated by the string of Christmas lights decorating the bar were all far too familiar.

She sighed. Loudly.

Loudly enough to catch the attention of her sister and Mike in the booth across from her. They slowly peeled away from one another and turned to face her.

"So, how's the fashion degree coming along?" Mike asked politely. He didn't see Maddie shake her head beside him.

"Jade switched courses to interior design," Maddie said.

Her sister's encouragement was unyielding, and Jade appreciated the support, but she could hear in Maddie's tone that this switching subjects for her online degree was getting old. From makeup artistry to special effects to fashion design to interior design... At twenty-eight years old, Jade had to get serious about her future career.

But this was it. Interior design was her calling. And it wasn't as though she'd switched from rocket science to botany. At least her attempts to find her "thing" had been in the same vein. And this final term assignment would prove that to everyone.

"It's going great, actually. We have a really fun assignment that accounts for fifty percent of our grade—decorating a business for the holiday season."

Mike glanced around. "It's already December. Are there any businesses who haven't been decorated since October? Ow!" he said, glancing at Maddie, who'd obviously kicked him under the table.

Jade refused to acknowledge the truth of Mike's words or get discouraged. Sure, she was getting a late start, but there had to be some shop in town in desperate need of her help. Noticing a bandage on Mike's forearm, she changed the subject. "Did you hurt yourself on a tour?" Mike was a tour guide for SnowTrek Tours and often led wilderness expeditions in the unpredictable Alaskan backwoods.

"No. I got a new tattoo," he said.

Jade wrinkled her nose. She wasn't a fan of body modifications. "What is it?"

Mike lifted the edge of the bandage to display a watercolor design of an ice fishing hut with the aurora borealis in the background. Obviously, a tribute to how he'd met her sister. As much as Jade disliked tattoos, the gesture was romantic, she'd give him that.

And it looked really well done, unlike the messy, unprofessional-looking ones that often left the Black Heart tattoo shop in town. "It looks good. Where did you get it done?"

"Redemption Tattoo—the new shop on Main Street."

Her mouth dropped. "The one opened by the ex-con?"

Mike shot her a look. "How about less judgment and more open-mindedness? Griffin's a good guy. A Wild River local who did some time for falling in with the wrong crowd, that's all. He's here to get his life back on track."

Maddie looked admiringly at Mike, but Jade wasn't so sure. Wild River was an accepting place, but she suspected Griffin would have an uphill battle in gaining back the respect of his hometown.

HE WAS LIVING in a holiday television special.

Wild River, Alaska, was a quaint tourist town, and despite it being his hometown, Griffin Geller stuck out like a sore thumb.

As he prepared his tattoo gun with fresh black ink, he stared out at the snow and the white mountaintops in the distance. He missed Las Vegas, the year-round mild weather, the bright lights of the city and the exciting, fast-paced lifestyle...but that wasn't the future he needed.

Moving there ten years ago right after high school graduation had felt like a dream. Striking out on his own, working his way up by apprenticing in local tattoo shops, learning the craft from artists he'd admired from afar, he'd been living his best life. Tattooing was the only thing he was ever good at.

Unfortunately, he hadn't had the opportunity to do much of it since opening his shop on Main Street the month before. He'd figured there was a market for his services, given that the only tattoo shop in town had been shut down twice in the last year for health code violations. But it seemed no one was looking for new ink...

The only customers he'd had all week were the two women sitting side by side, treating the experience like a spa day.

He snapped on his plastic gloves and rolled his stool toward them. "What are we getting, ladies? Matching roses? Inspirational quotes?"

"We actually just want our existing tattoos redone. They've faded," Cassie Reynolds, the owner of SnowTrek Tours, said. He recognized her from the one business association meeting he'd attended before vowing never to return again. The stares and judgmental looks had been too much.

He examined the faded *Best* and *Friend* tattoos on each woman's wrist. This would take all of three minutes and he could charge maybe ten dollars for the work.

Jail had been less painful.

His business would struggle to survive here in this small town, but if it meant living on the straight and narrow, staying far away from the trouble of his past, this was where he needed to be. He was lucky to be getting this new start.

Three minutes and forty-six seconds later, he removed the plastic gloves and forced a smile. "All done."

"We love them. Thank you," Cassie said as they approached the counter.

The other woman with her was some sort of doctor at Wild River Community Hospital. He'd nearly gagged as he'd worked when she filled her friend in on an angio-plasty she'd performed the night before. She was looking at the tattoo with appreciation, but she'd barely looked at him the entire time she'd been here. This had obviously been Cassie's idea.

The adventure tour owner scanned the shop as she paid. "You haven't decorated yet."

"Decorated?" He took the cash and handed her back change from the twenty.

She waved it away. "For Christmas. Not sure if you've noticed the abundance of holiday spirit all over town..."

He'd noticed. Just been desperate to avoid it. He cleared his throat. "Christmas isn't exactly my thing."

"Shocking," the doctor said under her breath.

It might actually shock her to know it used to be his thing. He'd loved everything to do with the holidays—the sights, sounds and smells. His family owned the local diner on Main Street, which was open every day of the year, so they hadn't celebrated in the traditional sense, but they'd gathered with the community on Christmas Eve and Christmas Day, families meeting up to eat together or lonely residents with nowhere to go. It had been a special time of year. One he'd looked forward to.

Getting arrested on Christmas Eve had quickly changed that.

"You at least need to decorate the window for the local business association competition," Cassie said, sliding back into a thermal winter jacket.

He shook his head. "I don't think I'll enter."

The doctor sighed and tried a more direct approach. "Look, if you want to draw in business, people need to be less afraid of you."

"Erika," Cassie hissed at the woman before sending him an apologetic look.

"What? It's true," Erika said. "The holiday decorations will show them you're one of us. You're not whatever embellished rumor they think you are."

He sighed. He'd rather tattoo a Christmas tree on his forehead, but she had a point. "I'll think about it."

Cassie smiled. "Great. If you need any decorations, I have a ton left over from my reindeer display."

"Thank you." Her kindness wasn't unappreciated. He suspected their tattoo touch-ups were more to help his struggling new business than because they'd really needed them.

Cassie offered an encouraging smile as they headed toward the door. "Hang in there. The first year is always the hardest."

She had no idea.

The bell above the door chimed as they exited onto Main Street, and Griffin sat on one of the plush leather waiting room chairs and stared out at the falling snow.

How the hell had he let his life turn out this way?

CHAPTER TWO

HAD *EVERYONE* IN town gotten an early start to their decorating?

Bundled warmly in her faux fur winter jacket and fashionable yet practical heeled leather boots, Jade carried her interior design portfolio down Main Street, eager to show off her holiday-themed ideas. But every business had their storefront displays completed already. She'd tried the local seniors' home, thinking they'd appreciate her help, but the decorating committee—a group of adorable, feisty little old ladies—had shooed her out of the complex quicker than she could say *Bah, humbug!* The Wild River Resort Hotel had claimed that they were going with the same decorators as last year. The fancy five-star accommodations boasted the same white trees and silver accents throughout the common areas every year, and Jade hadn't been successful convincing them to try something new.

Improving her sales skills would be her biggest challenge in this career. She was confident in her decorating skills, but her pitch to potential clients was somewhat lacking. She didn't have the experience, so she needed the work, but how did she get work without the experience?

Acquiring a location and gaining a business's trust were part of the assignment and she couldn't fail. She was personable, well-liked in town… She just needed to find a procrastinator who was too busy to do their own decorating.

As she passed Redemption Tattoo, she paused, seeing a man hanging fake sparkly green garland that looked like it had been reused over and over since the eighties from one corner of the window to the other.

Ho ho, hell no.

She hesitated briefly before squaring her shoulders and opening the door. That tacky eyesore of a decoration would bring down the property value on Main Street, and obviously this guy needed her expert advice as much as she needed the job.

A blast of heat hit her as she entered and looked around. It wasn't at all like the other tattoo shop in town. This one was clean and nicely furnished in leather and chrome. Tattoo designs were framed and hung on the wall, not held up with duct tape or displayed in faded old binders. The air smelled fresh and sterile as well. Definitely not what she'd been expecting.

"Can I help you?" the man from the window asked.

Confidence radiated from her as she said, "Actually, I'm here to help you."

"Doubt it. Look, whatever you're selling, I'm not interested," he said, his gaze landing on her portfolio.

"Is the owner here?" she asked. She wouldn't waste her sales pitch on an employee…no matter how attractive he was. She took in the dark brown hair, combed to one side, partially shaved underneath, the thin, muscular frame and eyes that were so dark they looked almost black from this distance. She didn't recognize him. New in town? Someone Griffin Geller had brought back from Las Vegas?

Maybe, if she secured the decorating opportunity here at the shop, the two of them could get to know one another…

Nope. She wasn't here for a date. She was here for a job.

"I'm the owner," the guy said.

She blinked. "What?"

"Let me guess—you were expecting some big, bald, burly guy with teardrop tattoos on his face?"

"Yes," she said honestly.

He laughed and her stomach was a field of fluttering butterflies at the gentleness of the sound. What the hell? This guy who looked like he couldn't harm a wasp if it was stinging him in the eyeball was an ex-con? Again, definitely not what she'd been expecting.

"What are you selling?" he asked in her silence.

Obviously, her blunt honesty had earned her thirty seconds of his time.

Repressing her surprise, she took a deep breath. "I'm an interior designer and I'd like to offer you my services to create your holiday window display."

He shook his head. "Nah, I got it covered."

"You certainly do not," she said, eyeing the box of mismatched decorations in an old SnowTrek Tours box. Obviously, Cassie Reynolds's discards.

"It's not a big deal. I'm not really trying to win the contest or anything." He waved a hand.

Crap, this was her only shot unless she wanted to decorate a back alley. She thought fast. "But you are trying to build a business here in town?"

He tossed the ugly green garland back into the box. "I'd prefer to attract clients because of my tattooing skills, not because of my holiday spirit."

She sensed the holiday spirit wasn't something he had much of. "You need to get them in the door first."

He sighed. "Look, I can't afford your services. This space on Main Street is already depleting my savings and, well, business so far hasn't been great."

"I'll do it for free." She wasn't doing this for money, yet.

"That's bad business sense."

She sighed. "Look, I'm a student of interior design and I need to display my skills with an actual client as part of my term grade. Everyone else in town has already finished their displays. I'm running out of options." Maybe she sounded desperate, but she was willing to play that card if she had to.

Griffin looked like he was considering it, but then he shook his head. "I don't think it's a good idea."

Still, he'd been considering it, which gave her the courage not to take no as his final answer. "Give me one good reason why not."

He cleared his throat. "I'm sure you've heard who I am by now and all about my past... Do you want your first client to be...?"

"Someone with bad taste in garland?" she finished quickly, picking up the strand he'd been about to hang.

His expression softened slightly, and he sighed. "Okay. You're right. This isn't my thing." He gestured toward the box of decorations. "It's all yours."

She laughed. "Yeah, no. Those aren't going to work. I'll be back tomorrow morning at nine a.m." She headed for the door. "Your holiday display is going to blow your mind."

He nodded. "Okay...great...thanks, um...?"

"Jade. Jade Frazier."

"Thanks, Jade," he said, and the way he said her name had those damn butterflies doing cartwheels.

HE DIDN'T REGRET allowing Jade Frazier to volunteer to decorate his window. No, he was so far beyond regret that it was a distant dot in his rearview.

This was a bad idea for so many reasons.

He was a "bad apple," and despite hoping to reinvent his

future, write a new narrative and all the other life-coach-y things his prison reformation officer had spouted, he still had a reputation that no one was going to forget so easily. Damn, his own family had refused to talk to him or acknowledge the existence of his new shop, a block away from the family diner, in the three months he'd been back.

Jade seemed like a nice woman. She was trying to start her own career. Associating herself and her interior decorating company with him wasn't a great idea.

Unfortunately, when he turned the corner the next morning at eight forty-five and saw her standing outside the shop with three large cardboard boxes on the ground next to her, he didn't have the heart to tell her he'd reconsidered. If only she wasn't so attractive, this might be easier, but since she'd walked into his shop the day before, he'd had a hard time getting the image of her dark emerald green eyes out of his mind.

He scanned the quiet street for a vehicle but didn't see one. "Did you get dropped off?" Definitely harder to send her away now.

"Took the bus. I only live ten minutes away."

He eyed the boxes as he unlocked the door. "You took the bus with those?"

She grinned. "Not as weak as I look."

Determined, he'd give her that much. He opened the door and turned off the alarm as she bent to pick up the boxes. "Wait. I'll help." He went back out, stacked two and carried them inside.

She'd already removed her coat and scarf and hat, and his mouth went slightly dry at the sight of her in tight-fitting jeans and a snug holiday-red V-necked sweater that almost had him believing in Santa Claus again.

Damn, this was really not a good idea. He hadn't been with a woman in two years...

He cleared his throat. "So, how long do you think this will take?"

"Just a few days," she said, bending to open one of the boxes.

His eyes landed on her ass and he averted his gaze. A few days. He'd never last a few days. "That long? It's just some decorations."

"Great work takes time. Art takes time. Think of it as a full back piece. You can't do it all in one sitting, right? You do it over a few sessions, layer things in. Gain new perspective and inspiration as you work."

He swallowed hard. "I was just thinking it would only take an hour or two."

She waved a hand. "Don't worry. The contest judging isn't for another week and a half."

Right, 'cause that was what he was worried about. "Okay, well, I'll leave you to it. There will be coffee and doughnuts in the back room if you want some."

"Thanks," she called over her shoulder as she took things out of the boxes. She began to hum a Christmas carol and he headed into the back room. He started the coffee and then he turned on the store music.

But even the sound of heavy metal blasting through the speakers couldn't drown out the voice in his head telling him that having Jade Frazier around for the next few days was the most dangerous situation he'd encountered in a long time.

JADE HAD SPENT all afternoon coming up with a theme for the tattoo shop window. She'd spent all evening buying the necessary items for her creation, and the window display was coming along exactly as she had envisioned it. The upside-down black Christmas tree adorned with flickering white lights—not twinkling, but actually flickering like goth candles—was the perfect spin on traditional Christmas decor. She'd been lucky to find it, as it had been the only one in stock at the department store in town... naturally. Not exactly a bestseller.

And the statue of the mythical creature Zanzibar, which she'd found at the local hobby and collectibles shop, was the perfect addition to the display. The gothic dragon climbing a tall winter castle was similar to the shop's logo, tying everything together nicely in dark red, silver and black metallic hues.

She was more than confident that she could pull off an A-grade design, but she hadn't anticipated how hard it would be to work so close to Griffin.

The shop had been quiet all morning. Only a few teenagers had stopped by, planning tattoos they weren't old enough to get, so it had been just the two of them. He'd sat at a desk, drawing and sketching new designs, and a few times she'd caught him glancing her way as she worked. Each time their gazes met, her heart pounded in her chest.

Reminding herself that he was not a good match for her only went so far when he was exactly her usual type. Clean-cut, clean-shaven, thin but muscular and not too tall. He was gorgeous and friendly. A professional business owner with artistic talent. The only thing she could list in the Con column was "ex-con."

Which was arguably a big one, but didn't everyone deserve a second chance?

She knew through the rumor mill that he was the son of Carla Geller, owner of Carla's Diner on Main Street. The fifties-style restaurant was a popular place in Wild River, thanks to the delicious food and the warm welcome Carla bestowed on all her customers. Carla's daughters, Molly and Gillian, worked as waitresses, and the business was a family affair.

Therefore, even Griffin's family was a checkmark in the Pro column. Having been raised by their father, who passed away several years before, leaving Jade and Maddie without any other family in Wild River, Jade always longed for a big, close-knit family like the Gellers.

Of course, she was getting far too ahead of herself. She needed to focus on this window display, and then, maybe, she could focus on the hot guy who was making it hard to focus.

HE WAS DRAWING the line at holiday music. He played metal in his shop. Only metal.

But he was quickly losing the battle to the feisty, energetic woman standing in front of him. "It's Christmas. People expect to hear holiday music playing inside the stores."

He folded his arms across his chest. "Not in tattoo shops, they don't."

She sighed. "Maybe big, burly, bald men don't, but tattoos are more mainstream now. Everyone's getting one."

Didn't he know it. His only customer that day had been an eighty-two-year-old grandmother adding her third great-grandchild's name to the string of names already on her forearm. *She* might have appreciated the holiday music. She'd insisted he turn down the "crap" he was playing.

Still, he was holding firm to this. "Nope. Sorry. All of this is already too much." He gestured at the decorations all over his shop.

Jade sighed. "Okay, I can compromise."

Doubtful. He suspected she never had to. Those emerald green eyes could make a man do anything, if said man was in a position to allow himself to fall for her.

Lucky for Griffin, he was not that man.

He waited as she shuffled through the music on her iPod and then connected it to the speakers. The familiar tune of "We Wish You a Merry Christmas" started to play, and he folded his arms across his chest. "Sounds like the same old holiday music to me."

"Wait for it…"

He listened closer. Something was different in this remake. "Are they saying 'metal' instead of 'merry'?"

Jade grinned as the beat changed and the sound of screaming lyrics nearly blasted his eardrums.

Holy shit, she'd actually found a heavy metal Christmas album.

"So…we're good?" she asked with a cocky smile.

He sighed. "We're good." Unfortunately, he was far from good. He was falling for the sweetest, smartest, sexiest woman in Wild River, and he didn't deserve the chance to pursue her.

CHAPTER THREE

HER DELIVERY WAS here right on time.

"More stuff?" Griffin asked the next morning as Jade signed the delivery slip and carefully carried the box stamped Fragile to the window. She set it down and, using a box cutter, opened it.

"This is the best part," she said, reaching into the box and taking out a white frosted Christmas tree bulb. Even better than she'd hoped. She held the ornament up to show him. "What do you think?"

He squinted as he peered at the black-and-gray design on the bulb. Then his eyes widened. "Is that one of my tattoo designs?"

She nodded eagerly, handing it to him and then reaching into the box for another one. "Hope you don't mind. I took a few photos of the black-and-gray designs and had these rush ordered overnight from the imprinting store in town. They turned out so well!"

Griffin seemed slightly conflicted as he looked at the dozen bulbs inside the box. "You had these custom made? Overnight?"

She nodded, but her enthusiasm faltered. "You don't like them? I thought they could serve a dual purpose. Nice, fitting decorations for the tree and a way to showcase your work in the window... But we don't have to use them."

He shook his head quickly. "No! I mean, of course we

have to use them. They're incredible. I just can't believe you went to all this trouble."

Her smile returned. "I think it was worth it. It will really give the design a unique look." She was definitely taking a chance with the less-than-conventional color scheme, but she'd wanted to give Griffin a display that he'd be proud of. The bulbs would help elevate the overall design.

"They must have cost a fair bit," he said, looking at the rest of the bulbs.

A lot more than she was willing to admit, so she shrugged. "Gotta spend money to make money, right?" she asked, unloading the rest from the box.

"Well, at least let me cover the cost of these. You've spent enough and you're doing this for free."

"No way. I'm doing this for an A in my interior design class. Whatever it takes…" It was partially true, but she'd also wanted to do something nice for Griffin, to help generate more customers for the shop. His designs were fantastic. His artwork even had her contemplating a tattoo of her own… People just needed to see his work.

He nodded slowly and cleared his throat. "Well, at least let me buy you dinner."

She blinked, surprised by the offer. She wasn't opposed to dinner with him, but he'd seemed to be keeping a low profile. Before coming into his shop two days ago, she hadn't seen him around town at the grocery store or bar or anywhere.

Unfortunately, he misread her silence. "Bad idea… sorry."

"No! I'd like that. Um, I just thought you weren't going out much around town."

"I've been keeping a low profile…"

He looked like he was changing his mind, and she really

did want to have dinner with him. Maybe get to know him a little better. "Why don't we order in? Eat here?" she suggested.

He nodded, looking relieved. "I'll grab some take-out menus."

"And I'll get back to decorating the tree," she said, her chest light and fluttery as she went back to work.

HE'D ESSENTIALLY ASKED her out. Although, he wasn't sure ordering takeout to the shop as a thank-you was an actual date. Did Jade read it that way?

As he ordered their Chinese food, he watched her working in the window. He couldn't help himself. What she'd done was the best thing anyone had ever done for him. She couldn't possibly understand how much those bulbs meant.

She was wildly talented and creative to come up with the idea, and having his work displayed in the front window like that was something he was proud of. He'd worked hard to make it to where he was in the industry. There were a lot of artists who never got a chance to realize their dream. He'd been doing so well…until getting busted.

And now he was rebuilding his career and his life. Jade was like an unexpected holiday angel in his time of need.

But did he deserve an angel?

An hour later, the food arrived and he turned off the loud music as they prepared to eat.

"Aw, that was my favorite song," Jade said, singing the chorus lyrics in a deep, gruff, gravelly tone.

He laughed. "Yeah, right." He knew the music must be annoying her.

"No, really, it's growing on me," she said, her gaze locked on his.

He cleared his throat and looked away. "Let's eat. I'm starving."

"I think there's enough food here to feed the entire neighborhood," Jade said, sitting at the small table as he unloaded the Chinese food containers from the paper bags.

"I couldn't decide what dishes to get, so I basically ordered everything." He handed her a paper plate and plastic cutlery. "Dig in," he said.

She did, and once they'd filled their plates, he sat across from her. A silence fell over them while they ate.

It was a little too quiet. He cleared his throat. "This food is amazing." He shook his head. "You never appreciate just how good stuff tastes until you can't have it."

She laughed gently. "Prison food not so hot?"

"Let's just say ramen bought from the commissary is as valuable as gold."

"Remind me never to go to jail," she said with a grin.

Although it was a heavy topic for him, for the first time since getting out, talking about it, thinking about it didn't feel as heavy, not as hard. It was an aspect of his past—a thing he couldn't change. He had to learn to accept his mistake and move on. He suspected Jade was making the conversation a lot easier. She had a natural way of making him feel at ease, unjudged. She wasn't afraid to acknowledge it, but it wasn't a big, dark cloud over his head when she did.

His gratitude for her was growing, and his feelings went even beyond that.

HE'D OPENED THE DOOR, but could she really ask? Maybe he *wanted* to talk about it. Maybe it might help. She cleared her throat.

"Can I ask what happened?"

He shrugged. "It's no secret. It was all over the news. I robbed another tattoo shop."

She nodded. She'd read about the robbery. She knew the details, that he'd been working for a shop in Vegas and they'd asked him to get a job at the other shop so they could rob it from the inside. But she was interested to hear what had *really* happened. From him. "Things are never exactly what the media presents them to be."

He sighed. "I moved to Vegas after graduation. I always knew I wanted to be a tattoo artist. I was working my way up by doing odd jobs around a small studio—cleaning, greeting clients—and in exchange being mentored by some really amazingly talented artists. Eventually, I needed to start making cash and I'd put in my time apprenticing, so I applied at the Dark Rebels studio." His voice hardened at the mention of the shop. "I started dating the owner's sister. Fell head over heels for her, actually. Turns out it had just been an act on her part. She told me that there was a family heirloom that had been stolen from their shop—an antique tattooing gun—and they had an idea of how to get it back. I believed what they planned to steal belonged to them."

"So, you did it."

"At the time, I thought I was doing the right thing. In hindsight, I think I was still just trying to win over Kelly. Show her how committed I was, or something equally messed up." He shook his head. "Anyway, it was Christmas Eve when they pulled the job. I let them in, and instead of just grabbing the tattoo gun, they cleaned the place out of cash, tattooing supplies… They'd barely made it two blocks away before I came to my senses and called the cops."

"You turned them in?"

"No, I turned myself in, but the cops had been watching them for a while. They knew about other illegal activities going on behind the scenes at the shop, and now I was tied to all of that."

"You did the right thing." It would have been so easy for him to simply allow them to get away, leave and never look back.

"It was the only thing I could do. I would never have been able to live with myself otherwise."

"How long did you serve?"

"I was sentenced to eighteen months, but I was out in eight. Overcrowding in prisons, it was my first offense, I turned myself in and I had behaved myself behind bars."

"That had to be hard."

"The hard part wasn't jail. It was knowing that I'd thrown away my future. In one stupid bad decision, I cost myself my career...my family."

She touched his hand, and a bolt of electricity sparked between them. "I'm sure your family just needs time."

"I don't know... I've been back three months. Gillian's away on her backpacking trip, and I know Molly wants to reach out, but she's being loyal to my parents and I can't fault her for that."

"Have you gone to see them?" she asked gently. Maybe he needed to be the one to make the first move.

He shook his head, staring at his food. "I've walked toward the diner and then chickened out several times...a lot of times."

His openness and vulnerability meant a lot to her. This probably wasn't a conversation he'd have with just anyone. She felt an unexpected connection to him. More than she'd felt with anyone in a long time. She took a deep breath. "I lost my dad a few years ago. Believe me, I'd give anything to have five more minutes with him. Your family can't stay upset forever. It's the holidays. A season for redemption, forgiveness…"

"Yeah, maybe. I don't know." He turned his attention to the window. "What I do know is that the window looks wonderful. Thank you."

"You're welcome," she said, a warm sensation flowing through her at the praise.

"In fact, you're kinda wonderful, too, Jade."

His gaze burned into hers and she swallowed hard. Her heart was pounding like the beat of the heavy metal Christmas music. He was so attractive. She liked him. A lot. He was nothing like she'd expected when she'd walked through the shop doors a few days before, and he was someone she was desperate to get to know better, spend more time with.

"The feeling's mutual," she said.

He dropped his head as though he didn't believe it. Couldn't believe it. Suddenly, it was her mission to make him believe it. She reached across the table and touched his hand.

His gaze shot up with a fiery intensity that almost scared her, but she didn't pull away. "One mistake doesn't define who you are," she said softly but firmly.

Standing slightly, leaning over the table, he reached for her, his hands cupping her face. She nodded once to answer the silent question in his expression, and then his mouth was crushing hers.

Ho ho hotness.

She wrapped her arms around his neck and deepened the kiss, savoring the taste of his lips, the smell of his aftershave filling her senses with an urgent desire.

The damn table prevented their bodies from touching, which was probably a good thing. If she pressed her body to his, she may not stop at just a kiss.

How long had it been for him? There was definitely a hunger on his end, but she believed it was because he was kissing *her* and not just anyone.

He pulled away abruptly and a look of panic entered his expression. "Shit, sorry."

"For what? The best kiss of my life?"

He relaxed just a little but still looked regretful. "I shouldn't have done that, but you're just so easy to be with, and I'm insanely attracted to you at the same time."

"Again, the feeling is mutual." She kissed him once more. "There's no reason to apologize."

He looked longingly at her lips but held back. "Gossip spreads quick around here, and I don't want people thinking you're mixed up with a guy like me."

"A guy like you? You mean someone successful and hardworking and attractive?"

"Jade..."

She kissed him again and his resolve broke. He moved around the table and took her into his arms. The embrace was long and passionate, full of desire and vulnerability. Her body sank into his and she could feel the reaction the kiss was evoking.

The chiming of the bell above the front door had them both reeling backward, nearly knocking over the table of food.

"Shit," he mumbled.

She wiped her mouth quickly and forced a smile, desperate to act natural, despite the fact that she was on fire. "Hello, Mrs. Silverman." Of all people to catch them in that moment, it had to be the biggest gossip in Wild River. The head of the business association committee, she knew virtually everyone and had no problem spreading local "news" around town.

"Hi," the older woman said slyly, eyeing the two of them with unconcealed pleasure. They'd given her the juiciest story of the week. "I just stopped by to drop off the official entry form into the window display contest."

Griffin cleared his throat. "Oh, right… Thank you." He took it and stared at it intently. "I'll fill it out and drop it off?" he asked when she made no motion to leave.

"You do that, dear," she said, glancing back and forth between them with a grin. "Bundle up if you go out. It's a lot colder outside than it is in here." She winked and pushed through the door.

Mrs. Silverman paused outside the window display, then waved as she headed down the street.

Griffin looked pained. "Tell me she's not the gossip she used to be?"

"By now, half the block knows," Jade said. Then, turning to him, she wrapped her arms around his neck. "And I don't care one little bit."

His look of gratitude was tainted with uncertainty and Jade kissed him again. She planned to keep kissing him until he stopped caring what the rest of the town thought.

CHAPTER FOUR

WALKING INTO HIS jail cell for the first time, with its cold, stark concrete walls and the faint smell of a decaying future, a heavy sense of foreboding weighing on him, hadn't felt as hard as walking toward his family's diner the next day.

Maybe because going to jail had almost been a relief. It was the first step in getting back on track.

This could totally blow up in his face.

But the day before with Jade had changed something in him. Sure, he was ashamed of his past actions. He was regretful and desperate to prove that he wasn't the sum of his mistakes, but she'd also helped him realize that he couldn't undo the past and that the people who claimed to care about him should be open to hearing his apology and moving past it with him…not continuing to shut him out or push him away.

Everyone deserved a second chance, Jade had said. And while he was struggling to believe that, he wanted to believe it, and that was a step, at least.

Kissing her in his shop had solidified the attraction he felt for her, and there'd been no denying she felt the same way. He wouldn't rush into things, but the day before had been one of the less heavy days he'd had in a long time and he wasn't going to let something that special go.

He pushed through the door and scanned the room. It was midafternoon, so it wouldn't be busy. Only a few booths were occupied, and a man sat at the counter drinking coffee and reading his cell phone.

Christmas music played and he recognized the old holiday soundtrack. The songs they played in the diner every year since he was a kid. All the popular, familiar classics brought feelings of warmth and nostalgia that nearly knocked the wind from his lungs. It might be too much to hope that he'd have the chance to spend Christmas with them. Baby steps.

Should he sit at a table? Or wait at the counter?

The kitchen was reserved for family members, and in the last conversation he'd had with his parents, they'd made it very clear that that title no longer belonged to him. The hurt and disappointment in their voices when he'd made that one phone call after his arrest had made him wish he hadn't reached out. But it would have been cowardly and unfair for his family to find out about it through news sources like the rest of the world.

Before he could decide where to sit, the door leading from the kitchen swung open and his sister Molly appeared, carrying two plates of the daily special. It was Wednesday, so he didn't even need to check the board to know it was spaghetti with homemade meatballs and garlic bread. The smell of the familiar family recipe had his stomach rumbling, but the sight of his sister put all thoughts of food on hold.

He hadn't seen or spoken to her since he'd gone in.

He'd missed both his sisters but especially Molly. He missed talking to her. Missed her corny jokes. Missed the connection they'd once had.

He knew she'd called him a couple of times over the last three months and hung up. She hadn't blocked the diner's number. He'd waited each time, wanting to say something, but afraid he'd say the wrong thing.

Season of redemption... He was ready to do whatever it took to redeem himself.

Would his family be ready to forgive?

"Hi," he said, opting for a stool at the counter before his wobbly knees decided to give out.

"IIi," she said, and the pain in her tone made all his regret come surging back.

He watched as she delivered the food and then headed toward him. She glanced into the kitchen. "Hungry?" she asked.

Starving, but too nauseous to eat. "Just coffee?"

She nodded and he noticed her hand shake as she poured the cup.

"How've you been?" he asked. Her back was to him as she ripped open two packets of sugar and dumped them in.

"Fine. Nothing changes around here," she said casually as she added the creamer and stirred it. She still hadn't turned back to look at him. She was procrastinating.

He needed the time, too.

Unfortunately, when she did turn, it was just in time for them both to see their mom enter the diner. He'd never seen a person's expression change so quickly—from surprise to hope to pain and then anger—as when his mother's gaze landed on him.

"Hey, Mom," Molly said, still holding the coffee cup.

His mother didn't take her eyes off him. "You're not welcome here," she said bluntly.

"Mom..."

"Don't call me that. The son I raised disappeared two years ago."

He shivered at the chill in her tone. She was the sweetest, kindest, most welcoming woman he knew, so her words hit even harder. "I made a mistake…"

"You did time in jail. You shamed our family and now you're back in town, running a tattoo shop." She shook her head. "You should have stayed in Vegas."

"I didn't want that lifestyle anymore. I'm trying to put my life back together, and I want to make it up to you." She was upset. He didn't fault her at all for that, but he wasn't prepared to give up. He loved them. He'd spend forever making it up to them if she'd let him.

Unfortunately, she stared at him as though he were a stranger. "You're not part of this family anymore. And I heard about Jade Frazier." She pointed a finger at him. "She's a good person, soft heart and gentle soul. She'll try to save you. Be man enough to refuse that help," she said, walking away from him and heading into the kitchen.

Molly suppressed a sob as she disappeared into the kitchen after their mom.

Griffin's chest ached so hard he thought it might explode. Getting up from the stool, he stalked out of the diner.

He never should have stopped by. Not knowing whether there was hope of reconciling with his family had been hard, but knowing there wasn't completely crushed his spirit.

LATER THAT NIGHT, Jade shivered as she pushed through the door of The Drunk Tank, where she was meeting Griffin. Since Mrs. Silverman had told the town about their kiss, there was no point in hiding that they were getting to know one another. She was in a fantastic mood and couldn't wait to see him. She'd submitted her photos of the window display to her professor and a celebratory drink was in order.

She scanned the crowded pub for Griffin and saw him

in a back booth. The dim lighting made it a more comfy, cozy place to sit. She smiled as she headed toward him. "This seat taken?" she joked as she removed her coat and hung it on the hook.

His expression was dark when he lifted his gaze to hers, and a chill ran through her. She noticed several empty beer bottles on the table. He'd started without her and, reading his mood, she suspected *he* wasn't celebrating.

"Everything okay?" she asked cautiously as she slid in across from him.

"Fine," he grumbled.

"This is your 'fine' face? We're still getting to know one another, so I'm not sure." She was desperate to lighten the mood. It was as though a storm cloud was brewing above his head, threatening to break any second.

He didn't look at her as he said, "Yeah, hey, I stuck around because I didn't want you to think I'd stood you up." He cleared his throat. "But I have to go."

She frowned as he slid out of the booth.

"Go? Already? I thought we were having drinks?"

"I don't think that's a good idea."

"Since when?" The day before they'd made out. A lot. That morning, he'd agreed to meet her for drinks. What had changed since then?

He lowered his head and shoved his hands deep into his pockets. "I'm not the guy for you, Jade."

"According to who?" She should have a say in that, shouldn't she? Obviously, he was still nervous about the two of them being together. What people would think. What they'd say. She didn't care about any of that.

"Things are just complicated right now, and I don't think you and I are a good idea."

"You're dumping me before we even have an actual

date?" He had to relax. Within a week, the town would have moved on to new gossip. In time, no one would care.

"I'm sorry, Jade." He did look sorry, but also unfortunately resolute in his decision. "Have a nice holiday," he said, and walked away.

Jade just sat there, mouth agape, watching him leave. Confused and conflicted, she released a deep sigh as she slumped against the booth.

What the hell had just happened?

CHAPTER FIVE

December 23...

THE LARGE GROUP gathered outside his shop had Griffin resisting the urge to turn and walk in the other direction. They didn't look like they were lined up for tattoos.

From a distance he recognized Mrs. Silverman and several other members of the business association. He forced a polite smile as he stopped next to them. "Good morning."

"Congratulations!" Mrs. Silverman said. "On behalf of the business association of Wild River, we'd like to present you with this award for first place in the window display contest." She extended the gold-plated plaque toward him, and an unexpected sense of pride welled up in him at seeing his shop's name engraved on it. A small validation of sorts.

"I won?"

"Hands down," another woman on the committee said. "This is fantastic! So unique."

He couldn't take the credit. "It was Jade Frazier's design. She did all of it. I had nothing to do with it."

"Well, that girl is talented. I expect you might lose your decorator to some other businesses around here next year, if you're not careful," the other woman said with a wink.

Mrs. Silverman shot him a mischievous grin. "I don't think he'll have to worry about that."

He swallowed hard. Unfortunately, he doubted Jade

would be interested in helping him next year after the way he'd abruptly ended things the week before.

The last seven days had been torture. He'd wanted to reach out to apologize or at least explain what he hadn't been able to that evening at The Drunk Tank, but he wasn't sure what he could say. Jade had said it didn't matter what everyone else thought of the two of them together. Maybe it wasn't important to her now, but his mother was right.

He wasn't the guy for her. She deserved so much better.

Unfortunately, that had been easier to believe up until now, when he was staring at the first place plaque with the casual, good-natured group of business owners congratulating him. He'd won, and in a small way, he felt as though the community was accepting him back. He still had a long way to go to fully earn the community's trust, but it was a start.

And he owed this first gesture of acceptance to Jade.

SITTING IN A booth at Carla's Diner, she hit the refresh button over and over on her email. The term grades would be posted any minute. Jade guzzled her coffee, then tried to counteract the caffeinated buzzing throughout her body by taking a deep breath.

The store window was incredible. She was so proud of how it had turned out. Unfortunately, her chest ached whenever she walked past it. She was desperate to reach out to Griffin, but he'd been pretty clear that he wasn't interested in pursuing things. He hadn't reached out to her either. She knew the attraction between them was real, that they'd formed a special connection, but what could she do?

He wasn't ready yet and she couldn't force him into a relationship.

She hoped maybe…in time.

She hit the refresh button again and the term grades loaded on the screen. She scanned quickly, and her heart rose for the first time in a week.

She got an A! She'd done it!

"Yay!" It was a small victory after getting dumped just before the holidays, but she'd take it. Finally, the validation she'd needed to know she was on the right track with this profession. It was something she truly enjoyed and was good at.

"Good news?" Molly asked, stopping next to her booth and refilling her coffee cup.

She nodded. "Yeah. Term grades came back. I passed my interior designer class," she said with a smile. She wasn't going to brag about the A, tempting though it was.

Molly's smile was sad as she nodded. "That's amazing and well deserved—congrats. I saw the display in my bro— in the tattoo shop window," she said, lowering her voice. "It is really wonderful. He definitely deserved that win."

"He won the business association window display contest?" Wow. She hadn't heard yet. Too bad they couldn't be together to celebrate their good news. Maybe she could stop by...congratulate him? Nope. She needed to let him come to her if and when he was ever ready. She cleared her throat. "Have you talked to him?" she asked Molly gently.

Molly glanced toward the kitchen, where Carla was working. "He stopped by a week ago."

He had? Her gut turned. "And..." She didn't mean to pry, but she suspected that maybe that was where his bad mood had stemmed from that evening at The Drunk Tank.

"Mom basically kicked him out," Molly whispered, busying herself with the salt and pepper shakers, her red braid falling across her shoulder.

"Of the diner?"

"Of our lives," Molly said sadly.

Jade's chest ached for him and she felt more than a little responsible. She'd encouraged him to try to reconnect with his family. He'd thought they weren't ready to forgive him yet and he'd been right. She shouldn't have interfered. "I'm sorry, Molly." She hesitated, opened her mouth to say something, then slammed her lips back together.

Nope. No more interfering. She'd done enough.

Damn it! She couldn't help herself. Griffin was a great guy and this family was hurting. They obviously wanted to reconcile…and didn't know how. "You know, just because your mom is still unwilling to forgive and move forward doesn't mean you and Gillian can't."

Molly toyed with the string on her apron as she shook her head. "Our family doesn't work that way. Siding with Griffin would be a slap in the face." She gestured around her. "This is my life."

Jade nodded. "I understand."

Molly walked away and Jade sighed. She closed her laptop and tucked it into her case. She'd lost her appetite.

"Leaving, Jade? You haven't eaten yet." Carla's voice, as she delivered that day's special to a nearby booth, made Jade pause.

She turned with a polite smile. "I'm not hungry today."

Carla eyed her. "Everything okay, dear?"

Obviously, the woman had heard the gossip about Jade's kiss with her son. Everyone had by now. "Fine," she said simply. It wasn't fine, but there was no sense getting into something that was no longer happening. She climbed out of the booth and headed for the door. Resisting the urge to turn back took all her effort.

Just leave. Their family dynamics are none of your business.

She turned back. "You know, everything's not really

okay." She took a deep breath and pushed on before she could lose her nerve. "This place has always welcomed people with no place to go. The Christmas after our dad died, that was Maddie and I. We were sad and facing a holiday season without him, and we came here for Christmas dinner. Everyone, especially you, Carla, welcomed us with open arms, open hearts… We've never forgotten your kindness toward us. Your kindness toward everyone." She paused. "Can't you find it within your heart to offer that same love to your son?"

Carla cringed, and Jade could see tears burning the backs of the woman's eyes. She glanced around the diner, avoiding Jade's gaze. "This is different."

"And absolutely none of my business, I know. But all I'm going to say is, Griffin made a mistake. Don't make one yourself." She touched Carla's hand gently, and then turned and left the diner.

CHAPTER SIX

APPARENTLY, TATTOOS WERE the new Christmas gift idea.

His shop hadn't stopped with walk-ins all day. It being Christmas Eve, Griffin hadn't expected to see anyone at all, but his waiting room was full.

Winning the window display contest had obviously been a bigger deal than he'd thought.

Men, women, some old and some barely old enough to sign the waiver for themselves, flocked in, and six hours after opening, Griffin was exhausted and calling it a day.

"First thing the day after Christmas, I'll be here and ready to give you that sugar skull, Mrs. Kingsly. I'm just afraid I won't do it justice after all the others I completed today," he told the last customer waiting.

The woman looked grateful. "I appreciate that. So, ten a.m. on the twenty-sixth?"

"Perfect." He walked her to the door and, after shutting it behind her, flipped the sign to Closed. He was happy about his productive day, but he couldn't dull the ache in his chest that it was Christmas Eve, and he couldn't get his mind off Jade. How great would it have been to spend the holidays with her?

Still, his mother was right. He didn't deserve her. She'd not only decorated his window and won him the contest, but she'd also inadvertently shown the town that it was okay to accept him as one of them again.

A knock on the door had him sighing. *Damn, people. I'm closed. Read the sign.*

He turned and, seeing his mother outside the door, his stomach lurched. She offered a quick, uneasy wave through the glass and he opened the door. "Hi…" How could one single syllable hold so much emotion? He thought the word might actually strangle him.

"Can I come in?" she asked, looking nervous—as though she was still contemplating whether or not to be there.

He didn't want her to leave, so he stepped back quickly to let her enter.

A long moment of awkward silence followed as she took in the shop, the tattoo designs on the wall, the chairs… anything to avoid his eyes.

He waited. He had no idea why she was here, but he'd let her say what she came to say. Good or bad, at least she was here. Getting to see her on Christmas Eve, no matter what the reason, was an unexpected gift.

She took a deep breath and stared at her hands. "The shop looks great."

Her praise meant everything, and he nearly choked on the lump rising in his throat. "Thank you."

She opened her oversize purse and took out an old poster. She handed it to him. "It doesn't really match the window decor, but the contest was over, so… I wanted to drop this off… Just in case you wanted to have it."

He unrolled the old familiar poster he'd given her for Christmas the year he'd turned nineteen and gotten his first tattoo, to ease the sting.

The image of a buff Santa Claus with the word *Mama* in a heart tattoo on his chest made him laugh. "This was your gift. Your poster."

She nodded. "I just found it among the decorations this year."

And she hadn't immediately destroyed it or thrown it away. That meant a lot. "Thank you for bringing it," he said. "I'll definitely use it next year." It might be the only decor in his shop the following year. A thought that depressed him on so many levels.

His mother nodded and cleared her throat. "Jade stopped by the diner yesterday," she said slowly.

His chest tightened at the mention of her name. He wanted to do the right thing, and now he wasn't even sure he knew what that was.

"She had a few things to say." His mother paused. "And she was right about it all. You going to jail broke my heart, as I know we raised you better than that. You were so smart and talented, and I thought you'd gone and thrown your life away. I felt helpless and that had to be the hardest part of all—knowing I couldn't fix things for you. It felt as though I'd lost you," she said, looking pained.

He nodded. "I know, Mom. I'm sorry."

"But I didn't lose you. You made a mistake, did your time, and now I realize that one choice doesn't define who you are. You're still the smart, talented, caring son I know. You were also brave enough to come back here and try to make amends, and I'd be a fool to shut you out when all I want is to be a family again, have you home again." Tears burned in her tired-looking eyes even as a hopeful look lit up her expression.

He swallowed hard, and dared to step forward and open his arms.

She hesitated, then stepped into them, clinging to him tight. "I'm so happy you're home, son," she said.

He didn't trust his voice, so he kissed the top of her head.

"And the thing I said about Jade." She pulled back to look at him. "Forget every word. That girl is special, so don't do anything to mess that up."

He sighed. The advice was coming a little too late.

CHAPTER SEVEN

CHRISTMAS EVE AND all alone.

Jade scanned the crowd inside The Drunk Tank for the annual Christmas Eve party. Had everyone in town coupled up overnight? She stared wistfully across her candy-cane martini at her sister and Mike cuddled up in the booth across from her, dressed in matching ugly Christmas sweaters. For the first time in her life, she understood completely why the Grinch decided to cancel Christmas.

For a brief few days, she'd been enjoying the season, launching her new career, falling in love unexpectedly...

She scanned the bar, but there was no one she wanted to talk to, dance with or really be around, and her mood would only ruin Maddie's night. If she knew Jade wasn't having a good time, her sister's protective instincts would kick in and she'd spend the night trying to make Jade feel better.

That wouldn't be fair. So, she faked a yawn and stretched. "I'm exhausted. I think I'll call it a night."

Maddie tore her eyes away from Mike and checked her watch. "It's only ten thirty."

"This school semester really took it out of me, but you stay and enjoy, and I'll see you under the tree at six a.m. for gifts," she said, forcing a smile and sliding out of the booth. Unfortunately, she wasn't really looking forward to the early-morning Christmas Day tradition with her sister. Mike would be there, which would be fine if Jade wouldn't once again feel like a third wheel. She and Maddie hadn't discussed it yet, but she knew the time was coming when Maddie would be moving in with Mike. They'd been seeing one another for a while, things were serious, and eventually it would happen. Jade would be alone. They were adults now, and that was how life went.

Mike quickly kissed Maddie and started to climb out of the booth. "I'll walk you home."

Jade pointed at him. "You will not. You will stay with my sister."

Mike hesitated.

"You sure you'll be okay, Jade?" Maddie asked.

"Absolutely. Have fun." She zipped her winter coat as she crossed the wooden floor toward the door. She pushed through and stepped out into the frigid night air. Large fluffy snowflakes fell to the ground on the quiet street, and she sighed as her boots left a solitary trail down the snowy sidewalk.

HE'D SCREWED THINGS UP. But these days he wasn't so afraid to admit it and try to fix it before it was too late. Climbing the steps to Jade's apartment, Griffin held his breath and knocked. A long moment passed, and no sound came from inside. He knocked again and waited.

Nothing.

It was Christmas Eve. Of course she wasn't home. She had family and friends to celebrate with. She wasn't home pining over him.

Unfortunately, there was no way he could let this night end without finding her and telling her how he felt. Apologize for pushing her away, thank her for everything she'd done for him and tell her he was falling in love with her.

Descending the stairs two at a time, he headed toward

Main Street. Most stores were closed until after Christmas and the street was quiet, illuminated only by streetlights. The sound of holiday music grew louder the closer he got to The Drunk Tank. The bar was the only place still open, hosting its annual Christmas Eve party, so it made sense that she might be there. He pushed through the door and rubbed his hands together for heat as he entered and scanned the bar.

Couples were everywhere, dancing, singing holiday tunes, drinking holiday-themed cocktails. A full, festive mood enveloped him. He'd love to be here with Jade. Celebrating a different kind of Christmas—one full of hope and the promise of a better life, a better future. If she was here, maybe it wasn't too late.

In a booth toward the back he spotted her, and his heart pounded as he made his way toward her. His gut turned seeing her cuddled into another guy... Mike? The man he'd tattooed a few weeks ago?

Then relief washed over him seeing that it wasn't her. But a striking resemblance. Her sister, Maddie?

Mike glanced up and waved him over.

"Hey, man...how's the tattoo healing?" he asked, still scanning the bar. If her sister was here, maybe Jade was, too. A candy-cane martini sat on the table across from where the couple was sitting.

"Great. No issues at all. Here alone? Want to join us?" Mike asked.

"Um...is Jade here?"

Maddie shot him an unimpressed look. "What exactly are your intentions with my sister?"

He deserved the overprotective sister drilling. "I messed up and I wanted to apologize." He looked around. "She here?"

"She left about half an hour ago. Headed home," Maddie said, seeming reluctant to let him off the hook so easy, but caving just a little.

"I was just there… No answer."

Maddie's face now took on a look of concern as she reached for her cell phone. She dialed and they all waited… No answer. "Damn, voice mail."

"Maybe she's asleep already," Mike said. "She did say she was tired."

"I should go." Maddie reached for her coat and Mike nodded.

But Griffin held out a hand. "Why don't you stay in case she decides to come back, and I'll head out to see if she's still walking? It's a nice night. Maybe she just needed some air."

Maddie hesitated, then nodded, still looking concerned. "Okay, but text us if you find her, and I'll try calling again." She scribbled her cell number on a napkin and handed it to Griffin.

"Will do," he said, tucking it into his pocket. He walked away from the table and headed out of the bar.

Outside, he looked up and down the street, then headed in the opposite direction of her apartment. He hadn't seen her on the street on his walk to the bar.

He walked along Main Street, and as he went, he quickly surveyed his competition for the window display contest. There were some seriously impressive designs. Flippin' Pages, the local bookstore, had stacked books in the shape of a Christmas tree. The Chocolate Shoppe had used hollow chocolate figurines to create a scene with Santa and his reindeer… Great stuff.

None as amazing as Jade's, though.

He continued walking, and when his own shop came into view, his heart pounded. There she was. Standing outside looking at the display. Dressed in the faux fur coat she'd been wearing the first day she'd walked into his shop, her heeled leather boots and a festive red hat, she took his breath away.

He smiled as he approached. "An incredibly talented woman designed that one," he said.

She turned, and a slight look of hope reflected in her green eyes as she shrugged. "Wanted to take another look before you dismantled it."

"I was actually thinking of leaving it up year-round," he said.

"That's an idea."

"But then I thought if I did that, there'd be no reason for you to design a new one next year."

"Next year's won't be free," she said with a small smile.

Damn, he wanted to reach out and kiss her, but first things first. "Jade, I'm sorry. I guess I panicked a little."

"I understand. You're not quite ready…"

"No. I thought I wasn't good enough for you. But, selfishly, I'm also not ready to give up the best thing that's ever happened to me." He moved toward her and took her hands in his. "I came back here looking for family. But family doesn't have to be blood. You made this homecoming a lot easier…"

She stared up at him and he kissed the snowflakes on her eyelashes.

"I'm sorry I interfered with your own family, though. I shouldn't have convinced you to see them when things were still too raw."

"You were trying to help. And you did," he said, staring gratefully into her eyes. He owed so much to her. He didn't even know where to begin in thanking her. "My mom came to see me at the shop." He still couldn't believe it. It was going to be a long road to healing, but at least they'd be on that path together.

"She did?"

"She did…and while we have a way to go, I think we can get there," he said.

Jade let out a happy sigh full of relief. "That's really great, Griffin."

"She also said that I better not mess this up with you and I'm desperate not to," he said, and paused. "Because I'm falling for you, Jade."

Her smile was wide and so incredibly beautiful as she stared up at him. "I'm falling for you, too."

"Is that your 'happy' face, because we haven't been together long enough—"

She cut off his words with a kiss. A deep, passionate kiss that beat any other kiss he'd ever had. He held her close and savored the moment, never wanting to let go of the best holiday gift he could ever have hoped for.

"So, you forgive me for being an idiot?" he asked softly as he pulled back.

"'Tis the season," she said with a wink.

He held her tight as the town square clock chimed with the sounds of midnight, signaling the beginning of Christmas Day and the beginning of his new life in his hometown of Wild River, Alaska.

* * * * *

SPECIAL EXCERPT FROM

◈ HARLEQUIN

SPECIAL EDITION

*Bethany Robeson already has her hands full with an inherited
house and an overweight pooch named Meatball. She doesn't
dare make room for Shane Dupree, her former high school
sweetheart, now a single dad. Bethany doesn't believe in starting
over, but Shane, baby Wyatt and Meatball could be the family she
always dreamed of...*

*Read on for a sneak peek of
the latest book in the Furever Yours continuity,*
Home is Where the Hound Is *by Melissa Senate!*

"I remember. I remember it all, Bethany."

Jeez. He hadn't meant for his voice to turn so serious, so
reverent. But there was very little chance of hiding his real feelings
when she was around.

"Me, too," she said.

For a few moments they ate in silence.

"Thanks for helping me here," she said. "You've done a lot of
that since I've been back."

"Anytime. And I mean that."

"Ditto," she said.

He reached over and squeezed her hand but didn't let go.
And suddenly he was looking—with that seriousness, with that
reverence—into those green eyes that had also kept him up those
nights when he couldn't stop thinking about her. They both leaned
in at the same time, the kiss soft, tender, then with all the pent-up
passion they'd clearly both been feeling these last days.

She pulled slightly away. "Uh-oh."

He let out a rough exhale, trying to pull himself together. "Right? You're leaving in a couple weeks. Maybe three tops. And I'm solely focused on being the best father I can be. So that's two really good reasons why we shouldn't kiss again." Except he leaned in again.

And so did she. This time there was nothing soft or tender about the kiss. Instead, it was pure passion. His hand wound in her silky brown hair, her hands on his face.

A puppy started barking, then another, then yet another. The three cockapoos.

"They're saving us from getting into trouble," Bethany said, glancing at the time on her phone. "Time for their potty break. They'll be interrupting us all night, so that should keep us in line."

He smiled. "We can get into a lot of trouble in between, though."

Don't miss
Home is Where the Hound Is *by* Melissa Senate,
available March 2022 wherever
Harlequin Special Edition books and ebooks are sold.

Harlequin.com

Copyright © 2022 by Harlequin Books S.A.

HSEEXP0122BMAX

Don't miss the first two books in the romantic and exciting Wild River series by

JENNIFER SNOW

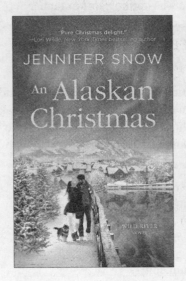 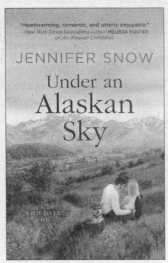

"An exciting contemporary series debut with a wildly unique Alaskan setting." —*Kirkus Reviews* on *An Alaskan Christmas*

Order your copies today!

HQNBooks.com

PHJSBPA0920Max

Get 4 FREE REWARDS!

We'll send you 2 FREE Books plus 2 FREE Mystery Gifts.

FREE Value Over **$20**

Both the **Romance** and **Suspense** collections feature compelling novels written by many of today's bestselling authors.

YES! Please send me 2 FREE novels from the Essential Romance or Essential Suspense Collection and my 2 FREE gifts (gifts are worth about $10 retail). After receiving them, if I don't wish to receive any more books, I can return the shipping statement marked "cancel." If I don't cancel, I will receive 4 brand-new novels every month and be billed just $7.24 each in the U.S. or $7.49 each in Canada. That's a savings of up to 28% off the cover price. It's quite a bargain! Shipping and handling is just 50¢ per book in the U.S. and $1.25 per book in Canada * I understand that accepting the 2 free books and gifts places me under no obligation to buy anything. I can always return a shipment and cancel at any time. The free books and gifts are mine to keep no matter what I decide.

Choose one: ☐ **Essential Romance**
(194/394 MDN GQ6M)

☐ **Essential Suspense**
(191/391 MDN GQ6M)

Name (please print)

Address   Apt. #

City   State/Province   Zip/Postal Code

Email: Please check this box ☐ if you would like to receive newsletters and promotional emails from Harlequin Enterprises ULC and its affiliates. You can unsubscribe anytime.

> Mail to the **Harlequin Reader Service:**
> **IN U.S.A.:** P.O. Box 1341, Buffalo, NY 14240-8531
> **IN CANADA:** P.O. Box 603, Fort Erie, Ontario L2A 5X3

Want to try 2 free books from another series? Call 1-800-873-8635 or visit www.ReaderService.com.

*Terms and prices subject to change without notice. Prices do not include sales taxes, which will be charged (if applicable) based on your state or country of residence. Canadian residents will be charged applicable taxes. Offer not valid in Quebec. This offer is limited to one order per household. Books received may not be as shown. Not valid for current subscribers to the Essential Romance or Essential Suspense Collection. All orders subject to approval. Credit or debit balances in a customer's account(s) may be offset by any other outstanding balance owed by or to the customer. Please allow 4 to 6 weeks for delivery. Offer available while quantities last.

Your Privacy—Your information is being collected by Harlequin Enterprises ULC, operating as Harlequin Reader Service. For a complete summary of the information we collect, how we use this information and to whom it is disclosed, please visit our privacy notice located at corporate.harlequin.com/privacy-notice. From time to time we may also exchange your personal information with reputable third parties. If you wish to opt out of this sharing of your personal information, please visit readerservice.com/consumerschoice or call 1-800-873-8635. **Notice to California Residents**—Under California law, you have specific rights to control and access your data. For more information on these rights and how to exercise them, visit corporate.harlequin.com/california-privacy.

STRS21MAXR2